Reflections of the Past:

A Story of
the Guardians of the Well

Vanda Inman

Reflections of the Past: A Story of the Guardians of the Well. ©

by

Vanda Inman

First published 2010

by

Vanda Inman's Write Space,

Rivendell, St Clether, Launceston, Cornwall. PL15 8QH
www.writespace.co.uk

First Edition

ISBN 978-0-9530733-3-7

9 780953 073337 >

Cover design by Hazel Brown, www.faery-art.com

Printed by T J International, Padstow, Cornwall.

All characters in this novel are entirely fictitious and bear no resemblance to any person alive nor dead – excepting those who lived over a thousand years ago upon whom I am unable to comment.

These words are written
in honour of
the Guardians of the past
and
those who journey
in the name of love, light and all that is good.

'The answers to all the questions
we might ever ask
can be found
in the ground beneath our feet.'

Reflections of the Past

A Story of the Guardians of the Well

Beginnings

Cornish Creations

The first line is always the most difficult to write. It is supposed to entice you into reading the second. And that, in turn, has the task of enchanting you sufficiently to continue onto the third.

So which words should I weave to tell a story over which you will linger and, when finished, feel an air of sadness akin to the departure of a dear friend?

Let me take you back, a thousand, two thousand years and more, to a frozen winter scene when snow lay on the landscape and the Pagan religion lived in harmony with nature. Jump forwards with me to the spring and new growth of Celtic Christianity, and then fall into a Medieval summer when knights set out upon their quests. Last, but not least, let us reach our fingers back to a time we can almost, but not quite, touch, the cataclysmic Victorian era – culminating in the story of today, the roots of which are interwoven amongst them all.

The characters and events in this book are a mixture of fact and fiction. Who can tell which is which? Even I am not sure at times, as the words fly onto the page and I have no idea of what is coming next. But surely once, long ago, a man stood upon high rocks above a valley and hurled his spear into the unknown. And for certain, another has spent a night in silent vigil in a little chapel, intent upon his quest.

Rowena's story is not all mine, yet some of it is, and the story of the chapel also - and there are shades of myself in all of the characters, as there are shades of you, whoever you may be who has picked up this book and are even now reading these words, linking into the thoughts and visions which I have as I sit at my desk writing these first few words in order to begin.

So there, I have written the elusive first line, second, line, paragraph, maybe even page. Don't stop now. Don't read the first line and abandon the magical and mystical journey which lies ahead of you, just around the next bend in the path, on the other side of the river or maybe even over the brow of the hill. Don't leave the second line unread, nor indeed the second paragraph, first page, first part... there are dark caves and moonlit nights to explore, the rushing of the river in dappled sunlight, the flight of the raven and the never ending search for truth. Take my hand, come with me and together we will discover the hidden treasures to be found in a little valley in Cornwall and, most importantly, within ourselves.

*   *   *

Reflections of the Past: A Story of the Guardians of the Well, has its roots in Cornish soil. The seeds were sown through the cycle of the seasons and from these the story blossomed into life, created and crafted by a Cornish maid, and you now hold the fruits of her labour in your hands.

It is for this reason I decided to publish the book myself and have it printed in Cornwall, and I feel a certain pride in this home produced effort, which bears the essence of my beloved Cornwall in every word, line and page.

In buying this book, you will have made your own contribution to the future upkeep of St Clether Holy Well Chapel - and for this I thank you.

And so, through this piece of Cornish craftsmanship, view the valley, savour the scents, reach out and touch the rocks, plunge your hands into the sparkling, holy water and – wherever you might be in the world – find your own, special peace.

Vanda Inman 2010

'Re bo kres ha kerensa a-hys an Norvys'
(May there be peace and love across the World)

Earth

Pagan Prophecies:

Cerridwen's Cauldron

The Sacred Pool
and the Lines of Power

The Rowan Tree

The Rowan (Sorbus aucuparia), Mountain Ash, Quickbeam, has the ability, perhaps more than any other tree, to help us increase our psychic abilities and connections. It has a beneficial energy which will aid us to receive visions and insights which in turn will enhance our communication with the spirit realms.

Its message is not to give up, but to hold on strong to what you believe in and to the power of the life-force.

Cerridwen's Cauldron

Once upon a time there was a Goddess, Cerridwen, who lived in Wales in the mountains of Snowdonia, beside Lake Bala. Cerridwen had two children, a girl, who was beautiful as the day was long, and a boy who was exceedingly ugly. Cerridwen decided if her son could not manage to enjoy good looks, then he should receive the gift of wisdom.

Druid alchemists known as the Fferyllt lived in the hills of Wales and Cerridwen heard that from them she could obtain a recipe to brew an elixir which would give wisdom to whomever tasted the first three drops, but the remainder would become poison.

6

As the mixture had to brew for a year and a day, Cerridwen chose an old, blind man and a young boy, named Gwion, to tend the fire beneath the cauldron. For long days and nights they tended the fire for Cerridwen while her cauldron bubbled and, at last, the time came when the elixir was ready to be used.

Unfortunately, as Gwion was tending the fire for almost the last time, three drops splashed out of the cauldron onto his hand. They were hot, he raised his hand to his mouth – and the three drops of inspiration from Cerridwen's cauldron were tasted by Gwion himself, rather than Cerridwen's son.

Fearful of Cerridwen's wrath, Gwion attempted to escape but Cerridwen chased after him. Gwion turned himself into a hare, the swiftest animal he could think of, but Cerridwen changed herself into a greyhound and pursued him across the land, up hill and down dale.

As she was about to catch him he turned himself into a fish, but Cerridwen turned herself into an otter and continued the hunt through the icy waters of the river and the stillness of the lakes.

And as she almost caught him once more, Gwion turned himself into a bird and soared into the sky. Cerridwen at once became a hawk and continued to pursue him as high as they both could fly.

Just before he was caught, Gwion made one final transformation into a grain of wheat, so small he hoped he would never be found. But Cerridwen turned herself into a hen, ate all of the wheat, and Gwion too.

Nine months later, the Goddess Cerridwen gave birth to a baby boy. She knew this was no ordinary boy but Gwion reborn, just as the sun is reborn every year from the earth mother. Unable to find it in her heart to kill the child, she placed the baby in a leather bag and set him adrift upon the ocean.

The bag finally came to rest in the mouth of the river Conwy and was found by a man called Elphin who became the baby's foster father. Elphin named the child Taliesin, which means Radiant Brow, and in time, Taliesin became the finest Bard in all the land.

One

There was fire in his head.

Fire stronger than he had ever experienced before, burning into his consciousness like the blazing sun at its height in the fullness of summer, calling him to another form, another time and place. Stronger even than the last time the moon had been full and the world shining around him. Now, in the brightness of the night sky it was back, blazing more fiercely than ever and calling, ever calling.

Fire in his head, and all around a bitter cold which reached into the depths of his soul.

The snows had started with the dark of the moon, the clouds gathering until the first swirling flakes fell, turning the landscape to white.

Deerman spent the entire morning watching the green and brown of the moorland steadily change colour. As the snow began he made his way to the peak of the tor, his body wrapped in animal furs to keep out the cold and wet, standing still and silent, a solitary figure clutching his staff of twisted rowan with white, frozen knuckles. The flakes had settled upon his face and eyelashes, turning him into a man of snow, before he finally made his way back to his shelter and the meagre warmth of his fire. And still the snow fell.

It finally stopped, leaving the world in silence. Then the clouds cleared to reveal a landscape of brilliant, twinkling light and bright blue sky, the air so sharp and cold it took his breath away. And when the moon rose, full and silver in the blackness of the night sky, he felt the call.

Taking his drum of wood and stretched animal skin he stood outside his shelter. It was impossible to walk to the tor, the snow lay as thick and deep as the tops of the stone circle on the moor. No human would be abroad and the villagers would stay inside, safe and warm with their stock, until it was time to venture out again.

Facing the rising moon Deerman began a slow drumbeat, slow as the rhythm of his heart, resonating into the shining, snowbound night. As he increased the pace an owl called in the distance, to be answered almost immediately by another, their eerie cries echoing all around. On the periphery of his vision the swift, shadowy shape of a hare bounded across the landscape, and still he maintained his drumbeat, slowly building to its crescendo, as he felt his heartbeat quicken with the rhythm and the fire begin to burn in his head.

Faster and faster until the sound of the drum filled his mind and echoed over the moor around him, the black and white of the surrounding landscape merging with the beat of the drum, the call of the owl, the racing of the hare, the fire in his head burning brightly. Deerman drummed to the heartbeat of the universe, breathing as one to the same rhythm.

The drumbeat ceased abruptly. There was a moment of complete silence as the world waited, before a rush of wings and a blur of whiteness moved into the dark, night sky. Then he was gone.

Two

Rowan lay quite still, peering into the sacred pool. She had been there for a very long time and her limbs felt as if they were turned to stone. The sun had moved across the sky casting a variety of shadows onto the water and the ravens croaked and tumbled high above, but still she was unable to make out anything other than the slow sway of weedy fronds on the pool's rocky floor and the odd scuttle of a tiny creature below. Occasionally she noticed a small, green frog, which made its home in the mossy crevices, swimming just below the surface of the water with swift, strong strokes before disappearing beneath the rocks on the other side.

Rowan sighed, rolled over and stretched her aching limbs. It was not much of a pool as far as she was concerned. And why it was so revered and seen as sacred she could not understand, although it had never been known to fail in the memory of the villagers, even through the terrible summer they often spoke of when she and Jun were born and people from all around came for water because everywhere else ran dry. That was fifteen summers ago and sometimes Rowan felt it could have been much longer than a lifetime.

Rowan opened her eyes and allowed her gaze to wander to the high pinnacle of rock on her right which guarded the valley, an ancient and immovable presence from which a number of rowan trees sprang, in summer a mass of greenery, now their branches heavy with orange and red berries as autumn began to prepare for the hardships of the winter to come. Below, the river snaked through the valley, flashing silver in the sunlight and to her left she could make out the tops of the villagers' huts huddled together, more rocks towering above them, mirror guardians to the pinnacle on her right. On the other side of the river the bank rose steeply to the sky, covered with low scrub of thorn and stilted oak, turning to brown now autumn was in full fruit.

'The rowan is the symbol of protection and insight.' She had heard this more times than the moon had risen during her lifetime, for her mother believed the birth of Rowan and her twin Jun that scorching summer to be the salvation of the villagers, an omen which portended their importance during the years to come.

Rowan, as daughter of the Chief, was destined to be the Guardian of the sacred pool and Jun as his firstborn son, named after the juniper which could be found further along the valley, would one day be the leader of the people. But both secretly knew their roles should have been reversed.

Rowan felt as if she had been bound to the sacred pool since birth and simply could not understand why the care of it had fallen to her, while Jun spent his days learning how to shape the shaft of a spear and even carve his own spearhead. Rowan sat up as the usual feeling of jealousy gripped her. It was not fair. She would have preferred to spend more time with the other women weaving the cloth, crushing the wheat or baking, all practical tasks for which at least she could see some result at the end of the day, rather than tending the pool, gathering herbs and spending most of her time either gazing into the water or watching the clouds rolling overhead and dreaming of being the great warrior her brother would undoubtedly one day become.

There was a fighting spirit inside Rowan but she often felt she had nothing to fight for.

As she lay back once more a shadow fell across her, blocking the light of the sun. She opened her eyes to find Jun standing over her, a mirror image of herself, tall and slim with curling dark hair, although his held a reddish glint in the sunlight. Rowan jumped up. 'On guard.'

Jun raised his arms in defence, a grin on his face, but a second later found himself winded on his back, Rowan triumphantly astride him.

'You'll have to do better than that, brother,' she laughed.

'And so will you.' Jun pushed her aside and Rowan cursed as she became entangled in her woven underskirts, wishing she were allowed to wear leggings like her brother, securely strapped around his long legs and allowing ease of movement. Jun rolled over peering into the pool, becoming still and silent. He remained there for several moments until Rowan began to fidget and fiddle with the small basket of herbs she had gathered earlier. She popped a sprig of yarrow into her mouth and began to chew, savouring its bitter flavour.

Jun plunged his hand into the pool and pulled something out. A long, narrow crystal, yet like no stone the twins had ever seen before, for parts of it were translucent, starting with a base of green at one end, like the green of the valley in springtime, moving through to the violet of the rainbow and ending in a brilliantly sparkling tip. It lay in Jun's hand, as long as his palm and wide as two fingers, and Rowan gasped. 'Where did you find that? I didn't see it.'

Jun sighed and shook his head. 'It was lying

towards the back of the pool, beneath a clump of weed. But if you'd taken the time to look you would have noticed it when the weed shifted slightly and...'

Rowan grabbed the crystal from Jun's hand and held it up to the light, where it caught a stray sunbeam and flashed with all the colours of the rainbow.

'The only time I've ever seen anything remotely like this,' began Jun, mesmerised by the colours which continued to swirl and flash around the crystal with a life of their own, 'was when Crowe used his ceremonial staff, the powerful one he only brings out on special occasions and which he says is filled with magic and...'

'Let's not talk about him.' Rowan dropped the stone back into Jun's hand and the flashing ceased, leaving nothing but a beautiful crystal shining in the sunlight.

'But don't you see...'

'Oh, no more.' Rowan snatched the crystal and tossed it into the pool, where it fell with a plop and a gurgle. 'There, it's back in now. When you've gone I'll do my job properly and spend a long time staring into nothing but a pool of water and then I'll find it and everything will be all right again.'

Jun shook his head. 'You know it doesn't work like that.' He sat, cross legged, gazing at the rocks before him. The cliff, three times the height of a man, from the top of which the sacred spring burst forth, towered above them. Years of trickling water had changed the rock face to grey black in contrast to the white of the surrounding stones, and clumps of green moss fed by the never ending water supply clung to the rocks all the way down. The rock face always entranced Jun, as the water had found a hundred different channels and worn the surface away with its gentle caress over the years, eventually forming the sacred pool at the bottom.

When the sun shone in the morning, the light stole over the rocks above and lit the surface of the pool, sending fingers of gold into the ferns which surrounded it. The water was always warm - even in the depths of winter it never froze - and in the evening as the sun sank beneath the hill on the opposite side of the valley, a warmer, golden hue infused the pool, shadows flickering across its surface hinting of hidden depths.

Jun noticed too, although he was sure Rowan had no idea, the way in which the pool itself changed with the turning of the year. In the springtime when new life was abundant there was a fresh, pure feel to it, as if the water was unable to run fast enough, as though it had the whole valley to nourish. By midsummer when the crops lay abundant in the fields and greenery was all around, interspersed with summer flowers, the pool appeared more languid, as if resting for a moment, enjoying the fruits of its labour earlier in the year. And by autumn, when the harvest had been gathered and the world was moving towards the time of darkness, the water, although always trickling steadily, felt a little slower, as though waiting to rest. Now, approaching the time of the festival of the ancestors and midwinter no more than a bend in the path away, shadows flitted across the surface of the pool, some swift and deft, others darker and more lingering. By midwinter the valley would be covered in snow, icicles hanging long and twinkling down the cliff face, the water of the pool still strangely warm to the touch.

There was a toad which appeared from time to time, as if sharing the guardianship of the pool with the frog, its slow movements and jewel like eyes speaking of an ancient wisdom. If Jun lay for long enough he could sometimes see the movement of shadows in the water's clear depths and even the faces of people. On one occasion he had seen a woman with hair fashioned from the flight of the swallows and a garment of meadowsweet. But he blinked in amazement, the vision vanished and he never saw her again, no matter how long he waited.

'Don't forget the crystal,' he reminded Rowan as he rolled back from the edge of the pool and they lay side by side surveying the valley. 'I have a feeling someone from a very long way away left it there.'

Rowan shrugged. 'Don't worry. I can pull out a crystal as well as anyone.'

'I just think it's important.' Jun turned away. How could he ever explain that when he plunged his hand into the pool and the waters swirled around his fist, for a split second amongst the sunlight and the shadows, he had seen a great ship sailing over a sea, something only heard of in tales, and he knew the crystal to be more important than Rowan would ever realise.

'Come on.' Rowan pulled him to his feet, unable to sit still for more than a few moments. 'We've done all we need here. You promised to give me another lesson in spear throwing.'

Jun sighed. There was no arguing with his sister when she was in this mood. But as he turned away from the pool and they made their way into the valley, he wished for the thousandth time with all his heart, it was he who had been entrusted with the care of the sacred pool rather than Rowan, who appeared to have no affinity with it at all.

Three

Samhain

It was at the time of the final harvest of the year when Rowan first noticed the stoat and the owl.

The fruits hung heavy on the trees, augmenting a hard winter to come, the elderberries bowing in dark clusters on the branches, ripe sloes tinged with hoar as the first frosts appeared, causing Rowan's fingers to bleed and her blood to mingle with the redness of their juice as she harvested the fruit for the coming months. Hawthorn trees turned to twiggy brown branches, stark in the crisp air, their shining red berries clustered closely, and there was an abundance of apples all around which the villagers carefully stored for the winter.

The crops had been safely gathered and it was as she made her way home one day when Rowan first saw the stoat on the path before her, eyes bright as jewels in the late afternoon sunlight.

She stopped in her tracks, almost holding her breath and the stoat had surveyed her for long moments before turning and disappearing into the undergrowth, its tail dark against the lighter fur of its body. Since then she had noticed it on several occasions as she made her way to the sacred pool and at times almost felt it was waiting for her. She wondered if it was searching for food and once held out a piece of unleavened bread, but the stoat turned and disappeared into the undergrowth, taking no notice of her offering at all.

Then, one night when the days had darkened to

the point when she always made her way back to the huts in gathering twilight, she first noticed the white owl, swift and silent against the darkness of the trees. She had paused and the owl perched on the twisted branch of an oak tree above her. She resumed her footsteps and the owl flew ahead as if showing her the safest path to take. This happened time and time again, until Rowan began to look for the stoat as she walked to the pool in the mornings, and the owl on her journey home at night. And they were almost always there, one or the other, silent guardians, watching over her.

'And so, little sister, what are your plans on this night?'

Rowan turned to find Jun standing behind her. It was Samhain, the time of the final harvest of the year, a time for turning inwards, of gathering crops, animals and children, of barring doors as darkness descended and the thoughts of the villagers turned to surviving whatever nature might decide to throw at them until the midwinter festival and the return of the sun.

If they were lucky. No one was ever sure why the sun disappeared every year and could only assume it was by their efforts, and their efforts alone, that it returned just when the nights were so long the people began to believe the world would remain for ever in a state of perpetual darkness. This was when Crowe, the village Magician, came into his own, banishing the darkness, summoning the light, and making the world safe once again.

But now was the time of the ancestors. The time just before the final descent towards the darkest night when the villagers honoured those who had walked before and asked for their benevolence during the coming months. No moon hung in the sky but Rowan had never been afraid of the dark and felt a shiver of anticipation of events to come.

'Less of the little if you don't mind,' retorted Rowan. 'You know very well I am the older of the two of us.'

Jun drew a rueful expression which soon resolved itself in a smile. 'As if you'd ever allow me to forget,' he laughed as he deftly twirled his spear in the air.

'What's that?'

'What?'

'Don't play games with me.' Rowan made a grab for the spear which Jun held aloft and just out of her reach.

'My new spear of course.'

'Show me!'

'Why?'

Rowan scowled and Jun relented, handing the spear to his sister who turned it over in her hands, admiring the smoothness of the wood and the symmetry of the delicately carved spearhead inserted into the end, fashioned from hard flint, slim, pointed and dark, shining brown. She felt a sudden shiver, a premonition of this spear's place in the destiny of events to come, the history of the future, which was nothing to do with the chill of the night. 'Did you craft the spearhead?'

Jun nodded, a shy smile on his face. 'It took me two whole moons.'

Rowan sighed. 'You're so good with your hands. I wish,' she began, 'I just wish...'

'Shhh...someone's coming,' interrupted Jun, as Crowe, the village Magician appeared, bearing a flaming brand in one hand which cast both light and shadow over the deep ravines of his face and caused his ceremonial dress to appear otherworldly in the firelight.

Rowan reluctantly relinquished the spear and as Jun took it from her, he felt a shimmer of power not experienced in all the time he had been crafting it. The feeling he sometimes had when he lost himself whilst gazing into the sacred pool.

Simultaneously, each twin shared the same thought. They both felt something momentous was about to happen, but, apart from the ceremony of the ancestors and the return of the sun, neither of them had the slightest idea what it might be.

The villagers had built a huge bonfire. It was, thought Rowan, the largest ever, made up of everything which needed to be cleared away before the final dip into darkness leading to the shortest day.

This was the practical side of it. The other reason was to keep the village safe from any wayward or evil spirits which might be abroad on this night and finally, to welcome the ancestors who, everyone knew, returned from the Otherworld at this time. There would be feasting, stories to be told around the fire and oracles spoken. Crowe sometimes saw visions in the flickering flames or in the wood smoke which rose into the dark night air, bearing aloft thousands of orange sparks. He often spoke a prophecy for the cycle of the year to come, passed messages from the ancestors and gave general advice, none of which the villagers would dare ignore.

There was a general excitement in the air but Rowan always loved the time when the ceremony was almost over and the villagers, tired from feasting and storytelling, began to yawn and return to their huts. This was when the flames of the fire turned from bright orange to a mellow yellow, gently caressing the wood and turning the embers from deep red to white as the ash formed upon them, continually moving like writhing snakes within the flames. This was also when the fire was at its hottest, it was difficult to get close, and when she felt more at one with the world than at any other time during the celebrations.

But now the evening was just beginning. Twilight was deepening and everyone gathered to enjoy the fruits of their hard work. Having toiled all summer over the crops, this was a special evening when they were to roast the hog they had been fattening all year and Crowe had intimated he had something important to reveal afterwards.

Crowe. Rowan watched as he approached bearing his flaming firebrand, for as village Magician it was his duty and honour to light the ritual fire. Rowan's brow furrowed. She had never trusted him, ever since she was a little girl. There was something she could not quite define, but only identify as a feeling deep inside which she was unable to ignore. Crowe and her father were the two most powerful men in the village, but whereas she watched her father, as Chief of the villagers, carry out his duty to protect the people to the best of his ability, although Crowe was held in awe and viewed with respect, something told Rowan he was more interested in himself.

And he knew that she knew. She did not know how or why. She simply did.

Now he was dressed in all of his raven feathered finery, his skin daubed with deep blue signs and symbols of which only he knew the meaning and had hitherto not passed on to another being. Around his shoulders he wore the sacred deerskin and on his head a pair of antlers. Rowan had a vague memory these once belonged to her father, but lately seemed to have been in Crowe's possession. All around his waist hung the feathers of ravens, crows and magpies – symbols of the birds of carrion.

Something troubled Rowan, like the sting of a wasp on a summer's day, sudden and unexpected, or the bite of the horsefly which would fester as poison gathered in the wound and became an itchy mound, relieved only when the tension was finally broken and the poison drained away.

Rowan shook her head. Fanciful, she told herself. She was the twin who wanted to be the warrior, not some girl sitting around with sights and visions of the future, for which she fully admitted she had no skill at all. But just the same, every time she looked at Crowe the feeling of disquiet returned. It was more than simply a young girl being frightened by the garb of the village Magician and, try as she might, nothing she could do would make it go away.

'Now, which is which? Sometimes even I can't tell the two of you apart.'

Rowan and Jun turned to find their father standing behind them, a fond smile upon his face. He could be forgiven, thought Rowan, for from the back they did indeed appear similar, especially on a dark night and wearing cloaks. Although it was traditional for the women to allow their hair to grow long, during the summer Rowan had rebelled, chopping her dark hair until the curls lay in a tangle around her feet. This had come about in a fit of pique when she had not been

22

allowed to join Jun in learning how to craft a spear and throw it straight and true.

Rowan fumed with fury and, although she reluctantly returned to the sacred pool as bidden, from her vantage point could clearly see Jun on the hillside across the valley and wished with all her might she could have joined him. Running her hand thorough her shortened curls and admonishing herself for her temper, she mused how the act had done her no good at all.

She had been in trouble for disobedience of course, but for now she and Jun, bearing in mind her tall, willowy figure which did not yet show the curves of the other village girls, looked very much alike. In fact, Rowan rather enjoyed playing the game of drawing up her hood and pretending to be her brother, drifting on the outskirts of the groups of men, listening to their conversation and talk of livestock and farming, weapons and fighting, without anyone realising who she really was.

Which was how she came to learn of what Crowe was to speak that very night.

Four

Deerman had dreamed of the valley long before he ever saw it in reality, often waking from a trance induced state to find the lingering essence of the place still with him. Something about rocks and rivers, lush vegetation and always on the peripheral of his vision a girl, guarding something, and he was aware she needed his help and he had to find her. As time progressed the dreams became more frequent, until he knew his drumming and trance like state would transport him to the place, although he had no idea where it was in reality.

He visited for more than the entire turning of a year, more lately under guise of stoat and owl, until the feeling became so insistent he realised he needed to search for the valley himself, as a man, for whatever was waiting there was a part of his destiny.

Deerman finally found the valley and the girl on the night of the festival of the ancestors. For days he had been walking, leaving his high, moorland stone circle and striding to the south, towards the green of the trees and the valleys and hills. And it was at the brink of twilight on a late autumn evening when he finally came upon it.

He recognised the place at once. There was something about the curve of the hill and the pinnacles of rock, the rushing river below and the small village nestling amongst the greenery, which confirmed this was what he had been searching for. He had visited it so often in other forms, swift and instantaneous, although this time he had been walking for days led purely by blind intuition and trust, each step bringing him closer to his destination. It was as if a path of silver led the way, shining faintly before him whenever he faltered, and he followed it implicitly, logic admonishing him for being fanciful, instinct assuring him otherwise. He had always sensed the lines of power which ran beneath the surface of the earth, criss-crossing at special, sacred points, and intuition told him it was towards one of these he was being led.

Finally, he found himself on the uppermost pinnacle of rock with a view of the valley below, and it was obvious the villagers were preparing for the great feast of the last harvest and the honouring of the ancestors before the onset of winter.

Although he longed to be closer, Deerman knew any stranger would be treated with suspicion, especially on this night and certainly a stranger such as himself, dressed in animal skins, his kilt of stoat tails, white owl feathers entwined in the dark plaits of his hair and bearing his twisted wooden staff and sacred drum.

He could make out the forms of people below, amidst which he noticed two figures in dark cloaks who looked similar but which he knew instinctively to be different. There was a solid, enduring looking man who he immediately took to be the Chief of the people and finally, standing out because of his attire, because of the antlers upon his head and the animal skin wrapped around him as well as his stance of self importance, the village Magician. Deerman narrowed his eyes. Even from where he was standing, when he looked at the figure he sensed danger and he saw death.

Deerman knew he had been guided to the place for a reason. He touched the stoat tails hanging from his waist, felt again the strong, wily power and the essence of the creature within, briefly smelt the raw, animal smell of stoat, the rush of energy, the sudden fire in his head - and then he was gone, leaving only a rustle in the undergrowth as he made his way towards the gathering below.

Deerman settled himself at the edge of the circle of firelight to watch the proceedings, near enough for his nut brown eyes and sharp ears to take in all which was happening, far enough away to make his escape if necessary. Before long the villagers had partaken of the roasted hog and consumed copious amounts of drink, brewed from crab apples and sweetened with blackberries and elderberries, the combination of which made them increasingly noisy despite the solemnity of the occasion. He sniffed and his heightened sense of smell detected another odour amongst that of hog, alcohol and human. Herbs, which he recognised from his shamanic travels, had been added to the fire. Herbs, which Deerman knew would induce a trance in the initiated and allow access to the hidden realms, but when used on the unwary could cause drowsiness, and he wondered if their burning by the village Magician served a two-fold purpose.

From his vantage point Deerman could see the Magician strutting amongst the people, an air of self importance about him, his ceremonial dress causing him to stand out in the flickering firelight. He also noticed the two figures he had seen before, the same yet different and, to Deerman, in his guise as a stoat and with heightened intuition and perception, these seemed to be the three most important people in the entire gathering.

Deerman sensed a change in atmosphere and noticed the Magician had struck his staff into the ground and was standing beside it, arms held wide to the night sky. At the top of the staff a crystal glowed, blood red in the firelight, reflecting the light in a thousand spirals of energy. The Magician moved not a muscle, but one by one the villagers fell silent, aware the time of solemnity was upon them.

As the evening drew to a close and the fire burnt lower, the orange sparks no longer raging into the blackness of the night sky with their cloak of grey smoke, a hush descended upon the crowd. No moon could be seen, for it would be three days before the new crescent appeared above the horizon; and for the first time in her life Rowan realised how she waited for the moon to return, feeling a shiver of relief to see it hanging low on the skyline following the darkness beforehand.

'People, heed my words.' Crowe's voice rang out into the night and there was a respectful hush. He glanced around at the faces of the villagers, serious and a little ill at ease in the remaining glow of the firelight, their previous good spirits and revelry completely forgotten.

'The ancestors are calling,' he began, dropping his voice so they all strained to hear and were impelled to move a step closer.

'They have messages for us which must be heard. Important messages.' He paused, eyes peering around with relish, feeling the power within him, the power of manipulation of the masses, the power he knew would soon be his.

'Ignore these words at your peril, for their prophecy is thus.' He allowed his voice to rise in strength and deepen in resonance, waiting just a moment longer than was necessary, aware of the silence in the valley save for the crackle of the fire and the far off hoot of an owl. Somewhere nearby a fox barked and in the undergrowth an animal rustled the dryness of the bracken. Then all again was still.

'When the sun disappears on the day when night is at its longest...' Crowe paused dramatically, allowing a moment of complete silence before continuing. 'When the sun disappears on the day when night is at its longest,' he repeated, 'this time, it will not return. The world will remain for ever in darkness.'

There was a collective gasp. Crowe smiled, a slow, cynical smile, taking in the confusion of the villagers, allowing them a few fear filled moments before he spoke once again. 'But there may be some way to avoid this,' he continued, before anyone had a chance to ask any questions. 'If you will pay heed to my words and the advice of the ancestors.'

Rowan narrowed her eyes. It was all falling into place now. The conversation she had overheard earlier as she passed a small group of men, her cloak covering her head in the darkness on the outskirts of the firelight, slowly began to make sense. She only heard snatches, but it had been enough to cause her heart to fill with dread.

'Treasure,' she overheard Crowe whisper to his group of followers. 'Beneath the sacred pool.' He held out his hand and on his palm something glinted in the firelight.

Rowan had frowned, a memory stirring in her mind. Was it only a moon ago when Jun had pulled the sparkling crystal from the depths of the sacred pool and warned her to take care of it? And what had she done? As far as she remembered, tossed it back and promptly forgotten all about it. Perhaps Crowe himself had discovered it. Perhaps, despite her derision at Jun's words, it really was treasure and maybe - the thought rushed into Rowan's head on wings of fear – maybe Crowe wanted to plunder the sacred pool to discover more treasure for himself.

For an instant Rowan realised this would be her key to freedom, an end to her sacred duties, something she had wished for as long as she could remember. And yet, something told her it was intrinsically wrong. The thought of the sacred pool being plundered caused her stomach to knot so tightly she felt physically sick and the knowledge the people were being led astray by Crowe, a thought she was unable to tolerate.

Now, it all began to make sense. Crowe was using his position to his own ends to gain more power over the villagers and claim the treasure he believed to be beneath the sacred pool for himself. And only Rowan could stop him.

She grimaced into the darkness, a dark parody of a smile, because for all her thoughts of being a warrior, she simply did not know what to do. That Crowe had made his plans well she had no doubt. How to stop him, she had absolutely no idea.

'What must we do?' Rowan's father was speaking now, his strong tone of leadership calming the people into a sense of security, trusting all would be well in the end. 'Tell us and we will do your bidding.'

Crowe smiled, then frowned. This was much easier than he had expected. They were fools all of them, hanging onto his every word. By the time the day of darkness arrived the sacred pool would be no more than a muddy ditch, the water running away into a boggy marsh. The villagers would believe he had saved them and when the sun returned – as it always did - he would be far away with the treasure he was certain was buried beneath the pool. He raised his arms to the sky once more and stood for long moments, trance like, before he spoke again. 'In order to save the village, the people, our valley...' his voice rang out loud and strong into the silence of the night and not a sound could be heard save the tiny rustle of a creature in the undergrowth. 'To save the village, the people, our valley - we must dig up and sacrifice the sacred pool.'

There was silence, then a sudden uproar. Voices

raised in confusion and outrage.

'What will we do without our sacred pool?'

'This cannot be so...'

'Never...'

Rowan glanced around, hope springing into her heart. The people would not allow it, would never listen to Crowe. Her sacred and beautiful pool would be safe. For the first time in her life she realised how much she loved it.

Crowe raised his arms once more and one by one the people fell silent.

'The ancestors have spoken,' was all he said.

Glancing around, Rowan saw a look of confusion on the faces of the people, uncertain now they were confronted with the wishes of the ancestors. This, she realised, was Crowe's best ploy yet. Even her father was standing deep in thought, and suddenly Rowan knew with those few, simple words, Crowe had won the people over. In time, he would have his way.

'Noooo.' Her voice rang out, as unexpected to herself as those around her. Rowan strode forwards, her cloak flying behind her. She turned to face the people. 'I am the Guardian of the sacred pool,' she cried. 'And I tell you all, this cannot be allowed to happen.'

At first she thought she had made a difference. She saw Jun glance about him, caught his eye through the dimness of the night and for a moment they were as one, for she knew he wanted to stop this desecration and treachery as much as she. In that second, after all the years of fighting, Rowan understood her role in life and realised just what it was she had been guarding.

Crowe threw back his head and laughed, a hollow sound which rang eerily into the night sky. 'You?' He pointed one long, knobbly finger towards her and Rowan felt herself shrinking before him. 'You? Whose idea of guarding the sacred pool is to lie in the sun all day, watching the clouds and tossing pebbles into the water? You? Who would prefer to change your sacred duties for those of a warrior, rather than learn the mysteries to which you should by now have been initiated – had you been worthy.'

In the remaining heat of the fire Rowan flushed, for Crowe was right. What had she done with her guardianship of the pool? She realised now how shoddily she had treated something so precious.

'You will not only have Rowan to answer to, but me also.' Jun stepped forwards from the shadows and there was a collective gasp. As the Chief's firstborn son and prospective leader of the people he held a little more sway. He glanced towards their father, expecting him to take the matter into his own hands, but found him looking strangely disorientated and he made no move to help.

Suddenly, from beneath the folds of his animal skin Crowe drew out the sparkling crystal he had stolen from the sacred pool. He held it high in the air and the firelight glinted upon it, sending out a rainbow of colour and causing it to glow with a life of its own. 'He who bears the sacred crystal shall be all powerful,' he cried into the night sky. And so beautiful did the crystal appear in the flickering firelight against the blackness of the night, none dared question him.

'The ancestors have spoken,' repeated Crowe simply, a cruel smile playing about his lips as he replaced the crystal once more within the folds of his clothing, and both Rowan and Jun knew in that moment their battle had only just begun.

Five

It was a few days after the night of the festival of the ancestors when Rowan found the stoat. She had been on her usual journey along the footpath to the sacred pool, swishing through the brown, dying bracken and twirling a stick between her fingers before throwing it high into the air and catching it again. She imagined holding a spear, hurling it as hard as she could, higher than anyone else, allowing the energy to transfer through her arm to the spear, which finally met its target with precision. But what would a young girl such as herself ever be expected to defend in such a way?

A movement in the undergrowth caught her attention and Rowan stopped short. Probably nothing more than a bird, maybe a rabbit of which there were many to be found. Perhaps she could use her hunting skills to capture and take it home for the cooking pot, which might help to find favour with her father once more after the recent events which had left her in disgrace. The events on the night of the ancestors were still rumbling around the village causing talk and disbelief amongst the people. For Rowan, one of the worst things was that Crowe's words concerning her were true and she clearly recalled the knowledge and sadness reflected in her father's eyes.

Rowan stopped. No sound. She waited. A rustle. Bracken moved and silence descended once again. Holding her breath, Rowan crept closer, one step at a time, carefully, making no noise – and then she peered down through the bracken at the place she had heard the last rustle. Staring back at her were a pair of nut brown eyes.

Rowan gasped. No bird or rabbit then. The creature stirred, aware of Rowan's presence. She felt its fear, but saw its light brown coat was matted with blood and it was wounded, unable to move.

Slowly she reached out her hand towards the animal, part of her knowing it was entirely the wrong thing to do, for however badly wounded, the stoat would fight for its life and cause her serious injury should it sink its sharp teeth into the pale and vulnerable flesh of her arm. She had seen it happen to some of the villagers who returned wounded from hunting, the wounds swollen and filled with foul smelling pus and more than one man had lost his life – but something told Rowan there was no danger and without even thinking she followed her instinct.

'There, it's all right.' She slipped her hands around the warm body, feeling for the first time the rough, wiry hair of a living stoat. As she lifted and cradled it to her chest the stoat turned and settled itself into her arms. It gazed up, a look of utter trust in its eyes and Rowan's heart filled with wonder.

'There,' she repeated. 'Come with me and we'll see if we can make you better.' She headed for the sacred pool, for once not minding her duty, only knowing her actions were worthwhile.

Beside the pool with the stoat curled trustingly in her lap, Rowan examined its wound. It looked as if it might have been in a fight with some other creature, a fox maybe, and sustained a bite causing the loss of a good deal of blood which matted its fur but, in the process, staunched the flow.

Painstakingly, with a piece of cloth torn from the bottom of her tunic and soaked in water, Rowan gently dabbed at the dried blood. Initially the stoat winced, then after a while, perhaps soothed by the rhythmic movements, its eyes closed and it lay completely still, save for its gentle breathing.

Rowan worked on, completely absorbed in her task. When, finally, all the blood had been cleared away she could see that the wound was not as bad as it had first appeared. Now, what would her mother have used? She racked her brains, wishing she had paid more attention to the skills of healing, as she had repeatedly been told but stubbornly ignored. Finally, she remembered juniper was good for cleaning wounds and yarrow for the clotting of blood, both of which grew nearby so, laying the stoat in a safe place amidst a bed of bracken and dried grass, she went in search of the healing herbs further along the valley.

After collecting what she hoped would be enough juniper berries and a bunch of yarrow, Rowan returned to the pool and peeped at the stoat. It lay just as she had left it, curled upon a bed of bracken and grass, but there seemed more of a rested air about the animal now, its nose turned into the dark hair of its bushy tail and its little body rising and falling steadily.

Rowan worked swiftly and deftly. She ground the juniper berries, their tangy scent assailing her senses, then added water, mixed some more, added the yarrow, mixed yet again into a smooth paste, and finally it was ready.

Before applying it to her patient, Rowan placed her little earthenware bowl containing the salve by the side of the pool and walked to the edge of the enclosure. She stood for a moment surveying the valley before her. The river rushing below, the rise of the hill on the other side and the tops of the villagers' huts to her left. Further along lay the remains of the fire, now a dark circle of ash. But even the memory of recent events and her disgrace could not take away the feeling of wonder and contentment Rowan felt in rescuing the stoat and mixing the salve. She was certain now the animal would live and its survival would be partly due to her.

She turned back to the pool. Maybe at last she had discovered her place in the world. Perhaps she was destined to become a healer rather than the warrior she had always longed to be.

Humming softly and feeling unusually at one with everything around her, Rowan arrived at the pool and stopped short. The little bowl containing the salve had completely disappeared and, when she peeped into the bed of bracken and grass where she had left it safely sleeping, of the stoat, there was no sign at all.

Six

The wheel of the year turned slowly as winter took its grip across the valley, bringing grey days and dark skies. A sharp wind whipped through the bare branches of the trees and around the corners of rocks, stinging eyes and causing the villagers to gasp with each intake of breath.

Rowan continued her duties at the sacred pool. She had been admonished over her outburst on the night of the ancestors, her words counting as nothing against those of the Magician's and, her father told her, brought disgrace upon the family when her shortcomings as the Guardian of the sacred pool were brought to everyone's attention. Following this he said no more, but Rowan knew it to be only a matter of time before a decision was made concerning her future. For the first time in her life, Rowan began to respect the trust which had been placed in her through her simple work of tending the pool and to understand its importance to the people. She wondered if she had lost both before she had known what they really meant.

Crowe had said nothing further, but she was aware of his presence and the fact he was continually watching her. Watching and waiting.

It was on a morning when the clouds hung low on the horizon and the scent of snow was in the air when Rowan found the man. Huddled beside the sacred pool, wrapped in animal hides, he lay sleeping, but by some instinct Rowan knew this man slept no healthy sleep, the taut, whiteness of the skin stretched across his high cheekbones and the rapid rise and fall of his chest pointing to the fact he was nearing his life journey's end.

She threw down her basket and ran to him, touching a brow which burned hot and cold at the same time. After a moment his eyes fluttered open, brown as the nut of the hazel, she thought, as another part of her mind raced for the knowledge to save him.

'Come. Can you stir?' She touched him gently, he winced, and Rowan realised the skins covering his shoulder were soaked in blood. An image stole into her mind of the tiny creature she had rescued only a short while before, which had so bewilderingly disappeared, taking her salve with it.

The man grunted, whether in agony or response she could not tell, but Rowan understood the need to keep him warm and once again prepare a salve to heal the wound and a brew to lower his fever.

But she could not do it alone. There was a movement at the entrance of the enclosure and Rowan turned to find Jun staring at the man, aware her twin's presence was due to the unmistakeable link between them.

'Thank the Gods,' she whispered. 'Come and help. I need a fire built so I can make a salve and brew some herbs, and this man needs to be kept warm or he will die.'

'Can we...'

Rowan shook her head, knowing Jun's question before it left his lips. 'No one must know of this.' She did not understand why herself, only that keeping his presence a secret was of imperative importance. 'And anyway,' she continued, 'he cannot be moved.'

Jun stood for a moment, then turned to carry out Rowan's bidding.

'I won't be long,' promised Rowan, and she was gone.

This time she knew exactly where to look for the herbs she needed. Once again the antiseptic berries of the juniper and the blood clotting properties of the yarrow were required, which she also proposed to use in a brew to reduce the man's fever. It occurred to her that his wounds were very similar to those of the disappearing stoat.

Feeling for the first time she was doing something useful, Rowan cut the last of the yarrow and placed the stems carefully in her basket alongside the juniper berries. When she returned Jun would have lit the fire and the water would be heating. She straightened up and stopped dead, aware she was no longer alone. Turning slowly, she found Crowe standing right behind her.

'Get out of my way.' Rowan's voice did not waver although her heart was pounding. Her body quivered and she was certain Crowe sensed her discomfort, although she determined to hide it as best she could.

Crowe smiled. 'And why are you in such a hurry this dismal morning?'

'None of your business.' Rowan made to pass but he stepped into her path.

'Remember,' he whispered, 'your days are numbered. The ancestors have spoken and the sacred pool must be sacrificed to the Gods.' He grimaced. 'At best, moved to another place.'

'You have spoken, you mean,' responded Rowan. 'I know of your plan, you don't deceive me. You seek the treasure which lies beneath.' For a moment she wondered if she should have kept the information to herself, but the flash of respect for her knowledge, swiftly followed by anger in Crowe's eyes confirmed she was correct.

Crowe's hand snaked out and grasped Rowan's throat. He was so quick she did not have time to react and could only gasp in pain as his grip tightened and the colours around her blurred as the world began to spin. She grasped his wrist and struggled to release herself, aware that in a few moments she would be in a dead faint. With the last of her strength she jabbed her knee sharply upwards and, with a curse and a groan, Crowe loosened his grip and Rowan wrenched herself free. But before she could escape, Crowe grabbed her foot and brought her tumbling to the ground once again, rolling over and imprisoning her against the clumps of reeds amidst the mud of the riverbank.

'You,' he hissed, his voice low, 'you will all pay for

this. Your silly little pool and your family and your village and your valley. And as for you, I curse you in the name of the ancestors who watch over us.'

Rowan felt a swift stab of fear for these were strong words indeed. She read the pure hatred and intent in Crowe's eyes, wondering what had caused this man to turn his back on the community he had served for so many years. She remembered how frightening Crowe appeared when she was a child and recalled he was never granted the position of Guardian of the sacred pool, although throughout the years he had made it clear to be his desire.

Summoning all her strength Rowan spat in his face, knowing that, after all her longing to be a warrior, the Guardian of the sacred pool was her destiny and hers alone. And for the first time in her life she had something to fight for.

She pushed Crowe aside with a strength she was unaware she possessed, taking them both by surprise, then turned and looked him straight in the eye. 'And you,' she whispered, 'if you do one thing to harm the sacred pool, the villagers, this valley, then I swear...' She paused and the greyness of the day closed in around them, the first fluttering flakes of snow falling and whipping away before they were able to touch the frozen ground. The sharp wind whistled and played in the branches of the willow trees, singing a mournful melody as the icy river continued its incessant rushing. Rowan drew a deep breath. 'I swear,' she continued, 'by the rocks above us and the water below, that if you do one thing to harm the sacred pool, the villagers, this valley... then I will kill you.'

And she was gone, grabbing her basket of herbs and running as swiftly as she could back to Jun and the wounded man, as if not only her life, but the lives of all around her depended upon it.

Rowan arrived at the entrance to the enclosure gasping for breath, her throat aching from the pressure of Crowe's hands. Glancing back towards the river she could see no sign of Crowe and felt relieved. If Jun had lit the fire and heated the water she could begin her work. But when Rowan reached the sacred pool there was no fire, no Jun and no wounded man. Once again, it was as if they had vanished into thin air and there was no trace of either of them, save for one white feather which lay on the grass beside the trickling water, moving gently amidst the ever increasing snowflakes.

Seven

It was almost the time of the darkest day and the villagers were preparing for the ritual of the return of the sun. Despite Crowe's repeated attempts to persuade them to destroy the sacred pool, nothing had yet occurred and Rowan felt they were hanging on until the last moment, fearful of what might happen if they carried out Crowe's instructions, afraid of what would happen if they did not. But Crowe was merely biding his time for Rowan knew he was confident his wishes would come to pass. At one point she requested an audience with her father in an attempt to explain everything, but he had been ill of late with a sickness which caused him to turn inwards on himself, his body wasting and wracked with pain.

The snows came, turning the valley to white.

Rowan's fingers froze and icicles hung like daggers from the rocks around the sacred pool – but still the water ran as crystal clear as always and was surprisingly warm to the touch when she plunged her hands into it.

Even her daily trek to and from the sacred pool became difficult as snow lay higher than her waist in places, and the villagers cut paths to the areas they needed to visit regularly. In the sunlight the snow was a twinkling, silver blanket lying over the land, causing the branches of the trees to bow down, the spikes of the gorse with its tiny golden flowers seemingly the only plant not entirely covered in white. Rowan imagined the plants beneath, waiting, curled in the ground until it was safe to venture out. But when the skies darkened to slate grey and the fat flakes began to swirl into the deepening gloom she sometimes found the snow a little frightening.

However, Rowan found no time to take much notice, except to be thankful she was left well alone, because her thoughts had been on other matters.

When Rowan returned with her basket of herbs following her encounter with Crowe to discover the man had disappeared, she wondered briefly if she was going mad. People and animals did not simply vanish into thin air, whisked away by the spirits, and just as she was beginning to wonder if this had truly happened, there was a low whistle and she turned to find Jun standing outside the enclosure beckoning her to follow him.

'Come quick, before anyone sees,' he hissed. 'This way.'

Grabbing her basket, Rowan followed Jun up the hillside to a dense patch of undergrowth that looked impenetrable but through which a small path had been cut, opening into a space leading to the entrance of a low cave reaching back into the rock. Inside, lay the man.

'I had to bring him here for safety,' explained Jun. 'After you left Crowe was lurking around and...'

'What place is this?' interrupted Rowan, as she knelt beside the man and placed her hand on his still burning brow. 'How on earth did you find it?'

Jun shrugged. 'I've known of it for a long time,' he admitted. 'Sometimes I just need to be alone and here is as good as anywhere.' He paused and Rowan realised Jun had been aware of the secret place all his life. She imagined in the summer the leaves of hazel and beech would form a shady bower, cool respite from the hot sun, and in winter the cave would remain dry as a bone. She wondered how she had spent her time so close to the place, yet never discovered it herself.

'He's worse,' confirmed Rowan. 'But you did the right thing. I've just met Crowe and, well, it wasn't good. Now, have you any hot water?'

Jun nodded and Rowan set to work. She made her salve and placed it upon the man's wound. The brew would follow later when he was able to sip the cooling potion.

'There.' She finally sat back, feeling more exhausted than ever before in her life, the shock of her encounter with Crowe and the concentration on healing the man overcoming her. 'Now, all we can do is wait,' murmured Rowan, as her eyes closed of their own accord and Jun gently covered her sleeping form, positioning himself at the entrance of the cave, tending the small fire, watching and waiting.

When Rowan awoke she felt completely disorientated. She recalled collecting juniper berries and yarrow, remembered Crowe's hands about her throat, then saw the man lying beside her and everything came flooding back. 'How is he?' She struggled to sit up but Jun placed a gentle hand upon her shoulder.

'Sleeping easily now – thanks to you.' His eyes held a measure of respect. 'I managed to get him to take some of the yarrow brew and his temperature has lessened.'

Rowan nodded. The man did indeed appear better, the taut, white skin across his cheekbones looser now with a little more colour, and even the braids of his dark hair which hung almost to his waist seemed less lifeless.

'You did well, sister,' murmured Jun, as he tended the small fire.

And for the first time in her life Rowan experienced a feeling of true satisfaction.

By the time the shortest day was almost upon them, Deerman, as they learned he was called, was sitting up and growing stronger with every passing moment. But that his name was Deerman was not the only thing Rowan and Jun discovered.

Finally Rowan understood what happened to the stoat, when Deerman explained how the great white owl and the stoat which she had encountered were actually himself in different forms.

'I know it's hard to believe,' he told her, his dark eyes holding her entranced, the melody of his deep voice causing her to feel she could listen to him talking for ever, 'but there are many things on the earth which we cannot explain and all I know is, it is the truth. It's like a fire in my head, it consumes me, and then all of a sudden I find a different form and the more I do it, the easier it becomes.'

'So the injured stoat was you,' confirmed Rowan.

Deerman nodded. 'When I awoke by the sacred pool I was back in human form. I remembered something about being picked up and then sleeping, sleeping, and then I wasn't sure where I was and, before anyone came, took the bowl and crept away. I'm sorry.' He smiled gently. 'It must have been frightening for you, but not as bad as if you'd turned your back on a stoat one moment and found a fully grown man there the next.'

Rowan nodded, thinking the one aspect of Deerman which could never be hidden, whatever form he chose to take, were his eyes, brown as the hazelnuts which fell from the trees around them.

'And although the salve helped,' he continued, 'the wound opened again and I knew I had to return to the pool in the hope you would find me and be able to finish the work you began.' He reached out and pressed her hand briefly, yet firmly. 'Thank you,' he finished gravely. And Rowan knew he meant it from the bottom of his heart.

'Bad times are coming,' Deerman told them on another occasion. 'It is why I felt the need to come here. I don't know what and I don't know how I can help, but it is to do with the dark of the year, to do with the moon and the sun and darkness and light. Something will happen in the heavens and everything will be different on this earth.

Rowan told him the tale of Crowe, the treasure he believed to be hidden beneath the sacred pool and his prophesy to the villagers.

'I disliked him the moment I first saw him,' said Deerman, 'but all we can do is watch and wait.'

'What will happen if this befalls us and how can we prevent it?' asked Jun.

'I don't know any of the answers,' replied Deerman. 'But something tells me we must remember our world is not the only one. There are ways into the Otherworld. Your sacred pool is one of them and there is another at the base of the highest rock. It looks like a cave, but it isn't. It doesn't go in very deep, yet if you venture there, if the Gods allow it, you will find the entrance to a world which is like our own, only different.'

'Have you been there?' asked Jun, his eyes alight with interest.

Deerman nodded. 'Many times through different portals.' He paused. 'There are lines of energy all over the earth, although we cannot see them, and the places they cross are of great power, the sacred pool being one. Two strong lines cross there. But the Otherworld is not a place to linger for fear you might not find your way back and, as I said, things are... different.'

He paused and both Rowan and Jun had the feeling it was best to leave him to his thoughts.

'You must rest now,' said Rowan firmly.

'One final thing,' continued Deerman, as his eyes began to close. 'It might be an idea to leave a weapon of some kind there, near the portal beneath the rocks, just in case you need it.'

As Deerman sank into the oblivion of healing sleep, Rowan and Jun looked at each other and shared the same thought. There was much yet to happen and, despite all which had already come about, their true battle had not even begun.

Eight

Midwinter Solstice

Whilst Deerman was sleeping, Jun climbed to the foot of the tallest pinnacle of rock in the valley and found the cave which was not a cave. It was strange, for it appeared to recede beneath the rocks yet was simply a shadow. But he would have trusted Deerman with his life and so hid his special spear in the undergrowth beside it. And he took time to instruct Rowan further in the use of the weapon. Just in case.

Rowan trusted Deerman too. So much so, she found herself sitting for hours by his sleeping form, watching his strong features, the way his dark hair, which she had painstakingly replaited, snaked around his face, how the muscles rippled beneath his tanned skin, tattooed with signs and symbols of nature and the elements. Once, she took an owl feather which had fallen from one of his plaits and, rather than weave it back into his hair, tucked it into the little pouch she always carried about her, in memory of their time together.

Rowan continued to visit the sacred pool and Jun ensured he was seen around the village so as not to arouse suspicion, but all appeared quiet and they almost began to imagine nothing would come of the previous events. The only problem was the news their father's health continued to fail and none of the village healers appeared able to cure him. Rowan could not help but suspect Crowe's hand in this.

It was on a cold morning when the snow was

once more beginning to fall and Rowan, Jun and Deerman were struggling to keep warm, when Deerman's eyes shot open and he sat bolt upright. 'It is time,' he said, and Rowan and Jun knew from his tone the day they were waiting for had arrived.

'The light,' continued Deerman. 'And the rhythm of the earth, the heartbeat deep inside...' His voice trailed off, but Rowan and Jun felt it too. There was a change in the air around them, to the extent Rowan almost imagined she was in the Otherworld of which Deerman so often spoke. If she closed her eyes she could feel the ground beneath her feet beating in time with her heart and when she peered out of the cave between the bare branches of the trees, the light seemed dimmer. No sound could be heard and the valley held an air of anticipation.

It was then they heard the beat of the drums, at odds to the heartbeat of the earth, slow and steady but filled with a menace which could not be ignored.

'They are coming,' whispered Deerman, struggling to stand, but Rowan pushed him gently back, although her body trembled with fear.

'Stay still,' she murmured, noting his white features and the sheen of perspiration upon his skin.

'Rowan.' Jun's voice was urgent. 'They're heading towards the sacred pool. The time has come to dig it up. Crowe...' His voice trailed away in horror as he peered down from their hiding place and watched the band of villagers weaving their way along the path below them, fear mixed with grim determination on the faces of the people, triumph on that of Crowe. 'We must protect it,' hissed Jun urgently. 'Come.'

Leaving Deerman in the cave, Rowan and Jun made their way down the slope, arriving at the sacred pool just before Crowe and the villagers. Rowan's heart sank. Here were people she had known all her life. The women who had helped to raise her and the men who told her stories on dark, firelit nights. She wondered where her father was in her hour of need, what ill Crowe had caused to happen and how, with his magic, manipulative words and quest for treasure, he had turned the hearts and minds of the people against her family.

'Go home.' Jun spoke with all the authority he could muster. 'Go home now and forget this treachery.'

The villagers paused uncertainly, but Crowe continued to advance.

'I have the magic crystal,' he wheedled, triumph in his eyes. 'And he who holds the magic crystal wields the power.' He turned to the villagers, holding the brilliant green and violet crystal high above him.

The villagers nodded. 'Aye.' It was one of the elders who spoke, although his eyes would not meet Rowan's. 'It is as we have agreed. He who holds the magic crystal wields the power of the ancestors.'

'And the time has come!' Holding the brilliant crystal aloft and turning it slowly so it gleamed brightly in the ever dimming light, Crowe raised his other hand to the skies in a gesture of power. 'Begin your work in the name of the ancestors,' he cried. 'Destroy the sacred pool.'

Rowan took a deep breath in one final attempt to change their minds, show them how they had been tricked by Crowe, but before she could utter a sound there was a rush of wings and a great white owl swooped low over the small group of people, grasped the crystal from Crowe's outstretched hand in its huge talons and disappeared swiftly down the valley into the increasing darkness of the day.

Rowan faced Crowe, the villagers stunned and huddled behind him.

Crowe gathered himself, clearly shocked but determined not to lose face. 'I warn you for the last time,' he continued in loud, ringing tones, turning to the villagers. 'Unless you sacrifice the pool, the sun will disappear and never return. Your world will remain in darkness for ever more. These are the words of the ancestors.'

There was a flurry of snow, the flakes falling suddenly thick and fast, the sky darkening, crowding in on the valley as if night had truly come in the middle of the day.

'Seize her,' he screamed, as the skies darkened even more. 'And when you have taken her set about your work, before it is too late.'

Rowan turned and fled. She ran faster than she had ever run in her life, hampered by her skirts and the snow which was now swirling thickly around her. She headed for the rock high above the valley, for the portal to the Otherworld of which Deerman had spoken and which she knew to be her only chance of salvation, intent upon reaching the portal and the weapon she knew to be hidden there.

Behind her she could hear the shouts of Crowe and the villagers, and Rowan felt a rush of relief that, for the moment, Crowe was more interested in her capture than the destruction of the sacred pool. Her breath was ragged and she was aware she could not run for much longer but must reach her destination.

At the base of the pinnacle of rock, Rowan surveyed the patch of darkness of which Deerman had spoken. Flinging herself into the undergrowth, her hands scrabbled furiously until they closed around the wooden shaft of the spear Jun had left there only days before. She heard a shout as the villagers converged upon her, urged on by Crowe.

Rowan waited, realising that indeed, something was terribly amiss with the valley and the ever deepening light in the sky. Closing her eyes, she sent a silent prayer for help to the Gods, but still Crowe and the villagers advanced. Crowe stepped forwards, arms aloft and wide open to the sky, a triumphant look upon his face. His time had come for revenge and power.

Rowan turned towards the river, took a deep breath and howled. In sheer anger and frustration, she found a voice she had not known existed, her anguish echoing through the valley, swirling around the trees, riding upon flakes of snow, bouncing off the crystals of ice which clung in frozen steadfastness to the rocks and skimming over the surface of the water which rushed through the river bed. Her cry echoed around the valley despite the ever thickening snow and the villagers momentarily stepped back.

Rowan turned to face Crowe, felt the smoothness of the spear's wooden shaft in her hand, aware of the sharpness of its point as she balanced it above her shoulder. 'I warned you what would happen if you harmed this valley or any of the villagers,' she shouted, her words dancing upon the snow which swirled around her.

Crowe laughed. 'And what could a mere slip of a girl like you do?' he countered, a mocking tone to his voice. 'That useless brother of yours cannot even protect you. A fine pair you have shown yourselves to be.' He laughed again, a dry, mirthless sound which echoed along the valley on the heels of Rowan's howl, riding on the increasing strength of the wind as the day darkened even further into twilight.

'Destroy the pool,' he shouted, and as the villagers, unable to think for themselves, finally turned to do his bidding, Rowan raised the spear and aimed straight at Crowe.

'Stop them,' she commanded. The spear was finely balanced, waiting only for her to draw back her arm and hurl it towards its target. Thunder rumbled and a flash of lightning lit the darkness of the surrounding countryside.

'Stop them, or I will kill you,' she repeated. Her words were whipped away on the wind, swirled into the sky then dropped again for all to hear.

Rowan held the spear steady, well balanced, just as Jun had taught her.

Crowe laughed and Rowan knew he would never give up until he had achieved his goal. She drew a deep breath, pulled back her arm and hurled the spear towards him, the spearhead speeding high into the air, arcing through the snow filled sky until it found its target with a sickening thud.

The last vision the villagers had was of Rowan standing above them whilst a great white owl swooped low over their heads. She raised her arm, feeling the weight of the owl upon it as a fork of lightning illuminated the body of Crowe lying inert upon the snow, a pool of red spreading around him. Then the portal opened and the world, as Rowan knew it, disappeared.

Nine

Rowan's eyes fluttered open. In stark contrast to the thick snow which had swirled around her only moments before, the sun warmed her face from a brilliant blue sky. Deerman was lying beside her.

She blinked, struggling to remember. She recalled the snow, the darkening of the day, Crowe and his ultimatum, the brilliant crystal of power snatched from his outstretched hand by the great white owl. She remembered Crowe ordering the villagers to destroy their sacred pool, the raising of her arm, the rush of the spear as it left her grasp and flew towards its target - the thud as it found its mark. She recalled the great white owl, flying fast and low, landing heavily on her arm, and then...

Deerman stirred, opened his brown eyes and smiled. 'You did it,' he said.

'Did what?' Rowan was still unsure quite what had happened.

'Found the portal, entered the Otherworld. And just in time too, I believe.'

Rowan looked around in amazement. 'So this... is the Otherworld?'

Deerman nodded.

'But it's just like our world, only the weather's different,' said Rowan, gazing around. It was strange. The light was dimming rapidly, as it had in their own world, but here it was unmistakeably summer.

'Not quite,' responded Deerman. 'Take a moment to look.'

And then Rowan realised the Otherworld wasn't like her world at all.

To begin with, the light was subtly different. Even though the sky was clear and blue the colours were muted, more brooding compared to the freshness of the landscape she had left behind. And although this was unmistakeably the valley with the rushing river below and topped by the same white rocks, the oak trees had disappeared and so had the huts of the villagers. In fact, compared to her world, this valley, although covered in swaying green bracken, felt like a wasteland.

Her gaze travelled along the contours of the hillside and stopped short. 'What's that?' She pointed to a structure nestling behind some trees to the left. 'Surely it's where the sacred pool should be?'

Deerman nodded. 'I've seen it before when I've travelled here. The sacred pool is still there, and yet it isn't...' He jumped up, seemingly filled with energy. 'Come on, I'll show you. Take my hand.'

'Is it safe?' asked Rowan in alarm, reluctant to leave the rock and the portal she knew was nearby, fearful they might be unable to return.

'Trust me,' said Deerman. 'It will be all right.'

'Wait.' Rowan paused, her hand in Deerman's, puzzling to make sense of it all. 'The owl...' She stared at him. 'The crystal... Where is it?'

Deerman frowned as if trying to remember. 'I had it,' he began, 'and then as I flew along the valley it slipped from my grasp, and then... and then all I knew was I needed to get back to you.' He shrugged. 'It can't be helped. Maybe it will turn up again in our world. Stranger things have happened. Now, come on.'

They scrambled down the slope, Rowan glancing fearfully around. When they reached the place where the sacred pool should have been she simply stared at a building, square, stone built and sturdy, yet appearing to waver in the air, and when she tentatively tried to touch the wall, her hand passed straight through.

A woman appeared from behind the structure and settled herself beside a man who was sitting cross legged on a large woven piece of cloth. They were people such as Rowan had never seen before, but she had no time to look more closely for she realised the day was dimming rapidly and wondered if this was indeed the end of the world.

'Take my hand.' As Deerman uttered the words, Rowan noticed the woman had taken the man's hand also as the darkness closed around them.

Then Deerman pulled her straight through the wall and Rowan found herself inside the stone built structure with corners instead of curves. There was a huge slab of granite at one end - an altar she realised. All around in the dimness of the little building were flickering flames, points of light shining in the darkness and Rowan gasped at the beauty of it all.

'Come.' Deerman gestured for her to follow him. They passed through another wall and found themselves where the sacred pool should have been, but now, although the water gushed as crystal clear as ever, it was surrounded by stonework. Corners everywhere. Rowan knelt down, wondering what had happened. And then she saw it. Lying within the depths of the pool, the sparkling crystal which Crowe had held aloft, which Deerman, in the form of an owl, had snatched and dropped somewhere along the valley.

Rowan gasped. 'Can I touch it?' she asked, reaching out, then remembering the wall.

'Try.' Deerman's voice was a whisper, and Rowan plunged her hand into the pool and grasped the crystal.

The water felt unusually icy to the touch.

'I have it.'

'Perhaps it is to do with the sacred water, maybe...'

'Someone's coming,' whispered Rowan, and sure enough, the woman she had seen previously appeared around the side of the building.

Rowan stood stock still, taking time to look more carefully at the apparition before her. Never had she seen a person quite like this, dressed in the blues and greens of the valley, yet Rowan sensed a familiarity about her. The woman knelt before the water and plunged her arm in right up to the elbow, searching for something. As she withdrew it, the water glistened in the bright sunlight, a cascade of twinkling diamonds running back into the pool. The woman appeared puzzled, thrust her arm in again and Rowan knew with absolute certainty that she was searching, searching.

'Come,' said Deerman. 'We must go back. It doesn't do to stay too long here and we have all we need.'

Rowan's hand tightened around the crystal. She knew the woman had been looking for it too, but Deerman was urging her away, back up the slope to the portal, their feet stumbling on the grassy tufts, the alien air rasping in their lungs. There was a feeling of urgency as the world around them seemed to quiver, as if they were viewing it through water. Rowan almost fell in her efforts to keep up with Deerman who was making swift progress. He turned to see her floundering below him and reached towards her. 'Take my hand,' he shouted, his words hazy and indistinct, and with the last of her strength Rowan reached out her own.

'How...' gasped Rowan, but Deerman was holding

her tightly, his strength seeping into her, his face turned towards the sky in a mixture of agony and ecstasy as he gave a massive cry and, once again, the world closed in upon them both. There was a rushing in her mind like the pounding of a great river and Rowan put her hands to her head, unable to think or understand what was happening.

As the feeling subsided, she found herself once more in her own world, this time standing by the sacred pool and surrounded by the villagers who looked set to begin its destruction. The illness of their Chief, Crowe's predictions, his death and the ever increasing darkness had proved too much for them and they were taking the only way out they knew. Tools gleamed in the dim light and their faces held a mixture of fear and grim determination.

There was a collective gasp as Rowan appeared, seemingly out of thin air, the great white owl once again upon her arm, the crystal of power in her hand which she held aloft for its rainbow of colour to be seen by all. At the same moment the clouds rolled back and the villagers witnessed a shining halo of light in the sky with a centre of deepest black surrounded by fire – and then the sphere of the moon began to move across the sun and the light to return once more.

The villagers turned back to Rowan, her arms outstretched and bearing the brilliant green and violet crystal which they believed to hold such power; and at that moment a shaft of sunlight illuminated it, causing a rainbow of light to shimmer all around.

The clouds swept away to reveal a shining blue sky and the people stood silently in awe, watching the sparkling landscape revealed before them in the ever increasing sunlight – and in a rush of wings, the great white owl took flight and disappeared silently along the valley once again.

Ten

Imbolc

'And so, all is well.' Jun gazed into the sacred pool, a slight frown upon his brow. The snows were melting slowly, patches of green appearing here and there to herald the end of the long, hard winter. A pale sun struggled to stretch its light across the valley in welcome of the life which was beginning to appear all around. Although it was cold, there was a feeling of hope in the air.

'Is it?' Rowan searched Jun's face as he turned back towards her. 'Not with you, I feel.'

He sighed. 'Only a few short moons ago you would not even have noticed, but no, things are not well with me,' he agreed.

Rowan made no comment but waited patiently. A skill which was new to her but one upon which she was working. She gazed into the sacred pool, its waters running crystal clear as ever and thought she saw a shadow cross the surface, swiftly, like the running of the hare, but shook the thought away. Sometimes she wondered if she had become a little too fanciful.

'You've found your place,' began Jun, 'and it's what is fitting and expected of you. You have shown you will fight to the death to protect the sacred pool and that is the mark of the true Guardian.' He sighed. 'I have loved this place and perhaps possess some of the skills you are now discovering, but to stay here is not my destiny.'

'But...' Rowan knew Jun was no warrior as their father had expected, although since his recent illness, which had miraculously disappeared upon the death of Crowe, he seemed much more tolerant of the wishes of the twins. 'So what is your destiny?' she eventually asked.

'My destiny is to follow in the footsteps of Deerman,' Jun replied. 'To be at one with the earth, the sky and the creatures which live beneath and within it. And my skills of scrying and healing will help the people here, or wherever I might travel.'

They both fell silent. Rowan knew Jun and Deerman had spent many hours together, both before and after her journey with him to the Otherworld, and harboured an increasing suspicion he and Deerman often travelled there together. She had sometimes seen the great white owl, accompanied by a huge buzzard, flying swiftly along the valley and imagined Jun's skills to be growing daily.

'And so,' continued Jun, 'something, somewhere is calling me and I have to leave. I've made my decision, taken my choice.' He thought back to the moment he finally realised he was no hunter and would never become a warrior.

He had spent all morning hunting the deer, following it along the valley beside the river and up into the undergrowth and low woodland, but every time he got near something stopped him. Once, a wild duck had flown up from the rushes, causing the deer to start and bound out of range. Another time, he had been at the point of throwing his spear, arm poised, body tensed, when he heard the sound of voices nearby, his concentration was broken and the moment lost.

And finally, finally, he was close, very close. The deer was grazing in a copse of low trees and Jun remained crouched, half hidden and clutching his spear tightly for what seemed an eternity. Eventually he straightened up and leaned forwards, slowly and carefully, lost in the moment, his brown, flint spearhead ready to claim its prize. He pulled his arm back, eye intent on his quarry, and then... And then the deer raised its head and looked at him.

Jun had frozen, his hand clasping the spear, completely unable to move as his eyes met those of the deer. It stood, silently chewing, watching him trustingly, completely unaware of the danger it was in and totally unafraid.

Jun remained in the same position for long moments until the deer lowered its head and began pulling the grass once more, at which point, with a will of its own, Jun's arm dropped slowly to his side, the spear falling from his stiff fingers.

He simply could not do it.

There was something Deerman had told him about the web of life, and although Jun knew hunting and killing were all a part of the great cycle, there was more, about the sanctity of life, of every single thing, man, animal, plant and stone, having its own spirit, and in that moment the essence of the deer had shone through, sang out to him in its gentle way and Jun saw a kindred spirit rather than an animal to be hunted.

He stooped, picked up the spear and turned away from the clearing. He fingered the flint spearhead, the best he had ever made, which had already taken one man's life, running his fingers along the serrated edges, wondering if he would ever find the courage to use it again. Knowing deep inside he never would.

Rowan nodded. She knew the pull between duty and personal choice was hard, but in the end Jun's heart had won.

'I only hope no ill comes of it,' said Jun softly, and Rowan saw the swift vision of a cloud passing before the face of the sun.

She grasped his hand. 'You must follow your heart, wherever it might lead you,' she replied. 'It is the only way to true happiness.'

'Like you?'

'Yes, like me.' Rowan nodded quietly and was silent for a moment. She too, had made her choice. Her destiny was to be the Guardian of the sacred pool, even though Deerman had asked her to go with him to his stone circle upon the moor, even though she loved him with all her heart and knew with an utter certainty she was carrying his child inside her, although little time had passed since their union.

Following the return of the sun, Rowan and Deerman had finally made their way to the cave and fallen into an exhausted sleep, each waking to the knowledge of a strong and enduring love which neither could put into words but which bound them together, body to body, mind to mind, spirit to spirit. Rowan would never in her life forget the feeling of being completely at one with another soul, as surely as the earth and the water, the sun and the moon, merged together in her beloved valley to create such beauty. She traced the lines of Deerman's face as she gazed into his brown eyes and knew that, for as long as she lived, he would be her one and only love.

But despite such intensity of feeling, her ties with

the sacred pool were so strong she knew she would remain there until the end of her days.

Rowan shook her head, thinking of the last time she had seen Deerman, when she bade him farewell. She pressed the brilliant crystal into his hand, a memory of their time together – and he handed her his twisted staff of rowan, for protection, then turned and walked away towards the moors and his own people, his kilt of stoat tails swinging in the wintry sunlight. He never once looked back, walking steadily forwards the whole time, although Rowan's gaze followed his retreating form until he was no more than a speck in the landscape and she knew within her heart she would never see him again.

'He has his own life to lead. Maybe we just weren't meant to be together. Perhaps it wasn't our journey.' She touched her belly softly. 'But I will have something to remember him by and this child will follow in either my footsteps or his.'

She did not tell Jun of the vision she had seen in the clear waters of the pool, of a woman whose hair continually moved with the flight of the raven, her gown of white snowflakes interlaced with the gold of the gorse, her presence giving Rowan the strength to carry on. If she had not seen this, Rowan doubted she could have lived without once more looking into Deerman's brown eyes and feeling his gentleness as he held her to him, their bodies and spirits entwined as one.

After seeing the vision for the first, and last, time in her life, Rowan crafted a knot of rowan leaves and dropped it into the pool, a sacrifice to the spring, for she knew without a doubt she and Deerman would always be together in spirit and they would indeed meet again, although perhaps not in this lifetime.

The sun was setting, beginning to dip behind the hill, streaking the sky with fingers of gold and yellow as the final light of day caught the clouds. The world was still and silent.

Jun climbed to the top of the highest pinnacle and surveyed the valley around him. The river rushing below, gleaming in the dying rays of the sun and the starkness of the trees at the end of winter, yet with new life pulsating within, waiting to burst forth. It was beautiful. All so wonderful he felt his heart must surely burst with happiness.

He felt the sting of tears in his eyes as the overwhelming feeling exploded in his chest, unsure if it was elation or frustration or a combination of the two. He felt heavy and he felt light. In his heart he held the sadness of the world and the ecstasy of being alive.

A movement caught his eye as a hare bounded along the valley below, ears flat against its back, intent upon its quest. Jun was filled with the knowledge of his life's destiny, sure his choice between duty and intuition was the right one. He thought fleetingly of Rowan and Deerman, still certain Deerman would return to her.

Now was the time for Jun's final sacrifice of his old life for the new. He had brought with him the spearhead so lovingly and painstakingly crafted but it was time to let it go, relinquish it to the land from which it came.

With a mind of its own his arm raised, his eye aligned down the shaft of his spear and with a massive cry deep from his heart which echoed through the stillness of the valley, he hurled the spear through the gathering twilight; his special spearhead, knowing he would never again find it once it disappeared into the undergrowth, but aware it was his own personal sacrifice to the Gods. As it raced through the air, Jun's cry embraced all the love and the hurt, the pain, the passion and the beauty of the world, and as it arced high above him, the spearhead caught the last of the sun's rays, causing it to flash brightly for an instant before turning towards the earth and its final destination.

Deerman had travelled across the countryside for several days, each step taking him further from Rowan and the sacred pool. The tug of his destiny, his stone circle and the people of the moors had been strong and it was only on the day when the moon disappeared from the sky to leave the world without her silver light for three nights, he realised he needed to return. Of all there was in life, Rowan mattered most. Living without her was like facing a world without moonshine or sunlight, without the gentle falling rains or the scent of summer flowers. As the day turned to twilight and streaks of gold appeared in the sky, Deerman knew what he must to do. Becoming the swiftest animal he could think of, he turned back towards the valley, moving as fast as he could, back to Rowan and his destiny.

As Jun's cry subsided, absorbed by the valley, becoming part of it and the great web of life, another high scream reached his ears, mingling with his own. Jun wondered briefly if his spear had, quite by chance, found the hare he had spotted bounding along the valley - and then he was running, running downwards through the undergrowth, his feet not moving fast enough to keep up with his body, with the knowledge he must run faster than ever before, a feeling he could not recognise bursting from his chest.

But as he reached the spot where he knew with an uncanny certainty his spear had landed, there was no hare to be seen. Only, amongst the brown fronds of bracken, the figure of Deerman spreadeagled upon the ground, the spearhead piercing his heart, his eyes wide open to the deepening twilight, the brilliant green and violet crystal lying at his side.

Air

Celtic Christian Chaos:

The Story of St Clederus

The Holy Spring
and the Village Church

Hawthorn

The Hawthorn (*Crataegus monogyna*), has long been used to increase fertility. Because of this power it is incorporated into weddings, especially those performed in the spring. The leaves, curiously enough, are also used to enforce or maintain chastity or celibacy.

The hawthorn is also known as the Queen of the May, and was banned from the early Christian church due to its association with witchcraft.

The Story of St Clederus

Once upon a time, a man walked through a remote and hidden valley. He had travelled far and wide, away from his homeland on a quest of his own to find a very special place.

He arrived at the valley in the springtime of the year. Above him white rocks towered, one a pinnacle akin to a miniature mountain, swathed in green and crowned with gold. Below, a silver river rushed along the basin of the valley, flanked by swaying willow trees and rushes. The white of the blackthorn flowers, the deep, shimmering gold of the gorse and the green of the newly budding trees caused his heart to sing and, as if in harmony with his thoughts, a raven flew overhead, wings whistling on the cool air, its harsh croak pronouncing the coming of the man for all to hear.

Walking through the valley, new life unfolding before him, the man eventually came to the clearest pool of water he had ever seen. Running from high up on a cliff face and filling a rough stone basin surrounded by delicate ferns, the water was sweet to the taste, yet warm to the touch. The man drank of the water, then turned to survey the valley, knowing he had found the place he was searching for.

The man decided to remain in the valley for a year and a day, during which he witnessed the passing of the springtime, the scent of the hawthorn and the call of the brisk wind through the trees. He felt the warmth of the summer sun upon his face, listened to the drowsy drone of bees and watched the tall swaying foxgloves, whilst enjoying cool respite beside the river in the heat of the day.

Summer passed and turned to autumn, bringing warm gentle rains and fruits hanging heavy on the bough, black sloes and red hawthorn berries finally giving way to winter's crisp white snows and the deep green of the holly.

Throughout this time the man revelled in the beauty of nature all around him, in the passing of the seasons and the turning of the year, the cycle of new life growing, reaching fruition and resting before beginning once more.

During the year and a day, the man became well known to the local people as one always willing to listen to a trouble, heal a wound to the body or soul and ever ready to share the little he had with those in need. He loved the place so much he decided to stay.

The people of the village were happy for him to remain in the valley and looked up to him as a man of pure heart and spirit. He built a hermitage, erecting a simple granite altar which was to remain in place through the wind and the rain, the sun and snow, for hundreds of years and he finally became known as a Saint, leaving his altar, his love for the valley and the little hermitage as his legacy for generations to follow.

His name was Saint Clederus.

Eleven

Imbolc

Rhiannon peered through the low, spreading branches of the beech tree at the line of robed figures weaving their way along the valley towards the little church. She leaned against the moss covered bough, a thin layer of snow still clinging to it, noticing a shining patch of bark where her touch over the months had rubbed it smooth.

At last she was rewarded. Even though the brothers wore their habits of undyed wool with their hoods up against the frosty air and hems close to the ground, there was no mistaking Cleder as he brought up the rear of the procession – and no mistaking the furtive glance he made towards Rhiannon's hiding place.

She smiled, a slow, satisfied smile. Although Cleder had told her to stay away and leave him in peace, one glance towards the place they had spent so many hours together assured her his words meant no more than the rustle of the wind through the trees, and as soon as the snows vanished and the leaves began to bud, she would lie in his arms once again.

Rhiannon moved away from her peephole and leaned dreamily against the tall rock behind her. Such a wonderful little hidey hole, perched above the path along the valley yet completely hidden and only accessible by taking the secret, scratchy way through the dense undergrowth. But once there, the small, grassy plateau sheltered by the white rocks behind and massive beech tree in front provided a safe haven from the world. There was even a small cave which was useful when the mists descended over the valley, soaking everything else but leaving the interior dry.

In spring the primroses would provide a yellow carpet to lie upon, their sweet scent rising all around, and now clumps of snowdrops pushed their way through the frozen earth, their delicate, white heads bobbing in defiance of the frost and snow. All year long the ivy stems twisted and turned up the weathered rocks, clinging precariously, allowing a tumble of glossy, green leaves to shade the entrance of the little cave, keeping it sheltered in winter yet cool in summer.

Rhiannon liked to pretend she and Cleder lived there. She preferred to block out the knowledge of his religion, his beliefs and the calling he was always talking about. She did not understand the God he spoke of who, as far as she could see, was simply taking over the old festivals and giving them new names.

Once, whilst walking along the valley, she had found a crystal lying in the undergrowth. A beautiful green and violet crystal which shimmered with a life of its own when she plunged it into the river water to wash it. She showed it to Cleder, offering it to him as a token of her love, but he had taken scant notice and eventually Rhiannon pushed it into the earth at the back of the little cave to keep it safe, subsequently forgetting all about it.

Rhiannon sighed. There was no fun in his religion. Last year, when the villagers lit the Beltane fires and everyone knew it to be a time for lovers and couples to meet with no retribution, she had been so excited. She had twisted her long, dark hair into a thick plait, entwined with spring flowers of celandine and daisy, crowned with a circlet of mayflowers. She felt beautiful, her dark eyes catlike in her impish face, aware of the way her deep blue smock clung to her ever more curving figure. But Cleder had done no more than hold her hand and give her a chaste kiss, muttering something about needing to get back for prayer.

Since then... Rhiannon sighed once again, wondering if the rest of her life would be spent sighing and waiting for him. Since then, although she had lain in his arms gazing up at the sky through the tangle of leaves and branches and, on occasion, been gently kissed... She relived once more the kisses they shared - so tender and warm – although she felt the passion rising within her, a delicious and unstoppable force, Cleder always drew back as if a boundary had been reached and he could go no further. Could not or would not, Rhiannon was unsure. All she knew was the more he tantalised her, drawing near then pulling away again, the stronger became her desire to break his iron will, despite his religion and beliefs, because deep down, Rhiannon was sure he wanted her as much as she yearned for him.

It seemed hours until the line of Brothers made their way back along the valley. Hours during which Rhiannon became increasingly chilled as she waited impatiently for them to appear, the day beginning to darken, the sky streaking with gold and purple as the sun sank behind the brow of the hill. Rhiannon often wondered what on earth the Brothers found to do in the little church for so long. Of course there was the chanting and the prayers and sometimes villagers in need of help waited for the Brothers to administer simple medicine, a word of advice or a blessing.

Rhiannon snorted. In her grandmother's time and for as far back as anyone could remember, the holy spring which formed behind the little church had been tended by women who served the community and fulfilled its needs. Tales still abounded on firelit nights in the depths of winter of healings and prophesies made by the women of the spring.

There was a story, the one Rhiannon loved the very best of all, of a girl who killed an evil Magician with a spear, then travelled to the Otherworld to bring back a crystal of power. She was the first Guardian of the spring and it was said her spirit guarded it to this day, although she sacrificed her true love, whose spirit sometimes took the form of a great white owl, which was occasionally to been seen flying swiftly and silently along the valley.

Well, thought Rhiannon, she was not doing much guarding at the moment, was she? Because the spring and the church were taken over by the Brothers, their prayers and chants. Yes, they ministered to the people and the sick, but so had the women before them. It was the same old story. The men were taking the power from the women and calling it their own, just as the new God was taking the Old Ways and giving them new names.

For a moment Rhiannon felt a surge of anger. By rights she should be the Guardian of the spring now, just as the line of women in her family had been before her, back into the mists of time. But St Clederus had arrived, built his hermitage and erected the granite altar. Although he was long gone across the oceans to spread his word, the Brothers, Cleder amongst them, now controlled the valley and all that was left of the women Guardians of the spring existed only in stories and legends.

In moments of insight, Rhiannon sometimes wondered if her obsession with Cleder was to do with the man himself or the religion and ideals he stood for. And when she was not thinking about the warmth of his arms or the gentleness of his kisses, she further wondered if it was really Cleder she loved or whether she simply wanted to gain back the guardianship of the spring for the people of the valley - and for herself.

Twelve

'He knows you're there but he won't come to you.' The words floated down the cliff behind Rhiannon and she turned to see Brother Dominic standing at the top, grinning at her.

'Go away!' She flapped a hand, pretending to shoo him off, but they were both laughing.

'Come on, forget him and help me in the gardens instead,' urged Dominic, jumping into the little clearing from the rock above. 'You know you're wasting your time pining after Cleder. He's married to his faith, we all are, and you'd be better off finding a nice village lad to settle down with and have a brood of children running around your legs and clinging to your skirts.' Dominic sank down onto a stone and pulled thoughtfully at a strand of ivy, eyeing Rhiannon carefully as he did so. 'You know I'm right.'

Rhiannon sighed and smiled, as always finding wisdom in his dark brown eyes and whiskery face. 'I know.' She was immensely fond of Dominic, whose presence had been a part of her life for as long as she could remember and she recalled many happy hours as a child spent listening to his stories. His patience and understanding, combined with his great knowledge of the plants and animals, the sun and the stars, the moon and the turning of the seasons, never failed to intrigue and fascinate her. Except when her thoughts turned to Cleder.

'Where's he going now?' Rhiannon realised she had missed her moment, for Cleder was already passing back along the pathway, hurrying as if he was late.

'Lessons with Brother Jeremiah,' replied Dominic shortly. 'He's supposed to be teaching Cleder the ancient scripts and showing him how to illuminate a manuscript or some such thing. Bah!' Dominic threw the ivy strand down in disgust. 'What they want with all these scripts and learning I don't know, when all any of us needs to know can be found around us whenever we care to open our eyes and look.' His gaze wandered over the valley to the hills and the river he loved so well.

Rhiannon thought of Brother Jeremiah and his parchments and scripts. She imagined being close to his massive bulk, podgy fingers and red, glinting beard and shuddered. But then she thought of Cleder's slim figure bent over his work, hair the colour of ripened corn and eyes, blue as the summer sky, his slender fingers holding the quill and scratching the parchment in concentration. She sighed.

'Do you suppose Brother Jeremiah would give me lessons?' she asked hopefully, although her stomach recoiled at the thought.

Dominic threw back his head and laughed. 'Nice try, little one,' he chuckled, 'but I think Brother Jeremiah would see through your plan straight away. And so would Cleder.' He stopped laughing. 'Seriously,' he continued, 'you're wasting your time. Like I said, he's married to his faith.'

Rhiannon nodded slowly, deciding perhaps it was best to allow Dominic to think she accepted his words, but knowing deep down she would find a way eventually.

'Come on.' He punched her arm. 'It's almost time. Are you coming?'

Rhiannon grinned and together they scrambled up the side of the cliff until they reached the highest point in the valley, standing silently for long moments as the sky continued to darken from gold and pink to a bruised purple as twilight gathered.

They heard them first, their incessant chattering on the moorland behind, which all of a sudden stopped, giving way to a moment of complete silence – and then they came. In a swift and whispering rush, thousands of tiny bodies, wing beats whistling on the air, almost low enough for Rhiannon and Dominic to reach out and touch, the flock of starlings flew overhead towards their roosting place on the distant moors.

When the final bird passed in a flurry of beating wings, all was still again. Rhiannon and Dominic turned to one another and, without uttering a single word, shared a moment of complete and utter understanding, before retracing their steps to the valley and home.

The Brothers had long since given up on Dominic. Numerous attempts were made to bring some decorum into his life, to stop him whistling so loudly as he hoed his beloved gardens, persuade him not to spend quite so much time fishing in the river he found so fascinating and, above all, show some pride in being one of the

Brotherhood. Yet he still loved to wander through the valley calling the animals by name as if he expected them to reply – which indeed they did. The buzzard was known to land upon Dominic's outstretched arm and a fox regularly appeared when he sat high upon the rocks and made his special cry. In the darkness, it was said, a great white owl was sometimes to be seen perched silently upon his shoulder.

Brother Dominic was, in some people's opinion at least, a lost cause. But to others, he was all the new religion stood for, because like the first Christian hermits who settled in that part of the world, like St Clederus himself, Dominic revered the world around him. He loved the turning of the seasons and the cycle of the year. The way everything was born, lived and died, only to be reborn again, whether it be animals or the crops he worked so hard to nurture all summer so the Brothers and any villagers who needed help would have food for the winter. He had no time for learning or books because he believed all he needed to know could be found either in nature, the ground beneath his feet or his heart.

And the villagers loved Dominic above all others, turning to him when they needed a potion or a salve for a wound, calling him when their livestock were ill and indeed, Dominic always seemed to have a number of animals in his care which he slowly but surely nursed back to health. It was whispered he had healing hands and, despite the view the Brothers took of him, the villagers trusted him implicitly.

Brother Jeremiah was not impressed.

If truth be told, Brother Jeremiah was not very impressed by much except his manuscripts, parchments and intricate lettering.

And of course, Rhiannon.

Brother Cleder and Brother Jeremiah glanced out of the doorway to see Brother Dominic and Rhiannon emerge from the vegetable garden together. The year was turning, clumps of snowdrops covering the greenery in a drift of white and there was a certain warmth in the air. Rhiannon often felt the weather was not quite sure whether to be warm or cool, wet or dry, and indeed, the days were a strange mixture of soft, warm rain flashing with miniature rainbows and the unexpected warmth of spring sunshine. The birds were singing, a sure sign spring would soon take a firm hold on the valley, and Dominic proclaimed this to be his favourite time of year.

Although it was against the rules of the Brotherhood for Dominic to spend so much time with one of the village girls, especially alone, he had repeatedly ignored warnings from Jeremiah and continued to teach Rhiannon the skills of the garden and his knowledge of nature, a passion he knew she shared, despite the added incentive of being closer to Cleder.

'Finished at last.' Cleder put down the quill with which he had been scratching the parchment for the last hour and surveyed his handiwork, a slight frown creasing his forehead. He glanced at Jeremiah anxiously. He had successfully copied the first book of the words of St Clederus, written following the Saint's departure. It was decided by Brother Jeremiah and Prior John to make a number of copies for posterity but it was a long and arduous task and this was only the first.

The Brothers occupied a low, wooden framed,

thatched building on the outskirts of the village, the church being on the other side of the huddle of huts in which the villagers lived, which meant Rhiannon had plenty of opportunity to see the Brothers as she carried out her tasks each day in the local community. Around the building lay the vegetable gardens which Dominic tended, providing food for the Brothers and anyone who went hungry during the hard winters.

The little room the Brothers used for their writing was furnished with a rough, wooden table upon which the parchments could be spread. Today, as always during the winter months, it was bitterly cold. In the summer a pleasant coolness could be attained. Cleder loved being indoors, for the sun caused his eyes to water if it shone too brightly and the first heat of the year invariably brought him out in a rash. He had no desire to spend his days grubbing around in the garden getting his hands dirty, although it appeared all Dominic wished to do. Cleder shivered slightly but not with the cold. He liked things to be clean, neat and orderly.

Brother Jeremiah grunted, resting his hands across his ample stomach. 'Most neat,' he commented. 'Tomorrow we will begin the illuminations. You have worked hard.' There was the sound of laughter in the air and his gaze strayed to the couple outside, the illuminations completely forgotten.

Cleder, realising he no longer held Brother Jeremiah's attention, began clearing everything away, trying desperately to ignore Rhiannon's presence.

Rhiannon. How he wished he had never become involved with her. Never spoken to her that day almost a year ago, which was to prove his undoing. His flesh had been weak and the memory of the few stolen kisses he had enjoyed with her rankled. He crossed himself fervently, wishing all thoughts and memories of her would vanish and he could return to his faith and his studies with a clear conscience. Perhaps he should confess to Prior John next time he called, but always his nerve failed at the last moment. Even Brother Jeremiah might have been able to absolve him but he appeared so preoccupied of late.

Cleder collected together the last of the parchment, quills and inks, deciding to spend the remainder of the afternoon in silent prayer, concentrating on the words of St Clederus and of God, doing his best to erase all thoughts of Rhiannon with her inviting dark eyes, long black hair and warm, tanned flesh, from his mind. Glancing towards the garden again and noting her attention was fully taken with Dominic, he hurried from the room to his prayers.

Following Cleder's departure, Jeremiah was able to fully concentrate on Rhiannon and Dominic. Their chatter became louder as Dominic showed Rhiannon a tool he had repaired, explaining how he honed the wood to fit the handle and what it would be used for.

Brother Jeremiah sighed. He simply could not stop thinking of her dark, swinging hair and the way her clothing clung to her curves despite the layers she was wearing on this chilly spring day. As always, he could feel the passion and heat rising in his body and, as happened more and more often of late, began to feel the tug between duty and pleasure deep inside. He tried to concentrate on God, his vocation with the Brotherhood, crossing himself several times and muttering prayers as he did so, but it made no difference. Eventually Rhiannon and Dominic disappeared from view, leaving nothing but a fiery burning in Brother Jeremiah's body and an uneasy feeling in his mind.

In all his life, Jeremiah had never felt this way before, nor experienced how one person could infiltrate every waking moment, wherever he might be or whatever task he might be occupied with, and his dreams too. But rather than brushing those thoughts and feelings firmly aside, he willingly succumbed and now all he lived for was a glimpse of Rhiannon which, rather than soothing his soul, turned his body into a raging monster and twisted his mind with longing when it should have been filled with nothing but religious thoughts.

Thirteen

Spring Equinox

It was the time of balance, when day and night were equal. Rhiannon was always grateful when this time of year arrived because it meant the long, summer evenings were just around the corner.

The villagers celebrated the growth of the light with bonfires on the hills, decorated eggs and made special cakes - much to the disapproval of the Brothers - all the while revelling in the signs of spring around them, hanging small bunches of dusty yellow catkins and tiny posies of flowers above the entrances of their homes for good luck. Yellow chicks hatched, birds sang and the early morning frost soon gave way to a carpet of greenery amongst which the first spring flowers of celandine, primrose and dandelion began to appear.

The gorse became a glory of gold and the blackthorn abounded. The great pinnacle of rock at the far end of the valley was swathed in yellow, green and white, a tower of colour and beauty; but the Brothers did not like the blackthorn flowers, nor the delicate may blossom of the hawthorn and would not allow them inside their church.

As evening approached and Rhiannon was sure the Brothers were safely engaged in prayer, evening meal and yet more prayer, she made her way along the valley to the little church.

Shivering slightly in the cool breeze Rhiannon decided she would be relieved when the days lengthened properly, allowing more time for wandering along the valley, fishing in the river or even helping Dominic with his interminable hoeing and weeding if the other Brothers did not make too much of a fuss. Anything was preferable to the spinning, weaving and cooking which was usually expected of girls her age. She was lucky she was often able to slip away unnoticed with only a mild, albeit frustrated, admonishment upon her return.

Rhiannon had never known her father, having lived all her life with her mother and grandmother in their little hut. But they scraped a living and, in times of hardship, food always appeared on their doorstep. Rhiannon sometimes questioned her mother about her father but could only learn he had been a man of the woods who needed to follow his own destiny. As she was growing up this, at times, gave Rhiannon a feeling of otherworldliness and she spent much of her time wandering the valley alone. She was also lucky no mention had yet been made of marriage, although some girls of her age were married with children of their own.

On this evening her mother had asked her to collect the eggs before darkness fell, being busy with the care of her own mother who had found the winter months hard and Rhiannon obediently picked up the wicker basket, although her mind was intent upon visiting the church and the spring which ran behind it.

As she was about to leave, her grandmother called from her pallet in the corner of the room. Rhiannon knelt beside the tiny, wizened frame, knowing she was near her journey's end and had been lucky to survive this long. But, if the Gods permitted, maybe she would live to see the flowers bloom again in the summer sun.

'Here, take this.' She beckoned Rhiannon closer and whispered in her ear, her bright eyes darting around to ensure they were alone.

'It is your heritage.' She fumbled beneath the pallet of straw and brought out a small, leather pouch, which she pressed into Rhiannon's hand. 'When the time comes, you will know what to do,' was all she said, and then her eyes closed and she fell into a sudden sleep.

Knowing there was no point in questioning her further, Rhiannon stowed the pouch in her clothing and continued on her way, ignoring the clucking chickens and their eggs but taking the path to the church instead.

She pushed open the plain, wooden door to find the church still and peaceful in the gathering twilight, save for one beeswax candle burning on the altar, casting a yellow glow through the gloom.

The Brothers had spent much of their time persuading the villagers to attend what was now called the village church, on Sundays, when they were supposedly free of their daily chores, although Rhiannon knew well enough daily chores never ended.

In Rhiannon's mind the people would have been better to spend the time working their own patches of ground to feed the mouths of their families than praying, but to have said as much would have been, in Cleder's words, blasphemous – he had become quite agitated when she shared the thought with him – although she had the feeling Dominic's ideas ran along the same lines as her own. As far as he was concerned, all anyone needed was around them in the fields as much as in a building, even one dedicated to God.

As Rhiannon's eyes became accustomed to the gloom, the granite altar with the intricately carved wooden cross above it stood out against the shadows. Even she had to admire it. The stone surface of the altar sparkled with star like glints in the light of the flickering flame, and the wooden cross, carved of course by Brother Dominic who was skilled in such matters, added a beauty all of its own, the cross set in a perfect circle, inscribed with plants and animals.

Rhiannon knew when Dominic was not working in the gardens he spent many hours carving the wood he collected as he walked the countryside, and had fashioned the crosses which the Brothers wore outside their habits.

The building was tiny but scrupulously clean, the walls whitewashed, giving an eerie glow in the dim interior. But to Rhiannon, the wonder of sitting in the little church was hearing the trickle of the water which burst its way from the rock face behind the building and ran down to the river, passing the church on its way. Although she never really understood why, Rhiannon always felt this to be of great importance and the true essence of the place and all it stood for.

Pulling the simple wooden door closed behind her, she made her way around the rear of the building to the square, granite basin into which the water trickled. Perhaps the Brothers were aware of its significance, although their worship was focused on the altar and cross inside the chapel, for they had constructed a place for the water to collect before it continued to the river.

Although the villagers shared a communal well, many preferred the water found behind the church and the women made regular visits there. Under this pretext offerings were left in and around the spring, a twist of grass and a flower or a few strands of hair tied to a nearby tree, for the people had more faith in the spirits of the spring coming to their aid in times of trouble than in the God of which the Brothers spent so much time preaching.

Rhiannon knelt to run her fingers through the warm silkiness of the water and felt a stab of anger. There should be women here offering advice and healing, as there used to be, as she should be doing, as was her birthright and heritage, rather than the Brothers, despite their good intentions. The women of the village should have no need to come under cover of collecting water to make their offerings, then bowing to another God on one particular day of the week because they had been told to do so.

Rhiannon sighed and straightened up, brushing her wet hands against her skirt. A fox barked in the distance and an owl hooted. Somewhere nearby the undergrowth rustled and she imagined it to be the brown stoat she sometimes saw when no one else was around. It was at times like this when Rhiannon felt at

one with the land, with the valley, the spring, with...
God, if that was how the feeling could be described.
Brother Dominic was right. There was no need of
scripts and learning, everything was right here, just
waiting to be touched.

She thrust her hands deep into her clothing and
her fingers closed upon her grandmother's leather
pouch, which she had completely forgotten.

Carefully undoing the drawstring, she tipped the
contents into the palm of her hand. The first object to
fall out was a spearhead. Dark brown, smooth and
beautifully carved, slim with serrated edges and a sharp
point. She knew it to be too large for an arrowhead for
it lay strangely heavy in her hand and she frowned.
Why had her grandmother given her this, what did she
mean by it being her heritage and what was she
supposed to do with it?

Rhiannon's hand close tightly around it, the
warmth of her body mingling with the coolness of the
stone itself and suddenly, as if standing and watching
from a great distance, she saw a young man upon a
high rock, hurling a spear into a golden sunset. She
blinked, brought back to the present with a jolt,
unaccustomed to such visions and disturbed by the
intensity of the sight and colours, and she carefully laid
the spearhead on the mossy granite of the spring's
basin. Still feeling slightly dazed, Rhiannon knelt over
the water, intending to wash her face in its warm
silkiness and clear her mind, soothed by the constant
reflections of the light upon its surface; but just as she
was about to plunge her hands into the water she
paused, unable to move, for the face staring back at her
was not her own.

Rhiannon blinked – the face in the water blinked

also but did not fade. Rhiannon smiled and so did the other girl, for girl it was, perhaps slightly younger than herself with short, dark curling hair and, overcoming her initial fear, Rhiannon found herself totally entranced.

'Who are you?' she finally asked, but the girl only smiled, then looked grave and held something up for Rhiannon to see.

She gasped. It was the spearhead which even now lay on the moss covered stone beside her. Rhiannon darted it a quick glance then looked at the girl once more, shrugging helplessly, for she could not understand what was required of her.

The vision changed. The world within the spring opened up into a landscape of snow, the girl standing with a great white owl upon her arm, a spear in her hand – and all at once Rhiannon knew this to be the girl who had been the first Guardian of the spring, so long ago, the one in the story she loved so much.

The vision began to fade and the last thing Rhiannon saw before the waters returned to normal was the girl, once more holding the spearhead and gazing imploringly at Rhiannon. Then she was gone.

Rhiannon sat back on her heels, drained by the events of the last few moments. Her hand closed around the spearhead and, without thinking, unable to comprehend what it could all possibly mean, she fumbled to return it to the leather pouch. But as she did so, her fingers brushed another object lying inside which she gently shook onto her palm.

This time she looked at the object with complete puzzlement, for in her hand lay a wooden pendant, delicately carved with a tree, spreading its perfectly balanced branches all around.

Rhiannon blinked again, slowly beginning to

comprehend the message of the girl. Everything began to make sense, the tradition of the women of the spring and the need to fight for it, just as the first Guardian had so long ago – and indeed, it was her heritage and perhaps this was a message the time had come to fight again for what was rightfully hers.

Rhiannon jumped up filled with expectancy, renewed hope and determination. She was a Guardian of the spring, she had seen a vision telling her so and held the very spearhead from the stories of old.

She thought briefly of Cleder. Much as she loved him, he was wrong, so wrong. Rhiannon raised her face to the sky. She could catch the scent of springtime on the air and the days would now lengthen until they became much longer than the nights. Perhaps then things would change. For the first time in her life Rhiannon felt a power surge through her. It seemed to well up from the depths of the ground below and sing in her head like the trickling music of the water beside which she was standing. If things did not change with the turning of the year, it would be no more than her duty to make them.

But as to the meaning of the carved wooden pendant, she had no idea at all.

Fourteen

Brother Cleder had almost finished copying the writings of his namesake, St Clederus. It had been a long and arduous task but the slight smile on Brother Jeremiah's face and the slow nod of his head were reward enough. Brother Jeremiah did not give praise often but when he did, as far as Cleder was concerned, it was worth waiting for.

Cleder arranged his parchments precisely, a glow of satisfaction spreading through him. Next, Brother Jeremiah might show him how to bind them together, another task which would take some time and allow Cleder to savour Jeremiah's company a little longer. He hoped when this was completed he might become Brother Jeremiah's assistant, entrusted to copying out more scripts and they could spend many months and even years working together in perfect harmony. This task had enabled Cleder to prove himself, to show Brother Jeremiah his true worth and was the best thing he had ever done. Although pride was not an attribute he should have allowed into his life and he would certainly need to confess his sin, proud was undoubtedly how he felt.

Glancing outside, Cleder noticed the shadow spreading across the square of grass and the single toll of the bell reminded him it was his turn to prepare the church for evening prayer. At least now the days were drawing out, the walk along the valley was a little more pleasurable, as long as he did not encounter Rhiannon. Collecting all he needed, but finding time to stop for a short prayer on the way, Cleder left the building and hurried towards the church, oblivious to the beauty of the sunshine filled afternoon, his thoughts full of manuscripts, prayers and Brother Jeremiah.

'I knew you'd come.' Rhiannon jumped down from behind the hawthorn tree where she had been waiting for Cleder to pass, lying with her back against its gnarled trunk, enjoying the trickle of sunlight through the fresh green leaves and admiring the tightly closed buds waiting to burst into flower. 'Come with me now, up to our special place.' She smiled invitingly. 'The afternoon is warm, we can lie and watch the sky and clouds through the leaves.' She paused. 'No one will know we are there.'

Cleder brushed her arm aside and scowled, all thoughts of manuscripts and Jeremiah banished from his mind. 'I've told you over and over again, leave me alone.'

Rhiannon pouted, scrutinizing him through narrowed eyes. 'You don't mean that.'

'I do. I've told you.'

'But what of the times we spent together? When you kissed me...'

'It meant nothing, a mistake. Now, go away before anyone comes.'

Cleder turned and hurried along the path towards the church, his heart racing with anxiety, focusing on the prayers he knew would calm him.

Rhiannon stood for a long time staring at the spot where he disappeared around the bend in the path, humiliation burning inside her which slowly turned to cold anger. It fed the spark of the fire which had been ignited the previous evening, after kindling for such a long time whenever she thought of the sacred spring, the church and the way the Brothers had robbed the women of their heritage; and one fed the other until Rhiannon knew without a doubt that one day she would make Cleder sorry for his words. One day, in the not too distant future, she would make them all pay.

The day of balance passed and the time the Brothers called Easter was upon them. They had made some effort to explain to the villagers how their God had been crucified at this time, only to return to life a few days later, and the importance of this story to all good Christians.

Although she understood the cycle of life and death, Rhiannon failed to see why this God died at a time when everything was bursting with new life, even if he did return. It made no sense and, on questioning Brother Dominic, found he had few answers and appeared to feel much the same as she did.

It was as they roamed the valley searching for herbs for one of Dominic's salves, they saw the first swallow of the year. They spotted it at the same moment, swooping down out of the clear spring sky, then another appeared, and another.

Dominic sighed, his thoughts returning to Rhiannon's questions. 'It is simply the same tale retold,' he began, in an attempt to explain the story of the Resurrection of Christ. 'Look all around, nature lives, dies and is reborn in one eternal cycle – nothing is lost forever. As the sun disappears on the shortest day, so it returns and the days lengthen. Just as the swallows leave in the autumn they return again in spring.' He picked a dandelion, a few days before, golden in the sunlight, now seeded into a mist of white. He blew and some of the seed heads dispersed while others floated towards Rhiannon and tickled her nose.

'Don't concern yourself overmuch,' continued Dominic. 'Things come and go, everything passes in time, and it is for the moment we should live, enjoying the beauty we see around us.'

Rhiannon nodded, wondering suddenly if she should confide in Dominic and tell him of her vision – but he was one of the Brotherhood and perhaps this was where his loyalty lay. 'I wish,' she began after a long and torturous pause. 'I wish I had known my father...' She stopped, blushing, wondering where the words came from, for they were not in her mind seconds before, but tumbled out unbidden.

She glanced at Dominic, waiting for the wisdom he usually imparted, but found him staring into the distant hills. 'There are more coming,' he stated, pointing towards a number of swallows swooping towards them. And then he turned and walked away as if, Rhiannon thought, she had never spoken at all.

'And then he rose to Heaven...' Brother Jeremiah told the villagers on Easter Day - a day which fell very soon after their own festival of the balance of light and darkness.

Rhiannon had been thinking about this ever since her talk with Dominic and calculated that this dying, then rising from the dead, then going to heaven, all seemed to coincide with their own festivals, the dying coming soon after the balance of day and night, and the rising to heaven falling when the Beltane fires would be lit. It seemed the Brothers would yet again be taking over and trying to change one of the festivals the people had celebrated for generations.

As she stood, crushed in the huddle of villagers on this special day, enduring the extra special church service they were all expected to attend, Rhiannon's thoughts were elsewhere. Her grandmother had taken a turn for the worse during the night and it was almost as if, since she had given the leather pouch and its contents to Rhiannon, she ceased to care if she lived or died, as if her life's work was over and she was free to leave. Rhiannon had wanted to remain at home, but her mother insisted she attend the service. This was difficult to understand for her mother hitherto would have nothing to do with the church or the Brothers, despite the trouble it caused over the years. But now Rhiannon determined to ask her grandmother about the contents of the pouch if she possibly could, before it was too late.

Squashed tight in the group of bodies crushed inside the church listening to Brother Jeremiah pontificating, Rhiannon began to feel weak and light headed, until Jeremiah stared straight at her and she was unable to look away. She already knew he had a passion for his religion, being the one of all the Brothers who spoke most zealously and emphatically about his God, the light of fanaticism shining in his eyes – but as he spoke, his voice raised to the small congregation and the heavens, she realised all his attention was upon her.

Feeling like a rabbit mesmerised by a fox and unable to run for its life, Rhiannon finally tore her gaze from Brother Jeremiah's large bulk, his podgy fingers held together in prayer and the thin sheen of perspiration upon his ruddy face; but was left with an unsettled feeling in the pit of her stomach and the certain knowledge there was more to be afraid of than she realised. She longed to be outside, to feel the cool air, heavy with the scent of gorse and hawthorn, upon her face. She wondered how her grandmother fared and longed to be at home.

From his vantage point Brother Jeremiah found it difficult to contain his excitement and raised his voice and arms to the heavens in ecstasy. He had seen the expression on Rhiannon's face, noticed how she was unable to look away and knew, without a shadow of a doubt, she felt exactly the same as he did.

Fifteen

The valley was a drift of yellow, white and green. All around, the flowers of the blackthorn mingled with the gold of the gorse and the fresh, spring green of hawthorn. The pinnacle of rock guarding the valley was crowned with gold, the pathway a carpet of green, strewn with flowers of gold and white, celandines and daisies and, in the distance, the slope of the hill was covered in a shimmering grey blue hue as bluebells swept across it. Dainty primroses nestled in clefts of wood and rock, and overhead the ravens croaked their raucous cries in ecstasy of the spring filled days.

Rhiannon hurried along the path towards her mother's hut, hoping to find her grandmother taking a turn for the better, wishing she had paid attention and asked more questions in the past. For once she was grateful to leave the church and the Brothers behind, not even the chance of a stolen word with Cleder causing her footsteps to falter.

'There is nothing more I can do,' murmured her mother, as Rhiannon entered the tiny hut and sank quietly to her knees beside the frail figure.

'Is there no one who can help?' she began, her mind racing to the women of the village, wise in herb lore – or even the Brothers. Brother Dominic especially was known to aid the sick more than anyone else.

'There is but one who might have the skill to bring her back,' replied her mother, 'but I would not ask it of him.'

Rhiannon was about to question who, and why not, when her mother, unbidden, continued. 'Because of times long past,' she murmured. 'Because of what he gave and that which he took away. And because I did much the same to him.' She paused and Rhiannon was about to ask who this person was, what he had done and if it bore any relation to the contents of the leather pouch, when there was a soft sound at the doorway, the light shifted and she turned to find Brother Dominic standing before them.

What puzzled Rhiannon was the way her mother, who hitherto would have nothing to do with any of the Brothers, calmly accepted his appearance and moved to one side as he knelt beside the old lady, placing a hand on her forehead and closing his eyes. After some time, during which no one moved at all, her mother raised herself gently to her feet, pressed one hand on Dominic's shoulder and gestured for Rhiannon to follow her from the hut.

'What, why...' Rhiannon began, but her mother simply put a finger to her lips, causing Rhiannon to subside into silence.

'Dominic is not truly like the others,' murmured her mother eventually. 'He has healing hands, a gift which cannot be explained and is, in truth, one of the Old Way. Leave him to his work and we will all be the better for it.'

'But you will have nothing to do with the Brothers,' insisted Rhiannon. 'Why have you invited him in, why...' Something clicked in Rhiannon's mind. A feeling difficult to put into words but which lay in the complete trust and unspoken understanding which passed between her mother and Dominic the moment he entered the hut. She thought of Dominic's skill at carving, the fact she had never known her father but only heard him referred to as a man of the woods - or should it have been wood - the realisation her birth had fallen shortly after the arrival of the Brotherhood, and the delicately carved pendant in the pouch.

'What was it he gave you and what did he take?' Rhiannon asked suddenly, the question forming upon her lips almost before she thought of it. They had been sitting in silence for a while, the sun warm on their faces and the birds busy with their nesting in the spring sunshine. Rhiannon glanced at her mother, wondering if she had overstepped the mark or if this was a rare time her mother might answer some questions.

'He took my guardianship of the spring,' began her mother, 'for I was no longer a maiden able to carry out my duties, even if I had been allowed when the Brothers came. In times long past it might not have mattered but with all this talk of Heaven and Hell, fire and brimstone... But,' she paused and smiled, taking Rhiannon's hand in hers in a rare gesture of affection. 'He gave me you. And I in turn took his faith from him, yet also gave him something to live for.'

There was silence for long moments whilst Rhiannon digested this information. 'Why didn't he marry you?'

Her mother smiled sadly. 'It was impossible. We would have been outcasts. Where would we have gone? What could we have done? One of the Brotherhood and a mere village girl? No, it was better as it has been. I remember well the scandal caused by one of the other Brothers falling in love with a village girl and I would not have put him through that. No, he stayed close by, for I could never deny him seeing you grow up no matter how difficult things might have become between the two of us.' She paused. 'Ah, daughter,' she whispered eventually, 'I have not been much of a Guardian of the spring. I have not...' She glanced down at their hands, still entwined. 'You have his healing hands,' she murmured, her thoughts taking a different direction, 'and one day you will be a great healer too.'

There was a movement and they turned to find Dominic standing at the entrance of the hut.

'She has passed,' he murmured slowly. 'But she left in peace and told me she was content she had done the right thing.' He spread his hands. 'What that means I do not know, but maybe you do.'

Rhiannon's mother rose to return to the hut and as she passed Dominic, pressed his arm briefly. In return he smiled a slow, wistful smile, then looked at Rhiannon and in that moment she knew, whatever battles lay ahead, there was one person in the world who would always stand at her side.

Sixteen

With the return of the longer days, Rhiannon received a sudden insight into the world around her. Everything was, she realised, a balance. And the only way for things to work properly was for them to remain in balance. As Dominic had so often told her, all things were present in nature and it was to nature people should look to know what was right.

Thinking about the lengthening of the days, the cycle of the seasons and the year, Rhiannon began to see the symmetry of it all, the way for half the year, days were longer than nights, but for the other half, nights longer than days, and there were two perfect points of balance in between. Neither had dominance over the other, rather, each had its turn.

Similarly, during the summer months the earth was abundant with crops and fruits, the air warm and life good, whereas at midwinter little grew, it was cold and times were hard. But these times were necessary in order for the good to return again.

Even as she looked around she saw the contrasts. The gold of the buttercups, dandelions and celandines reminiscent of the sun, sprinkled through the grass beneath her feet, contrasting with the silver of the daisies and blossom of the blackthorn, so like the moon. And Rhiannon began to understand how everything had its place and created a perfect balance of the whole.

So why, she asked herself, were the Brothers working so hard to disrupt the balance, to make their God the one and only and to force their beliefs onto the villagers, rather than allowing them to continue as they always had, revering nature and working with the turning of the year? To Rhiannon, the idea seemed like living in perpetual summer or eternal winter – one could not exist without the other. Only Dominic understood but the others took scant notice of him, holding the view he kept them fed from his vegetable patch and the villagers happy with his salves and potions, leaving Brothers Cleder and Jeremiah the more important tasks of copying out the scripts of St Clederus in order to leave his words for posterity. Words, she could not help but feel, of a man long dead, when surely it was the people here and now who mattered. As far as Rhiannon was concerned, Dominic was the only one who spoke any sense. Cleder, however much she loved him, had his head buried in his scripts and Jeremiah was simply obsessed.

Brother Jeremiah would not have said he was obsessed with Rhiannon, he was simply unable to stop thinking about her. And although he had no lurid thoughts or evil intentions, whenever he saw her his pulse raced, he could feel his heart pounding in his most ample chest and a flush rising to his already ruddy cheeks. And when he closed his eyes at night, willing sleep to come, or even at prayer when his mind certainly should have been on a higher level, all he could see was an image of Rhiannon, the darkness of her eyes and the tantalising curl of her long, dark hair. He had been known to reach out his hand to touch it, only to hear a discreet cough from Brother Dominic bringing him back to the present – and the thought of caressing her soft skin caused him to sink into a fever of ecstasy.

No, he was not having unholy thoughts at all. In fact, Rhiannon's very presence had caused Brother Jeremiah to focus on his vocation within the church, spending many hours in prayer concerning his faith and place within the Brotherhood. He also endured a number of long nights thrashing about in his small cell thinking of Rhiannon and questioning where his true path lay in life, torn between the duty of the mind and the passion of the flesh.

And he was so sure she felt the same, by the little signs she had given, like the way she looked demurely aside when they met despite the minx like quality of her smile, or how she sometimes pretended to shrink back when he was near - that of late he had seriously considered giving up the Brotherhood and requesting her hand in marriage.

As far as Brother Dominic was concerned, it was all a complete waste of time.

Brother Cleder either had his nose stuck in his scripts, was kneeling in prayer or searching for Brother Jeremiah in order to show him some page he had written.

Brother Jeremiah was... where? Increasingly absent, as far as Dominic could tell. And when he did join them at prayer, he often recited the wrong parts and had been known to make strange movements as if he were reaching out for something.

Brother Dominic sighed and stabbed his hoe into the ground much more viciously than usual. He was seriously beginning to doubt not just the intentions, but the sanity of the other Brothers. He had a good deal of planting to do and then some salves to make for the villagers, and if he did not cook the evening meal, simple though it was of stewed turnip and herbs, sometimes supplemented with rabbit if they were lucky, they would no doubt all starve.

He disliked the way all the preaching and prayers were detracting from the real meaning of life and appreciation of the world around them. Brother Dominic sighed again, deciding the birds and beasts of the field had much more sense than men, especially monks, and wondered how he could resolve the matter.

Seventeen

Beltane

It was Beltane Eve.

For days the villagers had been busy preparing to drive their cattle through the herb infused smoke of the fires, which would both protect and relieve them of parasites before their journey onto the hills and moors for the summer.

There was an air of excitement all around. The hard winter months were over and new shoots of green spreading throughout the valley faster than the blink of an eye. The white flowers of the blackthorn were dying now, leaving the fresh green of the hawthorn leaves, blossoms shining in all their delicate glory, waiting to be picked by the young girls to weave into head dresses and wreaths in celebration of the beginning of the summer months. Cow parsley danced, heads of lacy white tossing in the slight breeze and the red campion was beginning to appear, mingling with the bluebells which arrived in abundance.

Wherever Rhiannon looked she saw beauty, from the unfurling of the ferns in the clefts of the rocks to the yellow, pink and white of the flowers which adorned the valley. Dominic felt it too. She could see it in the smile upon his face as he collected newly sprouting herbs for his remedies. He had promised to teach Rhiannon more herbal lore this summer and the villagers were visiting him frequently for help with their ailments. Since her discovery of his real identity they had spoken little of it, although Rhiannon felt a sense of awe whenever she looked at him.

'You never went away,' she said at one point as they sat quietly in the sunshine upon the highest rock, the ravens circling above them. 'It must have been difficult for you.'

'And miss watching you grow up?' Dominic shook his head. 'Never.'

Another time, as Rhiannon pondered recent events, she had turned to him as they collected wild garlic by the riverbank. 'How will I know what to do?' she asked.

And Dominic, seemingly finding this a perfectly normal question to be asked completely out of the blue, told her that when the time came she would be told, and be in no doubt at all.

Hiding behind the hawthorn tree above the path to the church, Rhiannon watched the Brothers as they made their own preparations for the day they called by another name but was in fact, still Beltane. That morning, Rhiannon had plaited her long dark hair and entwined it with flowers of celandine and daisies. She wove a circlet of mayflowers for her head and, along with the other young girls of the village similarly dressed, walked the length of the valley at first light, their footsteps dispelling the early morning dew, the sun gaining strength as their procession continued. Rhiannon felt the touch of spring upon her face and felt at one with the world. A heron started up from the riverbank as they approached, heading down the valley on slow, flapping wings and swallows swooped overhead, while other birds sang noisily in the clear morning air.

Although the Beltane fires would be lit and followed by the usual singing, dancing and merrymaking, the Brothers had announced that first, there would be a special church service in honour of the Ascension of their Lord to Heaven. There was a muttering amongst the villagers, yet no one challenged the decision. At least when it was over, events could continue as usual.

Now, with the time of yet another special service drawing near, Rhiannon noticed Cleder hurrying along the path, a bundle beneath his arm.

'Cleder.' She jumped down from her hiding place. 'What are you carrying?'

For a moment he hugged the bundle to him. It was large and square, wrapped in a piece of sackcloth. A hostile look crossed his face as he noticed Rhiannon's crown of mayflowers.

She touched it, smiling prettily. 'Do you like it?'

Cleder shook his head, clutching his bundle more tightly, then, remembering Rhiannon's question, his face relaxed into a smile and he smoothed the cloth lovingly. 'It is my work,' he said simply. 'The very first copy of the writings of St Clederus.' He pulled the sackcloth aside to reveal a large, square stack of parchment. 'And this,' he continued, pointing to an even older looking bundle, 'is the original copy of St Clederus' words from which I have been working.'

Rhiannon reached out her hand, but he drew away, as if afraid her touch would sully the writings, holding the scripts so she could see the illuminations and lettering but ensuring they remained a suitable distance apart.

Rhiannon frowned. 'And this is...' It all looked very pretty, she supposed, but she struggled to understand how these squiggles could be the words of someone as important as St Clederus, although Dominic had spent some time attempting to explain the concept to her and even taught her which signs made certain sounds.

'Brother Jeremiah is well pleased,' said Cleder importantly. 'These will be blessed this evening. It is said Prior John will be coming to take the service himself. It is indeed a great honour.'

Rhiannon watched him hurry along the path, her eyes narrowing. She sensed someone approaching and turned to find Brother Jeremiah standing behind her.

'A pretty maiden and a beautiful evening,' he greeted her. 'I trust you are on your way to church?'

Rhiannon nodded silently, fighting the urge to run as fast and as far as she possibly could from the man. There was something about him which made her insides knot and slither, like watching a dangerous snake writhing on the path, unsure if it was about to strike. She wondered why Cleder thought so much of him. All she could see was the light of fanaticism in his eyes which she somehow felt was directed towards her. She noticed how his fat fingers continually caressed the wooden cross which hung from his neck over his large stomach, and the way he thoughtfully smoothed the glinting red of his beard as he watched her.

'Of course,' she replied reluctantly, as they fell into step together. 'And what is this script which Brother Cleder has made?'

'A worthy piece of work, he is a clever young man,' replied Brother Jeremiah, 'although already married to God. He has no thoughts for other pleasures.' He caught her elbow as she stumbled, holding it a second longer than necessary before reluctantly letting go. 'I shall look forward to meeting with you later this evening,' he murmured. 'The Beltane fires should be enjoyed by one and all.'

Rhiannon felt a surge of horror at his words as they approached the church to find Cleder waiting at the little gateway. Cleder scowled at Rhiannon before turning to escort Brother Jeremiah inside, already pulling the cloth from his manuscripts and speaking in low, excited tones, leaving Rhiannon aware the time had come to act. But still she did not know what she was supposed to do.

For Rhiannon and the villagers the service was even more tedious than usual, with plenty of talk about Heaven and Hell and a God who died, returned and seemingly disappeared once more – Rhiannon lost the gist of the story at this point - and a neverending blessing of the scripts of the words of St Clederus copied by Cleder, along with the originals. After numerous chants by the Brothers, when finally it was all over, the scripts lay in pride of place upon the granite altar for everyone to admire. Much to Cleder's disappointment Prior John had not appeared, although Cleder could have listened to Brother Jeremiah preaching for ever and felt a vague sense of sadness when the last prayer had been uttered.

Only when the service was over, were the villagers free to pursue their own celebrations.

As everyone dispersed into the twilight, much more quickly than they had assembled, Rhiannon wandered around to the back of the church to the spring. It always amazed her how the Brothers took so little notice of it. They were still inside the church, congratulating Brother Cleder on his scripts, or at least Brother Jeremiah was, and showing them to anyone who had been unfortunate not to escape quickly enough, whilst outside all was quiet and there was no one to be seen.

Rhiannon knelt beside the pool of water as she had before and took out the leather pouch, shaking its contents onto her hand, admiring once again the intricate craftsmanship of the wooden pendant and smoothness of the spearhead, then placed them on the stone beside her. Perhaps, she thought, if she gazed into the water hard enough, she might see the girl again, the first Guardian of the spring. Rhiannon had no doubt of the message of the spearhead – to fight for her heritage and restore the spring to the women. But she had no spear or other weapon and knew this not to be her way. There must be another.

Allowing her gaze to rest upon the surface of the water, Rhiannon willed the first Guardian to appear. But nothing happened. From inside the church she could hear the low murmur of the voices of the Brothers, and occasionally the words 'scripts' and 'writings' in Cleder's tones. Apart from this, all was quiet, save for the far off shouts of the villagers as they lit the Beltane fires. Dusk was closing in and again Rhiannon wondered what she was to do. She touched the spearhead, the pendant, gazed into the water, aware she was probably trying too hard, a feeling of panic overtaking her. Some inner instinct told her this was the time to act, but she had no idea how and time was running short.

As Rhiannon gazed, she saw swooping swallows reflected in the water, moving in ever increasing circles, their flight swift and precise. There seemed to be more and more of them. Rhiannon was just about to turn, to look into in the sky above her, when she realised they had disappeared and the spring was now filled with mayflowers, the delicate white of the hawthorn like froth upon the surface. Then, slowly, a face began to take shape – and she realised there had never been a swoop of swallows above her nor mayflowers upon the water, for the undulating flight of the swallows formed the hair of the woman she was watching and the mayflowers her gown.

Rhiannon watched, entranced. She almost held her breath, the vision was so lovely, the most beautiful thing she had ever seen in her entire life.

'Help me,' murmured Rhiannon. 'Please tell me what to do.'

The vision continued to stare steadily at her. Rhiannon was sure there was a message in the dark eyes but was unable to read it and began to feel frustrated with her failure. Then the vision abruptly faded, leaving only the reflection of a flickering flame upon the surface of the water.

Rhiannon sensed a movement and turned to find Brother Jeremiah standing behind her, a tall, beeswax candle in his hand, the flame of which lit his features grotesquely in the deepening twilight. 'Come, dear girl.' He held out a podgy hand. 'Come and I will show you the works of St Clederus and our dear Brother Cleder.'

Rhiannon felt a stab of disappointment. After the beauty of her vision, she still had no answer and the fire in the water had merely been a reflection of the candle held by Brother Jeremiah. She swiftly collected the spearhead and pendant, secreting them in the leather pouch before he had time to see what she was doing, noticing a tiny circlet of mayflower blossom floating gently upon the surface of the water. She picked it up and tucked it into her bodice, wondering where it had come from.

'This is indeed a special night,' began Brother

Jeremiah, as he took her hand and helped her to her feet.

'Indeed,' replied Rhiannon, removing herself from his grasp as swiftly as possible. 'For tonight is the time of the Beltane fires.'

And with those words, she knew what to do.

Eighteen

The Beltane fires were lit, the cattle driven between them and the villagers had jumped the flames in order to ensure good luck for the coming year. It was an age old tradition and for that evening at least, everyone was able to forget the presence of the Brothers, determined this was one ritual which would never change.

Dominic left the church soon after the service and made his way to the site of the celebrations, increasingly frustrated by the words and actions of the Brothers and deciding he preferred to join in with the villagers, doing something practical like tending the fires, while they turned their attention to their cattle, affairs of the heart and the fertility rites of the night.

As the evening progressed he wondered what had happened to Rhiannon. He assumed she would come to watch the cattle driven through the fires and to throw on herbs of medicine and magic to mingle with the smoke, but as yet there was no sign of her.

He mused on how beautiful she looked and felt inordinately proud. He might not have been the best father in the world but had done all he could, circumstances permitting, although he felt saddened events could not have turned out differently.

Dominic looked up, across the glowing firelight and gently billowing herb scented smoke, catching sight of Rhiannon's mother watching him. He paused in his work and the world seemed to stop, a timeless moment as they both remembered the night of the Beltane fires many years ago. Across the flickering firelight, Dominic smiled.

Rhiannon peered at Cleder's manuscript and tentatively touched it with one finger, only to have her hand pushed roughly away by Cleder himself.

'Brother Cleder, you should allow the young maiden to touch your work,' the voice of Brother Jeremiah quietly admonished. 'That is why I have invited her here.' Brother Cleder scowled as Jeremiah leant over Rhiannon, tracing the intricacies of penmanship and the beautifully coloured illuminations with one stubby finger. Rhiannon's dark head bent next to his, apparently exhibiting a great interest in all he was showing her.

Brother Cleder scowled again. He would have preferred Rhiannon to be nowhere near his precious scripts and to have spent the evening discussing them with Brother Jeremiah himself, just the two of them in the little church. But Rhiannon was showing an unusual interest in Brother Jeremiah's words – indeed, Brother Cleder would almost have thought she was flirting with him – and eventually, in an increasing rage of jealousy, he left the church and headed towards the Beltane fires.

The fires had died low, the burning of the herbs, driving of the cattle and revelry almost over. Most of the villagers had disappeared, either to their beds or into the darkness to celebrate the true meaning of Beltane and the fertility rites.

In the church, only a few candles remained lighting the darkness and, having spent some time in Rhiannon's company, Brother Jeremiah felt he could contain himself no longer. It was time to tell her exactly how he felt.

Brother Dominic raked the straying embers of the fire into a heap, whistling softly and wondering why the other two always disappeared when there was work to be done. But on this occasion he cared not, recalling the look he had seen in the eyes of the woman he had continued to love for so many years, and wondering if it was time for circumstances to change.

In Rhiannon's mind the plan had been simple enough. She would go into the church, take the manuscripts and burn them on the Beltane fires. This would surely cause such trouble the Brothers would leave the valley and allow the villagers to return to the Old Ways and the women to become Guardians of the spring once again.

But this plan had its flaws. Firstly, Brother Jeremiah's presence compelled her to accompany him into the church, making it impossible for her to simply take the manuscripts. Secondly, she was not sure if the Brothers would actually leave even if the scripts had been burned and finally, would she have the nerve to actually destroy the writings when the time came?

The more she thought about the situation, as Brother Jeremiah rambled on, pressing his large bulk increasingly close to her, the more Rhiannon wondered if she was doing the right thing and if she would even get the chance to burn the scripts in the first place. But she remembered the vision in the spring, trusted it with a deep understanding which came from somewhere inside herself, and was certain, as sure as she knew the sun would rise the next morning, that somehow on this night everything would be resolved.

Eventually, Brother Jeremiah could contain himself no longer. 'My dearest,' he began, resting a hand gently upon Rhiannon's shoulder in the soft candle light.

Rhiannon turned, finding herself trapped between Brother Jeremiah's large paunch and the altar behind her. He was standing so close she could feel his breath on her face and see the light of fanaticism in his eyes.

'I have waited so long...' began Brother Jeremiah, touching her cheek with one stubby finger and allowing it to run slowly down the curve of her neck. 'You know how I feel,' he continued, 'and I know you feel the same way. Our time has come.'

He pressed himself closer, his arm slipping around her slim waist and Rhiannon, knowing that whatever her plans might have been she could bear it no longer, felt frantically behind her for something with which to fight him off. Her fingers brushed the carved, wooden cross but it slipped from her grasp crashing to the floor. Brother Jeremiah, seemingly oblivious, pressed closer still. Rhiannon's hands scrabbled some more, finally coming into contact with the sacred scripts.

As Brother Jeremiah bent his head to finally kiss her, to claim the prize for which he had waited so long, Rhiannon brought her knee up sharply and, as he doubled up in pain, turned, grasped the sacred scripts and brought them down hard upon Brother Jeremiah's head, then ran from the church as fast as she could towards the Beltane fires. As she neared the glowing embers she ran headlong into Cleder who was standing in the darkness, his face as black as the night sky above.

'How?' Cleder gasped, realising exactly what Rhiannon was carrying and, after a moment of shock, began to wrestle the scripts from her. 'Give them to me.'

'Never!'

In the firelight the two figures twisted and turned, only to be joined by the figure of Brother Jeremiah, puffing and panting as he caught up with Rhiannon, grasping her about the waist in an attempt to pull her away from Cleder and force her to loosen her hold on the scripts.

From the corner of her eye Rhiannon caught a glimpse of Dominic watching from the other side of the fire and wondered why, in her hour of need, he did not come to her aid. But she had no time to think further, for at that moment with a great tearing sound the pages worked their way free from their bindings, the scripts fell to pieces and the pages scattered onto the ground, fluttering in the cool night air.

They all paused. Rhiannon panting, attempting to catch her breath, Cleder scrabbling about on his knees trying to collect the fluttering pages and Jeremiah bent double, gasping for air and wiping his face in his robe.

'Please,' cried Cleder, desperately. 'Help me, please.'

Rhiannon paused, suddenly realising what she had done. She looked at Cleder, the man she had given her heart to for a whole turning of the seasons, understanding finally where his love and duty lay and realising that, even if she were alone with the scripts and the most raging fire in the entire world, she would not have it in her to destroy something he loved so much. Her arms dropped to her sides, her body sagged and she knew that as a Guardian of the spring she was a failure. Just like her mother.

'What disgrace is this?'

They all turned, wild eyed, to find Prior John standing behind them.

'My Lord.' Brother Jeremiah bowed as low as he was able before the Prior, and Cleder followed suit.

'What disgrace is this?' repeated Prior John, taking no notice of the grovelling Brothers, his eyes resting on the dying Beltane fire and the young woman standing, defeated, before him.

Out of the corner of her eye, Rhiannon caught the movement of Brother Dominic on the other side of the fire, raking in the straying embers, steadfastly ignoring the presence of Prior John.

'My Lord, we can explain,' began Brother Jeremiah, wringing his hands together, the scripts momentarily forgotten.

There was a flurry of breeze on the night air which rippled up the valley, stirring the remaining embers of the Beltane fire, causing it to flare up and cast long shadows towards the small group standing a short distance away.

Then came the smell of burning and the faintest hint of white swirled into the air, like mayflower blossom on a spring breeze. As the particles settled upon her, Rhiannon found them not to be petals as she had first assumed, but tiny specks of ash, as on the far side of the fire Brother Dominic continued to rake the embers together, whistling quietly as he worked.

Rhiannon noticed a figure standing beside him, calmly feeding the flames from a bundle she carried in her arms and realised it to be her mother. Of the sacred scripts there was no sign.

Rhiannon smiled, realisation dawning slowly in the flickering firelight. 'Ah, Mother,' she murmured. 'You have in the end, shown yourself to be a true Guardian of the spring after all.'

And as the other Brothers stumbled behind the Prior back along the valley into the darkness of the night, Brother Dominic stood with the two people he loved best, feeling truly at one with the world around him.

Fire

Medieval Magic:

*The Legend of the
Maidens of the Wells*

The Sacred Well
and the Chapel in the Valley

Meadowsweet

Meadowsweet, (Filipendula ulmaria) has long been known to promote love and peace. Fresh meadowsweet can be placed on the altar for love spells or dried to be used in various love potions.

If gathered at Midsummer, the meadowsweet will give you information regarding thieves; if you have been robbed, place meadowsweet on water. If it sinks, the thief is a man. If it floats, a woman.

The Legend of the Maidens of the Wells

Long, long ago, all of the Sacred Wells of the land were tended by Maidens, who gave refreshment to travellers, from golden chalices. A traveller had only to arrive at a Sacred Well and a Maiden would issue forth to provide sustenance. These Maidens were sometimes known as the Voices of the Wells, for they were also oracles, forming a link between this world and the Otherworld, for at the sites of the Wells the veils between the worlds were thin. Because of the existence of the Maidens of the Wells the land flourished and was filled with beauty and contentment.

One day, the evil King Amangons raped one of the Maidens and stole her golden chalice, using it as a trophy for himself. His men did likewise, although it was their duty to protect the Maidens. Subsequently, the Maidens were forced into the Otherworld and from that day on they tended their Wells no more.

But without the Maidens, the Wells fell into disrepair, no sustenance was offered to passing travellers and the land became a wasteland, as the Maidens and the reciprocal link with the Otherworld had been lost. The land was overcome with drought and misery, no longer rich and filled with its previous abundance.

Many years later, King Arthur and his knights set out on the quest for the Holy Grail, searching for the court of the Fisher King where the grail was said to rest.

The Fisher King was bound to the land but, because he himself was wounded, his land was also a wasteland. The Fisher King spent his time fishing the unconscious world in order to discover answers, but could not be healed until he was asked specific questions and had given his reply.

King Arthur's knights vowed to rescue the Maidens of the Wells and indeed, found them not to be dead but living in the forest of the Otherworld, where they had been residing all along.

Nineteen

Beltane

The sun rose, a golden orb in the sky illuminating the remnants of the night's frost nestling amidst the landscape. As it steadily climbed above the towering rocks the sprinkling of white covering the valley rapidly disappeared, allowing the fresh green to shine through. Fingers of gold threaded the leaves of the hawthorn trees which guarded the enclosure, caressing their moss covered trunks and tingeing the newly opened leaves with light.

Rosenwyn closed her eyes, revelling in the first warmth of the early morning sunlight upon her skin. She was ready now, having risen well before dawn to undertake her rituals and preparations for the day ahead. She had bathed her face in the morning dew, walked three times barefoot around the chapel and finally, collected a cup of water from the sacred well, mixed it with dewdrops and held it aloft to the rising sun of Beltane.

Now she rested outside the chapel, surveying her surroundings and feeling, at that moment, the only person in the world.

Earlier Rosenwyn had braided her hair and wound it tightly around her head, piled high and woven with spring flowers of daisy and celandine. A crown of mayflowers waited for later, intricately laced with meadowsweet and rowan leaves. She pulled her woollen cloak around her, green at this time of the year to match the freshness of the valley. Come autumn, she would don a warmer cloak of russets, yellows and browns. Smiling contentedly, she thought of the turning of the seasons and the wheel of the year. Much as she loved the autumn with its rich tapestry of colours and abundance of fruits hanging heavy on the bough, she harboured an infinite love for the springtime with new life bursting forth and the sap rising in the branches, the sun gaining strength and a feeling of hope in the air.

'Are you ready my Lady?' asked a soft voice, and Rosenwyn turned to see one of the Maidens standing at the gateway.

'A moment longer.' She smiled as the girl retreated, respecting her High Priestess' wish for a little more solitude before the duties of the day began. As Rosenwyn watched her retreat, she noted the way the girl had braided her hair in one long, thick plait down her back and her thoughts traced back through the years to a time when she had been young enough to do the same and allow her dark hair to swing free and wild as the Beltane celebrations reached their height.

She could see herself clearly with the vision which came upon her more often as the years progressed, and was aware this had happened not in her present lifetime but one long ago.

Rosenwyn raised a hand and patted her head, ensuring everything was in place. Today, the Maidens of the Wells were journeying to her chapel. It was a rare occurrence for them to congregate, but as High Priestess it was fitting that on this particular day the Maidens who tended the Wells should travel to her for the Beltane ritual in celebration of new life and new beginnings.

'Without the Maidens of the Wells the land will become a wasteland...'

How many times had Rosenwyn heard those words, in her dreams, in her meditations, sometimes when she was sitting quietly in her chapel, at others when she was going about her daily business of gathering herbs or giving healing to a villager. The voice would come, whispering out of nowhere, taking her by surprise each time. Yet when she turned she knew no one would be there for she also understood it came from another time and another place.

The Maidens of the Wells. To all intents and purposes a group of young women who tended the sacred wells, of which there were many. Yet, everyone knew without it ever having been explained, their importance was not simply in the refreshment offered to passing travellers nor the fact the Maidens were also oracles, able to foretell the future to those who asked, or even their ability to prepare simple herbal remedies.

No, there was more, something indefinably linked with the land and the people, and the Maidens were representative of this. During the past hundred years the cult of the Maidens of the Wells had grown enormously in status and significance to the extent that Father Christopher was beginning to feel threatened – she could see it in his bright blue eyes, wary and awash with a shadow of fear when he spoke with her. And it worried her for she no longer trusted what might happen, was no longer secure in the knowledge the Maidens would be protected and revered as they had been for so long.

'Without the Maidens of the Wells the land will become a wasteland...'

The voice whispered in Rosenwyn's mind, jerking

her back to the present, bringing the realisation she had been on the verge of trance, immersed in her thoughts. Sometimes she tried to match a face with the voice, but it was always too elusive to catch.

One thing she did know with a certainty which never wavered. She was waiting for someone, waiting for a man to fulfil a destiny which was connected to her and, more importantly, the Maidens. And she knew, for she had seen his shadowy figure in her dreams, that when he came it would be when the blackthorn blossom was falling from the trees in drifts of white and the hawthorn shimmering green across the land. He would come when the bluebells, the red campions and the white of the cow parsley vied with the daisies and the buttercups to light up the valley – and she knew, with an ever growing certainty, his coming would be today.

Above her two ravens croaked and a buzzard gave its high pitched cry. A blackbird called and Rosenwyn rose to see the Beltane procession of villagers and Maidens wending its way through the valley towards her, drums beating and voices raised in song.

As she stood, she caught the briefest glimpse of movement on the other side of the river. She paused, attempting to focus but was too far away and could only make out the green of new leaves and the gold of the gorse.

Rosenwyn took a deep breath and raised her arms high and wide open to the sky.

Her day had begun.

Twenty

It had been a long and arduous journey. Justin had travelled throughout the night, pausing only to rest his mount and quench his thirst before continuing onwards. It had been clear, stars shining like distant jewels, the moonlight causing the landscape to appear as bright as day. Pools of silver interspersed with the blackness of long, low shadows lay before him as the steady sound of his mount's footsteps echoed through the landscape. A fox barked, a hare flashed across the open downland and at one point a great white owl flew low and ahead, pausing to rest upon the bough of a tree before moving on again, almost as if showing him the way.

Now the sun was rising, dispelling the coolness of the night, yet leaving a tingle in the air, the first fingers of gold creeping over the top of the mound ahead, and as he approached he could feel in his heart that he was close. Very close.

As he wound his way through the last bend in the valley, the sun rising before him, the full moon hanging in perfect symmetry, he saw it.

Justin halted his mount and stayed quite still for several moments as if in a trance, as if he could not quite believe his eyes. Amidst the tumble of greenery, he could make out a tiny roof surmounted by a cross at each end and he knew his quest to be over at last.

His mount snorted and stamped, bringing Justin back to the present and he became aware of the rushing river and the high call of two buzzards circling overhead. To his left white rocks towered, one a pinnacle, covered in greenery and white blackthorn blossom, surmounted by a crown of golden gorse; and quite unexpectedly Justin turned his mount away, unable to move closer.

Visions flooded into his mind, stronger and clearer than ever before, of a young man standing on a rock, hurling a spear high into the air, a feeling of exhilaration and ecstasy filling his entire being. And then he heard once again the high scream which had haunted his dreams throughout his life, and he knew without a doubt he had also returned to the scene of his nightmares.

Beneath his tunic his hand sought the brilliant green and violet crystal he had found thousands of miles away, the colours of which always reminded him of the place in his dreams. There was, he felt from the very first, something special about the crystal, and he kept it with him throughout his journeying, a talisman and bringer of good luck.

He recalled seeing a bridge further back along the valley and, turning his horse around, decided to cross to the other side, perhaps delaying the inevitable moment when he would finally reach his destination.

After crossing the river he guided his mount to the brow of the low hill where he had a much clearer view. Allowing his horse to graze, Justin walked to a point where he could see the whole of the valley spread before him, from the white rocks above the little chapel to the rushing river below. The bridge lay to his left, a little settlement along the valley to the right. A movement caught his eye as a woman appeared from the chapel and he knelt, fading into the greenery as she moved around the building before finally standing for some moments with her arms raised to the sky.

Justin swallowed and felt tears sting his eyes.

The scene was so beautiful and he had travelled so long and hard to reach the place. Along the valley he heard the first drumbeats of the Beltane procession and for a moment, although he was much too far away to be sure, had the impression the woman was aware of him for she was standing perfectly still and looking intently in his direction.

Justin blinked, made the sign of the cross, placed his hands together and began to pray.

As the procession wound its way along the valley Father Christopher stood, still as stone, lips pursed. His church normally saw a good congregation, indeed, the villagers would have been fined had they not attended the service every Sunday, providing him with a large captive audience.

But today they had deserted him for the Beltane celebrations and everyone's focus was on the chapel, the Priestess of the Well and her Maidens.

'Damn that woman. May she burn in Hell,' muttered Father Christopher in a most ungodly manner, running his hands through what was left of his thinning, fair hair. He had known Rosenwyn since she was a child and, inoffensive as she appeared then, he instinctively felt that one day she would be a force to be reckoned with. And how right he was.

The procession passed in a crescendo of drumbeats and singing, voices raised in harmony to greet the Beltane morn and Father Christopher retreated into the cool interior of the church, dim and comforting after the brightness of the day outside. He touched the smooth, round pillars of soft stone and once more admired the newly built tower.

The villagers had worked hard on the tower,

demonstrating their faith and love of God, carrying out Father Christopher's bidding at all times and he was justifiably proud of it. The only thorn in his side was the fact they had, at the final hour, rebelled against his wishes and also insisted on working on the little chapel and sacred well which nestled further along the valley, enlarging the building, adding a stone covering to the well and granite channels which directed the water beneath the altar. This was completely new and no one seemed quite sure who thought of it, but even he had to admit there was something special about the mingling of stone and water which added a spiritual quality to the place. They even made it impossible to stand in the position of power behind the altar, appearing to be more interested in playing a part themselves in the religious proceedings, rather than listening to just one person, such as himself, who was eminently more qualified to guide and direct their worship and prayer.

Of course, it had been explained it was in order for the water to run over the relics of St Clederus himself, secreted in a special chamber behind the altar - and indeed a number of pilgrims visited every year to pay their respects and drink of the sacred waters. The relics of St Clederus had remained in the little chapel, which had once been the village church itself, but this was not a situation to Father Christopher's liking and he fought hard to have the relics moved to the present church where he felt they should rightfully be and which the pilgrims should visit. But to his fury the villagers sided with Rosenwyn and he knew he was defeated. That was when he realised the ridiculous cult of the Maidens of the Wells must end.

The Maidens of the Wells. For the life of him he

could not see why they were so important and why the people turned to them in their hour of need rather than to his God, despite his repeated sermons in an attempt to save their souls. They attended his church, they listened to his words, they almost always did his bidding, but he knew deep down their hearts were not really with him but at the little chapel in the valley with Rosenwyn, or the High Priestess, or even the Lady, as some insisted on calling her. And it hurt, it stung and grew like the evil growth which had appeared on the face of one of the villagers last year, which God had seen fit not to heal, but Rosenwyn, in her herbal wisdom and against all the odds, had cured.

And now, seeing the procession of Maidens, their hair entwined with flowers, circlets of mayflowers about their heads and each carrying a chalice as a symbol of her position, Father Christopher was overcome with such frustration he should have sank to his knees and prayed for forgiveness.

But instead, he began to plot.

There was a whirl and a plop as a flurry of bubbles rose to the surface. Duncan sighed. He had been fishing since before dawn, spending most of the time in complete stillness, allowing his mind to wander into the murky depths where he often journeyed, but had not caught a thing.

Duncan pulled his line in, knowing it was not really fish for which he had been searching. The act of sitting on the riverbank appearing, to all intents and purposes, as if he were trying to catch a fish usually kept people well away, leaving him in peace and solitude and he was able to allow his mind to wander to places most people never knew existed. He was searching,

searching, but for what he was unsure, only aware that whatever it was lay just beneath the surface, like an elusive fish, too clever and slippery to be caught.

He stretched his leg, rubbing the stiffness away, wishing he had not been afflicted with constant pain and a limp which caused him to shuffle since childhood. And the problem was that as he grew older, the worse it became.

Duncan sighed again. It was Beltane and his mind was not really on the silver river rushing before him or the fish within. It was more on the little chapel which nestled below the rocks just above the pool of the river where he sat and on the priest who spent his time in the church plotting and planning.

For Duncan knew. With an intuition deep within his soul, Duncan had an inkling of events to come and also the feeling it was up to him to stop them. But how, he had no idea.

Today was the Beltane procession, the ritual at the chapel followed by the lighting of the Beltane fires and finally, feasting and merrymaking. And Duncan had his part to play in it all. Everyone was expecting him to appear, as he did at all village rituals throughout the year. The fool, the village idiot, the simpleton, whose job it was to make people laugh, with his shuffling gait and deep melodic voice, little knowing that beneath his antics lay words of wisdom with a deeper meaning than any of them could ever imagine.

The river swirled once more with a life of its own, tiny whirlpools forming here and there and a froth of white gathering in one particular curve of the riverbank. Soon the damselflies would be appearing, gliding over the surface and alighting on his hands and feet as he fished. Duncan spent many hours by the riverside fishing, thinking and learning. With his nut brown eyes and dark hair, dressed in clothes which subtly merged with the colours of the landscape around him and his ability to remain still and silent for hour upon hour, he learned much of the village people and their affairs without needing to speak to anyone or go anywhere. Duncan missed nothing and it was a mistake for anyone to believe him to be the fool he allowed people to take him for.

Once, sitting quietly and looking down at the valley, he had seen the shape of a great face in the movement of the beech trees, swaying in the summer breeze. The longer Duncan watched, the more definite it became and, rather than fade away to a mass of leaves, the face stayed with him until he, himself, felt the need to move his aching limbs. Duncan believed he had seen the Green Man of the forest, spoken of only in legend, and knew his own spirit also to be a part of the earth itself.

The sound of beating drums and voices raised in song drifted along the valley towards him. Duncan pulled in his fishing line, empty as usual and prepared to become another person.

His day had only just begun.

Twenty One

The villagers were understandably proud of their church with its newly built tower and felt a certain satisfaction on seeing it. But they were inordinately pleased with the work which had been carried out at the little chapel further along the valley. Everyone lent a hand, from the smallest child to the strongest labourer and most skilled craftsman, and now the time had arrived for the first festival since its renovation and the Maidens of the Wells were gathering from all around. It was an auspicious day indeed.

Although the chapel was now larger, there was scant room for more inside than Rosenwyn and her Maidens, so the people gathered outside in the little enclosure to take part in the ceremony as best they could. Following the ritual the Maidens would fill their chalices from the sacred well, offering sustenance to the people before the lighting of the Beltane fires and the feasting and merrymaking.

Inside the chapel the sacred water ran in a steady flow behind the altar, over the relics of St Clederus and into the well at the other side. Rosenwyn had spent many hours sitting quietly, listening to the trickle of the water which, at times, sounded like the lightest and most delicate of music, at others a symphony of birdsong. She felt the magic in the entwining of stone and water, and Duncan agreed when she broached the thought to him.

'Always look to nature for your answers,' he replied in his slow, deep voice. 'Look at the marriage of water and stone around you, in the fast flowing river and the sunlight on the rocks. The way water wears away stone, yet pebbles direct the flow.' And they sat for long moments in quiet contemplation, each understanding the other perfectly.

Now, the chapel had been dressed with all the flowers and greenery of the season. Beneath the tall windows, shot with sunlight and lighting the altar with a thousand tiny sparks, stood branches of hawthorn and flowers of may blossom, beautiful in the morning sunshine, reflecting the circlets upon the heads of the Maidens. Tall, white candles were placed all around, and the green spring foliage gave the chapel an air of cool tranquility.

The doors had been left open and for some time Rosenwyn and the Maidens sang and chanted songs to the Beltane energies, to the Goddess who, at this time of year, blessed the fertility of the crops and the people for the year ahead.

As High Priestess, Rosenwyn was expected to fall into a trance and deliver an oracle to the villagers. Indeed, all of the Maidens of the Wells possessed such skills which they used almost every day of their lives.

As the chanting rose to a crescendo, Rosenwyn felt herself slipping from reality. She had performed this so often it was now second nature to her, as she trusted in the wisdom and intuition deep inside to deliver the right message to help the villagers in whatever way was necessary.

Rosenwyn drew a deep breath. 'Heed my words, my children,' she began, and a hush descended inside the chapel until the only sounds to be heard were the call of a robin outside and the occasional croak of a raven overhead. The air was filled with the fragrance of smouldering herbs, their perfume reminiscent of the sweetness of new rain and the freshness of the first spring flowers. The Maidens knelt, heads bowed in reverence, waiting for the signal to proceed from the chapel to the sacred well to fill their chalices and present them to the people waiting outside.

Rosenwyn cleared her throat. If truth be told, she usually had a vague idea of her words beforehand, seeing it as part of her duty to guide the villagers to the best of her ability. Duncan, seen by most to be the simpleton of the village, was often able to give an indication to help her deliver the best possible advice.

She had planned to speak of the importance of the well and the chapel, and the balancing of the chapel and the village church over which Father Christopher presided. Duncan warned her on more than one occasion of his plotting and planning and Rosenwyn knew that unless a balance was found, ill feeling would prevail. But when she drew a breath and opened her mouth to speak, the words which came out were not those she had expected.

'Today,' she began, 'on this Beltane morn, I bring you a warning.'

There was a slight stir but the Maidens had been well trained and remained quiet, revering their High Priestess' every word.

'Without the Maidens of the Wells the land will become a wasteland...' Rosenwyn paused and it was as if the chapel itself held its breath. 'I call upon you, Maidens of the Wells, to take care,' she continued. 'Be on your guard and above all, trust no one.'

There was silence. No robin sang and only the rustle of the wind could be heard as a short, sharp breeze scurried around the chapel, swiftly brushing the flowers in the head dresses of the Maidens before hurrying on its way and lifting Rosenwyn from her trance.

She blinked, unsure of exactly what had happened. For the first time in her life she heard the words which had haunted her spoken aloud and realised with a growing horror that, although the voice in her head always belonged to someone else, the voice which finally uttered them was her own.

A cloud must have passed before the sun for the candlelight swayed and flickered amongst the greenery and spring flowers which ordained the chapel, giving the illusion of a dim winter's day with everything closing into darkness rather than the beginning of spring. Then all at once the sun appeared once more and the chapel was flooded with light. There was a collective sigh of relief as hope returned and for an instant Rosenwyn's words were but a memory, a passing shadow within the beauty of the surroundings. But in truth, they would never be forgotten by anyone who heard them.

Rosenwyn rose, lifted the ritual silver chalice from the altar and walked to the doorway. The Maidens fell into line behind her and, as she stepped outside, felt the warmth of the spring sunshine on her face. The golden gorse shone from the pinnacle of rock before her and the words receded into the darkest corner of her mind. Almost, but not quite, for despite the beauty of the day, there was a heaviness in her heart as she led the Maidens three times around the chapel before pausing at the sacred well to fill her chalice with its refreshing water.

As they walked there was a hush in the air, broken only by birdsong and the rushing of the river in the distance. Rosenwyn knelt at the edge of the well, but just before her silver chalice broke the clear surface of the water she caught a glimpse of another face gazing back at her. She paused, body still as, through years of practice, she allowed the vision to sharpen and define.

She saw faces, eyes wild with anguish, crying for help. Hands reaching towards her from the depths of the well, which had all at once become murky rather than running pure and clear. She heard cries in her mind which mingled with the sudden call of two ravens overhead, their croaks harsh against the softness of the previous birdsong.

'*Without the Maidens of the Wells the land will become a wasteland...*'

Yet again the words whispered inside her head and then she saw the final vision of a face streaming with tears and twisted in despair. And the face was her own.

Afterwards, Rosenwyn never quite knew how she managed to continue with the ritual, but somehow touched the surface of the water with her chalice and the well returned to its clear, pure state once again, after which she walked to the front of the chapel, the Maidens repeating her actions and following in her footsteps.

Rosenwyn held her chalice high, a replica of her personal ritual earlier in the day, symbolising the union of earth and water, and it sparkled silver in the sunlight. She took a moment to glance at her Maidens and felt a momentary pride both in their beauty, their beliefs and their work in the world. Then, with the inclination of her head they had been waiting for, the Maidens walked amongst the villagers, ensuring each one drank the sacred waters from one of the chalices, bestowing blessings for the coming year as they did so.

As the ritual drew to a close the festivities of the day began - the lighting of the Beltane fires between which cattle would be driven, a ritual which stretched back as far as could be remembered, followed by feasting, merrymaking and a night during which fertility rites abounded.

Rosenwyn moved away from the throng. She

was tired and her duties were, for the moment, over. As she rested in the shade of the hawthorn tree, heavy with the blossom of the mayflower, she realised not everyone had taken part in the ritual after all.

Two other figures stood, silent and alone at different points of the valley. One, a man in stark black, could be seen in the direction of the church, which she instantly recognised as Father Christopher. The other stood beside a horse across the river and she thought he wore a white tunic with a red and gold emblem upon it. Attuned as she was to the energy within the earth and the sky, Rosenwyn was aware the attention of both figures was upon her. From one she could feel such black hatred as she had never experienced before, and from the other the most strange and enduring love, which caused her heart to feel as if it might break into a thousand pieces.

Twenty Two

It was following the Beltane celebrations as the valley turned from the fresh green and white of spring towards the abundance of Midsummer, it began to happen.

The first time was a complete mystery which, although sending shock waves through the local community, was explained away by a variety of theories ranging from Marauding Knights to Acts of God, but no one really understood what happened.

All they knew was that one of the Maidens of the Wells had disappeared. And no one could find her.

Naturally, it worried Rosenwyn greatly.

By all accounts the Maiden had been about her usual duties the previous day, administering refreshments to passing travellers and giving advice and healing to those who sought it.

Everything appeared quite as usual, the people of the next village unanimously agreed, until in the morning their Maiden was nowhere to be found. On further investigation the earthenware cup she used each day for drawing water from the well was discovered lying broken in its watery depths – but of the Maiden herself or her ceremonial silver chalice, there was no sign.

Rosenwyn tried hard to find out what happened but it appeared she had simply vanished into thin air.

Eventually Rosenwyn asked Duncan his views as she came upon him fishing one afternoon.

'On the surface,' he mused in his deep, melodic voice, as a small fish jumped for a fly hovering above the slow flowing pool, 'all seems as if it could be a single incident. But beware what might be lurking in the depths.' He tugged hard on his line to reveal a huge trout, thrashing and wriggling in the sunlight, pulled it in, released it and allowed it to slide back into the water.

'Why do you do that?' asked Rosenwyn, her thoughts taken from the question in hand for a moment. 'Why not just catch them and eat them or not catch them at all?'

'It teaches me and it teaches them,' replied Duncan. 'It shows me what's in there and it shows them what's out here.' And he returned to his private musings.

Rosenwyn left him then, wondering if he knew more than he was admitting or if he was simply speaking in riddles to hide the fact he knew no more than anyone else; but he had been correct, for not half a moon later a second Maiden disappeared. And shortly after, a third.

Each disappearance followed the same pattern. By now, it was obvious some trickery was afoot. All appeared normal with the Maiden and her well in the evening, then next morning she was nowhere to be found, save for some small reminder she had ever existed at all – once a small posy of flowers on the pathway, another time a bunch of herbs abandoned a short distance away.

Rosenwyn decided something must be done.

The question was, what?

Once again, she consulted Duncan and once again, found him fishing by the river.

'Where are they, Duncan?' she asked, as she sank down beside him on the grassy bank, the scent of meadowsweet heavy in the air where her footsteps had crushed the flowers. 'What has happened to my Maidens?'

Duncan gazed thoughtfully at the swirling water and shook his head sadly. 'It is a truly bad thing which is happening...' he began.

'But don't you know anything?' Rosenwyn almost snapped in frustration. Sometimes his slow manner irritated her beyond belief, although deep down she knew the wisdom of his words in whichever form he chose to deliver them.

'Just remember,' he continued, 'things are not always lost for ever. Sometimes they simply can no longer be seen.' Which was all he would say, despite Rosenwyn's questions.

Truth be told, it was all he knew himself. Thoughts often rose to the surface of his mind, like the air bubbles from deep within the river which appeared with no explanation at all. Where exactly they came from he had no idea. His thoughts, like the bubbles, needed to be caught and collected, before they too disappeared.

Now, feeling the tug on his line once again and watching Rosenwyn make her way back towards the chapel, he was sorry he was unable to help her more. But he also understood that things unfolded in their own good time. Perhaps all any of them needed to do was watch and wait.

Justin's appearance in the valley shortly before the disappearance of the first Maiden had caused some consternation amongst the villagers. Yet it was not uncommon for travellers to pass through, not only on the trade route from the sea and the monastic island of Tintagel, but also due to the relics of Saint Clederus.

And so, although the little chapel continued to enjoy a steady stream of pilgrims, there was an air of unrest, a number of whispers were heard and, perhaps because he did not move on like the others, fingers pointed in the general direction of Justin.

As he approached the chapel Justin experienced the now familiar feeling of coming home. He had visited Rosenwyn on a number of occasions since arriving at the valley, the first of which was on the day of the Beltane fires following the Ceremony of the Maidens. It had been a busy morning and the procession a sight he would never forget, the line of Maidens followed by the villagers, wending their way along the path accompanied by the beat of drums, and when they had all left to enjoy the remainder of the day he tentatively approached the chapel himself.

'Welcome to our sanctuary. May I offer you some refreshment?' These were the words which Rosenwyn spoke to pilgrims and travellers, indeed she had surely uttered them a thousand times, yet she felt as if this was the first and knew this knight to be special. She looked into his eyes, framed by the rich, red of his hair and found a mixture of honesty, passion and humility there.

'Lady, I have travelled far to this place,' began Justin, dropping onto one knee before her. 'And I thank you for your offer of refreshment.'

Rosenwyn passed Justin her silver chalice filled with crystal clear water from the well and Justin knew the end of his quest was in sight.

And now, with Midsummer approaching, Justin felt the unmistakeable need to see Rosenwyn, his Lady of the Well, once again.

Twenty Three

'I could have told you long ago no good would come of this.' Father Christopher pursed his lips and maintained an air of righteousness as he conscientiously set everything required upon the altar in readiness for Evensong, feeling a slight resentment towards Prior Richard's consternation at the disappearance of the Maidens – events which now appeared to have taken on an importance far beyond their true worth.

Yes, three Maidens had vanished without trace

and the remainder were living their lives in fear - he allowed himself a small smirk at this - but such unfortunate incidents happened from time to time and life continued onwards. Perhaps now the villagers would understand the importance of regular church attendance rather than following the yearly cycle of festivals they still insisted upon and perhaps...

His thoughts were interrupted by a discreet cough from Prior Richard, and Father Christopher realised that in his furious internal tirade at Rosenwyn and the Maidens he had completely forgotten his superior's presence.

'It is a worrying state of affairs,' continued Prior Richard thoughtfully, holding his hands as if in prayer and allowing the fingertips to gently rest together. 'And I am sure you will agree the young Maidens should be given our protection. But,' he dropped his voice to a whisper, inclining his dark head towards Father Christopher's fair one, 'there is a further cause for concern I wish to discuss with you.'

Father Christopher turned in surprise, almost knocking over the brass candlesticks he was arranging. 'But of course,' he sputtered, privately acknowledging the great honour bestowed upon him by being included in Prior Richard's innermost thoughts. 'Anything I can do to help.'

Prior Richard glanced around to ensure no one was listening but the church appeared empty, save for a swift shadow which passed, unnoticed by the priests, leaving all as before. 'It concerns the relics of our patron, Saint Clederus.' He raised his eyebrows. 'Do you consider,' he whispered so quietly Father Christopher could barely hear him, 'them to be quite... safe... in the keeping of the chapel and sacred well?

After all, considering the disappearance of the Maidens and the fact our Lady Rosenwyn could be next...'

Father Christopher nodded slowly, understanding dawning, his heart pounding in excitement. 'I appreciate your concerns,' he replied steadily, careful to keep his voice on an even tone, 'and certainly share them. Come, let us take a goblet of wine together and discuss how they might best be safeguarded.'

Prior Richard and Father Christopher made their way importantly along the path from the church to the little chapel. As they walked, signs of high summer were evident all around. The willows hung heavy and cool over the river and oak leaves rustled in the breeze. Buttercups shone, waxy in the bright sunlight and the scent of meadowsweet hung heavy in the air. The sun riding high overhead caused a thin bead of perspiration to appear on Prior Richard's brow as he strode along, his portly frame unused to such exercise, whilst Father Christopher scurried behind in a desperate attempt to keep up. Across the valley the grass had been cut and men, women and children could be seen turning the hay before forming it into stacks.

At the top of the hill the Midsummer fire was being built, which would be lit in honour of the strength of the sun and the growth of the crops. Father Christopher sniffed and crossed himself briefly at the sight of such heathen activities.

As they approached the chapel they could see Rosenwyn sitting outside on her little wooden bench, a man in knight's clothing at her side, his tunic bearing the emblem of a golden lion upon a red background. A large sword hung in its scabbard at his side and his horse grazed quietly in the shade outside the enclosure.

Rosenwyn and the knight looked up as Prior Richard and Father Christopher opened the little gate, and a slight frown of annoyance appeared upon Rosenwyn's face.

Father Christopher smirked. This was the moment for which he had waited a very long time.

Twenty Four

'It was my calling,' explained Justin, as they sat together in the sunshine outside the chapel. 'I can explain no differently but it was in my heart. I have spent many years protecting the innocent, travelled to great castles far across the water, fought in combat, yet always I have dreamed of a tiny chapel with a stone altar beside which I would keep my vigil to truly seal my life as a Knight of the Realm. And it is all I thought it would be,' he continued softly. 'It is so very peaceful here. Truly, peace is the sound of heaven on earth.' He looked into her eyes and she saw love and vocation there, mixed with a passion for his quest.

'And you...' He paused, choosing his words carefully. 'Forgive me, my Lady, but you have long been at the centre of my search. Of you I have also dreamed, have known your need of protection and believe I have come at this time to your aid.'

Rosenwyn nodded, admitting to herself she too had felt a strong pull on Beltane morning when she first sighted Justin across the valley. She remembered the love she felt emanating from him and also the pure hatred she discerned from the other figure. In the warmth of the day, Rosenwyn shivered. 'And what of your vigil? You say you are here to aid me as best you can, although how and why, as yet we know not. Your presence is welcome and I thank you. But your vigil is important too.'

Justin nodded. 'I would like to undertake it on the night of the Midsummer celebrations,' he continued, 'if that is well with you.'

'And what will this entail?'

'Merely to spend the night alone, in the chapel, in prayer. I must contemplate my vows to God and my vocation as a Knight of the Realm and all it means to me.'

'There will be a full moon that night,' mused Rosenwyn. 'A powerful time indeed. The Ceremony of the Full Moon will be performed when she is at her height but we shall be on the hilltop above the rocks, as is our custom at special times such as this.' She smiled. 'The chapel will be yours and yours alone. I wish you well.'

'Thank you.' Justin paused. 'They say the vigil is a time of difficulty and of temptation. It is said visions appear before the very eyes and voices are heard, but it is important to separate fact and duty from fantasy, and to remain focused on what is right and upon God. Our duty means a great deal to us, my Lady, and our God, although I understand she whom you worship on the night of the full moon, differs.'

'But in the end all are one, even if some people refuse to see it,' replied Rosenwyn, her thoughts turning to Father Christopher.

'And I bring you this, a gift which I have brought across oceans and carried with me for many moons, for the moment I saw it I thought of the chapel and valley of my dreams and knew in my heart it belonged here.'

Justin produced the green and violet crystal and Rosenwyn gasped, completely taken aback by its unexpected beauty and the way it shimmered and sparkled in the sunlight.

'May I?'

'I would be honoured.'

Rosenwyn held out her hand and Justin dropped the crystal onto her palm. It felt icy cold and strangely heavy, and she had an unexpected vision of a girl holding the crystal high in the air, snow swirling about her, the crystal flashing a rainbow of colour all around. So profound was the vision that Rosenwyn drew in her breath sharply, the crystal dropping from her hand.

'My Lady?' Justin was on his feet at once. 'Can I help in any way? A drink perhaps?'

Rosenwyn nodded and gestured towards her silver chalice which Justin immediately brought, filled with refreshing water.

'It is indeed a crystal of enormous power,' murmured Rosenwyn when she had recovered herself a little. They both glanced at it, lying almost hidden in the grass and Rosenwyn bent to pick it up. It lay once more in the palm of her hand, glowing gently in the sunlight but she could feel its distant heartbeat connecting her to the earth from which it came.

'Please take it.' She offered it to Justin. 'And guard it for me. I fear the time will come when we will have need of it – and perhaps at the moment it is safer in your hands than mine.' She raised her eyes as the figures of Prior Richard and Father Christopher appeared at the gate to the enclosure.

Twenty Five

Rosenwyn and Justin did not rise to their feet as expected. Indeed, Rosenwyn appeared openly annoyed at the intrusion. Not, thought Father Christopher, the way she should be treating himself and Prior Richard in these troubled times.

'My Lady.' Prior Richard bowed his head briefly but made no attempt to skirt delicately around the reason for his visit. He paused, expecting some response, but finding none, cleared his throat and continued slightly self-consciously. 'Father Christopher and I have had a discussion and feel, due to current circumstances, particularly concerning the disappearance of the Maidens,' he paused once more, coughed delicately and drew a deep breath. 'I, that is, we, Father Christopher and myself, feel the relics of our blessed Saint Clederus are no longer safe in your care, that is, in the chapel and it is therefore in all our interests they be removed to the confines and sanctity of the church as soon as possible. In fact, Father Christopher is able and ready to transport them back to the church on your behalf, now, that is, this very afternoon.'

Father Christopher started. He had not expected to carry the relics himself at that precise moment and wondered exactly how heavy they were going to be. In all honesty, he had never actually seen them and had no idea of what they comprised. Rumour said there was a skull and some bones, but exactly how many he could not be sure. And how unsavoury might they have become after all these years?

Rosenwyn rose to her feet, appearing taller and

more stately than Prior Richard remembered, an uncompromising look upon her gentle features. 'The blessed relics have been entrusted to the care of the chapel for many years now,' she murmured. 'In fact, it was a decree of the Priory they remain here. Many pilgrims pass this way merely to drink of the sacred water which has passed over them.'

'Which they can do just as easily in the church. Such things can be suitably arranged,' cut in Father Christopher impatiently, refraining from rubbing his hands together now his dream was about to be fulfilled. 'And they will be much safer in my care. Especially,' he added piously, 'in these troubled times.'

'How?'

'Pardon?'

'How will they be safer in your care?' questioned Rosenwyn.

'Why, is it not obvious? You are a fragile woman with no strength to ward off intruders, whilst...'

'I see.' Rosenwyn surveyed Father Christopher's skinny form as his words dried upon his lips. 'And also you have a lock on your door to stop the people freely entering your house of God whilst I do not.'

'Enough.' Prior Richard clapped his hands. 'I have made my decision and we have come to claim the sacred relics. Father Christopher, if you would.' He nodded towards the chapel and Father Christopher scurried inside.

Rosenwyn stood pale and silent by the entrance, gazing steadily at Prior Richard. Eventually Justin stepped forwards, hand on the hilt of his sword. 'My Lady?' he questioned softly.

Rosenwyn gave a small shake of her head and he stepped back, but his hand remained upon his sword and there was a wary look in his eyes.

The door of the chapel swung open and Father Christopher appeared. 'My Lord,' he burbled, 'they have gone.'

'What?'

'The most sacred relics of our most sacred and worshipful Saint Clederus.' Father Christopher babbled incoherently. 'Beneath the altar, nothing but an empty space, my Lord. Glory Be To God.' He sank to his knees, crossing himself fervently. 'First the Maidens and now the sacred relics. What is to become of us all?'

It was not long before fingers were pointed and rumours began to fly once more. A number of theories abounded.

Some whispered that Father Christopher was behind the disappearance of the relics, his agitation being a cover for the fact he had already stolen them. Others wondered if they were hidden by Rosenwyn herself following the disappearance of the Maidens, whilst yet more pointed their fingers at Justin, the stranger in their midst who appeared just as the problems began. And even Duncan, who they had known all their lives and would hitherto have trusted with their very souls, was whispered to have become jealous of Rosenwyn's friendship with the knight and stolen the relics in order to punish her. The longer it lasted, the more ridiculous the theories became.

Twenty Six

Midsummer's Eve

Midsummer's Eve dawned with the mystery of the disappearing Maidens and the removal of the relics no closer to being solved.

'Mark my words, there will be trickery afoot tonight,' warned Duncan, as Rosenwyn paused by the river to speak to him.

'I do wish you would stop talking in riddles,' she snapped, then sighed. The whole scenario was making her irritable and she was unable to muster the feeling of enthusiasm and sense of wonder she usually felt at times such as this. The Midsummer festival of the longest day, coupled with the Ceremony of the Full Moon, made for a night of energy and magic. Some said spirits would be abroad on this night, others that it was a time of working high magic, and one or two insisted it was safer for all God fearing people to remain in their beds. She remembered the frown upon Father Christopher's face when he realised how the events were to coincide.

'Remember, many things are hidden or disguised,' continued Duncan slowly, taking no notice of her tone. 'Not always gone forever.'

Rosenwyn sighed again, knowing she would get no more from him than he was willing to give; and he felt a certain regret he could not tell her any more. His words, as always, came from deep within, like the bubbles which rose to the surface of the water and no one knew from whence they came, least of all Duncan himself.

From her vantage point at the chapel, Rosenwyn watched the swallows swooping low over the land and skimming the surface of the river in their never ending quest for insects. Along the pathway foxgloves grew, tall and stately, their vivid shade of pink standing out amongst the greenery of high summer, buttercups shone like miniature suns and the lacy white of the cow parsley mingled with the scent of meadowsweet on the air.

Rosenwyn knew in her heart the time had arrived to consult the waters of the sacred well, to ask for guidance and perhaps obtain some answers to recent events in the valley. It was Midsummer's Eve, a night of magic and anticipation of the day to come, and Rosenwyn was aware the energies would be especially strong for scrying.

Finally, when the chapel had been simply decorated in preparation for Midsummer's Day – a froth of meadowsweet and cow parsley amidst which stood the tall, stately foxgloves and a swathe of summer greenery - everyone left save for Rosenwyn.

With a sigh of relief to find a moment of peace following the hectic preparations, as the sun began to set and the moon to rise, casting a silvery glow into the dusk, she settled herself beside the sacred well and allowed her mind to still. Silently, from years of long practice, she called forth the previous Guardians of the well to whom she always turned in times of trouble and who never failed her.

There was a girl, her name lost in the mists of time, often seen holding a spear, a great white owl sometimes upon her arm. And there a young woman, hair plaited with spring flowers, fire and smoke swirling about her, mischief in her dark eyes. Around these two, legends had been woven throughout the years, stories which had created the very fabric of the cult of the Maidens of the Wells, for they were the first Guardians and each had fought, in her own way, to retain the sacred waters for the feminine.

There was another. Rosenwyn paused, wondering if she might see her on this day, for she appeared only at times of great need. Indeed, Rosenwyn herself had never seen this Guardian and only knew of her from whispers passed down through the generations. It was said she was the most beautiful vision of all, a wise and ancient spirit who invariably left some sign she had been present. Rosenwyn heaved a great sigh, thinking that if ever there was a time she needed guidance, it was now.

Long moments passed, the sun fading as the moonlight grew stronger. Inside the stone structure of the sacred well the water continued to flow through the square, granite basin and make its way into the chapel. The stones above and around the surface of the water were a cool green, their reflections continually changing with the shimmering moonlight and shadow, and a small, brown frog swiftly made its way from one side to the other, only to disappear into the stonework once more.

All was quiet, the perfect conditions for Rosenwyn to fall into a deep trance and contact the former Guardians of the well. Nothing happened. It was as if no spirit resided there, none ever had, nor ever would again. After some time Rosenwyn experienced, with a sinking heart, the realisation she had failed. Never before had this happened, for even as a small child she was always able to see visions in the waters, even if only spending a few moments focussing. And today, in her greatest hour of need, when she required help and guidance more than at any other time...

With a sob she pulled herself to her feet, struggling to fight back the tears feeling, for the first time in her life, completely useless, deserted and abandoned. Stumbling to the front of the chapel and down to the riverbank her eyes raked the length of the river, silver in the blackness of the surrounding shadows, hoping to catch a glimpse of Duncan who she knew would soothe her wounds. But of him there was no sign. Nothing stirred, save the gentle swaying of the willows in the darkness and the swift movement of the water. Never had Rosenwyn felt so alone in her life.

She sank to her knees, her dress wet and muddied, then amongst the reeds and the meadowsweet she lay down and cried. She wept for the loss of her vision, the disappearance of her Maidens and for the Guardians who were no longer with her. Where, she asked herself in anguish, had they all gone?

After a while she became quiet, exhausted, and it was then she felt the word in her mind.

Come.

Although Rosenwyn heard nothing spoken aloud, the summons was unmistakeable. Sitting up and glancing around she saw no more than the riverbank in moonlight and the gently swaying meadowsweet on the far side, then slowly became aware this was no ordinary meadowsweet but formed the flowing gown of a woman. Rosenwyn stared, entranced, as the vision grew more distinctive. The woman's hair reflected the undulating swoop of wild birds on a summer morn and the flowers in her gown danced with coloured butterflies.

Come.

Once again Rosenwyn felt the summons, rose to her feet and stepped into the cool depths of the river to follow her vision for this, she knew without a doubt, was the ancient Guardian for which she had waited so long.

Rosenwyn took a deep breath and moved forwards, reaching out her hands towards the vision, the icy water of the river drenching her dress as she began to wade across.

You will be safe with us.

The words lingered upon the night air as Rosenwyn felt an overwhelming sense of relief, of oneness with the world, the universe and a certainty that in the end everything would become right.

Behind her she sensed a movement in the darkness of the night, nothing more than an owl swooping along the valley, but enough to break the spell of the moment and Rosenwyn jerked out of her trance and back to the present, finding herself standing knee deep in water, hands stretched before her.

'You be careful now,' Duncan's low voice murmured in the velvet darkness. He reached out and grasped her arm, guiding her back to reality and steadying her as she struggled to the safety of the riverbank.

Rosenwyn blinked, vaguely aware of the moonlit shadows and shifting greenery crossing Duncan's face in the semi-darkness. 'I saw her,' she murmured. 'Just as you saw the Green Man, I saw the Lady, fashioned from meadowsweet and the flight of butterflies and birds...' Her voice trailed away in wonder as Duncan continued to hold her, gently grounding her in the real world.

'And what message did she leave?'

154

'She wanted me to go with her.' Rosenwyn blinked. 'But how could I? How could I leave my Maidens?' Her voice trailed away and she began to cry quietly, realising how very much she had wished to follow the Lady, and leave the world behind her.

'You be careful, now,' repeated Duncan. 'Such portals only open in times of great need and, once entered, lifetimes might pass before you are able to return.' He thoughtfully plucked a single stem of meadowsweet and presented it to her. 'She will come again,' he stated simply, 'although when you will return to this world might be a different question.'

Still stunned and half in a trance, Rosenwyn took the meadowsweet from Duncan and, leaving him amongst the moonlight and greenery, began to make her way back up the grassy slope towards the chapel. The little building glowed softly in the moonlight and her footsteps quickened for she felt the strong desire to be alone inside the chapel or beside the sacred well to ponder her thoughts. She reached the chapel to find Duncan sitting quietly, gazing across the valley.

'How... what are you doing here?'

Duncan regarded her with an air of quiet puzzlement. 'Waiting for you,' he replied slowly. There was a pause as the moonlight shone ever more brightly and an owl hooted in the distance. 'You be careful now,' he continued, 'this being a time of such magic and all. Even I wouldn't walk between the worlds on a night like this.'

Rosenwyn glanced in confusion from Duncan to the deep shadows of the riverbank, recalling his words and the moonlight which had played across his face only moments before.

She thought of the Green Man and the Guardian,

the disappearance of the Maidens and the danger which surrounded them all. And as the moon shone ever more brightly, a slow understanding began to form in her mind.

Twenty Seven

Midsummer's Day

The festivities of the day were over and the time had arrived for the lighting of the ritual fire in reverence to the strength of the sun and its importance in the abundance of the crops. On hilltops all around fires would be lit until the countryside was ablaze with light. Rosenwyn and her Maidens were then to proceed to the high pinnacle above the valley and perform the Ceremony of the Full Moon. And as the moon rose to her heights, Justin would take his place in the chapel for his night time vigil.

Although all three events should have been cause for celebration, Rosenwyn could not help but feel an unaccustomed heaviness in her heart, for things were not as they should have been in whichever direction she looked. Despite her faith and the visions of the previous night, she was unsure what lay ahead for herself and her Maidens, although she was beginning to understand the path which was opening before them.

Earlier in the day, Rosenwyn had taken from the pouch she always carried with her a brown, flint spearhead and a wooden pendant carved with a beautiful, spreading tree. She sat for long moments in the summer sunlight, weighing the spearhead in the palm of her hand and feeling its solidity. Her fingers caressed the serrated edges and smooth flint as she pondered on her next course of action. Finally, she placed the wooden pendant about her neck and spent some time in silent meditation beside the sacred well. When she finally came to a decision she returned both objects to the pouch, wrapped them with her ceremonial silver chalice and earthenware bowl in a cloth, and gave them to Duncan for safe keeping.

On the hilltop across the valley the Midsummer fire blazed. The villagers watched the next burst into life as the sun disappeared below the horizon leaving a smudge of gold in the sky. In the opposite direction the moon rose shining silver and Rosenwyn, from her vantage point on the rock high above the chapel, raised her arms in welcome.

In the valley the people were able to witness both the burning of the Midsummer fire and hear the singing which accompanied the Ceremony of the Full Moon, an auspicious time indeed and one, although they did not yet realise it, which would be recounted for many generations to come.

It was unfortunate that when the Maidens began to disappear, talk of Marauding Knights came to the ears of Father Christopher. Dark, hard men, it was told, who roamed the countryside, unashamedly taking what was not theirs and willing to carry out the most unsavoury of tasks for the right fee. Father Christopher had never been a violent man nor one who would wish harm to anyone, but the cult of the Maidens of the Wells, coupled with the disappearance of the relics and the fact he was fast losing his grip on any status he might once have held in the community, quite simply, turned his mind.

And so after spending some time in prayer, he finally felt perfectly justified in taking the required amount from the church coffers and organising the disposal of Rosenwyn and her Maidens, not for his own glory, but simply for the good of the church, the people and the future of the valley itself.

Justin reached the little chapel at dusk. Although the burning of the Midsummer fires was at its height and he could hear the voices of Rosenwyn and the Maidens raised in praise to the rising moon, as he approached there was a momentary lull during which nothing could be heard but the sound of the river rushing in the valley below and the croak of a lone raven, heralding the passing of the day.

A slow mist began to rise from the riverbed as twilight deepened and shadows lengthened, casting black fingers over the land.

Justin stood for a long time watching the waning of the day. As the light diminished the moon shone with increasing brightness, stars appeared and the landscape was bathed in brilliant white light, turning the valley to silver, reminding Justin of a magical, enchanted land. In the distance an owl hooted and he caught the rush of snowy white wings as it flew along the valley, then settled upon the bough of a nearby tree in its own silent vigil.

Justin pushed open the door of the little chapel. The first fingers of moonlight were creeping through the window and he knew that soon the granite altar would be flooded with silver, causing the stone to sparkle with an energy and life of its own.

The Midsummer decorations glowed in the moonlight, illuminating the tall, pale candles which Rosenwyn had placed upon the altar. Although the day had been warm, the chapel already felt cool and Justin was aware that as night progressed it could become icy cold.

Justin walked to the altar then knelt on one knee, his sword before him, hands clasping its hilt. The moonlight brightened with every second. Justin bowed his head and prepared to wait in total silence, still as a statue, until dawn.

As Rosenwyn and the Maidens began their ritual, the villagers on the opposite side of the valley noticed a cluster of black shadows congregating a short distance from the chapel and, so some were to say later, the sound of hoof beats drumming upon the dry, summer ground.

Justin had dreamed of this moment for so long. Would he be visited by spirits? Ghosts? An angel? The Lord himself? Other knights spoke of this as an experience from which they learned about themselves as well as God. With a feeling of deep anticipation Justin wondered what triumphs or tragedies he might encounter.

His quest. His search for the holy grail which lay deep within himself.

Justin closed his eyes and waited. Silence descended around him. Not even the sound of the rushing river or the rustling of an animal penetrated his thoughts and consciousness. He opened his eyes.

The interior of the chapel was bathed in silver, more beautiful than he had ever seen it before. All at once he felt a rush of pure ecstasy at the beauty, the stillness and silence around him.

For one fleeting moment he had a glimpse of himself standing high on the rocks of the valley, the same feeling of wonder coursing through his body, causing him to feel alive and at one with the earth itself – and in that moment he understood the link between man and nature, man and God, spirit and self.

This surely, was his grail, his journey on this night's vigil. It had not been difficult at all, his quest. He needed only to open his heart and allow love to flood in. The thought crept into his consciousness that it had all been too fast and too easy.

In his mind's eye he watched his self of another time draw back his arm and hurl a spear into the air, the sun flashing and glinting on its spearhead. Then there was a scream which mingled with his own. High pitched and lingering - and Justin realised with a shock he also heard a cry from outside the little chapel, resounding up the valley, the sounds in his imagination and in reality merging together on the night air.

He opened his eyes in confusion only to find the silver of the moonlight in the chapel had changed to red, the chapel bathed in blood and, unable to stop himself, his vow of silence was broken as a deep sob of fear and confusion burst from within him.

Justin was torn. He realised almost at once it was Rosenwyn's voice. He thought at one point he even heard her call his name. All his instincts told him to abandon his quest and rescue Rosenwyn, for surely it was his duty to protect her. Every inch of his being told him so.

And yet... This was his vigil. Was this real or was it a test? If he left the chapel only to discover there was nothing amiss, that it was merely a trick to lure him from his quest... what then?

The cry pierced the air once again and seemed to be joined by others, the calls of women from times long past, merging and mingling on the night air, moving up and down the valley. Desperate pleas for help. And mixed with the cries were the sound of hoof beats, drumming the dry earth on a quest of their own, closing in, as Justin himself had so often done in battle.

Still Justin hung on, his white knuckles clinging desperately to the hilt of his sword, his eyes, since that terrible moment when he had seen the blood red all around him, so tightly shut he thought they might never open again.

The voices of Rosenwyn and her Maidens rang out in one final song, beautiful and strong. Then, one by one the voices died away, their harmonies fading and the only voice in the stillness of the night was Rosenwyn's, until, like a single candle flame being extinguished, it too was gone.

There was sudden silence as Justin realised he was holding his breath, his body soaked in a cold sweat. He exhaled, long and slow. Had he passed the test? Was it over? Dare he open his eyes once more and, when he did, would he find the chapel peaceful and silver in the moonlight and would the terrible redness be gone?

There was no sound, not even the distant call of an owl.

Slowly, so slowly, Justin opened his eyes. All around was dull and red. He forced himself to look for the moonlight through the window but there was nothing. This was Hell. This was the hellfire and brimstone he had been warned of and suddenly he knew he could no longer remain there in silence for the rest of the night.

Gathering all his courage he moved to the door and stepped outside. The valley was awash with red and completely silent. Out of the shadows a figure emerged, which he discerned to be the simpleton, Duncan. Justin tried to form words in a futile attempt to ask what was happening, but could find none.

'They have gone,' said Duncan simply. 'And you are the only person who can find them.' Then he too, disappeared into the darkness.

Twenty Eight

Lammas

It was the talk of the countryside for a long, long time. Almost everyone had their own tale to tell of the night the High Priestess and the remaining Maidens of the Wells disappeared, and what was more, before the very eyes of a band of knights who had been reduced to quivering wrecks by the fact the women they were paid to dispose of had, quite simply, vanished before their very eyes. Questions were naturally asked, the truth inevitably coming to the surface, and Father Christopher found some explanations were necessary.

One good outcome was that the men in question, disturbed by their experience, threw down their swords and vowed to join Justin in his search for the truth, forming a band of knights which, in time, became known far and wide for their chivalry, justice and

162

honesty. But theirs is yet another tale to tell.

Over the years the story was recounted so often it lived on for centuries, added to the story of the girl who killed an evil Magician for her guardianship of the well and that of the young woman who fought the new religion and restored the well to the care of the women of the village. These stories were handed down through the generations, related to wide-eyed children around the hearth on cold, winter evenings and even continued to send a shiver of fear through many adults.

Following the initial furore, no more fingers were pointed and the whispers fell silent. If such a thing could happen to those so highly revered in the community then no one was safe and the villagers swiftly turned their attention to their work, kept their heads down and said nothing.

But the fact remained that their High Priestess and the Maidens had vanished and no one knew where they had gone. What would happen now?

Justin had taken pains to discover exactly what had occurred whilst he was intent upon his vigil. He cursed himself to Hell and back a thousand times for following his duty rather than his instinct – his heart – when he heard the tormented cries in the night. Why, he asked himself, had he not thrown duty to the winds and rushed to Rosenwyn's rescue? Now he had to rely on other people to relate what they had seen and always there was the question in their eyes, if not on their lips, as to why he was not there himself.

It appeared, when Justin pieced together the numerous accounts, already conflicting and some taking on supernatural proportions, that Rosenwyn and the Maidens began the Ceremony of the Full Moon, as planned, on the highest cliff above the chapel, a spot they often used at such times. They proceeded up the winding path to where a circle of stones and a small altar were in place. Rosenwyn often performed ceremonies at different locations throughout the valley, for she believed everywhere to be worthy of reverence, not just the location of the chapel and sacred well.

And so, as the moon rose to her heights and Rosenwyn and the Maidens began to sing, a strange occurrence had taken place. Slowly, very slowly, it was as if a shadow began to cover the face of the moon and as it progressed the silver of the night dimmed, turning the shining orb from full, to half, to no moon at all; but rather than the blackness of the night sky pinpricked with stars, all that could be seen was a bloody smudge in the sky which washed the valley in red. And every single person to which Justin spoke, told of the feeling of desolation which pierced their hearts.

The women had fallen silent at the point when the red and black of the night was at its height, a single cry rang from the cliff top, echoing around the valley, almost immediately followed by another and another until a cacophony of notes filled the night sky, blending together into a strange symphony, beautiful and terrible all at the same time. The voices echoed up the valley, rooting the villagers to the spot and then they ceased as suddenly as they began, the beautiful voices raised in unison one final time, only to be extinguished one by one until Rosenwyn sang alone, then her voice too died away into the silence.

As the villagers ran towards the cliff top, only to discover a confused and terrified band of knights riding in a disorientated fashion around the little altar, the sky began to change once more. The blood red of the moon started to lighten and, over the course of the night, returned to normal.

But of Rosenwyn and her Maidens, there was no sign. All anyone could remember was the strong scent of meadowsweet hanging heavy on the night air.

The year turned and it was Lammas. The leaves upon the oak, rowan and hawthorn were turning brown and shrivelling in the heat of the sun, the swallows preparing to leave – earlier than usual – but there was no denying the fact they were about to take flight.

'You are the only person who can find them.' The words of the simpleton, Duncan, repeated themselves in Justin's head so often that eventually, being unable to make sense of any of it, he searched Duncan out, finding him as usual, fishing by the river, shaded from the unnatural heat by the cool leaves of the willows. Even these, Justin noticed, were beginning to turn a pale yellow, sickly colour, as if they could not gain enough nourishment from the ground or the water itself.

'I have a question,' stated Justin. Confronted by the sight of Duncan calmly fishing in the midst of such tragedy, he was overcome with anger and appeared abrupt and rude.

Duncan stretched his leg to ease the pain and settled himself more comfortably. 'To ask is the only way to receive the answer,' he commented slowly, tweaking on his line.

Justin opened his mouth to form a stinging reply, then all the frustration left him and he sank down beside Duncan feeling weary and defeated. 'You said on the night when... the terrible night... I was the only person who could find Rosenwyn and the Maidens.'

Duncan continued to fish silently. A bubble rose

to the surface of the water, a small fish jumped and snapped at a hovering fly.

'Can you tell me how?' continued Justin. 'Can you tell me why?'

Duncan tweaked on his line. 'The whole picture is not for you to see,' he began in his slow, deep tone. 'There are pieces here and others there. Some are lost in the mists of time and have their roots in other lives. Yet more cannot be found until many lifetimes have passed. But be assured you are a part of the great pattern, the web of life, and the moment will come when you will again have your chance to save the Lady Rosenwyn and the vanished Maidens.' He paused for a long while and, just as Justin thought he had finished speaking, continued once more in the slow, melodic voice which had caused Justin to daub him a simpleton. 'Remember two things my friend. Firstly, without the Maidens of the Wells the land will become a wasteland, and secondly, although things are not visible it does not mean they do not exist. They might simply be out of sight.'

A cluster of bubbles rose to the surface of the river, swirled and were swept away. Duncan tugged on his line and hoisted a wriggling trout into the air, shining in a rainbow of colour. He nodded in satisfaction, then tossed it back in and Justin knew his audience to be over. A damselfly pitched briefly upon a delicate circlet of meadowsweet which floated gently down the river, before slowly sinking beneath the surface of the water without a trace.

'Thank you.' He stood, clasped Duncan's arm briefly and walked away, back to the empty chapel, bare now with no flowers or foliage to decorate it, and the sacred well which had taken on a murky look in its usually clear depths. As he walked he realised the land was badly scorched in the summer heat, the green of the valley turning to a sickly orange in places, the heads of plants wilting in the midday sun.

Justin stood before the sacred well and, taking the sparkling green and violet crystal which Rosenwyn had entrusted into his care, let it fall into the water, now still and stagnant, where it at once disappeared into the murky depths and was lost from sight.

He sighed, wondering at the significance of the crystal which seemed to have played no part in events at all, then turned and nodded to his band of knights who waited, saddled and ready, to follow him on his journey – perhaps, thought Justin fleetingly, the only good thing to have come of the whole sorry business.

As he shook the bridle and began to move away, giving one backward glance at the valley, so recently green with the hope of spring, now sickly and diseased, two thoughts came into his mind. Firstly, his quest would not be over for a very long time yet, and secondly, the simpleton, Duncan, was nowhere near as simple as he had first assumed.

Water

Victorian Values:

St Clether's Well

The Holy Waters
and the Ruined Chapel

The Wild or Dog Rose

The Dog Rose (Rosa canina), is often used in healing spells, and a rosewater saturated cloth laid to the temples will relieve headache pain.

In the past it was believed that fairies, by eating a rosehip and then turning anti-clockwise three times, could make themselves disappear. To become visible once more, the fairies had to eat another rosehip and turn clockwise three times.

St Clether's Well

'Through neglect this interesting and beautiful well, in its wild and picturesque situation, is falling into ruin; the water, not having a proper channel to run in, overflows all the ground around, and makes the spot almost unapproachable. One wonders how the possessor of such an interesting antiquity can be so indifferent.'

Ancient and Holy Wells of Cornwall.
M and L Quiller-Couch.

Twenty Nine

As Rose approached the site of the holy well an owl hooted in the distance across the valley, causing her to lose her footing and stumble slightly. She paused, listening for the sound of footsteps behind her or the telltale snap of a twig, but all was silent, save for the rushing of the river below and the call of another owl above.

Rose continued onwards, her breath rasping but increasingly confident she would reach her destination. Tonight the moon was full, the herbs she needed at their most potent and it was imperative she collected them by moonlight – despite the trouble it would cause should Jory discover she had been abroad without his knowledge. But why should she tell him when she knew so well his disapproval?

As the holy well came into sight Rose drew a sigh of relief. As far as she knew no one had followed her and, after picking her way through the boggy ground and over some fallen masonry, she sank down beside the granite basin in which the holy waters gathered and uncorked the small bottle she had brought. Having filled the bottle with spring water she set about finding her little knife with which to harvest the herbs she required - yarrow, comfrey, wild thyme, nettle leaves and fennel seeds - when she heard a slight rustle behind her and turned to see Davy standing on a piece of fallen masonry, grinning in the moonlight.

'I suppose you thought I hadn't noticed you

following me,' commented Rose tartly, although she was glad of his presence. One could never be too sure who might be around on a night such as this, many a good deal more dangerous than the resident gamekeeper.

'Indeed not. I came over the fields, not in your footsteps.' Davy jumped down beside her and settled himself cross legged upon the granite altar, the only part of the chapel which remained intact, save for a low piece of stone walling to one side. He placed two dead rabbits beside him. 'Tomorrow's supper,' he commented. 'A good night's work.'

'And I have mine yet to do,' replied Rose, gathering up her basket. 'I have a number of poultices and salves to concoct while the moon is full. And also...'

Davy nodded. 'You need to work your magic,' he stated simply.

Rose glanced at him sharply, unsure if he were poking fun at her but the expression in his dark brown eyes was, as far as she could tell in the silvery light, perfectly serious.

'I'll hang around if you like,' he offered. 'You never know who might be watching.'

'Thank you.' Rose felt a sense of relief at the knowledge he would be nearby. Close enough but not spying or interfering, although she had, on more than one occasion, offered to include him in her magic. But he always declined, preferring to remain in the shadows, watching and waiting.

She gathered her basket, knife and bottle. 'I'll be back shortly,' she whispered, before disappearing along the valley to where she knew the herbs could be found.

Davy nodded, settled himself more comfortably upon the granite altar stone and prepared to wait. He was good at that.

As he sat, Davy whittled away at a piece of wood. He also whistled, but softly, beneath his breath. To anyone passing, the sound might have been mistaken for the wind in the trees or the soft flight of insects on the night air. A movement in the undergrowth caught his attention and a brown stoat appeared, apparently unaware of, or perhaps familiar with, his presence as it searched the overgrown debris of the masonry for a meal. The water vole, which lived beneath the altar stone, would have to be careful. An owl hooted and Davy knew the stoat would in turn need to be wary, for the great white owl which frequented the valley and had been known to land silently and perch not far away, was more than capable of taking a stoat for its evening meal.

The hunter and the hunted, the cycle of life. Davy glanced at the pair of rabbits resting on the stone slab and thought of the meal they would make. Being gamekeeper had its advantages, especially with the hunting and the fishing which went with it.

The moon had risen higher now, her silvery beams illuminating the valley as brightly as day. The sound of the rushing river seemed unaccountably loud, the shadows a deep black in the silver of the night. There was a scrabbling noise and Rose reappeared.

'All done.' She arranged the herbs more carefully in her basket and pulled out a small stub of candle which she placed upon the altar.

'What you need that for? Moon's bright enough,' commented Davy as he jumped down and retrieved the rabbits.

'Just go and mind your own business,' replied Rose shortly. They repeated a similar conversation each time, Davy finding some question to ask and Rose telling him to mind his own business. Then she would perform her simple ritual in peace knowing he was keeping a look out for her.

When Davy had silently disappeared, Rose set the remainder of her tools upon the altar. Meadowsweet plucked from the marshes, its scent already filling the air, a brown flint arrowhead, a twisted stick of rowan and a small earthenware bowl filled with water from the well. Even though the chapel had been allowed to fall into disrepair, its stones in a tumble around the altar and the arch which once surmounted the holy well broken upon the ground, the well structure with its square basin of granite remained, although the water puddled into a muddy bog all around. It was, Rose often thought, as if the little chapel and well had been forgotten, becoming more inaccessible with every passing year.

Rose placed her hands upon the altar, mere feet from the holy well itself, and felt once again the shimmering of power which flowed through it. She closed her eyes, attuning herself to the energy. There was much work to be done tonight. A number of villagers had asked for help, ranging from lost animals, to sick relatives, to unrequited love, and although much could be cured by potions and salves, focusing her energy and intent brought about the healing much more quickly.

By the silver light of the full moon, Rose set to work.

Some time later, being careful to make as little noise as possible, Rose slipped quietly through the back door of her cottage and stowed her basket in the cupboard beneath the stairs. She hung her cloak, always good for moving around discreetly in the darkness, on its peg and stood for a moment in the silence of the kitchen.

The moon was high, casting bright beams through the small, square panes of the window, changing everyday colours to a monochrome of silver and black. Rose eased her boots from her feet, feeling the chill of the slate floor followed by the comfort of the rag rug which stood in front of the range.

Even from here, before climbing the narrow wooden staircase, she could hear Jory's snores rumbling in the bedroom above. At least he was sound asleep and, hopefully, had not missed her at all.

Besides, Jory disliked the full moon. He believed it made people a little strange in the head and was something to do with the Devil. 'Better,' he had told her on more than one occasion, 'for God fearing people to remain in their beds on such nights.'

Rose had shrugged and continued chopping vegetables for the stew she was preparing. She was not a God fearing woman so she assumed his words were not directed at her – but she was never quite sure how much he knew concerning her thoughts of God and always found it prudent to keep her opinions to herself.

Now, treading silently up the stairs and taking care to avoid the one which creaked, she thought of Davy, stealthily making his way back to his cottage with his booty of rabbit. With any luck he would appear tomorrow, handing a rabbit over the garden gate in return for a salve for a cut finger or bruised hand.

Rose and Davy shared an understanding. They worked well together but above all, viewed the world in the same way.

As she climbed into bed beside Jory and pulled the bedclothes around her Rose wondered, as she often did, if she was married to the right brother but it was far too late now. Her daughter was grown, her marriage to Jory had endured and she had witnessed a lot worse in her time. Settling down into the comfort of her bed, she was soon fast asleep.

When Davy arrived back at his gamekeeper's cottage the first pale light of dawn was streaking fingers of gold and pink across the sky. It was going to be another fine day.

He stood for a moment and drew a deep breath, filling his lungs with clear, sweet smelling air as he surveyed the countryside around him. The year was turning, there was no doubt about it, the first sharp nip in the air and the slight darkening of the evenings bore witness to the fact that autumn was on its way. The crops of high summer had been harvested and the fruits of nature, as he called them, were forming on the trees and in the hedgerows – blackberries ripening, sloes beginning to turn colour, rosehips and crab apples aplenty. This was Davy's favourite time of year, the colourful splendour of autumn when the world was filled with abundance.

He laughed. He was getting as bad as Jory, who would soon be holding forth about the Harvest Festival, ensuring he produced a good marrow or decent sized potatoes, so everyone would know what a good Christian he was.

Davy returned to his kitchen and surveyed the two rabbits lying on the table. His view of what a good Christian man should be and Jory's were never quite the same and they rarely spoke, although Jory never objected to Davy appearing from time to time with a rabbit or a shining, rainbow coloured trout for Rose.

Davy sighed. He often thought Rose had married the wrong brother, but there was nothing to be done about it now. Poking up the fire and pouring boiling water into the teapot, he set about making his breakfast before facing the new day.

Thirty

Jory loved Rose from the moment he first set eyes upon her, a young girl walking behind her father's hay cart in the summer sunshine. He had been passing through a neighbouring village on his way to market and felt an overwhelming desire to protect her, rescue her from the life she led and make her his wife. He loved her with a passion which, despite the years they had been married, never dimmed. In the early days some might have called it lust, but over time he was certain it had become pure love. But he also loved the Church and God with an equal intensity, which was the cause of all the problems.

Now, as he worked in his vegetable patch, tending his best marrows in the hope he would produce the biggest for the Harvest Festival and make the most money for Church funds in the auction afterwards, his thoughts turned to Rose and he wondered where she had gone wrong.

Sometimes he felt a real flash of anger when he thought about it. He had given her his best, and a better life than she would have endured had she married his good for nothing brother, always out poaching and taking what did not belong to him. *Thou Shalt Not Steal* was a commandment Jory lived by every day of his life, along with the other nine, which he knew off by heart and never tired of reminding Rose and their daughter, Rachel, of over the years.

As for, *Thou shalt not covet thy neighbour's wife...* Jory knew well enough Davy's feelings for Rose. He remembered clearly, before they were married, he had brought her to the village in the pony and trap and, on seeing Davy, put his arm around Rose, showing Davy she belonged to him. He felt a stab of pride at the time but, if Jory was completely honest with himself, a little ashamed of his actions afterwards.

He straightened up. It would soon be time to change his clothes before making his way to church to set out the sacraments and then join the bell ringers in summoning the villagers. Jory was Churchwarden and Captain of the Tower, both jobs he took very seriously. He only wished he could persuade Rose to accompany him but, try as he might, she would have nothing to do with it, only appearing by his side at Christmas, Easter, weddings, christenings and funerals, in a vague attempt to stop the villagers gossiping about her for at least some of the time - although he knew well enough they were glad to visit her for salves and potions – sometimes under cover of darkness.

Although Charles had lived in the village for a number of years, he still felt one removed from the villagers. It was all very well living in the manor house and the men touching their caps and muttering 'Mornin' Squire,' when they passed. Some of the women even bobbed the remnant of a curtsey if he came upon them in the road when he was out riding. His presence was required at church every Sunday to sit in the family pew and nod at everyone – but, truth be told, he was lonely and had been for so long.

Charles had never married and, after his parents died leaving him the manor house and enough land to bring in a reasonable income, retreated into his writing and books, content with his own company. And his books were all he needed. Charles spent hours reading, thinking, reading some more and debating with himself the meaning of life, religion and which was the true path, and although he had no one to share his thoughts with, had never missed the company of another person, never longed for the closeness of marriage or a woman to warm his bed. Until he met Rose.

And once Rose came into his life he could think of nothing else. For the first time, his books lay unopened on the desk before him. He longed for her arrival every day when she came to carry out her housekeeping duties, leaving instructions for the cook and the woman from the village who did the rough work, generally keeping an eye on the running of the place in her quiet, efficient way. He knew that without her the house would be empty and he sometimes thought of telling her how he felt - but how could he when she was married to the self-absorbed, self-righteous Jory, who believed God's word was law?

Charles sighed, his papers once again forgotten. Sometimes he was overcome with longing for Rose, albeit she was another man's wife, but it was more than simply lust. He was certain what he felt for her was pure, unadulterated, unrequited love. He just wanted to protect and look after her.

Davy spent a lot of time thinking of Rose too, when he was not busy being gamekeeper for Charles and bearing a grudge against Jory for marrying her in the first place.

And Rose, unaware as she was of any of it, was much more inclined to spend her time thinking about her magic.

Thirty One

The first time it happened, Rose had performed her ritual and was sitting in a peaceful and meditative frame of mind beside the granite altar. The moon was waning, the time for casting banishing spells to rid villagers of cases of warts, ringworm or anything unwanted. Davy kept watch as usual but, on this particular evening, soon disappeared due to other nocturnal activities requiring his attention and Rose elected to sit for a while in the diminishing moonlight.

'Don't worry, I'll be fine,' she assured him as he left. Although the days were drawing in and there was an autumnal nip in the air, it was not cold. The night was still and a feeling of peace permeated the valley.

Rose sat quietly, thankful to be away from Jory's snoring, even secretly glad Davy had left. She realised how little time she spent alone, being either in the company of Jory, Charles or Davy, not to mention the villagers who sought her help and guidance in one form or another.

Rose sighed heavily. She was tired and not simply due to her everyday work. There was a weariness in her spirit as well as her bones. She sank onto a fallen stone and rested her back against the tumbled wall of the chapel, brushing away the worries of the day as drowsiness begin to overtake her and soon her eyes closed.

When she opened them Rose thought she must be dreaming, for this was no place she had ever seen before.

First of all there was a pool and all around the world glimmered with snow. A great white owl perched upon the branch of a massive tree and a girl gazed into the depths of the shifting water.

Then, as swiftly as it had appeared, the scene changed. It was springtime and she saw a young woman, dark hair in a plait and braided with flowers, bending over what appeared to be an ancient book laid open upon the stone altar.

Again a change, a larger building and a woman with hair piled high upon her head attended by young girls, circlets of mayflowers upon their heads and carrying silver chalices.

Rose opened her eyes, called back to the present by the hoot of an owl and a scurrying in the undergrowth. She felt disorientated, dizzy, then it was upon her again and she was in the same building, yet different. The altar was still in place and the chapel rebuilt, at times silent and peaceful, at others, filled with candlelight and laughter. She saw men and women in a circle, singing, chanting, drumming in the moonlight, others taking Mass or sitting in peaceful solitude surveying the valley from a wooden bench beneath a rowan tree. Yet more knelt beside the holy well, its water running clear and pure, giving thanks, saying prayers and leaving offerings.

And finally she saw two people surveying the valley, their hands bound together, a feeling of joy and love in the air. The woman was dressed in a long, flowing gown, a crown of flowers upon her head – and it was a woman she recognised, yet did not know, a woman with a look of herself about her and yet was no one she had ever seen before. The man beside her she recognised too, in the darkness of his hair and the love and gentleness in his eyes, and a sudden breeze caused the hawthorn blossom to shed its petals which swirled around them like confetti.

Rose jerked back to the present. The waning moon had moved across the sky and she realised just how long she must have been sitting there. Her limbs were stiff and chilled and it took a moment to remember where she was and, more worryingly, who she was. For no more than a few seconds, but which seemed to stretch into eternity, she was unable to recall her name or her place in life. One moment she was a girl in the snow, feeling its icy chill upon her face, the next a young woman, the scent of springtime around her and then... Her mind groped for a fast fading image, akin to an elusive dream, as consciousness returned. It was more of a feeling perhaps, which settled somewhere in the centre of her chest and as it grew she recognised desolation, loneliness and longing.

'Without the Maidens of the Wells the land will become a wasteland.'

The words echoed through Rose's mind, unbidden, like the chill wind on a winter's night.

'Without the Maidens of the Wells the land will become a wasteland.'

Again. Rose wrapped her arms around her cold body and struggled to her feet. Around her the tumbled masonry gleamed in the dim light of the waning moon, the holy water trickled slowly, wending its erratic path down the slope to the river, pooling into bog and mud here and there, yet with an underlying freshness and purity which never failed.

Gathering her senses, Rose looked around, seeing the fallen chapel and holy waters as if for the first time, a lonely, forgotten place which had been allowed to fall into disrepair and become covered in brambles.

She felt the prick of tears. So beautiful, yet so sad. But she was a woman of few means, not even knowing who the building belonged to. The church, she supposed, although the thought of questioning Jory about repairing the chapel filled her with despair, for as far as he was concerned the church itself was the primary place of worship and nowhere else.

Rose sighed, defeated.

'Without the Maidens of the Wells the land will become a wasteland.'

There it was again, softer now, fading, yet those were words she would never forget. Who were these Maidens of the Wells, she wondered? What had happened to them and where were they now?

A memory tugged at the back of Rose's mind, no more than a shade of shadow, a passing fragment of thought to which she clung, nurturing each colour and movement, allowing it to grow until it finally became whole. A tale her grandmother had told of the holy wells and Maidens who tended them and something about disappearing. There was more. As the images flew through her mind, Rose became aware she had known the women in her vision before. The girl, the young woman, the lady with the chalice – all stories heard at her grandmother's knee and which she intrinsically felt to be a part of herself.

And then it happened. The thought, the knowledge, the absolute certainty that she, Rose, was the latest in this line of women and had a greater place in the scheme of things than practising her simple magic. For this was her place, a part of her very soul and she knew that if no one else cared, if no one else would do anything to save it, she would.

Rose drew a deep breath, suddenly exhausted as she often felt of late, an aching tiredness behind her eyes, yet refreshed within.

This was her time.

She looked about her as so many women had before, feeling the long line of her ancestry stretching back in time, allowing the strength of the women of the past to move into her. No longer alone.

Rose noted the waning of the moon and the year, reflecting the lessening of love and energy the little chapel and holy waters received, despite the fact the spring trickled staunchly onwards, hidden by mud and bog, yet still there.

Her thoughts returned to Jory, the parish church, back to the ruined chapel. There was a balance required in all things, in religion, beliefs, masculine and feminine. Man's belief and worship in God, the acknowledgement of the lost Maidens and all they stood for.

Rose raised her face to the moon, pulled back her shoulders and drew a deep breath of cool night air. Her time had come and she knew what she must do.

Thirty Two

'I need your help.'

Davy stared at Rose in surprise. It was not often she needed anything from him, let alone his help. He even suspected she only allowed him to keep watch for her as she worked her magic at the holy well because she had a kind heart. She could manage perfectly well without him. If anyone appeared she would have vanished into the shadows before they even knew she was there. He had seen her do it before, once in broad daylight as she was hurrying along a country lane. The Vicar appeared from a cottage gateway and Rose was gone in a flash. Davy never quite worked out where. One moment she was there, the next she was gone. It was as if she simply faded into the hedgerow. And of course, then it was Davy who was compelled to stop and pass the time of day with the Vicar, all the while cursing Rose for disappearing.

'Where were you? Where did you go?' he asked afterwards.

Rose smiled. 'I was there.'

'No you weren't.' He shook his head emphatically. 'You completely disappeared.'

'You just didn't see me. You weren't looking in the right place,' was all she would say, until eventually she got tired of him asking. 'Look Davy,' she said finally, 'some things are hidden, but it doesn't necessarily mean they aren't there.' And then she looked sad and he wondered exactly what it was she was talking about and raised the subject no more.

Davy sighed, wondering why he was remembering that particular occasion. 'What is it?' he asked, pulling himself back to the present. 'How do you need my help?'

Rose bent closer, glancing around to make sure no one was nearby. They were standing at the gate to her cottage and Davy was handing her his usual illicit gift, this time a shining rainbow trout from the river. It was almost mid September and the sun was pleasantly warm upon her bare arms. The garden was beginning to fade after the glory of high summer, but held the air of a job well done. Seeds had formed on the coriander, fennel and dill. The rosemary hedge, from which Rose always took a sprig to chew as she was passing, looked much the same as ever and would be a winter stalwart along with the sage and thyme. The sweet perfumed wild rose which twined its way around her window already held rosehips as its petals faded in the late summer sunshine. She noticed how brown Davy had become following a summer working in the sun.

'I need your help with a ritual.'

'Ah.' Davy nodded slowly, then jerked his head up. 'A what?'

'A ritual,' she hissed. 'You know, when I go to the holy well and the granite altar and work my magic...'

'All right, all right.' He glanced around uncertainly. 'You know I don't have anything to do with that kind of thing.'

'Yes, but I need another person, and I need a man and, well, I need you.'

'Can't you ask someone else?'

'Like who?'

'I don't know...' his lips twitched. 'Jory?' he finished, unsuccessfully attempting not to laugh.

Rose gave him a withering look although she was struggling not to smile, and Davy knew he would never be able to refuse.

'You know the ruined chapel.'

Jory glanced up from the Bible he was studying, his red hair glinting in the lamplight as he searched for a suitable reading for Sunday's service. He frowned at Rose, sitting by the range sewing quietly. 'What about it?'

'Does it belong to the church? And if so, why has it been left to fall into ruins?' She lowered her sewing onto her lap. 'Doesn't anyone care?'

Jory shrugged. 'What good is it?' he replied. 'Nothing more than a pile of broken down stones and a lot of bog and undergrowth. No one's been there for years. I expect it's all covered in brambles by now.'

Rose remained silent, unwilling to admit to her regular visits, much as she longed to explain to Jory the special feeling of the place and the beauty of the granite altar, especially by moonlight. She shrugged and picked up her sewing again.

'Not sure, really,' continued Jory a moment later. 'Could be it belongs to the landowner, your Mr Charles. He seems to own most of the parish and if that is the case, maybe how it came to fall down. I'm sure,' he continued, turning the pages of his Bible importantly, 'if it belonged to the church, the right thing would have been done.'

Rose nodded. 'Have you found a suitable reading?' she asked.

Jory blinked. Rose did not often show any interest in his church duties. Perhaps things were changing. 'As it happens,' he began, 'I have. Would you like to hear it?'

'Yes, it would be lovely,' murmured Rose, her

attention once more on her sewing, allowing Jory's voice, as he read the words of his Lord, to fade into the background. Under cover of semi-darkness Rose smiled. She was beginning to find some answers and knew where to look next.

Charles lived in the old manor house, down the hill, around the bend and over the bridge from the village, setting it slightly apart from village life, yet near enough for his land to stretch all along each side of the valley, touching both the village, the church and the ruined chapel. The house was, in fact, only a stone's throw from the chapel should anyone care to cross a field and the river, and it nestled in solitude, built of the same grey stone as the church, amid the tall trees of oak and elm which surrounded it.

When Rose arrived to carry out her housekeeping duties she invariably let herself in through a little gate, allowing her access into the cobbled courtyard and then through a door beside the small, round tower which housed nothing more than a staircase, and into the kitchens. The large, dark oak door, seldom unlocked and even less likely to be used, opened onto what was known as the great hall, which, although not so very great, boasted an enormous fireplace which would have heated the entire room. As it was, no one could recall the fire being lit in living memory. Charles, and his predecessors before him, lived in one small wing of the house, the remainder being left to dust, cobwebs and any mice who cared to make it their home.

Rose loved the house. From the moment she first stepped inside, it wrapped itself around her, as if knowing someone finally loved it. She liked to watch the dust motes dance in the beams of sunlight as they struggled through the leaded glass windows set in granite frames and loved the feel of the wooden doors and stair rail, smooth beneath her fingers, and most of all relished the air of tranquility which enveloped the rooms, content to be left to the lazy buzzing of a bee or the soft breeze through a partly opened window on a summer's day. Rose was enchanted with it all and could think of no one more suited to live there than Charles, who seemed to have become a part of the fabric of the building itself, with his piles of papers and books, clutter and bric-a-brac, each item important to him in its own way, although he often appeared in danger of disappearing beneath towers of paperwork. For Charles, although the last of a family who had lived in the manor house and farmed the countryside for generations, held no interest in farming and was at heart, a pure academic, content to spend his days wandering through the thoughts, ideas and conundrums of life, the universe and himself.

'And how are you today, my Rose?' Charles' face lit up when Rose entered his tiny study. He had, Rose noticed, taken to calling her 'my Rose' of late, a term she rather liked and, as he was a good twenty years older than herself, caused her no embarrassment at all.

'I'm well, thank you.' She fidgeted with the curtains, arranging them as best she could to allow maximum sunlight into the cluttered room, relating the arrangements for the day concerning his meals and the organisation of his household.

Charles nodded thoughtfully, uncaring so long as something appeared at some point and taking absolutely no notice of her words but contemplating how lovely she looked in the morning sunlight. Her manner did, however, appear a trifle agitated, as if she was working up to asking him something but could not quite bring herself to do it.

'Is anything the matter?' he asked eventually.

'Yes, no, I mean...' Rose trailed off and twitched the curtains once more before lowering herself onto a chair opposite Charles. 'Can I ask you something? I hope you don't mind...'

'Please do.' Charles smiled. As far as he was concerned, Rose could have asked him anything in the entire world, and if he knew the answer or could find it for her, he would.

'It's about the ruined chapel.'

'Yes?' Charles was surprised. He had walked to it on a number of occasions but found no more than a tumble of fallen masonry and a muddy stream which trickled down to the river. 'What about it?' he asked.

'Do you know who it belongs to? I mean, does it belong to you or to the church... only no one seems to know. And it's such a lovely spot and has a wonderful feeling, I just think it's a shame no one has ever bothered to take any interest in it or rebuild it,' she finished lamely, feeling suddenly foolish in the light of Charles' interested, yet puzzled, gaze.

'To tell the truth, I'm not entirely sure.' Charles put his fingertips together and rested his elbows on his desk. 'The land all around is mine, but as to the ruined chapel... I'd have to look at the deeds.' He smiled. 'Next time I'm in Camelford at the solicitors, I'll take a look. It would be interesting for me to know too.'

'You really are very kind.' Rose jumped to her feet, unsure what she would actually do once she discovered the true owner of the ruined chapel but feeling she had at least made some headway.

As he watched her leave, Charles sighed. There

was more to Rose than met the eye. He was well aware that, although married to the most zealously religious man in the parish, she was held in some respect by the villagers for her salves, potions and general healing skills. Charles wondered exactly what Rose did when she visited the ruined chapel, as she obviously had on a number of occasions, and decided maybe it was time he paid it another visit himself.

Thirty Three

Autumn Equinox

It was the time of balance, when the wheel of the year paused for a moment as day and night became equal, twilight arriving earlier each day before the darkness was longer than the light.

Rose unpacked her basket and laid a number of objects upon the granite altar.

'What's all this stuff?' asked Davy.   'I thought you usually lit a bit of candle or something.'

'I do, but this is different.'

Davy bent to inspect the objects. There was a brown, flint spearhead and a wooden pendant which appeared to have once been carved, although it was difficult to see the markings now – Davy thought he could make out the shape of a tree but was not sure. To these, Rose added a twisted wand of rowan, a small silver chalice and a brown earthenware bowl.

'Where did they come from?'

'Never you mind.   Handed down over the

generations,' she muttered. 'Now, are you going to help or just ask questions?' she continued sharply.

'All right, all right.' He held up his hands. 'You're the boss. What do you want me to do?'

'I wasn't expecting this.' Davy stood amongst the rubble, undergrowth and boggy ground, leaning on a shovel. 'I thought we were making magic.'

'We are.' Rose smiled sweetly. The brown, flint spearhead, the small, silver chalice which sparkled in the moonlight, two candles, the earthenware bowl and a bunch of herbs lay ready and waiting upon the granite altar. The wooden pendant she slipped around her neck. 'It should be the time of balance,' she explained. 'The light and darkness are of equal length and the world needs to be the same. Our beliefs, my work, are under cover of darkness, the church thrives whilst the chapel stands in ruins and no one seems to care.' Her hands stilled as she surveyed the muddy stream which trickled down to the river. 'The holy waters are muddied and cannot flow properly and the Maidens of the Wells are lost. It is time for balance to return.'

'Who?' Davy looked around anxiously. 'Who's lost?'

'The Maidens of the Wells,' repeated Rose. 'It's a legend which I heard when I was little, from my grandmother. The holy wells were once tended by Maidens but they were lost... I'll tell you another time.' She glanced at the waxing moon hanging in the sky. 'It is time, we must set to work.'

'And what exactly do you want me to do?' asked Davy, surveying his shovel. 'Rebuild the chapel? Find the Maidens?'

'Symbolically,' replied Rose. 'I shall carry out the

ritual but in order to find all which is lost, to bring it to us, we need to use the holy waters and to stand within them as they flow towards us, visualising everything coming back to life.' She smiled. 'When the time is right I simply want you to make a channel for the water to flow more clearly and strongly.'

'Okay, you're in charge.' He sighed. 'Is that all you wanted me for then?' he asked eventually. 'To dig a trench?'

'No.' Rose crossed to where he was standing and touched his face gently. 'I cannot do this without you. The balance of masculine and feminine is important at this time. Black and white, day and night, male and female. Balance is the only way forwards. That is why you are important.'

Davy nodded. 'Let's get on with it, then.'

Rose lit her candles, one black and one white, then placed the gently smouldering herbs upon the altar, filled the silver chalice with holy water and the earthenware bowl with earth. After sitting for some time watching the flickering candle flame, attuning herself to the energies of the earth, the moon, the stars, and the scents upon the night air, she felt the time to be right.

'Now,' she called to Davy. 'Make the channel wider.'

Davy took the shovel and began to clear mud away from where the little stream ran. Almost at once it became brighter and faster flowing, no longer muddied and running in different directions. Encouraged, he pulled at the undergrowth, finding it coming away easily. His spade struck something hard which turned out to be a small, granite trough and with a little more clearing, discovered it to run beneath the altar itself.

Hot and muddied, Davy continued, to be rewarded with a rough channel through which the water flowed swiftly, beneath the altar and through to the other side.

'Who would have thought it?' he murmured.

'What about up there, closer to the holy well?' asked Rose. The water was flowing more strongly now but still pooling in one place. Davy struck his spade, only to be met with what felt like a large rock or stone. He dug around, discovering a flat slate which he was unable to move.

'Never mind,' said Rose. 'We have more than enough. Time for you to rest. You have worked well. Now, take my hand.'

Together, in the waxing moonlight, Rose and Davy stood, his hand encompassing hers. Rose insisted on standing in the channel of water, taking off her boots and allowing it to flow over and around her bare feet, proving to be unexpectedly warm. She imagined all she wished to bring about, explaining it to Davy so he could visualise it too. The balance between the church and the chapel, people and beliefs, the restoration of the ruined building and the return of the lost Maidens which, she instinctively felt, was of more importance than anyone had ever realised.

Hand in hand, Rose and Davy visualised the chapel intact and used for its true purpose, the holy waters running clear and bright, the Maidens returned from their exile and taking their rightful place in the community.

Rose remained motionless until the visions swam into a multicoloured blur in her mind, the energy in their bodies and minds swirling all around them, her feet numb from the passage of the water. The great white owl hooted in the distance and then all was still. Rose felt a final tingle of energy pass between herself and Davy, then it was gone and she dropped his hand.

The moment was broken but the spell was cast.

'What will happen now?' asked Davy as Rose cleared everything away. 'I mean, will it really work?'

'Of course,' she answered simply. 'It always does, although not necessarily in the way you might expect.'

She smiled and he thought how beautiful she looked, longing to reach out and touch her, hold her once again in his arms, like... He brushed the memory away. 'It's a tall order,' he continued. 'Ruined chapels, lost Maidens...'

'We have asked,' replied Rose, 'and done our best in the name of love, light and all that is good. If it is to be, it will happen, but perhaps in ways we might not even begin to imagine.'

'Then,' he began, 'how come you don't just have everything you want in life?'

Rose smiled. 'You know better than that,' she admonished. 'You of all people know there needs to be a balance. Give and take. Win and lose. Otherwise everything's upset. And you should never, ever, use this or any knowledge to harm anyone or it will come back at you. Threefold.' And Davy knew the conversation was over.

All the same, he felt different. He and Rose had shared something special, rekindled the link which had been lost, or perhaps merely hidden, through the years. The moonlight glimmered upon her face and highlighted the silver strands in her hair. For an instant he saw the girl he had known many years before, even more beautiful now, the fine lines around her eyes etched by tears, laughter and... feeling.

'Thanks,' he ventured.

'For what?'

'Including me.'

'Thought you didn't really want to do it.'

There was a short silence. 'You know I did.'

Rose turned. 'Davy...' she began.

But he jumped down from the fallen masonry in his usual manner and the moment was lost.

'Thank you too,' said Rose quietly.

Thirty Four

Charles had spent many years pondering his beliefs. Or disbeliefs, for sometimes he thought he believed in a God almighty, just as Jory did, and at others, looked at the world around him, saw pain and suffering and was unable to understand how any God would allow it to happen.

At times he surveyed the beauty of the countryside, especially the valley in which he lived, and felt it could not have occurred by chance, the hand of someone or something must be behind it. And the more Charles read his books and searched his heart, the more confused he became.

Charles was no stranger to any of the religious theories, being familiar with both the Old and New Testaments and indeed, inevitably found a similarity between all the religions he studied. Yet he had not discovered his own truth. Was God – if indeed God existed – to be found in a building or in the outside world? Was He, if indeed God was male, an angry God or a sympathetic one? Did Heaven exist? Where was Hell? Or did the world simply turn of its own accord, everything working together in a way which was beyond the understanding of mere mankind who, Charles could not help but think when surveying village life around him, were not quite as important as they liked to believe.

And so one evening, with thoughts of Rose and her questions concerning the ruined chapel in his mind, the moon dark and the night filled with stars and shadows, Charles decided to visit the chapel to see what might be discovered there.

'What's that?' Rose surveyed Davy, standing before her, shovel in hand.

'I want to do a bit more digging.'

'But you've done all we need.' Rose bent and dipped a finger into the granite channel through which the holy water trickled. Already the ground was beginning to dry and there was a definite change in energy when she placed her hands upon the altar. The water in the holy well itself seemed to be flowing stronger than ever, the marriage between stone and water working its magic.

'It's that great slate slab.' Davy stuck his shovel into the earth and once again felt the jolt of metal upon stone. 'I want to know what it is, what's under it. It's just a feeling I have,' he continued, 'but I need to know. It might be important.'

'But...'

'Look.' Davy sighed in exasperation and leaned on his shovel. 'You have feelings and suchlike, don't you? Well, so do I. And I have a feeling there's something important here.' He stuck his spade in once again and Rose knew from the determined expression on his face there was no arguing with him.

'All right,' she conceded. Davy had helped her often enough and this was no time to say he was wasting his time. 'Go ahead, dig.'

Davy pushed on his shovel and heard the dull thud once more. Then he carefully shifted the mud and earth sideways taking, it seemed to Rose, infinite care, as if he knew something special lay beneath. After a while an oblong slate lay before them, embedded in the earth between the holy well and the one remaining section of wall of the ruined chapel.

'What is it?' Rose's voice was hushed now. Perhaps it was to do with the mist which was rising from the river on smoky fingers in the dim light of early evening, swirling around them like smoke, causing the sound of the shovel and their voices to fall bluntly into the night air; but Rose had a feeling now, an inkling they were about to discover something which had been hidden for a very long time and she was unsure if it should be disturbed.

Davy had no such qualms. 'Hand me the bar iron,' he commanded, and Rose heaved it across to him. With a lot of grunting, pushing and poking, Davy finally managed to lift the stone a fraction. Once, twice, it lifted, exposing a gaping, black hole beneath, then at the third attempt he managed to heave it right over and it fell backwards with a loud thud.

By the light of the flickering lamp, Davy and Rose gazed into the hole and stared.

They debated for a long time about what to do, until the mist from the river encompassed them and night truly arrived, casting a cloak of darkness all around. Finally, Davy shifted the heavy slate back into position and scattered some earth over the top.

'I think it's for the best,' commented Rose.

'We can always come back another time,' agreed Davy, reluctant to think the episode would be forgotten. 'But now I have to set some traps. Will you be all right?'

Rose nodded. 'I'll head back in a minute,' she replied. 'You carry on.'

Davy disappeared into the darkness leaving Rose in the silence, but after a while she had the distinct impression she was no longer alone. Perhaps it was the great white owl, the brown stoat or the water vole which frequented the chapel ruins. Or maybe – she told herself she was being fanciful but could not help wondering – the spirits of the place, the long ago Guardians she had seen in her visions. Rose shivered, the night air chilling her, and decided this was no time to sit and ponder on their find. Her warm bed beckoned and she would think about it all in the morning.

It was then she heard a soft movement nearby, no more than the scrape of shoe upon stone, but enough to alert her to the fact someone was near.

'Who's there?' Perhaps she should have remained silent and immediately regretted her action. Maybe the other person was unaware she was sitting amongst the shadows, but it was too late now. Rose turned this way and that, hoping to find Davy jumping down from a piece of masonry, laughing because he had given her a fright, but again, silence.

Rose picked up her basket. Perhaps she was mistaken. Maybe there was no one at all, for who except herself and Davy would be out on a night such as this? The mist had increased to a thick fog, sounds falling heavy and muted in the night air. But as she picked her way carefully over the trickle of the stream and moss covered stones her foot slipped and she stumbled, only to be saved by a swift hand beneath her elbow.

'Careful.'

Rose turned to find Charles standing beside her.

'Sorry, I didn't mean to frighten you.' His voice was muted in the fog as he held her arm, steadying her.

'It's all right.' Rose breathed a sigh of relief. 'But what...'

Her words were cut off by a sudden cry in the night, piercing through the fog, and they both froze. Charles' hand tightened on Rose's arm.

'What was that?' whispered Charles. 'It sounded human.'

And Rose, hearing it again, felt a rush of fear sweep over her. 'It is,' she replied, her voice rising in panic. 'It's Davy.'

Thirty Five

'What on earth were you thinking of?' Rose pressed the cold compress onto Davy's foot and he winced in pain. 'Serves you right, wandering around in the dark when you should have been in bed minding your own business,' she admonished sharply as her fingers felt anxiously around the swelling, but to her relief she could find no indication of a break. It seemed as if Davy had escaped with a bad sprain and a few cuts and bruises.

'Could you hold this, please?' She turned to

Charles who stood silently watching and he moved to do her bidding. Little had he thought when he set out earlier, he would end up helping tend his gamekeeper's wounds, sustained he had no doubt, whilst up to no good on his land.

The question crossed Rose's mind as to why Charles had been wandering around the valley in the misty darkness but there was no time to find out, even if she could have found the courage to ask.

'Like this?'

'Yes, good.'

Davy moaned in pain but Charles held the ankle still while Rose worked. She paused to gently wipe the perspiration from Davy's face with a cloth soaked in rose water.

'He'll be all right now.' Rose turned to Charles. 'Thank you for your help.' She smiled briefly and wrung out her cloth once more. 'He's just a bit stunned. I don't think he really knows where he is or what he's saying. He'll come out of it in time.'

'Are you sure...'

'No, really. You've been kind enough.'

Charles nodded, realising Rose was more than capable of dealing with Davy and his wounds.

'Come back to work when you're ready,' he mumbled, feeling suddenly awkward in Rose's presence.

'Thank you.'

'And if there's anything you need...'

'If you could just let Jory know I'll be home tomorrow...'

'Of course.'

'Thank you,' replied Rose, as she turned back to Davy, and Charles left, closing the door quietly behind him.

'I don't know what you were thinking of,' Rose repeated as she wiped Davy's face for the hundredth time, even though she knew he was taking not the slightest bit of notice. 'You, of all people, should know better than to put your foot down a fox hole or whatever it was in the middle of the night and then be fool enough to hit your head on the branch of a tree.' But it made her feel better even if she was telling him off and it was preferable to sitting silently. Secretly, she was concerned at the angle Davy's ankle had twisted and the length of time which had passed without him remembering what happened. The bruise on his head was coming out now in shades of purple and black, but she was unsure how much damage had been done.

There were times when he appeared confused and almost delirious. 'Where am I? It's so dark,' and, 'where are you, don't leave me alone again,' all featured in his mutterings, and Rose could make no sense of any of it.

For the remainder of the night Rose stayed by Davy's side, holding his hand in hers and, as the birds trilled their early morning chorus, she fell asleep beside him, a sleep of pure exhaustion but one to which she only succumbed once Davy had looked perfectly normally into her eyes and admitted what a fool he was. Then he fell asleep and she knew he was going to be all right; and when Rose finally opened her eyes she turned her head to find Davy awake, his fingers entwined in hers.

'You know I was always waiting for you. But when you married Jory there was nothing I could do.' It was a few days later and Rose was resting on the bed beside Davy, the late afternoon light fading around them.

Rose sighed. 'I knew, of course I did, and I realised what a mistake I'd made almost as soon as we were married, but...' She shrugged. 'What could I do? Imagine the scandal there would have been for both of us in such a small village. It isn't easy to move away and begin again. And then I had Rachel.'

There was a long silence during which the sounds of the gathering evening crept through the open window and a slight breeze caused the single candle to flicker. Davy shifted restlessly but Rose knew it was nothing to do with the pain in his foot which, although he found difficulty in walking and could only manage a slow hobble, was healing nicely.

She sighed in the dim light of the room and Davy could see the glisten of tears upon her face. 'She was your child, of course she was,' she whispered. 'But we only had one afternoon together and the wedding was arranged for the following week. At the time I thought it a moment of Midsummer magic and it was only after I'd married Jory I realised I loved you with all my heart.'

'So Rachel...'

She nodded again. 'She really is yours. I knew from the moment I first held her. There's something in the way she views the world, a look in her eyes at times, a wildness, just like you. And no one ever guessed, I'm sure of it, you and Jory being brothers...'

She trailed off. 'Oh Davy.' The tears began to flow and Rose sobbed with all her heart. 'I do so wish she'd grown up with you as her father instead of that Bible basher who's done nothing but chase her away and now I hardly ever see her except on high days and holidays...'

Rose continued to sob and Davy pulled her to him, attempting to soothe her tears whilst struggling to hold back his own, feeling his heart might burst with anguish for Rose, for the daughter he never realised he had, for himself...

'I'm sorry, Davy.' Rose wiped her eyes and sat up, wriggling from his arms, agitated and unable to settle. 'After all these years, it's difficult to let it out. Easier to keep it hidden away, forget it ever happened and pretend Rachel belongs to Jory, although of course I never could. Every time I looked at her I saw you. You must hate me, really hate me.' Rose burst into tears again and sank down upon the bed, crying as if her heart would break. But, she reminded herself, it would never break because it was already broken. It had shattered into a thousand pieces one summer's day all those years ago, when she and Jory were married in the church which meant so much to him and she finally realised it meant saying goodbye to Davy for ever.

There was a long silence, then Rose felt Davy's hand upon her shoulder. 'I love you,' he whispered. 'I've always loved you and I always will and I'm glad you told me about Rachel.' He laughed unexpectedly. 'I admit I've wondered all these years and hoped - how I hoped - she was mine and not his. But I've watched her grow and she's a part of me and a part of you and that's what matters. No.' He put his arms around her and pulled her close. 'Don't cry any more. The time for crying is over.'

Rose drew a shuddering breath. 'But what now?' she asked. 'What can we do now?'

'I don't know,' replied Davy slowly. 'I truly don't.'

'But what a waste. What a waste of our lives,' whispered Rose. Her fingers linked with his and he kissed them gently. 'If only I'd told the truth all those years ago about how I felt and not worried about what people would say or think. If only...'

'Are two of the saddest words in the whole world,' interrupted Davy. 'And you can't spend the rest of your life berating yourself for what you should or could have done. Hindsight is a wonderful gift but you did what you thought best at the time and it's all anyone can ever do.'

'I've robbed you of a family,' Rose continued. 'I've stolen your daughter and stopped her knowing her true father.' She bit her lip. 'I don't see how you can ever forgive me.'

'Look.' Davy tightened his embrace. 'I loved you then and I love you now and when you truly love someone forgiveness doesn't come into it because there's nothing to forgive. Love holds no record of rights nor wrongs. Every second I've spent with you has been worth it a thousand times over, from that mad, wild afternoon we spent together all those years ago, until now. It's been worth it simply to hold you again, to smooth your hair, to feel the touch of your lips on mine. Even if it's just this once.'

'If only we could have another chance,' whispered Rose. 'Why couldn't it have worked out for us? Why did it all have to be such a mess?'

'I told you, no more if only's,' admonished Davy, 'but you know what we both believe. We'll meet again next time round and then we'll do it properly. Get married, have a family and all the things we wish we'd done this time. We'll live somewhere near here and you can look after your well and visit it every day.'

Rose made a sound which was half a sob and half the beginnings of a giggle. 'But you don't have to wait until next time,' she replied. 'We're here now and we have each other.'

Davy smiled and a sudden breeze caused the single candle flame to flicker and die. 'I think I'm getting too old for this,' he whispered into the darkness.

'So am I,' replied Rose, 'but who cares?'

And outside, the great white owl flew swiftly away into the deepening twilight.

Thirty Six

'I need to ask you a favour.'

'Yes?' Charles half turned from the bookshelf where he was carefully replacing books in order. It was his section on myths and legends and Rose knew it to be one of which he was particularly proud.

'I don't want to disturb you...' She hovered in the doorway and, seeing her agitation, he put the last few books down and crossed the room.

'You could never disturb me, Rose, you know that.' He indicated a chair. 'Come and sit down. Now, what is it I can do for you? How's Davy?' Charles had finally come to hear the tale of how Davy had gone to set his rabbit traps but stepped unwittingly into a recently dug fox hole, spraining his ankle badly and, in the process, banging his head against a tree, resulting in bruising and concussion. Charles had secretly smiled at the irony of it and thought perhaps it would cause Davy to end his nocturnal habits.

'I need you to write something for me,' began Rose. 'I need it written down for my daughter. It's all been passed down by word of mouth but gets a bit muddled over time and I'm not even sure I'm going to see Rachel again and...'

'Slow down. Why might you not see your daughter again? Has something happened?' asked Charles sharply.

Rose shook her head. 'Just a feeling I have,' she murmured. 'But if you could spare a few moments...'

Charles nodded, already reaching for his pen and writing paper. 'For you, my Rose, anything,' he replied with a smile. 'Now, what is it you want to tell me?'

'I've made you something.'

'Oh?' Rose settled herself on the edge of Davy's bed and looked expectant. 'That's nice,' she continued. 'But it isn't my birthday.'

'Doesn't have to be to make you something,' said Davy. 'I just felt like it.'

Rose smiled. She did not often receive presents. Offerings, maybe. Thank you gifts from villagers she helped, although she never asked for payment and gave all she could willingly. A jug of milk, a loaf of bread, a comb of honey. But not presents, not the sort of thing which was frivolous and she had no need for but wanted all the same. She had a feeling this would be just such an item.

'Open it then.' Davy thrust his offering into her hands.

'All right, give me a moment. Don't rush me, I want to enjoy it.'

Davy sighed knowing when he was beaten.

He had wrapped his gift in a piece of blue cloth which, Rose imagined, might have been a curtain in a previous life, and tied a length of string around it which was knotted several times.

'Why did you tie so many knots?' she asked.

'So you could enjoy undoing them.'

She smiled. Sometimes Davy understood her more than she realised.

Rose struggled with the knots until finally, unable to bear it any longer, Davy produced a pocket knife, cut the string and Rose was free to open her present.

'Go on then,' he urged.

'Wait, I'm just savouring what might be in there.'

'Oh, for goodness sake!'

'All right.'

Rose allowed the fabric to fall away and found herself staring at a wooden box. The most beautifully carved wooden box she had ever seen.

'Like it?'

Rose turned the box over and over in her hands, admiring the intricate carvings on the top and around the sides. There were trees and animals, a hare, a fish, the sun, the moon and the stars. And in the middle a woman holding a chalice.

'It's beautiful,' was all she could bring herself to say. 'So this is what you've been working on while you've been confined to your room.'

Davy nodded. 'I wanted it to be a surprise. Something special.'

Her fingers traced the delicate carvings. There was something about them which awakened a memory but she was unable to grasp it, the images slipping elusively through her mind, like petals floating on a spring breeze. 'How did you think of it?' she asked eventually.

Davy sighed. 'I'm not sure. I had some strange dreams when I was ill, the night it all happened. It was as if I didn't know who I was or where I was. There was something about changing into a hare and then getting killed and...' he frowned, 'it was dark, so dark,' he continued in almost a whisper. 'And I was calling out to someone, I think it might have been you but I'm not sure, and it was such a long time before I found you again. And when I was carving the box, all of those things seemed important.'

'It's beautiful.'

'It's for your things, you know, those special ones you used on the night of the ritual.'

Rose nodded. 'Thank you,' she replied. 'Thank you so much.'

Davy smiled and kissed her. 'My pleasure.'

Thirty Seven

Samhain

'I need you to look after something for me.'

'And what would that be, my love?'

Rose silently passed Davy the wooden box he had carved. It felt heavy as he took it from her hands.

'Why?'

Rose shook her head. 'I don't know. I just feel it's the time for remembering the ancestors, those who have gone before and I can't see... that is, I don't know what the future holds for me. Don't ask me to explain,' she finished, seeing the question frame upon Davy's lips. 'Just understand I'm not sure what's going to happen and I want to leave this in your safe keeping, for Rachel, for the future.'

'Is everything inside?'

Rose nodded. 'Yes, and I've asked Charles to write some things down. He'll know what to do if...' Her voice trailed off and Davy pulled her to him.

'Nothings going to happen,' he murmured into her hair. 'I won't let it.'

'I know,' she replied, 'but just in case.'

It was as Rose was making her way back to her cottage, she first noticed the rosy glow in the sky. She hurried, aware something was very wrong and, by the time she arrived on the scene, the church was well and truly ablaze. Orange flames licked around the windows like the feasting tongues of demons and there was a fear the tower might collapse. Smoke billowed from the doorway preventing entry but the main problem, everyone agreed, was the roof. If the fire in the roof could be put out then perhaps there was a chance of saving the building; but the age old timbers were tinder dry, catching alight easily and it was far beyond the power of the villagers to rescue it.

Nevertheless, they tried. For seemingly hours, chains of men and women had attempted to douse the flames with buckets of water from the Vicarage well but soon discovered that, due to the inordinately dry autumn, it was rapidly drying up. And so the time arrived when it became apparent they would be unable to save their church and simply have to wait until the fire lessoned of its own accord and the church burnt to the ground.

It was then Rose arrived. There was a general atmosphere of panic in the air and, as she approached, was met by a throng of people milling around, fast losing heart in their task. She forced her way as close as she possibly could.

'There you are. Where on earth have you been?' Her arm was roughly grasped by Jory as he swung her around. 'I've been searching for you all over the place.' He glared at her, wild eyed. 'This is all your doing.' He jabbed a finger at her in the orange darkness. 'May the Lord have mercy on you for this.'

Rose gasped. 'How could you say that? How could you think I would, or even could, do such a thing?'

'You and your spells and potions and curses,' continued Jory as if she had not spoken. 'I've always turned a blind eye to your carryings on but this has gone too far. You heathen. You witch!' He backed away, such venom in his words and hatred in his eyes that Rose felt her throat constricting. She fleetingly remembered lying in Davy's arms a mere hour before, recalled the tenderness and the love she had found there and realised he and Jory had always been worlds apart.

There was a touch on her arm and she turned to see the Vicar standing behind her. 'Rose, I'm so glad you're here.'

'Don't touch her, Vicar,' interrupted Jory, pushing Rose roughly aside. 'She's the devil's spawn and I'm ashamed to call her my wife. May the Lord have mercy upon me for having anything to do with her.'

'Leave her be.' The Vicar's tone was sharp and Jory blinked in astonishment. 'Leave her alone and don't take the Lord's name in vain.' With an obvious effort he turned his back on Jory and took Rose by the arm, drawing her to one side away from the main throng. His face was white and she could see the fear in his drawn features.

'Rose', he repeated. 'I don't know how this began or what we have done to deserve it, but...'

She looked into his eyes and saw, not a man of the cloth, but simply another spirit such as her own, doing his best for humanity in the only way he knew how. And she knew he saw the same in her. She relaxed, feeling no threat, no blame or intimidation from him.

'Rose.' He swallowed. 'You can see how things are. There is no saving the church now. You are the only person left to ask. Will you help us?'

Rose stood on the rise of the hill above the church and calmed herself, breathing slowly and steadily, moving into the place between the worlds where simple magic was at its strongest and worked best. Slowly, a sense of order descended upon her and she felt her body and mind balance with her spirit, above and below, within and without.

She felt the energy of the ground root her and the night air swirl around her being. She was aware of the heat of the raging fire upon her face as she raised her arms wide to the heavens, calling in the element of water which was so desperately needed to save the church. For in the end it mattered not who, what, or how people worshipped. In the end all became one.

Rose's lips moved silently as she focused, bending her intent to her task. The breeze, which so readily fanned the flames, danced around her carrying orange sparks on the air which quickly turned to white ash, like confetti on the wind or the fall of mayflower blossom in spring.

The villagers had fallen silent, one by one

becoming aware of the woman standing on the rise of the hill behind the church, arms raised in supplication. Time stood still. The world waited. Only the flames continued to dance as Rose concentrated upon calling the rain, bringing the water which was needed to douse the raging flames. In all her years as village wise woman and healer this was her greatest challenge.

Rose slowly opened her eyes. Nothing had changed. The fire licked the building as ever and she was aware the villagers feared this last ditch attempt would also fail and they would finally lose their church.

Rose drew a deep breath, knowing she had done all in her power, aware that only a much greater and higher energy than hers could change events now.

And then she saw her.

She stood to one side of the graveyard, forming a triangle between herself, Rose and the burning church. At first Rose wondered who she could be, until she noticed this was no ordinary person, for the woman's body undulated in the flickering firelight and Rose became aware that her hair was formed from swirls of grey and black smoke, whilst her gown was the white rush of a waterfall. A swift breeze sprang up all around her, flattening the grass in a circle and causing the leaves on the trees above to shiver. Upon her head lay a circlet of wild roses - and Rose instantly knew this to be the Guardian who appeared only at times of great need and her heart soared as she felt the energy flooding into her, knowing, without a shadow of doubt, everything was going to be all right.

One by one, people began to notice the stars being obliterated as low clouds gathered in the night sky. The wind changed direction, swirling now from the north and, far away down the valley, the first low rumble of thunder could be heard.

Rose stood, intent upon her task. A hush fell over the villagers, the only sound the crackle of flames as they licked at the battens of the roof.

There was a louder rumble of thunder, a sudden flash of lightning, which, it was related in the telling, was so magnificent it would never be forgotten by any of those who witnessed it. Then the heavens opened and the rains pummelled the earth in a deluge of water and hailstones which engulfed the burning building, causing such a hissing and spitting as flames and water clashed it was, some said, a spectacle as magnificent as the fires of Hell.

In seemingly no time at all the flames were doused and the fire out, leaving the ruined church in blackness, save for the mists of smoke which swirled around it and the glow of embers fanned by the remaining breeze. The blackened walls stood stark and forbidding against the night sky but the tower and some of the roof remained intact and the villagers resumed their work, able to cope without the ever increasing heat, cooling the walls and ensuring every last spark had been extinguished.

Rose surveyed the scene before her, glanced across the graveyard towards the place the figure had been standing and found her still there, her hand outstretched.

Come.

The word echoed on the dying breeze.

Come.

Rose's heart swelled with love and, feeling an enormous sense of relief, passed into blessed oblivion.

The rain was fading to a misty drizzle and it was

obvious the church would be saved. Everyone felt a wave of relief, then out of the blackness Jory appeared, drenched to the skin, staggering down the slippery slope with Rose inert in his arms.

People rushed forwards, taking her from him and hurrying to the Vicarage where they laid her gently down and wrapped blankets around her in an attempt to warm her freezing body. But she remained pale and lifeless and every effort to revive her seemed to fail.

'Let me see her.' Charles pushed into the Vicarage, took one look at Rose and sent a man to ride immediately for the nearest doctor, although something in his heart told him it might already be too late.

Of Jory, there was no sign.

Charles sat with Rose, holding her hand. He wished Davy was with them. He would have known what to do to cause her eyes to open, bring warmth to her cold skin and make her smile again. But Davy was still confined to his cottage, unable to do more than hobble.

As Charles sat with Rose's hand in his, he felt a movement and Rose's eyes flickered.

'Rose,' he whispered. 'My Rose. You saved the church, you put out the fire. It's going to be all right. Hold on a little longer, just hold on.'

Her grip on his hand tightened momentarily and then relaxed, as if the effort were too much.

'Tell Davy...' she whispered.

Charles bent his head closer to hear her words which were soft as gossamer on an autumn breeze.

'Tell Davy it was worth it, even for just once, it was worth every moment... It was ours in the end and next time... we'll do it properly.'

Charles leaned closer still, but it was too late.

Rose's eyes stared at the ceiling and the fragile grip on his fingers slackened. She looked so peaceful and content, all Charles could do was gently close her eyes. Then he put his head in his hands and wept.

He found Jory in the church.

Despite the danger of the roof falling in, Charles knew there was nowhere else to look, and indeed, Jory was kneeling before the blackened altar, hands together in prayer.

As he ran up the aisle Charles glanced around him. The damage was not as bad as it appeared. The roof was, however, in danger of collapsing and it would be prudent to get Jory out as soon as possible. But the blackened pillars stood tall and proud, the stone font had suffered little damage save for its charred wooden cover and the tower was still in one piece. Nevertheless, it was with a combination of compassion and urgency that Charles placed a hand on Jory's shoulder, to feel it heaving with sobs.

'Come along. We must leave.'

'Rose?' The question was muffled and Charles knew he had no choice but to tell Jory the truth.

'She's gone. I'm so sorry. Exhausted, cold... but peaceful. Oh, so peaceful.'

He pressed Jory's shoulder, searching for the right words, knowing he would never find them. 'You should be proud of her. Proud of what she did for us all, proud she saved the church,' he murmured eventually.

Jory turned then, his face twisted and contorted in grief. 'May she rot in Hell,' he snarled.

Charles backed away, shocked at Jory's words, imagining they must be a reaction to his loss. He held out his hand. 'Come outside and we'll talk about it there. You don't mean that.'

'No.' Jory sprang to his feet and Charles could see the wildness in his eyes. 'She might have saved the building, but with what? Her trickery and her witchery. I'd rather the place had burned to the ground. At least it would have been God's will. I wish I'd never married the woman. I've spent my life torn between Rose and God, love and duty, and now, now... That was my test and this is my punishment. This is all my fault.' He took one long, shuddering breath. 'I should have chosen God, not the woman I loved, I should have...' He began to cry incoherently, great heaving sobs from the depth of his being. 'Now I'm glad the witch is dead,' he finished, as he turned and stumbled from the building.

Charles stood for a moment, shocked and stunned, until an overhead creak reminded him of the danger he was in and, taking one last look around, followed Jory into the cold, night air.

Thirty Eight

Come.

The woman had reached out, touched Rose's hand, and all at once she was free of her mortal body, light as a rainbow on the morning air.

Rose experienced a moment of pure ecstasy, but something tugged at her spirit, pulling it back to earth. *I must...* She glanced at the scene below her. Already her body had been moved, taken across the road to the Vicarage and she knew she had only moments before there was no return. *I must tell Davy...* became her only thought, her reason to live just a few heartbeats longer.

And then she was in the Vicarage and her spirit rose once again to survey Charles beside her, his head in his hands, weeping as she had never seen a man weep before. She had flown then, knowing she was going home. A final glance towards Jory on his knees in the blackened church, a longer moment with her beloved Davy, during which she gently touched his face and kissed his lips as he slept peacefully in the bed they had shared only hours before. And then she was flying home on the wings of the cool, morning air, the little chapel coming closer with every second until she was standing amongst the fallen masonry and the running stream – and they were all waiting for her. The girl, the young woman, the lady holding the silver chalice and the Guardian, fashioned of the elements and the essence of the valley, who appeared only at times of great need. Rose raised her face to the rising sun, feeling their love encompass her, then all became one and she was finally at peace.

And as the day dawned and a new era began, one single pink, wild rose petal floated upon the surface of the holy waters, glowing gently in the early morning sunlight.

Thirty Nine

'She's still here, I can feel her.' Davy pressed Rachel's hand as they sat together on a piece of moss covered stonework. The holy water trickled from the spring, flowing strongly through the channel he and Rose had cleared beneath the altar and making its way to the river.

Rachel nodded. 'I feel it too. I only wish I'd spent more time with her. If only...'

Davy put a finger to her lips. 'Are two of the saddest words in the whole world,' he replied, as he had once before. 'What matters is now and I know, in here,' he touched his heart, 'she is at peace. Anyway,' he smiled. 'I have something for you. It belonged to your mother and she left it with me for safe keeping, but it was always for you.' He passed Rachel a bundle wrapped in a blue cloth. 'And if I'm not mistaken,' he continued, 'the answers to everything you need to know are in here.' He handed her a large envelope, tied with pink ribbon and sealed with wax. 'I don't know...' he interrupted, as a question framed her lips. 'All I do know is Charles wrote a lot down for your mother, things she wanted passed on to you. Information for you and nobody else and it was the only way she could think of doing it. He asked me to give it to you.'

Rachel's eyes filled with tears. 'Why didn't she just tell me?'

'You know it was difficult with your father. There was no point complicating things even more. And something tells me she knew there wasn't much time left,' he continued. 'Very perceptive, was your ma.'

There was a moment of silence as they both remembered.

'And one more thing,' finished Davy. 'Charles said there's something in there from him. All I know is he said to be sure to tell you to keep it safe until her spirit returns once again.' Davy spread his hands and shrugged. 'Don't ask me,' he finished, 'but I think there might be more to our Charles than meets the eye too.'

Rachel turned the packages over in her hands but made no move to open either of them. 'Until...' she began, glancing at Davy.

'Her spirit returns once again.' He looked at her steadily. 'And we both know it will, don't we?'

Rachel nodded and Davy thought how like Rose she looked, but also, he thought with a touch of pride, he could see a little of himself in her too.

For a moment Davy felt his heart might burst. Images of Rose flew through his mind, as a young girl and the woman he loved so well. Then all at once he felt her presence, like the soft touch of a rose petal upon his brow and knew, without a doubt, they would meet again.

'Where did that come from?' asked Rachel some time later as they were preparing to leave. They had remained in silence for a long while, remembering Rose, as a strong sense of peace descended over the valley, a feeling of timelessness, as if, thought Davy, it was possible to reach out and touch the spirits of long ago.

Davy turned to where Rachel was pointing. Upon the granite altar lay a simple circlet of wild roses, entwined with leaves of rowan.

Spirit

Closing Circles:

The Green Man and the Guardian

The Holy Well Chapel

Honeysuckle

The Honeysuckle (Lonicera periclymenum) encourages us to reach for those desires sought while remaining true to the values and beliefs held, and will help you to tread safely. The sweet scent of the honeysuckle signals joy in the search for the self. If a honeysuckle plant grows outside near your home it will bring good luck.

When the honeysuckle vines wind around the branch of another tree, a spiral effect is produced, often found in twisted wooden staffs.

Fluorite

Fluorite is a highly protective and stabilizing stone, useful for grounding and harmonizing spiritual energy. Fluorite increases intuitive abilities, links the human mind to universal consciousness and develops connection to Spirit. Fluorite further anchors intuitive insights into the physical plane, allowing mental and physical coordination.

Green fluorite aids intuition, absorbs negative energies from the environment and can also shield the user from psychic manipulation.

The Green Man and the Guardian

Once upon a time there was a well, from which sprang the clearest, purest water to be found. Over thousands of years this well became sacred to many people, due to the beauty of where it lay, the inspiration it contained and the peace it brought to those who visited and drank of the waters.

The well had always been tended by a female Guardian, through times of abundance and times of hardship, but always the line continued and when the time was right, a new Guardian appeared.

One day, however, the line of the Guardians failed, there were none to care for the well and without its true and chosen Guardian, it slowly fell into decline.

The wind and the rain, the sun and the earth watched its demise and were saddened. They spoke with the spirits of the well which dwelt within its precincts, and finally, a man and a woman were fashioned from the essence of the valley in which the well rested. The man formed from the green of the willow leaves which swayed above the river in the warm summer breeze, the sunlight which dappled the shade and the movement of moonlight upon water. The woman was fashioned with the springtime mists in her hair and clothed in a gown of hawthorn and wild roses, a crown of rowan and meadowsweet upon her head.

At midsummer they entwined as one and, nine months later, as the lush growth of springtime spread throughout the valley a child was born, her destiny to continue the Guardianship of the well and carry it forwards into the future.

Forty

It seems a lifetime ago I first set foot upon this land – maybe longer, for who can truly measure time when years fly by like seconds and minutes tick slowly along, each a century in itself.

I first noticed how time could pass in the blink of an eye when I was but a child and also discovered how objects and people disappear and reappear again, although at the time they were nowhere to be seen – but maybe I had merely been searching in the wrong place.

Perhaps I always hoped my mother and father would one day appear to claim the tiny baby left on the doorstep of the farmhouse where I grew up. They had both disappeared – some say they never existed at all - but my eyes, as slate grey as the clouds which sweep low along the valley bringing the misty rain, and the feeling of being at one with the green trees which sway above the river in the moonlight, are enough to give me a sense of belonging. I have no recollection of my mother, save for a memory at the back of my mind whenever I catch the scent of the may blossom or meadowsweet and feel the misty spring rains upon my face. These almost take me to her. Almost, but not quite, for she remains a fleeting image in the corner of my vision, perhaps a cloud of dark hair, or is it a mass of grey clouds on the horizon, and is the brightness of her dress fashioned from may blossom and the petals of wild roses?

No matter. I was taken in and brought up well enough by a farming family whose son, Cornelius, at the age of ten, discovered me nestled in a basket of woven rowan on their doorstep one chilly, spring evening and named me Rowena. And if I felt a little at odds with the rest of the world, well, what did it matter?

I loved to wander the valley during the winter snows and the spring showers. During the hot summer days my haven was the cool shade of the willows on the riverbank, and in the autumn I picked the fruits of nature and retired to one of the many hidey holes of which only I knew and where no one would ever find me. On moonlit nights I spent hours leaning out of my bedroom window, arms resting on the warm granite sills, gazing at the moon, stars and shadows cast by the moonlight in the trees. There was a great white owl, which regularly flew down the valley, and in time I came to watch for its presence as an omen that all was well with the world.

One of my favourite pastimes was gazing at the stars and joining their pinpricks of light to make pictures in the sky. A house here, an animal there – the possibilities were endless and no two nights ever the same. From these pictures sprang stories which I spent hours writing or relating to anyone who cared to listen, and when Cornelius finally explained the constellations to me, realised my own pictures were nothing like those other people had seen in the heavens – but then, I did not always view the world as other people did.

The slow progress of the stars was also, I realised, reflected in the waxing and waning of the moon, the rising and setting of the sun and the changing of the seasons. Perhaps this was my first introduction to the cycle of life and the way in which everything appears to be a series of random events – until the dots are joined and the true picture emerges, which was there all the while, yet hidden from view.

And then, of course, there was the little chapel.

When I journeyed on the school bus as it wound its way down the long hill and up the other side, taking me away from the valley, I knew the chapel was just a stone's throw over the hedge and always felt a sadness to be leaving it behind. But in the evening, as the bus made its way down the little hill before winding its way up again, if I looked at exactly the right time and in just the right place, I could catch a glimpse of the chapel roof glinting in the afternoon sunlight, and the tense feeling which had been with me would disappear, leaving me at peace once more.

It was during these times I realised that, in the blink of an eye, time had passed and it would be the next day, week, month, even year. I came to understand how time does not move at the same speed but changes in loops and swirls, speeding up and slowing down, the seasons passing and, in another blink of the eye, returning again; and although those times seem long ago now, in the grand scale of things, perhaps they are not so very far away after all.

Forty One

'Rowie, Rowie, Rowena! Where are you?'

The bracken swayed above my head but was a safe haven and I knew Cornelius would never find me. Our game of hide and seek along the valley had continued for much of the afternoon and I knew he would soon tire of searching and his attention be taken with something else – the raven's nest high up in the white rock or the dragonflies which danced over the surface of the river. I knew if I stayed still for long enough he would wander off, leaving me free to visit the little chapel all by myself without interruption. Looking back I realise how patient Cornelius had been, for I was left in his care for much of the time and he rarely tired of keeping me amused and answering my childish questions, although by then he was a young man with better things to do.

There was a long silence and, poking my head above my canopy of green, I saw Cornelius' fair hair bobbing amongst the bracken on the way to the high rocks which towered over the valley. This was a favourite place of his, where he could watch the buzzards and ravens circling below or lie on his back gazing up at the blue sky, trying to answer all the questions the world had to offer.

I knew that for a short while, as Cornelius made his way towards the rocks, it would be safe for me to traverse the pathway and arrive at the little chapel unnoticed.

The valley lay quiet and still in the heat of the late afternoon sunlight, only the rushing river and the distant croak of the raven to be heard. It was as if all the world was asleep and Cornelius and I the only two people alive.

As always, I felt a surge of relief as I pushed open the rickety wooden gate into the enclosure. The chapel stood before me, its granite walls warm in the sunlight and the holy well peeped from behind, built of the same stone and housing the water which ran through the granite basin and underneath the altar, before reappearing in the little well at the front. I sank down and plunged my hands into the water, splashing my face and creating sparkles on the surface as the ripples subsided. Drawing a deep breath, I knew meadowsweet must be growing nearby for I was often aware of its heady perfume permeating the dusky summer air. Sometimes, I imagined I saw faces in the water and made up stories about the people I found there, people from long ago who led much more exciting lives than I ever would.

I felt the pocket of my dress and was reassured to feel the weight of the iron key there. The key to the chapel was always kept in the porch of the Old Vicarage, on the other side of the road from the church, and anyone wishing to enter simply took it from its nail and hung it back up upon their return. Fitting it into the lock of the wooden door and feeling the satisfying clunk as it turned, I pushed the door open and entered my sanctuary.

It was cool, always cool, yet seldom cold, as if the ancient walls held some semblance of heat in winter yet kept the interior blessedly cool in summer. I had seen it a hundred times, but each visit felt like the first, as if I could never get enough of the sparkling granite altar and the way the shafts of sunlight slanted through the leaded windows. There was a second, side door which I often pulled wide open to allow air to circulate through the building, and another tiny door above the second, smaller well where, it was said, offerings had once been left to the Saint. There was also a Visitors' Book in which I must have written my name a hundred times, never tiring of following the same ritual upon each visit - pausing at the entrance, touching the altar stone, opening the doors, looking through the book – and I must have spent hours gazing into the waters of the well, weaving tales of long ago in my mind.

'Rowie. Rowena. Time to get back.' Cornelius' voice drifted along the valley towards me and, looking upwards, I saw him silhouetted against the skyline, standing on the tallest rock. He waved his arms frantically, then disappeared into the swaying bracken, only to reappear shortly afterwards behind the holy well, making his way through a gap in the rough hedge and eventually appearing, hot and breathless, at my side.

'Come on, we'll be late for tea.' He draped himself over the stone arm of the well house and began to swirl the water with a stick, withdrawing it quickly as a frog swam to the surface then disappeared into a clump of weed, causing Cornelius to forget his words and lose himself in the moment of wondering and questioning. If ever there was a boy unsuited to a farming life it was Cornelius, whose mind was always searching for the answers to a hundred questions but never dwelling on the practicalities of life.

I closed and locked the doors of the chapel, wishing it a silent goodbye until next time, peeping through the trefoil in the entrance which so perfectly framed the altar and hurried back to Cornelius.

'Come on.' I poked him with a finger and he jumped good naturedly to his feet.

'Why are some frogs brown and others green?' he asked. 'And why do toads...'

'Come on!' I laughed, happy at that moment in the warmth of the sun with Cornelius by my side, teasing me as he always did, feeling I had all I needed in the world. There was a spot on the slope further along the path, perfect for rolling down through the bracken and as we approached it we both knew, from long experience, what my next words would be. 'Let's have a game of roly poly.'

He grinned. 'There isn't time.'

'Only one. Please,' I wheedled, knowing I would get my own way in the end.

He sighed theatrically, aware he would invariably be the loser, but nonetheless enjoying a few moments of childish pleasure which would keep me occupied for a little longer. 'Go on then,' he bargained, 'but give me a head start.'

'No.'

'Don't be mean.'

'Why should I?'

'Because you're younger than me.'

And then we were off and, of course, once led to twice, which led to three times and finally, hot and happy, we pulled ourselves back to the path, aware we were going to be so late for tea we would probably have missed it anyway.

As we headed for home my hand went to the pocket of my dress, as it instinctively did when I was in charge of the key to the chapel. It was empty.

My fingers scrabbled inside my pocket again and again, as if the key might magically appear, but it was nowhere to be found. A coldness slowly spread its way around my heart.

'Come on, Rowena.' Cornelius was already some way along the path and he turned, a puzzled look on his face at seeing me standing, stock still, patting my pocket over and over, looking wildly at the path around me.

'What's up?'

'It's gone. The key. Missing. Lost.' I looked at

him, a feeling of dread settling in the middle of my chest. 'What are we going to do?'

'It can't be lost. Things don't just disappear, it must be here somewhere.' He surveyed the swathes of broken bracken where we had been rolling. 'Oh.'

'What will we do?' I felt panic rising. It was the most terrible thing which had ever happened to me. I thought of the little chapel. No one would ever be able to unlock the door and go inside again. It would be closed up for ever, abandoned, would fall into ruins - and all because I had lost the key.

We frantically searched the path all the way back to the chapel, knowing if it had been lost in the bracken there would never be any hope of finding it. I was close to tears, although Cornelius did his best to assure me such things could be rectified. But his words were of no consolation and it was nowhere to be found. A fearful chill gripped my heart.

'Come on, one last roll.'

I was aware he was trying to cheer me up and we both knew he would never succeed, but just to humour him, I agreed. We rolled down the slope for the last time, both of us hoping we would miraculously find the key.

Eventually, we pulled ourselves up to the path and prepared to face the consequences. It was then I looked down and saw it, lying on the grassy path exactly where we had been standing earlier. I bent down and scooped it up, never having known such relief before nor having been so thankful to feel its cool weight in my hand.

Cornelius and I exchanged glances but said not a word. It was only some time later I realised it had never occurred to either of us to pretend we had not taken the key.

That was the first time I realised things which are lost can be found, even if you have given up the search. And some things are not lost at all, merely hidden.

'You were just looking in the wrong place, that's all,' said Cornelius, as we made our way home.

Forty Two

I never knew my mother, but did have a box which I always pretended belonged to her. Looking back now I see no one else was in the slightest bit aware of its importance. It must have once belonged to someone in Cornelius' family and I remember sitting in my bedroom at the farmhouse as a child, the heavy summer rain falling outside, as I opened the bundle which had been given to me with instructions to amuse myself for a while.

But as always the valley beckoned, and before long I slipped down the curving oak staircase and through the side door which led into the courtyard and from there, escape. I could hear the thumping of a rolling pin in the kitchen, but had no interest in domestic duties and soon found myself in the valley, warm and dry in my very favourite hidey hole, near the chapel and beneath the rocks.

It was the perfect place, sheltered from the rain and, due to a spreading beech tree, hidden from anyone who might be passing.

There was a blue cloth which I immediately discarded to reveal the most beautiful wooden box I had ever seen. Even at my young age I knew it to be special and took a moment to wonder at the trees and animals - a hare and a fish – and the sun, moon and stars so delicately carved. And in the middle of the top, a woman holding a chalice.

I lifted the catch carefully and felt a stab of disappointment, for inside lay a few items which seemed interesting enough, but then again were nothing special.

There was a brown, flint arrowhead. Or was it too large for an arrow? A spearhead, maybe. Cornelius would be interested, I thought, as I placed it to one side. And a sort of wooden pendant, which although I could see had once been carved, was now no more than a smoothed wooden disc with the vague outline of a tree upon it, as if someone had held it a lot and worn away most of the carvings.

Apart from those, a twisted piece of stick, a stub of candle, and then... this made me sit up and take notice. A small silver cup, no, chalice, was what it would have been called, tarnished with age, yet which I instinctively knew could be bright and shining, given a little attention.

And that was all. I wondered how I was supposed to amuse myself with these items and eventually lay back against the rock and closed my eyes.

It was then I found it.

The rain had increased. Heavy, summer rain and I pushed myself as far as I could beneath the overhang of rock for shelter. There was a surprisingly large space there, bigger than I had previously realised, almost a cave, and I felt a sense of security as I lay listening to the rain pattering on the leaves of the trees, hidden from the rest of the world and wondering if I was the first person to lie there or if others had done just the same before me.

As I lay, eyes closed, mind idly drifting into another place, my fingers came upon something smooth, at odds with the rough texture of the soil. I explored further, felt around the object and, finally stirring myself, found a long, pointed crystal of green and violet, lying cool and heavy in my hand.

It must have been there for ages, I thought, for it was cloudy with dirt and dust, and yet... As I held it I saw a shimmering in the weak sunlight and, after wetting my hand and rubbing the crystal with raindrops it shone brightly, giving the impression of returning to life after a very long time.

It was beautiful.

The rain cleared away then and I was able to step outside into the sunshine, holding the crystal up to the light, watching the way the green and violet twinkled and sparkled with a life of its own. I could not begin to imagine how it came to be in the soil beneath the rocks or who could have left it there, but had the strongest feeling it was as much a part of the valley as I was myself. And so, I placed it carefully in the carved wooden box with everything else and headed for home.

'Who does the little chapel belong to?' I asked Cornelius on our next visit to the valley. Summer was passing, the bracken turning to brown and dying back. Since losing the key we no longer played our usual game, perhaps we had grown up a little, and this time simply walked to the chapel to spend the afternoon gazing at the river and hillside opposite, until the day began to turn chilly and we decided to return home.

'I'm not sure,' he hazarded. 'The church maybe, or even our family. After all, we farm the land hereabouts.' He continued walking, as if it was of no consequence who owned the chapel; but as I passed through the gateway of the field in which the chapel enclosure stood, I could not help thinking how wonderful it would be to own the little field and, by default, the chapel itself.

Forty Three

Beltane

And so, in the blink of an eye the years passed, Cornelius and I were grown, the days of our childhood but distant memories, resurrected with affection at times but otherwise pushed beneath the clutter of work and everyday life. Neither of us moved away from the area. I lived in a little cottage in the village which had been left to me when Cornelius' parents passed away and still made up stories for pleasure. And if I felt something was missing from my life, it was a feeling I had always been familiar with and so thought little of it. Cornelius inherited the farmhouse and the land, which he continued to farm, so it came as a shock when he called one day to tell me he was planning to sell everything.

'But...' Words failed as I stared at him sitting casually opposite me, as if he had not just given me the biggest surprise ever. It was May, everything was bursting into life around us and we were relaxing in the pleasant warmth of the afternoon. The scent of wild roses drifted through the partly open window and I could see the rosemary hedge from which I could never resist taking a sprig to chew each time I passed. I had planted honeysuckle outside the window and its delicate scent mingled with the roses to create a magical perfume. The cottage had been in Cornelius' family for generations and I loved the cool, slate floors and the wooden staircase with its one creaking stair, leading to the two tiny rooms above. When I moved in, I had found a small, earthenware bowl tucked away at the back of the cupboard beneath the stairs, and this now rested on the mantelpiece, a link with times past.

'You can't...' I finally stammered feebly, knowing full well he had every right to do exactly as he wanted and I had no business telling him what to do at all.

'I have to.' His voice was low, but I perceived a note of quiet determination. 'I know it will hurt you, me, us, to see the house and the land in the hands of other people, but I simply can't make a living of it on my own. And you know very well I was never cut out to be a farmer. It's just a burden to me now. I want to start again, even though I'm almost forty and it might seem a bit late in the day. In fact,' he drew a deep breath, 'I want to join the clergy. I'm going to take a theological degree, then go into training. I can come back for weekends and during the holidays while I'm at University, and moving into one of the cottages will be much better than the farmhouse. Mother and Father would never have understood but my decisions can't hurt them now.' He paused and my heart went out to him, realising this was the first time in his life he was free to do as he pleased.

'It's been all right for you,' he continued, as if reading my thoughts. 'You've always been settled here with your job and your writing and you've been able to make ends meet by doing what you enjoy. I haven't.'

I nodded, wondering if he had any idea how many times over the years I had longed for parents with expectations of me, rather than being left to my own path in the world.

'I do understand,' I whispered. A thought occurred to me. 'But what about the little chapel? Surely you aren't going to sell it?'

Cornelius smiled, looking relieved now he had dropped his bombshell and the worst was over. 'There's something else I have to tell you,' he continued. 'You see, when I started sorting everything out and was going through all the paperwork and old deeds, I remembered you asking me years ago who the little chapel belonged to. Well, with a bit of searching around I discovered there was something of a mystery surrounding it. Apparently, my one of my ancestors named Charles gave it to someone called Rachel, and one of her descendants then married into his family, and it returned to us once again, so you see, it was ours after all.'

I nodded, wondering where this was leading. I felt sad as I had forgotten to visit for months. If I no longer made the effort, how could I expect anyone else to?

'Anyway,' he continued, 'I do feel slightly ashamed I haven't taken more notice of it over the years, especially in the light of my recent calling. But now...' Cornelius paused dramatically as his face broke into a smile. 'I'm going to give it to you,' he finished. 'So you see, even though I'm selling up, you still have the chapel and field. They're yours.' He grinned and I glimpsed the boy he once was, caring, gentle and protective of his little sister – and I suddenly understood he was exactly right to pursue his dreams and search for the answers to all the questions he had ever asked.

I gasped, not knowing what to say, tears pricking my eyes. Of all the things I could have thought of, I never expected this. 'You cared for it in your own way by simply keeping it safe,' I assured him, as I took his hand and gave it a squeeze.

'Something tells me you're going to do a much better job than me,' he replied.

'Thank you,' I whispered. 'And you're going to make a great Vicar.'

Forty Four

Midsummer

Once more the blink of an eye and time fast forwards. Where does the intervening time go, from one moment to the next, when there are days, months or even years between?

It seems so long ago, and yet as if mere seconds have passed since I walked to the chapel, the knowledge the little field, enclosure, chapel and holy well itself belonged to me. Did they belong to me? Could anything as timelessly beautiful belong to anyone? Perhaps I was a mere caretaker, a Guardian if you like, to cherish it and ensure it would never be neglected or allowed to fall into ruin again. I suddenly realised that, much as I loved it, I knew little of its history and as I walked along the valley felt the enormity of the task before me. Responsible for the place I might be, but it would need to be insured, the grounds required more attention than a single cut once a year, the gate was on the verge of collapse, not to mention the roof which looked decidedly dodgy. And what about the field? The path was downright dangerous in places, especially during the winter when it became a twisty, slippery slope.

The journey along the pathway felt different as I approached and as I passed through the gateway into the field – my field – I felt a surge of energy, as if the swaying bracken, the towering rocks, the calling ravens and rushing river welcomed me home. The sky was the bright blue of summer and the sun high. It was a perfect day.

I reached the chapel, pushed open the wooden door – my wooden door – and stepped inside. As always it was cool and the sunlight slanted warm fingers through the window. There were flowers on the windowsill, fading now, and a feeling of general neglect and dustiness in the air. I walked forwards, dropped the bunch of wild, pink roses and golden honeysuckle from my garden onto the altar and rested my hands upon the cool granite.

'I'm sorry,' I whispered. 'I'm sorry I've neglected you for so long.' I glanced at the cobwebs hanging in the corners of the windows, noticed the sheen of dust which lay on the sills and felt a lump rise in my throat as tears stung my eyes. How could I have forgotten how beautiful it was? How could I have lived so near and yet allowed my mundane, everyday life to take over? 'But I'm here now,' I ventured into the silence, my voice stronger, a feeling of determination within me.

The chapel wrapped itself around me silently, peaceful and comforting. 'It's all right,' it seemed to say.

'You've come home.' And it was then I had the feeling of complete oneness with the place, as if I were a part of every stone of the building and every stone a part of me. I listened to the steady trickle of the water running behind the altar, delighted in the lazy drone of a bumblebee which wandered in through the open door and knew this was a place I would give my life for and whatever I needed to do for it would never be a hardship.

Throwing out the fading flowers, I filled the jam jar with fresh water from the holy well. The water felt warm and silky as I plunged my hands into its depths and, on a sudden whim, threw off my sandals and stood right inside the well itself. This time the water felt tingling cold and I gasped with shock, then laughed out loud as a small frog swam across the surface right over my feet and disappeared into a clump of waterweed. I carefully stepped out, sunlight sparkling upon the droplets of water on my skin, and I knelt down, washed my face in the water and scooped up a handful to taste. It was as sweet and pure as ever. Holy water. My water.

Returning to the chapel, I arranged the honeysuckle and roses in the jam jar. Even now there was a different air about the place. A feeling of appreciation for what I was doing. It was almost as though the chapel had picked itself up, dusted itself down and was looking forwards to the future. 'I'll be back,' I promised, loudly now, uncaring of anyone hearing me. As I left, out of long habit, I gave one final glance through the trefoil in the door. The honeysuckle and roses winked at me in the shafts of sunlight and the clear water in the jam jar sparkled.

An hour later I returned with all I needed. A

bucket, a brush, some cleaning cloths and more jam jars. Plunging my bucket into the holy well, it soon filled with clear, sparkling water. I carried it back inside the chapel, threw open both doors and looked around, suddenly daunted as to where to begin. The windows, the sills, the altar, the floor... and then I knew what to do and a moment later buckets of water were sloshing and swirling all around, drenching the window sills, cascading onto the altar and swishing across the floor, followed by a brushing, sweeping and shifting until eventually the chapel lay damp, glistening and refreshed in the late afternoon sunlight.

After picking as much greenery and as many wild flowers as I could find - ferns, bracken, shining buttercups, vivid foxgloves, scented meadowsweet, delicate white cow parsley - and arranging them in jam jars, I returned outside and leaned against the wall, surveying the valley. It was a strange feeling. I felt cleansed as if I, along with the chapel, had been given a thorough cleaning and I felt fresh and new. Returning inside I was greeted with the beauty of the wild flowers, the musical sound of the trickling water and the perfume of roses and honeysuckle mingling together and swirling around me. A wave of thanks washed over me, from whom or where I did not know, and I too, gave thanks for the beauty of it all.

This was my new beginning.

It was Midsummer's Eve.

Forty Five

I soon discovered that being the Guardian of a holy well was not all it was cracked up to be. I had always thought of Guardians as people who stood tall and strong, perhaps stern, definitely unwavering, possibly holding the odd sword, viewed with awe by those who encountered them. And Guardians of holy wells and chapels would no doubt be beautiful women who smiled at their visitors, giving good advice in an otherworldly fashion, receiving offerings and revered and respected by all. No one had ever mentioned the other side of things.

For a start there were the snails. There appeared to be hundreds of snails living in the cracks and crevices of the well house, accumulated over the years and regularly dropping into the water. The sludge which had collected at the bottom of the well was inches think, which when finally cleared revealed a large grey slate set into granite surrounds. The grounds needed tidying, there were fallen branches of trees, a broken fence which allowed sheep in, rotten doors and cracked windows.

And along with everything else, the building was listed and the site a scheduled monument, which meant I had to gain permission to carry out any major works. There was insurance to be organised and paid for, and several people telling me what to do and how to do it. All at once I wondered if I was really cut out for this, until the realisation came to me that perhaps in this day and age the duties of a Guardian might have changed to encompass the twentieth century.

After the turning of a whole year and more I

became accustomed to the passing of the seasons, the energy of the valley and the weather, constantly changing but always beautiful. I began to understand the link between the people who worked the land long ago and their reverence of nature. There were deer on the other side of the valley, white tails bobbing in the sunlight as they swiftly traversed the bracken, and sometimes they could be seen grazing peacefully on the skyline. And there were no end of magical places to be explored and discovered – shady places beneath overhanging trees, high rocks which gave views of the entire valley and dappled, cool retreats beside the riverbank where it was easy to imagine I was in another time, another place.

No two journeys to the chapel were ever the same, no matter how often I visited. One summer's day could be completely different to the next and so it was never a hardship to tread the winding path through the valley, although I sometimes wondered how many miles I had covered should all my footsteps be added together.

At times it was total perfection, blue summer skies, fruits hanging heavy on branches in autumn, crisp winter days or the first warmth of the sun in springtime. But who is to judge perfection? The days when the valley was a swathe of warm, misty drizzle which soaked my clothes through to the skin were one of my favourites, and there was a raw energy to the howling wind which pushed me along the path or fought to prevent me leaving. At times I wrapped a scarf around my face, eyes watering with the chill of the air, fingers numb with cold – and always, at the end of my journey, the little chapel lay waiting for me, a haven of peace and a shelter from the ever changing elements.

I inevitably knew if people had visited as the atmosphere changed along with everything else. Sometimes it felt incredibly peaceful, at others a little ruffled, as if its silence had been disturbed, but always I was left with a feeling of tranquility, of having returned to my source however short a time I spent there.

As the year progressed I began to appreciate more fully the cycle of the seasons and the life of the valley. On a practical level I understood the work which needed to be carried out, cutting grass, painting fences, cleaning windows, and started to investigate obtaining the permission required from English Heritage for major work to be done. It all seemed so daunting and I often wondered if I would ever manage it but a small voice inside told me to take one step at a time, and I did, moving ever closer to my goal.

And so a whole year, maybe more, passed before my story even began.

Forty Six

Solar Eclipse

It was on the day of the solar eclipse I met him, when the first of the dots of my life began to join and the true picture to emerge, like the stories made from the stars all those years ago. Looking back now, I see we were merely renewing our acquaintance, picking up the threads we had left hanging a lifetime before. But I did not realise it at the time. Momentous meetings and events creep up on you silently, and it is only in

247

retrospect the enormity of what was happening becomes clear.

There had been a lot of hype about the solar eclipse, Cornwall being in the area of near or full totality. I was unsure what to expect or where to go, until Cornelius showed me the way.

'But surely you'll be going to the chapel,' he exclaimed, as if it were the most obvious thing in the world. And then, of course, it was. Cornelius himself was travelling to the far end of Cornwall, in order to experience the eclipse in all its glory. But once the thought to be at the chapel was in my mind, I could do nothing else.

The morning dawned bright and fresh, a sunny day, although there was some cloud and it was a little hit and miss whether we would see the eclipse or not. I chose a dress of blues and greens, the colours of the valley, and felt a part of the landscape as I approached the chapel, hoping to have the place to myself so I would have no need to make small talk with anyone else. The previous afternoon I had placed flowers on the altar and tea lights all around. Clutching my blanket and rucksack, I made my way to the enclosure. Although the eclipse would not occur until just after eleven o'clock, I left myself plenty of time to light my candles and enjoy the view of the valley.

When I arrived at the chapel there was no sign of anyone and I breathed a sigh of relief. Soon the candles were lit, my blanket spread on the grass and all was ready. Despite the occasional cloud cover the sun was warm and it was a perfect summer's day. I had brought bottles to capture some of the holy water – someone told me that following the eclipse it would be sparkling with energy. I did not know if it was true, but thought it worth saving some just in case.

After a while I became fidgety. There was plenty of time to spare, nothing more to do and the river looked inviting, so I made my way to my favourite spot, where the dragonflies danced above the surface of the water and sometimes alighted on my arms or legs as I sat amidst the cool greenery.

It was as I lay with my back against a willow, the feeling came upon me of no longer being alone. I glanced around but no one was there. Only the fast flow of the river, bubbles swirling on the surface, the occasional plop of a fish coming up for insects and the dancing dragonflies. Clouds floated overhead, patches of light and shade dappled the riverbank. I glanced at the huge willow to the right, leaves stirring in the slight breeze. I could see no one, yet the feeling persisted. I lay back, closed my eyes, heard a soft sound and sat upright to look again. It was then I saw him, although I could have sworn he had not been there a moment before. As soon as he realised he had been spotted he smiled, and in that moment the clouds shifted, casting sunlight and shadow over his face, blending him into the trunk of the tree and for an instant he disappeared once more, only to become clear as he stepped forwards and I saw a man, dressed in green and brown, holding a twisted staff in his hand.

'Handsome day for it.' His voice was soft, deep, melodic and I felt no fear at finding him there, more a sense of security and oneness with the day and my surroundings.

'Will you be coming up to the chapel to watch?' I asked.

He paused, shaking his head. 'This is my place,' he replied. 'I'll stay here by the river, in the shade.'

I nodded, feeling a slight stab of disappointment.

He raised his eyes skywards. 'I think it's nearly time,' he commented, 'you'd better be getting back.'

Glancing at my watch, I wondered where the time had gone, for it had passed much more quickly than I realised.

'Well, goodbye,' I ventured.

He inclined his head. 'Catch you later.'

I turned away, paused, glanced over my shoulder to once again invite him to join me. But he was nowhere to be seen.

Back at the chapel, the moment of the eclipse was approaching, the sphere of the moon just beginning to cover the face of the sun and although scattered clouds occasionally passed overhead, it would be possible to see the eclipse quite clearly.

Inside, the tea lights and candles were burning steadily and as the world began to darken, seemed to glow ever more brightly in the deepening gloom. I paused for a moment before approaching the altar. There was a strange atmosphere, as if the chapel was waiting, waiting... a feeling of reverence and, although the building was only small, it felt much larger, like a church or even a cathedral.

I suddenly remembered the green and violet crystal I had brought with me, the one discovered in the cave as a child, and returned outside. It was my intention to place it in the water of the holy well for the duration of the eclipse – people often bathed crystals in holy water and it seemed a good idea. I hurried out, leaving the darkening peace of the chapel behind me and stopped short. He was there again, the man from the riverbank. This time leaning against a rowan tree, gazing across the valley.

'You changed your mind, then.' I broke the silence of the moment, for the valley had quietened. As the day began to dim, so a hush descended and there was a feeling of evening in the air. I noticed the birdsong had ceased and one lone crow flew westwards, as if heading for home.

The man looked up in surprise and smiled. 'Hello,' he replied, in a soft, Cornish accent. 'I didn't realise anyone was here. I've only just arrived.'

'I know.' I smiled. 'I spoke to you earlier at the riverbank.'

A puzzled expression crossed his face but my mind was on my crystal as I searched in my rucksack. Finally I located it and he wandered over to take a look.

'Very nice. Fluorite,' he commented. 'Where did you get it?'

'Found it when I was little,' I replied, not wanting to go into detail. I was aware of the fast fading light, the moment of the eclipse approaching much more rapidly than I had imagined. 'I'm going to put it into the holy well,' I explained. 'Do sit down if you like.' I indicated my blanket and made my way around the chapel, leaving him watching the valley.

The day continued to darken. I stood for a moment, thinking of my mother, allowing my mind to wander back through the years, to her mother and her mother before her, and had the strangest sensation of being at the end of a long chain of women who had lived and loved and fought and survived, just so I could be there, at that precise moment. It was a daunting feeling, yet a comforting one, as if they were all around me and even though I had never known my own mother, my family was always with me, although I could not see them or ever know their names.

Kneeling before the water I gently dropped the crystal into the well, allowing it to slide from my hand and enter the water with no more than a soft plop, coming to rest on the bottom and wavering gently as shadows danced upon the surface of the water. Then, realising it was almost time, I returned to the front of the chapel.

Dan, as I later discovered his name to be, was settled cross legged on the blanket. There was an air of stillness about him which matched the silence of the valley. He was dressed in ordinary working clothes and his tanned face and arms spoke of a life outdoors. I put on my special glasses and looked up. The face of the sun was more than half covered by the moon now, the valley rapidly becoming a dim twilight. We sat in companionable silence and all seemed well until I noticed Dan's hands were trembling.

'You okay?' I removed my glasses, watching him with concern and detected fear in his eyes.

'I just hate the twilight,' he replied. 'I don't know why and it's bad enough in the evenings, but having it come in the middle of the day is... spooky... scary...' He paused. 'I didn't realise it would be this bad.'

I had to admit it was strange and was aware the moment was almost upon us, the dimness increasing with every second.

'Take my hand.' Without consciously thinking, I held it towards him, the words echoing in my mind as if they has been spoken a second later by someone else. Dan paused, grasped it gratefully, and then the moon finally moved to almost, but not quite, cover the face of the sun. It happened in a rush. One moment the day was dim, the next a roller coaster ride, the bit when you go down and up again – into the darkness, there for a few seconds as time seems to stand still - then the day began to lighten once again. Bands of light and shade shuddered along the valley and a strange breeze sprang up, departing almost as soon as it arrived. There was a feeling of relief in the air.

I glanced at Dan, looking calmer now and our hands fell apart, although the feeling of warmth remained.

'Okay?'

He nodded. 'Thank you.'

I left him sitting there and made my way around the chapel to find my crystal. The sun was shining as the day continued to lighten and I could smell the scent of meadowsweet as I approached the holy well. Bending down I peered in, but could see no sign of my crystal. Strange, maybe it had been moved by the flow of the water and was hidden by some fronds of weed. I plunged my hand in. For once the water felt icy cold and as I withdrew my arm, droplets of water sparkled like diamonds on my bare skin. Again and again I plunged my hands into the water, my fingers scrabbling in each corner, searching every crevice, my head assuring me it had to be there, my heart knowing it was not.

I returned to the front of the chapel and Dan.

'What's up?' he asked.

'My crystal,' I replied, looking around as if I half expected to find it lying on the grass, memories of the lost key of long ago in my mind. 'I've lost it.' I searched some more, on the ground, in my rucksack, even beneath the blanket, realising it was futile. I had definitely dropped it into the well earlier.

Dan frowned. 'Strange.'

'I just can't understand it,' I continued. 'I put it in

the well before the eclipse. And no one else has come except us and we've been sitting here the whole time.'

Dan shook his head slowly. 'It's a peculiar day and stranger things happen than we can ever imagine. Sometimes things do seem to disappear, but they normally turn up again, even somewhere else, and there's no rhyme nor reason to any of it.'

I sighed. There was really nothing more to say, so I returned to the well for one final search before filling my bottles with crystal clear water.

'Can I offer you some refreshment?' I asked Dan, as I settled down beside him, offering one of the bottles of sparkling water. It was all I had, but somehow it felt the right thing to do.

He smiled. 'Thank you. It's an honour to be here today,' he replied, as he took a sip of the clear, pure water. We sat in companionable silence as the world returned to normal and the birds resumed their song – and I had the strangest feeling I had done this many times before in the past.

'I'll just have a wander down to the river,' commented Dan. 'See what's going on.'

'I know, we met on the riverbank earlier, remember?' I began to wonder if Dan was quite right. How could he have forgotten so quickly?

But he shook his head. 'I arrived just before you came out of the chapel, and came straight along the pathway from the church.'

I did not press the matter. This was a strange day and, now I thought about it, wondered if it was the same man after all.

I smiled. 'Okay, see you later.'

He looked straight into my eyes. 'Thank you,' he said, and turned away. A moment later he had disappeared.

I sat a while longer, eventually returning to the well to look for my crystal once more, but however long I searched there was no sign of it and I wondered if I would ever see my beautiful crystal again.

Forty Seven

The day of the eclipse remained with me for a long time, not only the event itself, or even meeting Dan and the man by the riverbank. There was another element which linked into my soul, a story of long ago which lingered in my mind, waiting to be told. At times I had visions of it and eventually knew I had to write it down.

The Dawning

Place - A hidden valley in Cornwall

Her footsteps were silent, only their imprint in the dew-ridden grass marking her passing. Ferns swished aside and sprang back into place as she moved along the tiny pathway through the valley. Far below, the river snaked silver on its endless journey, its banks strewn with meadowsweet and rushes, and apart from the call of a buzzard wheeling silently overhead, the whispering river was the only sound to be heard.

It was high summer and although still early the sun had long since begun its journey into the heavens, having risen over the craggy outcrops of granite above her. All was as it had appeared on many a summer morning, but today something was different. The air held the shimmering of expectation as the last of the mists burnt away, as though the valley was holding its breath.

Elana paused at the grey standing stone which marked the pathway and the nearing of her journey's end. Now she was fully grown, it was exactly the same height as herself and as she passed she unconsciously, out of habit over the years, laid a hand upon its rough surface. At this hour it was still cool, but later, on her return journey when the sun had reached its height and begun its descent, it would feel warm and comforting.

She was almost there now. Almost at the sacred spring she tended every day of her life. The occupants of the village understood her duty which had been passed down through the generations. The care of the sacred spring, the healing, life giving water which never failed even in the hottest of summers. On more than one occasion the spring had been the saviour of the village.

Elana knew this place was special for she was bonded to the spring, and although she visited it every single day, she never failed to feel the shiver of energy as her feet neared the site, for she was in essence approaching a part of herself. A place undeniably linked to her very soul.

The shrill of the mobile phone broke through the heat of the morning as Ellie made her way through the ferns along the tiny path which led to the Holy Well Chapel. Angrily she switched it off. It would only be work, never giving her a minute's peace. Couldn't even come home to Cornwall for a few days without them bothering her. She was tempted to throw the wretched thing into the ferns, allow it to be swallowed up in the swaying banks of green, but common sense - or was it merely conditioning - made her slip it back into her skirt pocket.

Ellie's ruffled feelings were soothed as the magic of the valley began to work on her. She couldn't believe she hadn't been back for so many years. How could she have left it so long? University, followed by a job in London and now, five years on, she had found success. Money, car, promotion. But happiness? The question whispered through her mind, fed with memories of the valley from her childhood when it had been her playground. It had nurtured in her an energy which the child had not understood and from which the adult had been separated for too long.

Beneath her the river snaked silver amongst the rushes and meadowsweet and a buzzard circling on high gave its own mournful cry. She paused for breath and found her hand on the grey standing stone. A farmer had hung a rickety gate on it which swung permanently open, as though any attempt to close it would result in its demise, and as her fingers felt the slight warmth of the stone she found, to her surprise, that now she was fully grown the stone was exactly the same height as herself.

As she turned the final bend in the path the grey

slate roof of the tiny chapel came into view before her, then the walls hewn of Cornish stone. Soon she reached the little wooden gate and was inside the enclosure, swamped with a feeling of coming home, of finally arriving at a safe and tranquil place. The chapel looked just as she remembered, and as she raised her eyes to the roof silhouetted against the blue sky, Ellie noticed a clump of grass springing from between two slates, waving in the slight breeze.

Beyond the building was the holy well itself, still and crystal clear, and as she approached she could see the moving reflections of the water causing waves of light to dance on the moss covered stone arch above it. From here the water ran through the chapel and underneath the altar, to reappear on the other side in a tiny basin, above which a door was set in the wall over a granite shelf. This was where people used to leave offerings to their Saint. She knew all of this, had known it all her life. How could she have forgotten its existence for so long?

There was a new door at the entrance now, no longer the rickety one she remembered, but even this was showing the test of time, its rich wood already faded. She slowly pushed the door open and as it swung silently inwards, breathed a sigh of relief. It was just as it had always been. The cool air rushed out to engulf her and the altar, a plain slab of granite balanced on four rough hewn stone supports, stood beneath the window at the far end, surmounted by a simple cross.

The sunlight filtering through the tiny side window gave the small chapel a welcoming look and, without consciously thinking of what she was doing, she removed her sandals and walked to the altar. Someone had placed a jar of wild flowers there and a shaft of sunlight struck the water, making the glass sparkle and giving the foliage an inner light. Slowly, she placed her hands on the cool stone and closed her eyes.

The first thing Elana did each day was to wash her face and hands in the bubbling water which sprang from the rocks, forming a pool in the rough bowl of granite, and then she entered the building which the villagers had erected around the altar.

The altar. When she touched it she could feel the power shimmering beneath, for the spring had been directed to run underneath it. Four uprights of Cornish granite and a great slab balanced on the top, all simply covered with a rough building, but it was enough. This was her temple, the home of the spirit of the spring. As she touched the stone slab, the tingling in her body told her that today the power was incredibly strong, bubbling beneath the surface, waiting. But for what she didn't know. She had never felt it like this before, attuned as she was to its ebb and flow which changed with the cycle of the moon.

After some time she stepped outside. The day was darkening. What had been a bright summer's day was now almost twilight. The sky was dim but all around the horizon was an eerie light and it had become colder, a chill wind blowing from the east. The valley seemed to be waiting, holding its breath in anticipation of some terrible event. Frightened now, she retreated into the building and placed her hands on the altar, feeling the energy stirring restlessly beneath her fingers.

She felt the tremor of their footsteps first, and it was as though the tiny hut quaked at their arrival. They had thrashed through the undergrowth, trampling the ferns and small trees which she and the other villagers were so careful to preserve. Then she heard their voices, rough and harsh, no reverence for the place they were infiltrating, and then two men appeared, framed in the tiny entranceway. She realised how vulnerable she was, a woman alone with only the sacred spring for protection.

She realised from the shouts outside there were more following and soon the building would probably be alight, after she had been dragged from her temple and forced to watch its desecration, probably followed by her own.

She stood facing them, her hands on the altar stone although it was behind her now. The energy trickling through was her only comfort, the knowledge that whatever happened would only be the pain of mortal flesh. But to watch them desecrate her sacred spring would be the demolition of her very soul, which she would truly be unable to bear.

She realised that although the energy was strong today, it alone could not save her. As they advanced she saw very clearly the look on the faces of the two men, saw them laugh, the light of conquering and greed in their eyes and she could do nothing but stand with her hands upon the stone and silently pray.

Over the following weeks the memory had remained with Ellie, although at times she tried to forget, but always it crept back into her mind and she would find herself quietly reliving it, oblivious to everyday life going on around her.

The moment she had placed her hands on the stone altar she felt a stirring. Not a blinding flash or rush of energy, but simply a stirring, as though something which had long been asleep was at last reawakened. And she felt her body respond. Not a jolt or an electric current, but a tiny tingle, a response from deep within, and she felt alive and vibrant, as though for the first time she was in the place she belonged.

As the day of the solar eclipse approached, Ellie received many invitations from well meaning friends. A festival, a boat trip, climbing to the top of a hill. But none of them had interested her. She simply hadn't been able to summon the enthusiasm for an event which was no more than an excuse to party - Christmas come in the middle of August - and when asked to work on that day had agreed. She felt unenthusiastic and listless about the eclipse and couldn't see why everyone else was making such a fuss.

But as the day approached Ellie felt a strange uncertainty that she was doing the right thing after all. It wasn't just that the office was almost empty. Telephones rang, computers beeped, life continued much as ever, but something bothered her deep inside. There was feeling of anticipation within her. She realised she was waiting for something to happen, holding her breath almost, but she didn't understand why. It wasn't until the evening before the eclipse that she suddenly realised she had to go home to

Cornwall.

She spent the night behind the wheel of her car. The traffic was every bit as bad as had been predicted. No one had taken the advice to arrive early and the entire population, Ellie included, seemed to have left work at the same moment and started the long trek to the West Country. She spent the night on the road, snatching a few hours sleep in a lay-by when she could drive no further, and was once more at the wheel of the car as the sun rose.

Finally the traffic began to move again and Ellie was left with some hope she might get there in time after all. The mobile rang shrilly and she realised she ought to be at the office, but she let it ring, strangely empowered by its persistent tone which she studiously ignored. It was late. So late there wasn't even time to see her parents, announce her arrival and change out of the work clothes she was still wearing. Out of sheer habit she picked up the phone and slipped it into her skirt pocket as she left the car.

The sky was already beginning to darken as she stumbled along the path. Again she was afraid she wasn't going to make it in time, but knew she must. Suddenly, getting to the tiny chapel before the eclipse reached totality was the most important thing in the world.

As Ellie reached the standing stone she paused, fighting for breath. She leaned against it, her hand unerringly finding its resting place and as she caught her breath, tore off her shoes, flinging them into the bracken on one side, feeling lighter, freer as she continued on her journey, unconfined by the restraints of civilisation. Her hair had come loose from its pins and swung down her back in a way she never usually wore it. Breaking into a run she rounded the final bend and the chapel appeared before her.

As she thrust open the tiny wooden gate she realised that totality had almost arrived. The sky was darkening rapidly, birds ceased to sing and a sudden chill breeze had sprung up. All around was a sense of silent anticipation. The world was holding its breath, and at any other time she might have found it eerie, frightening, but now there was only one thought in her mind. With her last ounce of energy she pushed the door open and hurled herself towards the stone altar, and only when she had placed her hands upon it was she filled with an overwhelming sense of relief and thankfulness.

When the surge of energy came it frightened even Elana, used to it as she was. It seemed to well up from beneath the ground, through the holy water, through the altar, into her hands and straight through her body. She felt it pause in her belly and then shoot out from her chest and the top of her head. It was the same energy, strong, pure, feminine, alive, but it was a hundred times more potent and vibrant than she had ever felt it before.

It was so strong the men must have been aware of it, for a puzzled look had come over their faces, causing them to momentarily stop in their tracks. It didn't last long. They were barbarians, unattuned to the earth energy, but nonetheless, those few vital seconds during which they paused were enough. By the time they had gathered their scattered wits, the light, which had been steadily decreasing, was all but gone and the air outside filled with shouts and cries of fear. Dropping their weapons, pointing at her and gibbering words she didn't understand, the two men turned and fled from the tiny building.

The energy surge ceased and Elana left the altar to move outside, instinctively knowing she was safe. It was night. The stars were out and where the sun should have been shining brightly, was a black hole in the sky, surrounded by a fiery halo.

When Ellie emerged from the chapel, totality was over. She surveyed the scene before her, bands of light and shadow shuddering up the valley as the moon passed from the face of the sun and suddenly everything seemed so blindingly simple she couldn't believe she hadn't seen it before. This was where she belonged. This was what was important in her life. The phone rang shrilly and she took it from her pocket. For a moment she looked at it as though she had never seen it before, and then she drew back her arm and flung it away from her, a modern day sacrifice to the life she was leaving behind. As it arced through the air it turned and the black plastic casing caught the sunlight for a brief instant before falling into the ferns of the valley. Where it landed she could not tell, for it caused only the swiftest shiver of green fronds and then it was gone forever, and she knew with sudden relief that no matter how hard she might search she would never find it again.

After a while she knelt beside the water and washed her hands and face in it, as she had done so many times in the past, and she could feel the energy sparkling in the sunlight on the water. Ellie knew her destiny in life now.

This was home. This was where she belonged.

And the spring bubbled from its secret place deep beneath the ground as it always had, stronger now than ever before, for Elana had returned at last.

Forty Eight

Midsummer

In the blink of an eye the wheel of the year turned. I became more used to my duties as Guardian of the well, simple as they seemed at that point, and so it was Midsummer when I first met Jowan. I say first, for as with Dan, from the moment we met it was as if we picked up the threads of some long ago conversation which was resumed centuries later. And, as before, a few more of the dots of my life became joined to create another part of the picture which was beginning to emerge, although at the time much still remained unclear.

I had never been one to see ghosts or hear voices. Although I was susceptible to atmosphere and soon became aware, the moment I set foot over the threshold of the chapel, if anyone had visited and the energy they left behind, I never saw or heard any of the spirits other people so readily spoke of. There was a monk, I was told, who stood just inside the door and an ancient spirit who resided in the corner to the left of the altar. Try as I might, I was unable to see or feel either of them. And so, it was something of a shock to open the door one day to discover a knight standing before the altar, appearing perfectly at home as if his presence was nothing unusual at all.

I must have seemed stunned for he grinned good humouredly and I realised he was reading one of the little leaflets about the chapel. Would a ghost or spirit be reading a leaflet?

'St Clether.' He waved the piece of paper at me and smiled disarmingly. 'One of the twenty-four children of King Brechan of Wales.'

'Yes.' It was about all I could muster in reply. He was an imposing figure in his white tunic, bearing the red and gold emblem of a lion, and he even had a sword in a scabbard leaning against the altar, although the iPod tucked into his belt and ear plugs hanging around his neck somewhat spoilt the illusion. I noticed the sunlight filtering through the window glinted red upon his hair and judged him to be in his late teens, a good ten years younger than myself.

He stepped forwards, holding out his hand, and I had the impression of a large, playful puppy, all paws and filled with good natured energy. 'Re-enactment Society,' he explained, glancing down at his costume. 'Just on my way to Tintagel, but had a few moments to spare so thought I'd call in. I've heard about this place but never actually made it here before.' He glanced around. 'Awesome, isn't it?'

I nodded. 'Pretty much.' I could not help smiling. There was something so very familiar about him, the way he held his head, his stature, the timbre of his voice. Yet I was certain we had never met before.

'Have you lost something?' I asked.

He was glancing around, unable to remain still, as if he was searching, but he shook his head. 'Not really,' he admitted. 'It's more as if I've forgotten something but I can't quite remember what. Silly really, I only felt it when I arrived here and I don't think I left anything at home.' He shrugged and grinned. 'I usually do though,' he continued, 'lose things. All the time, but they normally turn up when they're ready. It'll come to me eventually.'

I nodded.

'Beautiful valley. Beautiful chapel. Just the sort of thing I love finding out about.' He grinned disarmingly. 'I'm at college at the moment, then hopefully going on to Uni to read law. Want to be a solicitor. Justice must be done and all that.'

The door creaked behind me to reveal Dan, holding a saw in one hand and the remains of a branch of a tree in the other, and in the distance I noticed Cornelius making his way down from the highest rock where I knew he had been sitting for most of the morning.

And suddenly, there we were. Looking back now, although I did not realise it at the time, the dots were joining together and we had met yet again in our varying guises, to work out our destinies, to save the Maidens of the Wells, to find our true selves and to discover all we had been working towards. But at that moment, none of us had any idea at all.

Forty Nine

Autumn Equinox

The blink of an eye and yet again time fast forwards. It seemed only seconds later we were sitting outside the little chapel enjoying the autumn sunshine. It had been strange, the way the four of us clicked so readily, despite the difference in our ages, as if we had known each other for years.

'I think it's a wonderful idea.' Cornelius lay, legs stretched out before him, resting against the chapel wall. There was no breeze and the valley slumbered peacefully in the late autumn sunlight. We had assumed Cornelius was dozing but his words proved us wrong. 'I'd love to do it myself but I'm flat out with my studies. You'll enjoy it though.' Cornelius had completed the first year of his degree and was spending his final few days at home before returning for the autumn term.

I smiled. The idea of researching the history of the chapel definitely appealed to Cornelius more than it did me, although I was beginning to feel pretty excited myself. Although I had discovered bits here and pieces there, the picture was far from complete and the more I searched the more interesting it all became.

'So much information,' continued Cornelius. 'I could point you in the right direction. Records Office, researching articles about the place, you know the sort of thing.'

'I'd love to help,' added Jowan. 'I like research and stuff.' He paused. 'Maybe I should be a historian instead of a lawyer. What do you think?'

'Wouldn't do for me, all those books,' said Dan. 'But each to his own. One man's meat is another man's poison. Why don't you just do what you want?'

'Because I sort of feel it's my duty, as my father's a solicitor and his before him,' replied Jowan.

Dan rolled his eyes heavenwards. 'Why?' he asked. 'No one has the right to run someone else's life. It's your life, your journey, you do what you want.'

'I agree,' cut in Cornelius. 'Don't be like me and wait until you're forty to begin. For goodness sake, do it now.'

'Anyway,' continued Dan turning to me, 'when you research all this stuff, how do you know it's right? It's only what someone else has written, after all. They're just words, and words written by someone long ago at that.'

'Somebody's got to record things,' interrupted Cornelius, 'else we'll never know what happened in the past.'

'And the past is fascinating,' added Jowan.

'But it's all in the feeling,' continued Dan. 'This is a wonderful place and what matters is the feeling you get when you're here. Never mind the books and the words. Yes, I know they have their place,' he glanced at Jowan and Cornelius before they could interrupt further, 'but one man's theory is another man's lie. For me it's all about the feeling. I work the land, have farmed all my life and spend my days in the fields and the woods, the rivers and the valleys, taking care of livestock and working with the cycle of the seasons, and I have that feeling every day – but never as strongly as I do when I'm here.'

'You're full of good advice today,' I was unable to resist commenting.

'There must be ley lines and stuff here,' interrupted Jowan. 'I bet there are.'

'Wouldn't be surprised at all,' agreed Dan, ignoring my remark. 'You can't see them, but they're here all the same. And I bet if you dowsed you'd find one going right through the chapel, another through the well and both crossing on the altar.'

'How do you know that?' I asked.

Dan shrugged. 'Just a feeling.'

'Anyway,' said Jowan, 'I have a feeling I need to do something to put things right with the world but I don't quite know what.' He paused. 'Perhaps being a solicitor isn't necessarily the thing for me after all.'

'I must admit, I can't really see you sitting behind a desk all day,' I agreed. 'You've too much fire and passion in you.'

'What then?' asked Jowan.

I shrugged. 'Wait and see how you feel when you've finished at college.'

'No need to rush into things before you know it's right for you,' added Cornelius.

We were silent for a while and it occurred to me how different they all were, yet each a part of the whole. Cornelius and his mind, his books and his words, Jowan and his passion for the past, whether searching out facts or taking part in his re-enactments, and Dan with his feelings, which I already knew ran deeply.

As far as I was concerned they were all right and they were all wrong. It was not one single thing, it was a fusion of all three. Mind, body and spirit.

'Well, I shall do it.' I leaned back against the wall feeling a decision had been made. 'I'll write a little guide book on the history of the chapel. It'll be good for me to know more about it.'

'Then what?' Jowan squatted down beside me and I closed my eyes. There was an energy which I always felt when he was nearby, as if he was plugged into an electric socket and giving off sparks. Perhaps it was because he was so young but it also seemed the way he felt about life, the quest he appeared to be on, continually searching to discover everything he could with such passion. Unlike Dan, who was more like a deep, slow running river, nothing much happening on the surface but all manner of things hidden beneath.

'I think I ought to get more people to come here,' I replied. 'It's such a special place and, although it would be nice to keep it just for me − for us − it somehow wouldn't be right. I've heard people say they come here with problems, sit for a while and feel better. No matter what religion they are, whether they believe in a God or in nothing at all, this is a place for everyone to find their own spirituality.' I stopped. I had never voiced those thoughts before but once uttered, realised how right my words felt.

'I told you. It's all in the feeling.' Dan smiled and looked up from the piece of wood he was whittling.

'All different paths up the same mountain,' added Cornelius.

'What's that?' I asked. Dan was always making something with wood. It was as if he was unable to keep his hands still and they liked to be busy.

He turned the sliver of wood over and shrugged. 'Dunno,' he replied with his slow smile. 'A pendant, maybe. Looks like what it's shaping into.'

'Don't you know?' asked Jowan. 'How can you not know what you're making?'

'You can't always know the outcome when you

begin,' replied Dan. 'Just go with the flow and see what happens.'

'But it's always good to have a plan.' Cornelius frowned. 'I make lists all the time, so I know what I'm doing and don't forget anything.' He laughed. 'I think I must have been a scribe or something in a former life.'

Dan held up his piece of wood which appeared to be shaping itself into a disc. 'Now I can take this home and sand it down and then do a bit of carving. But I don't know what's going to come out until it happens. It's hidden inside until it wants to show itself.'

There was a brief pause, during which nothing more than the rushing of the river could be heard and the croak of a raven, high above. Bracken swayed in the warm breeze and I thought I caught the scent of meadowsweet on the air.

'So, what are you going to do about getting these people to come?' asked Cornelius. 'I mean, you do need some kind of plan.'

'You could have days,' interrupted Jowan. 'Days when people come and see how lovely it is, meet you...'

I laughed. 'Who would want to meet me?' I asked. 'Why would they?'

'Because you're the Guardian,' said Dan.

'Lady of the Chapel,' added Cornelius with a smile.

'Maiden of the Well,' said Jowan. He stopped short and frowned, as if trying to remember something. 'Whatever that's supposed to be...'

'Never mind.' I could see another debate looming. 'We'll think of something but first I need to concentrate on this guide book.'

'Well, exactly how much do you know already?' asked Cornelius.

I paused. I had read bits here and there and a vague outline was forming in my mind but there were still a number of gaps. 'I know St Clether founded his hermitage here,' I began, 'and he was one of the twenty-four children of Brechan of Wales,' I glanced at Jowan and smiled, 'and a lot of his siblings also settled in these parts. I know somewhere along the line the chapel fell down and was restored by the Reverend Sabine Baring-Gould of Lewtrenchard, and the Vicar of Altarnun who was called Reverend Malan, in around 1899. But how it came to fall down and why they decided to restore it I have no idea.' I sighed, feeling rather lacking in knowledge. 'The church itself was almost destroyed by a great fire in 1865. Oh, and Rev. Baring-Gould wrote *Onward Christian Soldiers* and *Now the Day is Over*.' I glanced at Cornelius. 'Remember those from school?'

He nodded. 'Sounds as if you've got a general outline, but there's one heck of a gap in the middle.'

'I know. I need to do more research.'

'There are plenty of shelves of books which need sorting before I can move.' Cornelius turned to me. 'You know, the ones in what we used to call the study. You'd be doing me a favour if you had a look through. You might find something about the chapel and the immediate area. I don't know what I'm going to do with them all really. I don't want to throw them out but they'll never fit into the cottage when the farmhouse is sold. I think I need to have a bit of a bonfire to get rid of the really old junk,' he finished sadly, 'and then maybe get some shelving put up in the spare room of the place I'm moving into.'

'Don't know much about books but I'll give you a hand with making shelves,' Dan offered.

'And I'll help,' added Jowan with his usual enthusiasm. 'Especially with the bonfire. Sounds great.'

'Thanks.' Cornelius smiled. 'Now,' he continued, turning to me. 'What are you going to call this book of yours? How about, *A Guide to St Clether Holy Well Chapel.*'

'Sounds boring.'

'But it's what it's about,' responded Cornelius.

'I think it needs to be more... romantic,' I replied lamely. 'It needs a better title, although that could be a sub-title, I suppose.'

'What is it all about?' asked Dan. 'I mean, what's behind it all which we can't necessarily see?'

'St Clether, I suppose,' I replied. 'He built his hermitage here and gave the place his name, and...'

'It was sort of his legacy to the world,' cut in Jowan.

'*Legacy of a Cornish Saint.*   Perfect,' I cried. 'Thank you, what a lovely name.'

Cornelius laughed. 'You thought of it.'

'But I wouldn't have if it hadn't been for the three of you'. I smiled happily. 'You know, now I've got a title, I really think it's going to happen.'

'Of course it will,' said Dan. 'Everything always works out in the end. You just need to give it time and look in the right place for the answers.'

Fifty

Samhain

It was Samhain. The leaves had fallen from the trees and a chill hung in the air. Across the valley a bonfire was burning and the scent of wood smoke followed me as I made my way to the farmhouse. All around were signs of nature preparing to rest over the coming winter months.

'Where on earth are we going to start?' I surveyed the piles of books and papers which needed sorting before Cornelius could even think of moving out of the farmhouse. Although I had grown up surrounded by all the clutter, I felt suddenly inundated with the amount of stuff to sort through. 'I mean, who on earth collected all this?'

Cornelius shrugged. He was home for the weekend, especially for the Great Bonfire, as Jowan insisted on calling it. Personally, I thought Cornelius was worried about what we might throw out in his absence and wanted to keep an eye on us. 'Some ancestor of mine, obviously. Mother and Father never had time to read any of them so they just stayed here for years and years. I've delved in here and there and made a collection of the ones I'd like to keep, but haven't room for everything. The rest will need to be either taken to a second hand bookshop or burned. Seems a shame but some are so old and mouldy there's no hope for them.'

I picked up a book, blew a shower of dust from the top and made a face. The task of sorting Cornelius' books and having a root through for any information sounded simple enough, but was obviously going to be a monumental task.

'Don't be so negative.' Dan appeared in the doorway, looking like a man on a mission. 'I've built the bonfire. All you need to do is bring out anything you want burned. Quickest way to get rid of it.'

'That simple?' I asked.

'Life usually is,' he affirmed with a grin, 'unless you complicate it, which is what most people seem intent on doing. Just so long as you don't expect me to read any of them. You know what I think about books. Nothing but words.'

'People need stories,' I told him as I began dragging boxes towards the doorway. I pulled at a particularly large one which promptly fell apart at the seams, spilling books all over the floor. 'They need stories to make sense of the world,' I continued. 'They always have and they always will.'

'One man's theory is another man's lie,' replied Dan. 'Here, let me help you. And where's Jowan anyway? I thought he was coming to help.'

'Lost his car keys, I expect. He's always losing something and spending ages looking for it. I've never known anyone as scatter-brained as he is.'

Dan and I bent to shift another box and our gazes locked. I found a peculiar mixture of amusement and care in his nut brown eyes. He was about to speak but was interrupted by the slamming of the front door.

'Hiya.' Jowan's voice drifted towards us. 'Couldn't find my iPod, but I'm here now.'

'Never around when you're needed,' commented Dan, giving me a wink. 'Where's Cornelius disappeared to?'

'Looking at the bonfire you've built. I passed him

on the way in,' replied Jowan. 'He says there are all sorts of nooks and crannies and shelves and cupboards in this house with nothing more than a load of old junk in them, and if he can't sell it, recycle it or give it to charity he's going to burn it.' He grinned. 'I'm game. Love a good bonfire, me.' He stuffed his ear plugs in, switched his iPod on and went in search of Cornelius.

By the time Cornelius and I had sorted piles of stuff to save or burn, the bonfire was well underway. Dan decided he needed to be in charge of keeping the fire under control. 'Jowan will have the entire place burnt to ashes if he's left on his own with it,' he commented, and the two of them disappeared outside.

'Such a lot of stuff,' said Cornelius with a sigh. 'And every time I think I've come to the end I find some more.'

I nodded. It seemed as if the pile we had pulled out and sorted was far greater than the space it came from and still it looked as if nothing had been shifted.

'What are these? Keep or chuck?' I held up a package of papers, grey with dust and tied in a faded pink ribbon with a wax seal. They were so old and covered in cobwebs I was afraid they might fall to pieces in my hands.

'Chuck, no, keep.' Cornelius pulled a face. 'You never know. We must check everything, especially if it's going to be burned.' He peered at the bundle more closely. 'Actually, those look quite interesting. May be an idea to have a look later.' He threw them onto one of the piles as Jowan appeared.

'We're sure to get there in the end, one day...' muttered Cornelius, throwing more stuff randomly behind him.

'No. Cornelius,' I called. 'Wrong pile. You're

getting them mixed up.'

He groaned. 'Right hand doesn't know what the left hand's doing,' he commented. 'It's all this dust getting into my brain, and...' He stopped short. 'Where's the pile?'

'What pile?'

'The pile with the package on. The wrong one, the one to be burned...'

We both noticed Jowan's retreating back at the same time.

'Jowan,' I called. 'Don't take those, they're mixed up.'

There was no reply.

'Jowan!' Cornelius' voice bellowed through the hallway but all we could see was the opening of the outer door and the orange flames in the distance, accompanied by billowing smoke. Dan made his way steadily around the fire, raking in the ashes, keeping it safe.

'Jowan!' I began to run, realising he was plugged into his iPod and would never hear, no matter how loudly we shouted. 'Stop him.' I burst out of the doorway, waving my arms frantically, only to see the dark smoke swirl afresh as he threw the contents of the box into the heart of the fire, a sudden gust of wind causing the flames to flare and greedily consume all they were given. Around the outside the flames burned orange, at the bottom were red embers, but in the middle a white hot ash reduced everything to a twisting, writhing mass. I reached the fire and stopped short.

'What's up?' asked Dan. 'Good fire, eh?'

'Awesome.' Jowan pulled out his earplugs. 'Were you calling me?'

'I... you...' I stopped, out of breath, realising

there was no point in saying anything. It was not Jowan's fault, he was only doing his job. The package might not even have contained anything important. 'Nothing.' I panted. 'Yes, brilliant fire.'

'Plugged into that thing all day so you can't hear and now your eyes aren't working either,' commented Dan with a nod in Jowan's direction. 'Take a look at what you're doing, half the stuff, missed the fire.'

And so it had. The elusive sheaf of papers had been caught by the sudden gust of wind and were now strewn all around the garden.

'Oops, sorry,' gasped Jowan, dashing off to retrieve them. Dan looked at me, grinned and winked as Jowan returned, out of breath but with the grubby papers in his hands. I held out my arms before he had a chance to throw them onto the fire and he delightedly thrust them towards me as if he were giving me a pile of treasure.

Which, of course, he was.

Fifty One

It was evening and darkness had fallen. Cornelius stoked up the range in the kitchen of the farmhouse and Dan raked in the bonfire, which now slumbered gently. Jowan, in a fit of enthusiasm, insisted on brewing a pot of tea and we sat around the kitchen table, the bundle of papers before us.

'It appears,' said Cornelius after peering over the tops of his glasses at a seemingly ancient script in copperplate writing for some time, 'as though these were written on behalf of someone called Rose, by an ancestor of mine called Charles. Fascinating.' He continued to scrutinise the papers closely, shuffling the sheets which had been scattered across the garden into some semblance of order.

'Well,' asked Jowan, impatiently. 'What does it say? Is it about buried treasure? Or ancient spells, or...'

Cornelius looked at me. 'Would you like me to have a go at reading it?'

I nodded. 'Yes please.'

He settled his glasses more firmly on his nose and began.

My dearest Rachel,

I have asked Charles to write this for me as I do not know when I shall see you again and have the strangest feeling that perhaps I never will. Somehow I feel my time might be coming to a close, although I know not why, how, or when.

All I do know is life can be difficult at times and I have never blamed you for staying away, although I wish I had seen more of you. But there are some things I should have told you many years ago and this is why I am writing to you now, so that should anything happen to me, I will have passed my knowledge on to the next generation.

There are stories which I heard at my grandmother's knee, told to her in just the same way, and all are centred around the chapel and the holy well along the valley.

These are only stories, legends passed down and no doubt changed through the course of time but I will leave it to you to interpret them as you choose.

Firstly, from before the dawning of time as we

know it, there is the story of a young girl who defended the sacred well against an evil Magician and retrieved a crystal of great power, although she had to journey to the Otherworld to do so and in the end sacrificed her one, true love.

There is another tale of a young woman who outwitted a band of monks to claim back the well for the Old Ways, becoming a great healer, and finally, a story set at the time when worship at the chapel and the celebration of the seasons was at its height, but one night the Priestess and her Maidens mysteriously disappeared, never to be found again.

It had been foretold that without the Maidens the land would become a wasteland, and indeed, in my time the chapel is no more and the well runs into a muddy pool covered in brambles. I have done my best to change this, but mine is a simple magic and I can only hope and pray it is powerful enough to bring about the changes we need and for the Maidens of the Wells to return, reforging the link between nature, the Otherworld and the people of today.

I have cast a simple spell for the resurrection of the chapel, the return of the Maidens, and for life, spirit and hope to come back to the valley, the chapel and holy well once again.

One more thing I must add. It has always been said that the relics of St Clether disappeared at some point in the past but there has been a mystery surrounding where they were. We recently discovered some bones buried near the holy well. Whether these were the relics of St Clether I do not know but there was a strange feeling as we found them and we covered them over again, feeling it was the right thing to do. I will leave it to you, dear Rachel, or whoever reads this at whatever time in the future, to decide what to do when the time comes.

It breaks my heart to see the chapel and well so neglected but I have done all I can and only trust that when this is read, some change will have occurred.

At times in the past the bloodline of those who care for the chapel has failed, yet always another appears to continue the work, for the forces which guide us and care for the place are infinitely more powerful than we ourselves.

One last thing. There is a carved, wooden box containing some items which have been passed down through the generations along with the stories. Treasure it with care, for although I do not know the history of all the pieces, I feel them to be of great importance and some are of a great age.

And finally, never forget the sun, the moon and the stars. The eternal cycle of the seasons, the four elements of earth, air, fire and water, the ground beneath your feet upon which we all depend for nourishment, the earth mother and the green father.

Remember to journey in the name of love, light and all that is good - and to be aware of the magic which lies all around, a simple magic but always there for those who are chosen.

Take care my dear,
Your loving mother,
Rose.

We sat in silence for a while, the words of Rose clear in our minds, as if she was in the room with us.

'Some lady,' commented Jowan eventually. 'It's sort of magical, isn't it? Wish I'd known her.'

Cornelius nodded. 'Apparently Charles had no

offspring and on his death the house and land went to a nephew and at some point one of the family must have married one of Rose's descendants.' He looked up, understanding dawning in his eyes. 'Do you remember I said he'd given the chapel to someone called Rachel? It's all beginning to fall into place now. If the families intermarried, it would account for the letter being here. I started researching some family history a while back and - of course - Rachel was Rose's daughter. And I do believe you now live in Rose's cottage, Rowena. It's always been a part of the estate.'

There was a silence as we all contemplated Rose's words and their implications.

'When you think about it,' I began, 'shortly afterwards the Reverend Baring-Gould and the Vicar of Altarnun restored the chapel.' I paused. 'Do you think it was anything to do with Rose?'

Cornelius shook his head slowly. 'It's an interesting thought but we'll never truly know.'

'Pure and simple magic is the strongest,' cut in Dan in a firm voice. 'And things often come about in ways you least expect them.'

'It's an amazing story anyway.' I picked up the papers and carefully folded them back into the package. 'I wish I'd known her too, I wish these papers could tell me more. I wish...' A tear trickled down my cheek. I would never have expected to become so emotional but it was as if all my longing for the mother I never knew had risen to the surface in Rose's writings.

'But you know more about her than you realise.' It was Dan who pulled me gently back to reality. 'You look after the chapel she loved so much, you even live in her cottage...'

'And I have her box,' I interrupted. 'The one

mentioned in the letter.' My mind wandered to the small, earthenware bowl I had found in the cupboard beneath the stairs, and briefly wondered if it had also belonged to Rose. I decided to add it to the contents of the box when I got home.

'I think,' said Cornelius, 'you should keep these papers, Rowena. You heard what it said about someone always coming along to look after the chapel. Well, it's you. You're the next in the line.'

'She really is a part of you,' said Dan. He reached out, briefly touching my hand and I felt comforted.

I smiled at him. For an instant our eyes met but I was unable to fathom his expression and turned away. There was an understanding, maybe a love, but definitely a deep knowledge which stretched back further than the short time we had known each other.

'Awesome,' breathed Jowan, completely oblivious to my emotional turmoil. 'What are we going to do now? Can we dig up the relics? Cool.' He appeared about to jump up and rush straight out with a spade to begin.

'Can't,' I told him, 'even if I wanted to - and I'm not sure they're something to be disturbed - but the chapel and the enclosure are scheduled, which means we can't dig without proper permission, and that would take ages, even if it was granted at all.'

'Oh, blow.' Jowan looked crestfallen, then smiled again. 'It's obvious to me,' he continued, before any of us had time to even begin to grasp what he was talking about. 'We have to solve the mystery. We have to find the Maidens.' He grinned, as if he had just solved a puzzle and was expecting the prize.

'And how exactly do you propose to do that?' Dan met Jowan's enthusiasm with a rolling of his eyes, a gesture I had come to expect when Jowan launched into one of his unlikely plans. 'They aren't actually a group of women waiting to be rescued, you know. They haven't just broken down at the side of the road, waiting for a lift. It's a legend, that's all.'

'Have you stopped to think,' began Cornelius in a reasonable tone, 'what this legend is really about?'

Jowan gazed at him. 'Lost Maidens, of course,' he replied. 'And when you come to think of it, I'm the obvious one of us to find them. After all, I spend most of my spare time dressed as a knight and it's just, well, fitting. It's my quest, my duty.'

Cornelius sighed. 'There's more to it than that,' he began. 'The legend of the lost Maidens of the Wells is really all about balance being restored. Look, it's here in one of these books.' He rifled through a box, the contents of which he appeared familiar with and, pulling out a well thumbed volume of Celtic lore, began to read.

The Story of the Maidens of the Wells

'From the beginning of civilization, water has been considered the 'home of wisdom,' and prophecy and wisdom went hand in hand in the ancient world. In classical Greece priestesses took up residence within a nearby grotto or cave and drank the water before going into trance for oracular knowledge.

Once, so the legend goes, every well had its attendant priestess. These were the mysterious 'damsels of the wells' described in a medieval Grail text. The story goes that long ago in the rich country of Logres (an archaic term for Britain), tired hunters or travelers found refreshment at sacred grottos where a spring gushed out. Here they were given food and drink by the 'damsels of the wells,' maidens who were the guardians − or perhaps the spirits − of these holy places. But one day an evil king raped one of them and stole her golden cup, and his followers treated the other maidens likewise. After this the grottos were empty, the wells dried up, and the countryside was stricken with drought:

The land was dead and desert...
So that they lost the voices of the wells,
And the maidens who were in them.

The 'voices of the wells' suggests that the maidens were also oracles. Like the priestesses of ancient Greece, they sat at the entrance to a sacred well, one of the gates into the Otherworld, where they had a direct line to the spirit within the earth. When the Damsels of the Wells were violated, the channels to the Otherworld were severed, leaving the world cut off from its wisdom. Its spiritual riches once so accessible to humankind, were withdrawn: and since then the court of the Rich Fisher which made the land to shine with gold and silver, with furs and precious stuffs, with food of all kinds, with falcons, hawks and sparrow-hawks could no longer be found. In those days when the court could still be found, there were riches and abundance everywhere. But now all these were lost to the land of Logres.'

(Extract from 'Kindling the Celtic Spirit' - Mara Freeman)

'So you see,' he finished, 'it's all really about the

balance between the masculine and the feminine being restored. About the need for both, not one or the other.'

'Sounds about right to me,' cut in Dan. 'I always say if you want to know what's right, you look to nature. And there's always a balance.' He pulled himself to his feet. 'Now the bonfire is well and truly finished, I'm going to leave you good people to your books. Thanks for the tea.'

Cornelius followed Dan to the front door and Jowan turned to me, a deadly serious look in his eyes. 'I'll find them,' he murmured softly. 'I'll find them and then you'll have your Maidens of the Wells back again.'

I laughed, but Jowan shook his head. 'It's my duty, as a Knight of the Realm.' He touched my arm. 'I'll do anything for you and justice will be done. You just wait and see.'

Fifty Two

Lunar eclipse

It would soon be my birthday and I found it impossible not to look back over the past couple of years and marvel at how much had changed since the day the chapel first came into my care - meeting Dan and Jowan, discovering Rose's letter. The year continued to turn, the February snows clearing away to leave drifts of snowdrops and bulbs beginning to shoot, fresh and green in the crisp air.

My birthday, or the day on which Cornelius found

me, was the 4th March and this year fell on the full moon which was also to be a lunar eclipse. And I had plans. I wanted to go to the chapel, spend time there in the moonlight and then, later in the night, experience the eclipse. And I wanted to do it alone.

'I'll come with you,' offered Cornelius, who had returned for a few days especially for my birthday.

I guessed he would offer and was ready. 'Thanks, but I really want to go alone. I want to get the feel of it there, find the magic if you like.'

'It's all in the feeling,' agreed Dan, 'but if you want me to just be around to keep watch...'

'What's the point of that?' asked Jowan. 'You're afraid of the dark.'

Dan sighed. It was a sore point but he really did have an intense fear of darkness. 'I've got a big torch,' he said eventually.

Again I smiled but shook my head. 'Nothing's going to happen to me. What possibly could?'

'You might disappear forever and we'd never find you again,' suggested Jowan, as usual over the top with his ideas. 'You need me to protect you. I'll dress up in my knight's costume and bring my sword and frighten off any unwelcome visitors.'

I laughed out loud. 'You've been listening to too many legends, the lot of you. I'll be perfectly fine and it will be good to have a bit of time there to myself. I've always wanted to go by moonlight. Well, this is my birthday and it's what I'm going to do.'

The matter was settled and as the day passed into evening I prepared for my vigil.

It was a clear night as I set off for the chapel, but as it was still only March I wrapped up warmly. I had left a sleeping bag and blankets there earlier in the day, and now carried a large flask of tea. Any ideas of romantically sitting in the moonlight in a long, flowing gown had vanished long ago.

The moon was well risen as I approached, the lunar eclipse timed for the early hours of the morning and I did not want to spend too long waiting. Just enough time to enjoy the silver moonshine for a while and attune myself to the valley at night. Secretly I hugged myself. This was the best birthday present ever.

The river glinted in the moonlight below me and the dark shadows made the silver of the landscape stand out. To my right the towering rocks stood like shining sentinels and a great white owl flew low over my head along the valley, as if showing me the way.

All was still as I passed through the wooden gate, the catch sounding unnaturally loud in the night air and I finally pushed open the door of the chapel. It was just as I imagined it would be. The moonlight filtered onto the altar stone, transforming the cluster of snowdrops left earlier into silver and the altar glowed eerily with a life of its own. The musical sound of trickling water was all which could be heard and, as always, I felt a sense of safety, of coming home. I laughed to myself at the thought of the others being so concerned at my wellbeing, for what ill could possibly befall me here?

There was a deep silence, save for the sound of the water which blended into the night. Otherwise, all was cold and shining silver. I laid my hands upon the altar, ghostly pale in the moonlight and lit three candles, causing the chapel to spring into light, shadows flickering all around. I almost felt myself to be a spirit of the chapel already.

Outside the moonlight touched the water in the holy well, scattering diamonds over the surface which fell in a silver cascade as I allowed it to trickle through my fingers. I wondered, if I remained long enough gazing into the water, I might see some Well Maidens of the past looking back at me, sending a message down through the years, but there was nothing save the gentle flow of water and the moonlight shifting upon its surface.

My mind traced back to the solar eclipse, when my crystal had so mysteriously disappeared and I almost imagined that, should I plunge my hand into the well on this magical night, my fingers would grasp it lying at the bottom in wait for me, returning through a doorway in time - but a part of me knew this could never happen.

After a while I made my way back into the chapel, pulled out my sleeping bag and poured myself some tea. I had no intention of becoming cold during the wait for the start of the eclipse, and suddenly the enormity of my actions began to sink in. I wondered exactly how safe it was for a woman on her own in the middle of nowhere on a cold spring night, and I also began to wonder exactly what I would see or hear. How many people in the past, I wondered, had carried out a similar vigil and what had become of them? For an instant I wished I had taken up Cornelius' offer of company, Dan's of watchfulness or Jowan's of protection. But it was too late now, and eventually I decided to go outside to experience the moonlight and wait for the eclipse to begin.

I was looking out over the valley when I first sensed the movement behind me. There was a prickle at the back of my neck and a tingling sensation, causing me to turn towards the chapel and he was standing there in the moonlight. I breathed a sigh of relief.

'Thank goodness. You scared me for a moment then. What do you think you're doing creeping up on me like that? And what are you doing here anyway? I thought you were afraid of the dark.'

He grinned. 'You be careful now,' he said, 'this being a time of such magic and all.'

'I'm fine.'

'I'll hang around for a bit if you like, just make sure you're safe.'

'No really, it's something I need to do on my own.' I was touched, half of me wanting him to stay, but I knew this was something which had to be done alone.

'All right, but just be careful of the portal,' were his last words before disappearing. I was unsure where he had gone, not through the gate, I was certain. I imagined he must have climbed up behind the holy well to walk back along the top of the valley. But it was strange, I thought, Dan coming out, knowing how much he disliked the darkness.

Time ticked onwards, for it waits for no man, woman nor Well Maiden, but is merely marked by the turning of the stars, the rising of the sun, moon and ever changing seasons. I was musing upon this as I wandered back into the chapel to refill my cup with tea and as I did so, thought of the Maidens of the Wells and the way they had offered refreshment to passing travellers. But that was merely symbolic, I realised, to the nurturing of the spirit they gave, and in that moment I understood the true link between the Otherworld and the everyday, subtle yet strong, and realised how desperately mankind was reaching out for spirituality, for balance, for an end to disillusionment and fighting.

I noticed a slight darkening in the air. The glow of the candles appeared brighter and I returned outside. The shadow of the earth was beginning to make its way across the face of the moon. There was a strange feeling in the air as the night darkened even more and I hoped Dan was safely home.

As the shadow moved, almost covering the moon, I felt a foreboding in my heart, a desolation and fear, greater than any I had ever felt before in my entire life. The valley had turned from silver, to black, to red. Blood red and it was as if the light had gone out of life itself. There was no sound, even the rushing river appeared to have been dampened by the heavy, oppressive feeling and, unable to bear it any longer, I fled back into the chapel.

'What are you doing here?' I stopped short, surprised by the sight of Jowan, kneeling before the altar, dressed in his tunic, forehead resting upon the hilt of his sword. I breathed a sigh of relief. 'I know I told you not to come,' I babbled, 'but I'm really glad you did. It's spooky out there. Don't you think? Jowan?'

There was no reply, nor did he move or show the slightest acknowledgement of my words, remaining still as a statue in the ever increasing redness of the night, until finally he gave one, long sob, filled with fear and confusion, which burst from deep within him. I stood, unsure whether to touch his shoulder in an attempt to comfort him or if it would be best to leave him alone.

After a few moments I made my way outside again and around to the holy well, almost stumbling as my hands touched the chapel wall for guidance, the night red around me, the shadows darker than they had ever been before.

The surface of the water in the holy well

glittered, but dully now, as if glinting with blood in the moonlight, which was no longer moonlight, but a parody of all that was good.

It was then I saw them and heard their voices. It began as a note on the trickle of the water, mingling softly with others, until my head was filled with sound and the cries of women, and then I saw in the shifting shades of the water, their hands reaching up, begging for freedom, needing to be rescued.

'*Without the Maidens of the Wells the land will become a wasteland.*'

The voice rang out clear and strong, echoing down the years, reaching out to all the women who had gone before me – and I realised the voice was my own.

I pulled back. Nothing like this had ever happened to me before. I was not a person who saw spirits or heard voices from the Otherworld. But there was no mistaking the vision and I knew that for as long as I lived, it was a moment I would never forget.

My mind raced back to Jowan, alone in the chapel, and suddenly I wanted nothing more than to be with him, for him to rescue me from this nightmare, to laugh and assure me there was nothing to be afraid of. Then we could make our way home together, leaving the desolation of the night behind us and think about it all in the morning when, in the clear light of day, everything would seem better.

I stumbled back to the chapel doorway, my eyes blinded with tears and pushed the door open. 'Jowan,' I croaked, his name sticking in my throat. 'Jowan, I...' I stopped short, stunned. The chapel was empty and there was no sign of him at all. 'Jowan?' I surveyed the flickering candlelight, the place he had knelt before the altar, empty now, reflecting the feeling within me - and then I became aware the light was changing. The chapel was a little less red, the moonlight growing stronger and I ran outside to see the shadow moving across the moon, the shades of redness passing along the valley, the brightness of the night returning.

'I think it's time to come home.' I spun around to find Cornelius standing at the gateway. The latch clicked as he entered and I was never so grateful to see anyone in my life. I flung myself into his arms and he held me tight, protecting, comforting. 'I thought you might have had enough by now,' he continued in a matter of fact sort of voice. 'The others wanted to come but I told them there'd be trouble if they did, so I took it upon myself...' He paused, briefly holding me away from him as he scrutinised my tear stained face. 'Looks as if I made the right decision,' he commented.

'The others?' I was feeling better now, safer, the presence of Cornelius bringing me back to reality. 'But they were here,' I protested. 'They must have come anyway without telling you. Earlier, Dan was here. I couldn't understand him coming out in the dark like that, and not long ago Jowan, in the chapel...'

Cornelius gave me a strange look and his arm tightened around me. 'Let's pick up your stuff and get you home,' he said gently. 'You've been deluded by the moonlight. Dan and Jowan have been at my cottage all evening fretting about what might be happening to you. Jowan was all for charging out here to rescue you or some such thing and Dan kept muttering about keeping an eye on you and you never knew who might be about in the dark. Couldn't do a thing with either of them.'

We gathered everything together and Cornelius blew out the candles, leaving the chapel in darkness.

'But they were here...' My voice trailed away.

Perhaps I was going mad. After all, I had heard the voices of the Maidens of long ago, an experience I felt unable to relate to Cornelius at that moment; but as we stumbled back along the pathway and the silver moon began her descent in the night sky, I knew what I had to do.

Fifty Three

The Awakening
Being the Story of the Maidens of the Wells

The moonlight shimmered on the water and caressed the rocks with silver as Ellie walked softly along the path. Her shadow cast a dark smudge on the dim grass and in the sky above a thousand stars twinkled, only obliterated by the bright halo of the full moon. As she rounded the curve in the path the standing stone shone white before her and she paused, her hand resting on its cool surface, feeling the enchantment of the night air. In the distance an owl hooted.

As she approached, the chapel loomed dark and slightly foreboding, protective of its treasure in the brightness of the night, but as she gently opened the door moonlight flooded through the window, bathing the altar in pure, white light. Ellie shivered. It was cold as ice. Walking towards the altar she felt a tingle – not from the coolness of the floor beneath her feet or the air around her, but from the sheer power which emanated from the place.

Ellie paused. Tonight was the night of the lunar eclipse, the full moon falling on her birthday, and she knew without a shadow that it would be special. The synchronicity was amazing and she briefly thought back over the last seven years to the solar eclipse, when she had first felt the power of the chapel; and the link between herself and the women of the past had coursed through her. Tonight, seven years on, she wanted to feel the power again.

She had nurtured that link of course. During the intervening time Ellie had tended the place and grown to love it more than she loved anything else. She had cleaned the well, swept the floors, brought fresh flowers to the altar; always aware this was the reason for her being. It was as if she was a part of the place itself, at one with the power which lay latent beneath the trickling waters and the sheer beauty of the valley.

Outside, the holy well lay in dark shadow, occasionally catching a sparkle of moonlight as it overflowed and gushed through the chapel. The flow was strong tonight and Ellie felt a wave of anticipation for events to come. All was as it should be. All was waiting.

Inside, Ellie settled herself, hands upon the altar. The water played its own symphony as it trickled beneath and Ellie fancied she heard the voices of women and snatches of music hidden amongst it. Sometimes high notes, at others low, mingling together in a wonderful cacophony of sound. A gentle breeze rustled through the open door and the granite altar glinted and sparked in the moonlight.

Ellie waited. Slowly, the moonlight began to fade,

the altar becoming less luminescent in the darkness until she could no longer see her hands before her. She breathed deeply, awaiting the rush of energy which would connect her to the women of the past, anticipating that feeling of being at one once again. But as the light dimmed, Ellie felt the first stirring of a foreboding deep inside her - a feeling of unutterable pain and misery. Just as previously she had felt an upsurge of power, now she felt repression, depression and despair.

Ellie snapped her hands from the altar as if they had been scorched. Running to the door, she found the moon overcast by the shadow of the earth, blood red in the sky. As she watched, a bank of low cloud closed in, turning the moon from red to dull pewter, eventually leaving a murky smudge in the sky, like grey ash.

Slowly, Ellie gazed around her. Gone was the enchantment of the moonlit night. Now, all she could see was deep, dark, blackness.

During the days which followed, the unbearable sense of sadness continued. Not only did Ellie feel she had lost her link with the past, she found herself losing faith in all she believed. The anticipation of the lunar eclipse had come to nothing and as the days wore on she found herself questioning her destiny, wondering why she had spent the last seven years thinking she had a role to fulfil, believing she had a special place in the greater picture.

She dreamed. Colourful, vivid, lucid dreams of the valley, not as it was now but subtly different in landscape; of women, their faces appearing before her and their voices calling out of the darkness, at times soft and sad, at others hard and filled with distress. She awoke and walked, anything to escape the nightmares, yet always found herself back at the chapel, looking into the dark depths of the well and catching flashes of faces in the water, hearing voices in the rushing of the stream, crying out, wanting to be heard – but Ellie could make no sense of it all, again and again turning away despondently only to begin the cycle once more.

She tried to forget the living nightmare which had woven itself around her, infiltrating the fabric of her life, weaving insidiously into her subconscious, a reminder of her failure and loss of faith, but nothing could shift the visions from her mind nor the emotion in her heart.

Weeks later, she discovered a small book lying on the altar, old and well thumbed, almost falling to pieces when she touched it. The pages felt damp to the touch but she took it outside into the sunlight and settled herself upon the wooden bench, feeling the warmth upon her face and watching the river flash diamonds below her. Above, the ravens called and tumbled against the bright blue sky and for a moment Ellie felt soothed, forgetting the haunting misery, once again revelling in the beauty of the valley and her love for the chapel and well.

A gentle breeze stirred, caressing her face and bringing her back to the present, and Ellie looked down to find that in the warmth of the day the pages had dried, now crackling like autumn leaves, and beautifully scripted illuminated letters shone like jewels.

The Legend of the Maidens of the Wells

Long, long ago, all of the sacred Wells of the land were tended by Maidens, who gave refreshment to travellers from golden chalices. A traveller had only to arrive and a Maiden would issue forth from the Well to provide sustenance. These Maidens were sometimes known as the Voices of the Wells, for they were also oracles, forming a link between this world and the Otherworld, for at the sites of the Wells the veils between the worlds are thin. Because of the existence of the Maidens of the Wells the land flourished and was filled with beauty and contentment.

One day, the evil King Amangons raped one of the Maidens and stole her golden chalice, using it as a trophy for himself. His men did likewise, although it was their role to protect the Maidens. Subsequently, the Maidens were forced into the Otherworld and from that day on they tended their Wells no more.

But without the Maidens, the Wells fell into disrepair, no sustenance was offered to passing travellers and the land became a wasteland as the Maidens and the reciprocal link with the Otherworld had been lost. The land was overcome with drought and misery, no longer rich and filled with the abundance of before.

Many years later, King Arthur and his knights vowed to find the Maidens of the Wells and indeed, discovered that they were not dead but living in the Otherworld still.

This legend is a part of the Grail Legends and can be found in many of the texts relating to the stories from this time.

It speaks of the repression of the feminine aspect and the need for balance in the physical and spiritual world. It is about understanding the importance of the two worlds, the masculine and the feminine, and their coming together to make a whole. When the Maidens of the Wells were abused and no longer perceived as sacred, the reciprocal link between the worlds was broken, their voices fell silent and the land perished.

As in all cycles, the time will come when the Voices of the Wells will be restored and the offering of sustenance, both physical and spiritual, will be given to all who are in need.

Ellie's fingers shook as the book slipped from her grasp, momentarily disorientated, feeling she had returned from another place, another time. Now she understood the reason for the dark foreboding in her heart.

The women who had passed before her, the voices which called through her dreams and in the trickling of the water, were the Maidens of the Wells, repressed, forced into the Otherworld - and she felt it too. As surely as she had experienced the surge of pure energy at the solar eclipse, now she shared their degradation and despair. Ellie's eyes burned with tears.

But with her new found knowledge Ellie felt a flicker of hope. She hadn't lost the link after all. It was pure and true, stronger than ever before and pulsating with life. The Maidens of the Wells had disappeared but were still alive – in her. Ellie jumped up. She wanted to sing and dance, shout her discovery throughout the valley, to the river below and the rocks above. Two ravens flew overhead calling in acknowledgement, their blue-black wings whirring in the sunlight; and Ellie felt the enormity of the tradition of which she was a part.

A living legend – a legend which had never died but simply been hidden – now returned to continue into eternity.

Ellie laughed out loud – a laugh of pure happiness. She was a modern day Maiden of the Well. She would bring the legend alive once more. In this day and age, people needed spiritual refreshment more than ever before, and she realised this was what the chapel and the valley were all about. A sacred space to reconnect with the past and restore the balance.

Around her the trees shone with the bright green of spring, the hawthorn heavy with the delicate white blossom of the may. The rustle of new life was all around her, the eternal cycle continuing as it always had and always would.

For the second time in her life, just as seven years ago she had finally understood where her true destiny lay, Ellie knew what she had to do.

She reached for the book, but it was nowhere to be seen. Only a tiny scattering of brown dust lay upon the bench beside her as a reminder it had ever been there at all.

And a moment later, that too, had disappeared.

Fifty Four

Beltane

It was early on Beltane morn when I walked to the chapel along the riverbank. The sun glinted upon the heavy dew, causing the droplets to flash like jewels of yellow, orange and red. As I made my way along the path I spotted a movement amongst the drooping willows and my mind was taken back to the day Dan and I first met. Was it by the riverbank or at the chapel? I never really understood what happened that day, but as he stood and waded across the river I saw this was unmistakeably Dan and he smiled in welcome, climbing out of the water to give me a guiding hand through the last of the boggy ground - taking slightly longer than necessary to let go.

'You're out early,' he commented.

'May morn,' I replied. 'It seemed fitting to come to the chapel.' I surveyed the pinnacle of rock towering above us, swathed in white blackthorn blossom, green hawthorn and crowned with golden gorse. Below, on the slope down to the river the first bluebells shimmered.

'I've brought a few flowers.' I held up my bunch of fresh cow parsley, bluebells and red campions. 'You?'

'Been doing a spot of fishing.' He paused. 'Peaceful. Helps me think.' He glanced towards the chapel. 'Can I come up with you?'

'Of course.'

We made our way along the grassy slope together, the valley slowly coming to life around us, patches of frost and mist rapidly dispersing as the sun

302

came through more strongly. A heron rose from the riverbank, its wings flapping heavily in the cool morning air. When we finally arrived Dan sat on one of the wooden benches whilst I arranged the flowers, as always rejoicing in the simple beauty of the altar, the sparkling water and the sunlight filtering through the windows.

Suddenly Dan chuckled. 'Jowan and his Maidens.' He shook his head, an amused smile playing around his lips. 'He really thinks he's going to find them, you know.'

I nodded. 'I hate to disillusion him,' I agreed, sinking down onto the bench, 'but what can we do?'

'He's young,' commented Dan. 'He'll learn.'

'Learn what?' I asked. The chapel felt cool in the early morning air and I shivered. Dan hesitated for a second, then put an arm around me.

'That magic isn't quite as he thinks.' His arm shifted but he did not let go. 'I know I'm always saying it's in the feeling but it's true. It's subtle. A clue here, a hint there, and if you aren't looking out for it the magic can be right under your nose and you wouldn't see it. There are no flashes of light or puffs of smoke. It's all in here.' He put his hand to his chest.

'Look at Rose,' he continued. 'She was an ordinary woman, but a wise one. Hers was a simple magic, carried out for good and the healing of the local community. And it worked. She might not have received many thanks for it and if she did, it would only have been a loaf of bread or a comb of honey, but these things are not done for payment. People who create real magic, real healing, go about their work quietly, they don't shout about it and tell everyone how wonderful they are. There are no thanks and no rewards. It's just something they have to do.'

I gazed at him, realising there was so much more to Dan than met the eye, so much more for me to learn about him, and suddenly I wished with all my heart I would have the opportunity to do so, for in that moment I realised I loved him.

He took my hand in his. 'And the real magic,' he continued, as he looked steadily into my eyes, 'is the way I feel when I'm with you.'

Fifty Five

Midsummer

It was Midsummer's Eve when Jowan found the Maidens.

Dan and I were sitting outside the chapel. I had been given a present, a simple, wooden bench inscribed with the words, *Peace is the sound of heaven on earth*. It was fashioned of oak, fitted its surroundings perfectly and was placed beneath the rowan tree at the corner of the enclosure, giving a view of the chapel to the left and the valley to the right. Dan and I had enjoyed a simple picnic and life could not have been better.

'So peaceful,' murmured Dan. He took my hand. Ever since Beltane we had grown closer and now our lives were entwined as one. He smiled at me and there was no need for words. The sun was setting behind the brow of the hill across the valley and I wondered, as I often did, what stories the other side of the river held. How many people had gazed across at the chapel over the years, finding it nestling beneath the tall rocks in the shelter of the valley, and how many had crossed to the chapel, perhaps not knowing what it held but always, as I was beginning to discover, it held the power to change lives.

'What about these 'days', then?' Dan stirred beside me and I pulled my attention back to the present. 'When are you thinking of beginning?'

I shrugged. 'I know it was ages ago we thought of it but time's slipped by and other things got in the way.'

'But it hasn't been wasted. You've done a lot.' Dan surveyed the new gate which replaced the rickety old one, fashioned in oak and carved with a Celtic cross. And the new, wider path which traversed the most dangerous part of the field where people had often slipped in winter. This had been constructed to allow safer access to the chapel so more people could make the journey.

'It's the roof next. Every time I find a slate's come off it worries me. They say it needs doing within the next five years but it's going to cost a bomb. Grants are difficult to obtain and take an age to come through and I might not get one anyway.'

'Look on the positive side,' replied Dan. 'Make a plan. You've got a few years in hand. Start now. Look at grants and help and suchlike and in the meanwhile, start these 'days', get people interested and coming just like you wanted and make it a two-fold thing. Raise money for the roof too.'

'How?'

'I don't know. Sponsor a slate or something. Anything which raises money towards getting the roof fixed, let's people know what you're doing and makes them feel a part of it. I think you'll find they want to help. A lot of people come here and you shouldn't have to bear the brunt of it all by yourself.'

I surveyed the undulating roof, remembering how worried I always was someone might be injured. 'I think you're right,' I began, a slow certainty growing within me which rapidly ignited the first spark of excitement. 'When shall we start?'

'No time like the present,' said Dan.

'No.' Once again, I was overcome with the enormity of it all. 'We need a bit of time to get organised. We need to do it properly.' I thought for a moment, my gaze resting on the gate with the Celtic cross carved in it, then smiled. 'How about St Clether's Feast Day? November 4th. Also close to Samhain and the beginning of the Celtic New Year. It all fits perfectly. Let's start then and do them all.'

'What do you mean, all?'

'The eight Celtic festivals of the year.' My excitement was taking hold now. 'Midwinter Solstice, Imbolc, Spring Equinox, Beltane or May Day, Summer Solstice, Lammas, Autumn Equinox and back to Samhain and St Clether's Feast Day again.'

Dan looked at me in amazement. 'You been doing your homework or something? You seem to know a lot.'

I grinned. 'I've been talking to Cornelius. We've had long discussions about religion over the Internet, especially the way so many of them reflect the same ideas but with different stories, even falling on similar dates. There's so much conflict in the world, especially between religions, but as Cornelius always says, and he's right, it's all just different paths up the same mountain. That's why these days should be for everyone. A time when anyone can come and be welcome.'

We were silent for a while as the sun sank lower on the eve of the longest day of the year. 'Very wise, is Cornelius,' commented Dan. 'Jowan could do with a bit of his common sense. But he's young.' He grinned. 'I wonder if he's found his Maidens yet.'

We both laughed. Since the day of the bonfire, Jowan had been on his own special quest to find the lost Maidens with a passion which, Cornelius commented dryly, he would have been better putting to his studies. But that was Jowan, half of him seemed to be in one place and half in another. And as his relentless search for the lost Maidens appeared to take the form of dating as many young women as he possibly could, just in case one was a lost Maiden in disguise, he had been having an entertaining time.

'Rowena,' began Dan, taking my hand again and gently tracing the back with his finger. 'There's something I've been meaning to ask you.'

I turned to him. The moment was magical, soft rays of sunlight fading to pink and gold in the sky, the valley mellow from the heat of the day. A lone bird flew along the skyline and I heard the croak of a raven overhead. Apart from this there was silence, save for the rushing of the river below as the valley settled into itself for the night. I felt at one with the world, sitting with my hand in Dan's and such peace and beauty around us. In that moment everything was perfect.

'Rowena,' repeated Dan, gazing into my eyes, 'do you think...'

There was a crash as the wooden gate banged open and the spell was broken, the magical moment lost. Jowan stood before us, dressed in his white tunic bearing the red and gold emblem of a lion, his sword at his side. He looked wild eyed and his mouth opened and closed as if he was unable to find the right words but was desperate to get them out.

'Jowan.' I rose to my feet, ran over to him and took his arm, guiding him to the bench. 'What's happened? Are you all right? Is something wrong?'

He was agitated, gasping for breath, having apparently run all the way along the pathway from the church.

'Calm down,' advised. Dan. He glanced at me. 'Get him a drop of water or something. He's out of breath, that's all.'

I hurried into the chapel to find a plastic cup and dipped it into the well, where it filled with clear, pure water. 'Drink this.'

Jowan grasped the cup gratefully and downed it in one gulp, but his breathing became steadier and we were finally able to understand what he was saying. 'Found them...' he began.

'Found what?' I wondered what he had lost this time. His car keys? House keys? Important documents? iPod? There was no end to the stuff Jowan might have lost and found.

He gave me a pitying look. 'The Maidens of course,' he explained importantly between gasps. 'I've found the lost Maidens of the Wells.'

Dan and I exchanged glances. I paused, choosing my words carefully. 'Jowan,' I began, 'have you been drinking...'

'No.' He jumped up, grasped my shoulders and looked straight into my eyes. 'I've found them,' he repeated in almost a whisper. 'I've found them for you.'

'Where are they then?' asked Dan. 'And where

308

did you find them?'

Jowan looked smug, seeming to return to his normal self. 'You just wouldn't believe it,' he began, recovering his breath and getting into his stride. 'They're on their way here now, coming along the path from the church. That's why I ran on ahead, I wanted to tell you before they arrived. So you'd know who they were,' he finished.

'How did you know we'd be...'

'Cornelius,' interrupted Jowan, 'on his way here to join you and Dan. We picked him up and he's bringing them now. Can't let them escape this time, you know.'

I had the sudden vision of a line of Maidens bound with rope, being herded along the path by Cornelius. 'Perhaps,' I suggested, handing Jowan another cup of water, 'you'd better sit down and tell us what happened. Right from the beginning.'

'Well,' began Jowan, obviously relishing every moment of his tale, 'you know I've been on this quest to find the lost Maidens of the Wells for you...'

'Yes,' I replied hastily. 'We know all about that.'

'And you know they say when you stop looking for something you find it.'

I nodded, a smile twitching my lips. If I had a pound for everything Jowan had found when he was searching for something else, I would have been able to pay for the roof myself.

'Well, I decided today I'd probably never find them. I mean, it was a bit of a wild goose chase after all. Fun though.' He paused and grinned. 'But I reckoned it was about time to knuckle down and get on with some work and then decide what I want to do, just as Cornelius suggested. In fact,' he smiled shyly, 'I've made a bit of a decision. Unusual for me, I know, but

I've come to the conclusion I don't really have to be a solicitor to bring justice to the world, and you're right, I don't really see myself sitting behind a desk every day. Surely I can do something I enjoy which helps other people too. Maybe to do with museums or something, but anyway, it's my duty to myself to find my own path in life and do something I really want.'

Dan winked at him. 'That's my boy.'

'Anyway,' continued Jowan, 'I was on my way to a re-enactment at Tintagel and just as I was deciding to stop all this running around looking for Maidens and concentrate on my studies a bit more, I went round a bend in the road – I was a bit late as I couldn't find my keys earlier and took a short cut through some back lanes - and almost ran into the back of this van which had broken down there. It was a VW camper van,' he explained. 'You know the sort. And I got out and found these three girls there.'

'So you found the Maidens broken down at the side of the road waiting for a lift,' commented Dan dryly.

'No.' Jowan turned to him quite seriously. 'They were slap bang in the middle of the road blocking the way. No one could get through. One was peering into the engine – it's in the back you know,' he added importantly, 'and the other two were looking sort of lost and helpless.'

'But you don't know anything about engines,' cut in Dan. 'You don't know a spare tyre from a spanner.'

'I know that, and you know that, but they...' Jowan tapped his nose and grinned again. 'Well anyway, what's a knight to do when there are three damsels in distress? There was no signal for them to phone for help and they were broken down and lost.'

'Lost?' I asked. 'Didn't they have a map?'

310

'That's the odd thing,' explained Jowan slowly. 'They were on their way to Tintagel too, for the re-enactment, but they'd come from miles away and were completely in the wrong area considering where they'd come from. And when I asked if they had any idea at all where they were they said they'd been lost for ages. Apparently they'd stopped for a picnic earlier on, had a bit of a walk and just got back in time to see some yobs on bicycles making off with their food, drink, cups, plates and map.'

'So they were lost, hungry and thirsty, had their cups stolen, you found them, a knight in, sort of, shining armour, and decided they were the lost Maidens,' finished Dan.

'Not exactly, there's more.' Jowan looked as if he was about to produce a white rabbit from a hat. 'You see, I poked about with the engine a bit but nothing much happened – obviously. Then I wandered round to the front, just to check their tyres, you know,' he explained, 'and I saw it.'

'Saw what?' I was beginning to wish he would get to the point.

'The writing on the van, of course. On the side of their van was painted in great big letters, along with a lot of purple and yellow flowers, nicely done though, in a hippy sort of style, but in great big letters it said, *The Maidens.*'

'And?'

Jowan looked at me in exasperation. 'Do I have to explain everything?' he asked. 'They're a band. A trio, called *The Maidens.* On their way to a Midsummer's Eve gig at Tintagel, miles out of their way, lost, alone – and rescued by me!'

'But if you and the girls were on the way to the

re-enactment at Tintagel,' I began slowly, desperately trying to sort it all out, 'what are you doing here?'

'Ah, that's the tricky bit,' replied Jowan. 'I know, I really do know I should have taken them to Tintagel so I could be in the re-enactment and they could play their gig. I did know,' he repeated, a slightly troubled expression crossing his face, 'but it's been my quest to find the lost Maidens for so long. And in the end I just couldn't take them to Tintagel, I had to bring them to you. I just had to,' he finished quietly.

'You could have brought them another day,' I suggested gently. 'Tomorrow, maybe, or the next.'

'But it's Midsummer's Eve,' replied Jowan. 'I don't know why, but it was like a big crossroads in my life, a bigger decision than it could ever really have been, and although my head told me I should have taken them to Tintagel, I did what I felt was right. Here, in my heart.'

'Oh, Jowan.' I flung my arms around him and hugged him tightly. 'You really are a knight with a true heart and I thank you from the bottom of mine.'

'Here they come now,' commented Dan, and we turned to see Cornelius making his way along the path followed by three young women. And indeed, as they approached I could see why Jowan had been so taken with them, for they were dressed in Medieval costume, each with flowing hair entwined with flowers, and carrying an instrument. In that moment I had to admit, if ever the Maidens really were to return, this was exactly how they would have looked.

Cornelius ushered them through the gateway and Jowan all but ran over to them.

'This is Morwenna,' he began, introducing a pretty girl with long, black hair, a green dress and carrying a violin. 'This is Tamsyn.' Tamsyn smiled and nodded, her golden tresses shining in the evening light. She wore a white dress and carried a flute. 'And this is Demelza.' Demelza was auburn haired with a deep, blue dress and slung across her back was a small harp.

I stared, entranced.

'Nice to meet you,' began Tamsyn. 'I don't suppose you have drink, do you? We're parched.'

'I'm so sorry, I'm forgetting my manners,' I replied. 'Only water, though. Would that be okay?'

All three nodded gratefully and promptly settled themselves upon the wooden bench as I hurried into the chapel to find some more cups.

'Lovely place,' commented Morwenna. 'Glad we got lost now.'

'Glad we got found, you mean,' added Demelza, with a wink in Jowan's direction.

I filled the plastic cups with water from the well, clear, pure and sparkling in the sunlight and carried them to the Maidens. 'Drink and be refreshed,' I murmured and they each took a cup and drank gratefully.

There was a moment of silence and I looked up to see Cornelius, Dan and Jowan staring at us all, different expressions on each of their faces. Upon Cornelius' was a look of profound understanding, as if an idea had finally slotted into place. Jowan wore an expression of absolute pride as he gazed at the four of us, and Dan... Dan looked as if he was about to burst into laughter and was unable to hold it back very much longer.

'What?' I asked, unable to fathom it all. 'What's the matter?'

'I found the Maidens for you,' said Jowan.

'They've returned,' said Cornelius. 'Symbolically,

of course,' he added, as the trio looked at him, puzzled expressions on their beautiful faces.

Dan burst out laughing. He laughed as I had never heard him laugh before, until the tears ran down his face and the valley echoed with the sound of it. 'For goodness sake,' he finally sputtered. 'Must I do everything? Jowan, you've found *The Maidens* and very well done indeed. And yes, Cornelius, it has all slotted into place, quite amazingly in fact. But the thing we've all missed is what's been right under our noses the whole time.'

We stared at him in complete bewilderment.

'The real, living, Maiden of the Well has been here all along.' Dan reached over and pulled me into the centre of the little circle. 'Who cares for the chapel and loves it more than anything else in the world? Who's written books and stories about it, who's keeping it repaired and open for visitors and who's going to get more people to come and one day have the roof repaired so it's safe for another hundred years? Who,' he finished with a flourish, 'pulls the snails out of the well, washes the floors and keeps flowers on the altar all year round?'

All eyes turned upon me and suddenly I was aware of all I had done, that being a Maiden of the Well was not simply sitting around looking beautiful and giving oracles, but a role which changed with time – this was my time, there was a lot of hard work to be done – and I was doing it.

"Scuse me,' said Tamsyn, breaking the stunned silence. 'But would anyone care to explain exactly what's going on?'

Fifty Six

We remained there all through the night until the sun rose on Midsummer's Day to find us laughing and talking still, and we toasted the sunrise with water from the holy well which I handed to each of the others.

During the course of the night, *The Maidens* played their music, the violin, the flute and the harp, and sang, their voices echoing through the valley, filling it with moonlit magic, whilst inside the chapel the musical notes mingled with the trickling water.

'Truly a night of Medieval magic,' commented Jowan, as *The Maidens* played a particularly lovely piece and the sun rose above us.

'What is that?' I asked them. 'It feels so fitting, yet I've never heard it before.'

Morwenna smiled shyly. 'It's a song we've composed especially for you in honour of this night. It's been so wonderful we felt it should be remembered somehow and so...' she shrugged. 'This is our offering.'

'Play it again, please,' I begged, 'so I can hear the lovely melody and listen to the words.'

'We can sing them in Cornish and in English for you,' replied Demelza with a smile, 'for we are all Cornish speakers.' They picked up their instruments and, once more, began to play and sing.

Fenten Glether

Orth Fenten Glether ha ni ow 'sedha,
Ha klywes spyrys an tir,
Han Bronn Wennyli yn hons dhe'n gelli,
Warnedhi 'ma kommol pur hir.

Yma Dowr Ynni ha son an bryni,
'Kesseni war alsyow a-dro,
Ha'n redden ow sia, an eythin a via,
Ow poppya yn tedhes an howl.

An teylu a Glether a dheuth 'mes a Gembra,
Dhe gavoes Sansoleth Kernow,
Y kevyn y enev, pyth eus hwath genev,
Pupprys pan av yn-dann y do.

At Clether's Well whilst we were sitting,
And hearing the spirit of the land,
And Brown Willy yonder the wood,
On top of her there was very long cloud.

There is Inny Water and the sound of the crows,
Echoing on the surrounding cliffs,
And the ferns are buzzing, and the gorse would be,
Popping in the sun's heat.

The family of Clether came out of Wales,
To seek the sanctity of Cornwall,
We find his soul, that is still with me,
Always whenever I go under his roof.

The music ceased and we remained silent for a while, enjoying the sounds of the valley around us.

'Oh, we forgot to give you this.' Tamsyn felt around in her bag. 'Where is it?' she murmured. 'Have you got it, Demelza? Don't say we've lost it?'

'Lost what?' I asked, feeling a replay of Jowan's antics coming on and wondering how young people always seemed to be losing things and getting lost.

'Something we were given earlier,' explained Morwenna. 'For you.'

I looked surprised and Tamsyn began to explain. 'When we wandered down to the river late last night, there was some bloke there, standing in the moonlight, and he asked us to give you this. Blow it,' she continued. 'What on earth did I do with it?'

'Some bloke?' I asked in surprise. As far as I knew there had been no one around but ourselves. 'What sort of bloke?'

'All dressed in green and holding a stick,' cut in Demelza. 'Nice sort of chap, I thought, and there was a woman too, but she was on the other side of the river and we couldn't make her out very well. Wearing a long dress though.'

'Looked pretty in the moonlight,' added Morwenna. 'Don't worry, I dropped it in the well to give it a bit of a wash.' She turned to me. 'Go and have a look, I think you'll like it.'

'What did this bloke say, exactly?' I asked. 'I mean, did he tell you who he was and why didn't he come up here and give me whatever it is, himself?'

Demelza shrugged. 'Dunno. But he did say something about it needing to be returned to you.'

'Go on,' urged Tamsyn, her beautiful eyes shining. 'Have a look. I think you'll like it.'

I smiled, humouring them but feeling slightly excited nonetheless, wondering what on earth this mysterious object could be which the girls had been given to pass on to me by some unknown man on the riverbank. It all appeared very odd, but then again, today everything seemed strange.

I rounded the corner of the chapel and knelt before the gently flowing waters. The sun was rising steadily now, we had been awake all night and, despite the excitement, I was beginning to feel drowsy. As I knelt before the clear water there seemed to be a change in the light and other faces gazed back at me. A girl with short, curling hair, then one with long, dark hair entwined with flowers, a woman with hair piled high upon her head and finally an older woman, her hair traced with strands of silver. I blinked and they were gone, then remembering my reason for being there, I plunged my hand into the water and felt around.

My fingers closed over it almost immediately and I knew what it was even before my hand left the water, droplets of diamonds spilling back onto the surface like miniature waterfalls. But I had no time to ponder on the beauty of the early morning sunlight, for in the palm of my hand, as if it had never been away at all, lay my beautiful green and violet crystal.

Fifty Seven

We were basking in the Midsummer's Day sunshine, reluctantly deciding it might be a good idea to pack everything up and return to my cottage for something to eat and a rest, following the revels of the night, when I first noticed them approaching.

Something struck a chord in my heart, although at the time I could not understand why, but I suddenly felt chilled in the warmth of the sun and glanced around, grateful to be surrounded by so many friends, although they were all inside the chapel at the time.

There were four of them, dressed in black. Big men, the sort, I felt with a shiver, you would not wish to encounter on a dark night. The gate clicked as, one by one, they entered the enclosure and stood gazing silently at the chapel, then the eyes of the biggest and the blackest alighted on me, sitting alone on the wooden bench.

I shrank before his gaze as something inside me shrivelled up, fighting the urge to run, wanting to call out to Dan, to anyone who might come to my rescue, but I was frozen in time, trapped in a moment which had its roots centuries before and was unable to drag my eyes away. It must have been the blood pounding in my head or my heart beating, but I could have sworn I heard the sound of hoof beats, and the call of a bird in the distance reminded me of voices crying in the night.

He glanced around again and I noticed the tattoos upon his forearms, dragons writhing and twisting, as he took out a roll up which he slowly lit and took one long, deep drag, a look of satisfaction crossing his face.

'Jowan!' Why I called Jowan at that point I never knew, but he was the first to come into my mind. 'Jowan!' I repeated, panic beginning to grip me although I was trying not to show it. I rose to my feet, aware I was still alone and then the man spoke.

'Awesome place,' he murmured. He withdrew the

roll up from his lips, looked at me – and then he laughed, his blue eyes crinkling in his whiskery face, the sound ringing around the valley. 'Ain't it grand?' He turned to his companions who nodded and began to advance towards me - but the moment the first man had spoken I knew there was no danger, for it was as if the clouds had rolled away revealing the bright, shining sunlight.

'Art.' Jowan appeared from the chapel, a look of delight upon his face.

'How you doin' mate?' Art gave Jowan a manly hug which almost crushed him. 'Brought the lads, just like you said.'

The lads, almost but not quite as burly as Art, nodded, appearing to be men of few words.

Jowan turned to me, his face alight with excitement and pride. 'This is Arthur,' he began, 'but everyone calls him Art. And this,' he gestured towards me proudly, 'is Rowena.'

Jowan ushered me forwards and Art took my hand gently in his. 'Charmed, I'm sure,' he murmured softly and his blue eyes twinkled.

'Will, Sean and Stu.' Art gestured towards the others who, only moments before, had appeared so dark and foreboding, now smiling and handsome in the morning sunlight. 'Young Jowan here asked us to look over, seems you need a few jobs doing, clearing and suchlike and we'll be glad to help out.' He grinned. 'We've plenty of muscle between us and do a fair bit of this sort of thing, clearing land, felling trees, all for the good of the environment, of course. Call ourselves the Green Knights we do, although afraid we're dressed in black today on account of being at the re-enactment last night. Black Knights we were then.' He laughed.

'But we're ever so nice really. But for you, for a friend of Jowan's and for this awesome place,' he took another drag, gazing around as if he was unable to believe how lovely everything was, 'we're happy to help you out for nothing. Be a pleasure!'

I did not know what to say but could only do what I had done so many times in the past, invite them in and offer them refreshment – which they gratefully accepted.

'I really think we must be getting back now,' I commented, after the Green Knights had met everyone and appeared more than impressed with the Maidens.

'Great, isn't it?' commented Jowan.

We were sitting together on the bench once again and I felt a sudden rush of gratitude towards him. 'Jowan,' I began. 'You've done so well. You've found the lost Maidens and you've brought the Green Knights... Although I must admit, I was pretty scared for a few moments when they first appeared. But you've brought them here to help me with the work which needs doing. I just don't know how to thank you.'

'Aw, it's all right, you know I'd do anything for you.' Jowan looked shy and I put my arms around him, giving him a hug and a big kiss on the cheek, making him blush even more.

'I'll tell you what,' I began, 'all this talk of duty and feeling you have to do the right thing, well, you've fulfilled your duty as far as I'm concerned and now I think you should be free to do whatever you want in life. Whether it's being a solicitor, or a builder, or a brain surgeon, or...'

'As it happens,' interrupted Jowan with a slight

smile, 'I've been thinking of doing something along the lines of Art and his mates. Maybe to help the environment, you know, even change my college course or possibly take an apprenticeship but to do with protecting the land and making sure it's treated in the right way. And Art says I can help them out any time. What do you think?'

'Oh Jowan.' I gave him another hug. 'It's a brilliant idea, and just the sort of thing I can imagine you doing. Dan'll be delighted, you know how he loves the countryside.'

'Come on everyone, time to get home.' Cornelius' voice broke the moment and I rose from the bench feeling everything I ever wished for had come true all at the same time.

Picking up our stuff we made our way back along the valley, a long, straggling line of Maidens, Knights and Guardians, until we reached the church car park where Jowan had left his car and Art and the Green Knights their vehicle, a huge, black 4 x 4, gleaming in the sunlight. But on the ground beside it lay three bicycles and, to our horror, three youths attempting to break into the truck.

'Oy!' It was Morwenna who spotted them first and broke away from the rest of us, running towards the car park. 'Stop them,' she yelled. 'It's the yobs who took our stuff.'

The youths looked up, grinning smugly at the sight of her, then their smiles faded as Art appeared, surprisingly nimble on his feet, followed by the rest of the Green Knights.

'Not so fast.' Art's arm shot out and grabbed the largest of the lads around the neck. 'And what do you think you're doing, eh?'

The youth wriggled and squirmed but it was no use, and then the others were firmly captured by Stu and Sean, while Will checked to see if any damage had been done.

'It's them,' repeated Morwenna, jabbing her finger, eyes wild with rage. Tamsyn and Demelza nodded in agreement.

'What did they do?' questioned Sean.

'Stole our food, our map, our cups...' Tamsyn glared at them. 'Left us in the middle of nowhere with nothing to eat or drink and no way of finding our way...'

'Not a very nice thing to do, was it?' asked Art, and the lad he was holding shook his head mutely.

'I think,' said Will, after discovering no real damage had been done, 'they'd better come along with us for a bit, don't you?'

Art nodded thoughtfully. 'Nothing else for it,' he agreed.

Stu glanced at me and winked. 'Don't worry,' he said. 'We'll sort them out.'

Fifty Eight

We were in my garden, resting after the events of the previous night, unable to sleep and enjoying the scent of roses and honeysuckle around us. Following the discovery of The Yobs, as *The Maidens* insisted on calling them, we had retired to my cottage, Yobs and all, much to Morwenna's disgust, for she had been intent on marching them, bound and gagged, to the nearest police station.

But to my surprise Art intervened. 'We all make mistakes,' he told her, 'and these here Yobs, as you call them, just need something worthwhile to do. I have a feeling they'm not so bad as they seem. Misguided perhaps, but not all bad. Leave 'em with us for a bit and you'll see a difference.'

Morwenna said no more but shot them dirty looks, until I began to wonder if the Yobs ended up more afraid of *The Maidens* than they were the Knights, for I began to see a softer and more understanding side to Art than I ever would have imagined.

'They'm goin to be all right,' he assured me later. 'Bored, that's all they are. They'm coming to help me and the lads do a few jobs for you. Give 'em somethin' worthwhile to think about. And they'll replace what they stole from you and they want to apologise,' he added, turning to Morwenna, Tamsyn and Demelza.

'Well,' began Tamsyn, 'if you really think so.'

'Lance. Tristy. Perce. Come here,' called Art.

The lads appeared, looking apprehensive. 'Sorry we took your stuff,' muttered Lance.

'Yeah, and thanks for not calling the police,' added Perce.

Tristy nodded. 'We'd have been in dead trouble. We'll make it up to you.'

Demelza grinned, looking amused. 'Interesting names, you have,' she commented.

Lance blushed. 'Yeah, we're really Lancelot, Percival and Tristram. We're brothers. Our parents are great fans of the Arthurian legends.'

Morwenna snorted with laughter. 'Well, I think you might just have found the real thing, now you've met King Arthur, here.'

'You weren't very chivalrous,' scolded Tamsyn, 'so

you'd better change your ways if you know what's good for you.'

'But we're part of the Green Knights, now,' said Lance. 'For a bit anyway, aren't we?' he asked, glancing at Art.

Art grinned and clapped him on the shoulder. 'Course you are,' he replied. He looked at me and winked. 'Give me a year and a day,' he said, 'and everything'll be different.'

Fifty Nine

'Do you ever see spirits in the chapel?' asked Demelza. They had all finally left, and only myself and *The Maidens* remained. Demelza, Tamsyn and Morwenna were staying the night while the others retrieved their van and got it on the road again. It felt nice just the four of us at last, like old times, although we had only met the previous evening.

'I had the feeling of a monk standing inside the doorway to the right, and also of a Guardian, a feminine one with a very ancient energy,' Demelza continued.

I smiled. 'Funny you should say that,' I replied. 'Many people have spoken of the monk, but try as I might, I've never seen him. I'm in no doubt there are many spirits around but none have ever shown themselves to me.'

'But you wrote these lovely stories.' Morwenna had been reading *The Dawning* and *The Awakening*, which I had printed into little booklets and left in the chapel for sale, along with *Legacy of a Cornish Saint*, a small, token start towards funds for the roof. 'I have a feeling,' she continued slowly, 'you see and feel more than you realise. You might not actually see Spirit but you've written these stories which have come to life through you. And there must be hundreds of tales of people throughout the ages. I'm sure if you sat down and allowed them to come, you could write more.'

I nodded slowly, remembering the energy which filled me when I had written the first two, and indeed, always felt the words were not my own but came from a higher place.

'Perhaps I'll try,' I ventured. 'But how would I know where to begin?'

'What about your monk?' questioned Morwenna. 'He has a story, to be sure, and maybe he wants you to tell it. After all, he's a Guardian of the well too and who better to relate his story than you?'

I was taken with the idea, it stayed with me over the coming days, and almost before I knew what was happening, had written the story of the Monk and the Maiden, or, as it was eventually titled, *The Scent of Meadowsweet*.

The Scent of Meadowsweet

Many people had seen him in the little chapel over the years. So much so he was something of a legend, at least amongst those who could see spirits or ghosts. Time and time again a visitor mentioned him standing in the corner beside the entrance door or by the altar. It was thought from his attire he'd been there for hundreds of years - but for what reason? Was he a long ago Guardian still acting out his role or was he waiting? And if so, who or what was he waiting for?

She ran through the tall grasses of the fields, crushing meadowsweet underfoot and releasing its soft scent as she approached the river. Her breath ran ragged as she pelted helter skelter down the slope and, on reaching the river, plunged in and waded to the other side, the water icy on her warm legs. She was barefoot but certain of every step and, pulling herself up onto the grassy bank, paused for a moment to survey the roof of the church in the distance, further up the hill.

She could hear the low chanting of the monks, their voices riding softly on the warm breeze which stole up the valley on the late summer afternoon, touching the high rocks above, swirling around the church and carrying the melody down to the river. High above a raven soared, its croak strangely mingling with the low chant emanating from the church. Close to the surface of the river dragonflies swarmed and occasionally a flash of iridescent blue or green settled for an instant upon her bare leg. She smiled contentedly, sank down amongst the rushes and meadowsweet, and waited.

He knew she would come. Even after he'd told her not to because it was against his faith and the rules of his Order, she never stopped coming, and now he looked for her every day. Throughout the chanting of the Brothers and their daily rituals in the church, increasingly his mind was not upon his act of worship, but upon her.

He should have taken action, stopped her or told Prior John, but each time he considered it, something deep inside stopped him. Every day, after the Brothers had left him to finish his work at the church she had come, barefoot through the tall grasses, meadowsweet clinging to her legs bringing with her its own special perfume. He'd look up, pretending not to notice, only for his heart to leap as she made her way upwards from the riverbank and, more often than not, would be alerted she was near by the overhead croak of a raven.

And now, when she arrived, he had only to look into her eyes to know he was lost – and would wait for ever.

'So what is this legend about a monk here?' asked Lizzie as she wandered around the little chapel. It had been dark and cool to enter after the heavy heat of the day and the walk along the valley from the churchyard. Before entering it she'd instinctively kicked off her shoes and the cold stone floor had given her a jolt but was now refreshingly cool. She immediately felt a sense of peace, as if, just for a moment, her cares had been lifted from her shoulders and time stood still. The gentle trickle of water running through the chapel soothed her and the stone altar was cool to the touch. Someone had arranged vases of midsummer flowers, cow parsley, foxgloves and meadowsweet all round the chapel, and the sweet, heady perfume overtook her senses, making her feel slightly disorientated.

'He's standing by the door now,' replied Jo. 'When we came in he was beside the altar, then he seemed to be aware of our presence and came right over to us and now he's just there, in the corner. But I can't see below his knees. Maybe in those days the floor was lower than it is now.'

Lizzie stared into the darkness of the corner but could see nothing other than a mishmash of stones in various shades of grey. She sighed. She loved visiting places like this with Jo, but sometimes felt frustrated when Jo was able to see spirits or ghosts wherever they went, whilst she was never lucky enough to see a thing. 'What does he look like?' she asked.

'Youngish,' replied Jo, in a matter of fact tone, as if she were describing a real person. 'And he has a habit tied at the waist. And brown eyes.' She paused. 'Kind eyes, with a hint of sadness. He's looking at me... and now he's looking at you, looking right into your face, in fact.'

Lizzie tried very hard to tune in, to imagine the elusive monk which Jo could see so readily, but it was no use. In the end she wandered outside again, leaving Jo to commune with the monk, and sat on the low wooden seat overlooking the valley.

Although she knew they would both be in terrible trouble if their secret was ever discovered, she could never stop herself visiting the church to be with him whenever she was able to get away in the afternoons, when the Brothers had left and he was there alone. Sometimes they just sat and held hands, at others made their way through the high bracken to a place no one would find them and they could forget for a short while that she was a farmer's daughter and he one of the Brotherhood.

'It says here...' Jo's voice interrupted Lizzie's

thoughts. There was a feeling of timelessness sitting looking down over the valley. Ravens croaked overhead and the bubbling river could be heard clearly. The scent of meadowsweet hung in the air. 'It says here this used to be the parish church before the current one was built by the Normans.'

'I think some people are coming,' replied Lizzie, noticing a small group of heads bobbing along the path in the distance. She stood up. 'I'll just have another moment inside before they get here.'

He'd been waiting for months now and she hadn't come. Each day, with increasing frustration he watched the Brothers wend their way through the valley, perform their rites and make their way back again, dark, heads disappearing into the distance. High summer turned to autumn, a chill hung in the early morning and late evening air. The trees changed from green to golden brown, but still she did not come. Eventually the frosty nights and snow gave way to the new life of spring. Nothing. Each day he waited for her, longing to hear her soft footsteps on the slate floor and feel her gentle touch. But she did not come.

'You will wait for me, won't you?' she'd strangely asked at their last meeting. 'Promise you'll wait for me, whatever happens. And for as long as it takes?' He hadn't thought much of it at the time, he always waited for her and always would, and he kissed away her words as the shadows lengthened and they spent longer together than ever before. Maybe too long. Looking back, perhaps she'd

known something he hadn't.

'She was sent away.' He looked up, startled to hear the voice of Prior John cut through the quiet of the church. He must have waited until all the Brothers had left and returned alone. 'Please understand, I'm here to help you.' He placed a hand gently on his shoulder. 'She was with child, her father was furious and sent her away, although she refused to tell him who the father was.'

He was speechless with shock. Why had he not known before? Was this what she had spoken of at their last meeting?

'I'm sorry.' Prior John's voice was kind and low. 'She died in childbirth and will never come here again.'

'You knew?' His voice was hushed.

Prior John nodded. 'I worked it out in time,' he replied.

Lizzie wandered into the chapel, the floor soothing to her bare feet and walked to the altar. There was a deep sense of peace here, like she'd visited before and was coming home. And there was something else. She stood for a moment, only the faint trickle of water playing in the background. It was as if the place was telling her something, desperately wanting her to hear. She wished she had Jo's gift and knew what the monk wanted her to understand.

He'd seen her enter the chapel and known immediately who she was. After all this time waiting, he knew she would come again, one day. As she entered the *door his heart jumped and he felt alive once more, crossing the chapel swiftly to stand beside her, but she was unable to see him. Her companion had though, and he looked into her face willing her to pass on his message, then into his beloved's face, wishing he could hold her in his arms again, just once more, but of course it was impossible and she didn't even know he was there. Consumed with frustration he paced the chapel after she left. Now she was back again and he was standing right beside her. He put his arms around her and kissed her gently on the forehead just as he had hundreds of years ago, as overwhelmed with love as he'd always been and suddenly the frustration disappeared and he felt a great sense of peace. They were reunited again, however briefly. Every second of his waiting had been worthwhile, every moment which had seemed such an eternity dissolved in an instant, because just to see her face and touch her once again was all that mattered.*

Lizzie stared at the corner where she thought the monk was standing but still could see nothing. She sighed, feeling her time alone was limited before the walkers arrived and the silence shattered. She was suddenly overwhelmed with a feeling of love like she had never known before. It was as if arms had been wrapped around her and she was enveloped, loved and cherished for all eternity. A shiver ran through her and she felt the faintest touch of breeze upon her forehead, although the meadowsweet remained still in the vases and nothing stirred the delicate lace of the cow parsley. She sighed, feeling she had come home and was where she belonged.

'He's gone,' called Jo from the chapel as she closed the door. 'How strange, that monk, his presence was so strong but there's no sign of him at all now. Most peculiar.'

Lizzie was silent as she surveyed the valley. Outside, something had changed, although she couldn't quite define exactly what. Maybe it was to do with the shadows along the valley or the colours of the landscape but something was different. On leaving the chapel she felt as if she'd left a part of herself inside - where it belonged.

'I don't know what happened to your walkers,' commented Jo as they retraced their footsteps back to the churchyard. 'They never appeared. Hey...' she laughed. 'Perhaps after all this time you managed to see some ghosts of your own.'

Lizzie smiled. She didn't think so, but she had felt something very special back in the chapel, an intense feeling of peace, contentment, love - and an overwhelming relief she'd never experienced before.

She glanced down towards the river and saw a flash of movement. Two figures stood on the riverbank, their distant laughter hanging in the air and as she watched they jumped barefoot into the river to paddle. They were holding hands and then they embraced tightly as if they would never let each other go again.

But when she looked a moment later they were nowhere to be seen. And the scent of meadowsweet hung softly in the warm summer air.

Sixty

Autumn Equinox

It was autumn equinox, the time of balance when the days and nights are of equal length before tipping towards the darkness, heading for the winter solstice and the shortest day. Dan and I were walking along the valley by the riverbank in the late afternoon sunlight. The hawthorn was already heavy with red berries and the blackthorn bore sloes, waiting to ripen before being harvested for wine or jam. The swaying, green bracken was dying back and swallows swooped around us in final flight before their journey to warmer climes.

'I want to show you something.' I took his hand and led him from the path towards the rocks which towered above us, guarding the valley as always. 'This is where I found the crystal, years and years ago.' I ducked beneath the branch of the spreading beech tree, noticing the brown hazel nuts which already lay upon the ground - the colour of Dan's eyes - and leaned against the soft, white rock covered with thick trunks of ivy and green moss.

Dan hopped over the branch and joined me. 'What an awesome place.'

I nodded. 'And look, there's a little cave here, beneath the rocks. It doesn't look much but you can crawl right into it and that's where the crystal was, tucked inside, as if someone had hidden it there.'

Dan bent to examine it. 'I've never been here before,' he began. 'It's a sort of magical place, not far from the path but so well hidden – yet it feels familiar, like a safe little haven.'

I agreed. There had always been something about it which made me feel secure, ever since I was a child and used to hide there on rainy afternoons.

'Come on.' I took his hand once again. 'Let's go up to the high rocks and watch the sunset. I've brought something to show you.'

We scrambled back over the tree and followed a rough path through the bracken to the field above the chapel, heading for the highest pinnacle of rock. Once there, we wriggled our way to the edge and looked down. The view was fantastic. Despite spending so much time in the valley, this was a place I rarely visited but, whenever I did, never failed to be amazed at how much could be seen. The valley stretched before us, a strip of lush green, the river its centrepiece, whilst on the other side of the water a great expanse of hillside rose. Below us the granite rock fell away steeply and a number of rowan trees grew beneath, their leaves dark, berries of yellow and orange turning to red in preparation for winter. To the left the chapel nestled, safe and secure. It was, quite simply, yet another special place.

'Look.' Dan pointed and I squinted into the sunlight. 'Deer.' And indeed, two roe deer were making their way along a pathway through the dying bracken, walking at first, then bursting into leaps and bounds, their white tails bobbing.

'Dan produced a flask of tea and we lay stretched out on a blanket in companionable silence, watching the valley and enjoying the sunshine. 'What have you brought to show me?' he asked eventually.

I reached into my rucksack and pulled out the carved wooden box. 'I don't know what you'll make of this,' I began, 'but I've had it since I was a little girl. It was Rose's, but I used to pretend it belonged to my mother.' I paused, the loss of someone I had never known still with me. 'Anyway, some of it's quite old and I thought you might be interested.'

Dan raised himself onto one elbow and took the box, examining the intricate carvings on the lid, tracing them with his fingertip. 'Beautifully crafted,' he commented. 'Can I open it?'

'Of course.'

He sprang the catch and the lid lifted, revealing the contents inside. Dan stared at them for a long time before taking out the crystal. He turned it over and over in his hands. 'Is it the one you lost?'

'Yes and no,' I replied. 'I don't think it's the actual one, I mean, how could it have been? But it's so similar it's spooky. It could almost be it, in fact, if I didn't know the original had disappeared and couldn't possibly have been given to the girls, I'd say it was the same.'

Dan held the crystal to the light where it sparkled for a moment, catching the late rays of the sun, before laying it carefully upon a flat piece of rock and picking up the wooden disc, turning it over in his hands. 'Looks like a pendant,' he commented. 'See this is where there would have been a piece of leather threaded through. Very old though and I can't really make out the markings.'

I bent closer. 'I've always thought it looked a bit like a tree.' I traced the ancient lines with my finger. 'What do you think?'

Dan smiled slowly. 'I think I'm the one who's spooked now, because I've brought something to show you too.' He dipped into his pocket and I recognised the piece of wood he had been carving all those months before. He held it out to me. 'I made it for you,' he explained, 'with my love.'

He dropped the piece of wood into my hand and I gasped, for there lay another pendant, strung on a band of leather, round and beautifully carved with the spreading branches of a tree. He slipped it over my head. 'Yew,' he continued. 'For infinity.'

'Thank you.' I didn't know what else to say. Words seemed inadequate.

'Now,' Dan broke the spell of silence. 'What else is there?'

'Well, there's this little silver chalice.' I pulled it out and Dan examined it carefully.

'Very old,' he mused. 'You could get it valued although I don't expect you'd ever want to sell it.'

I laughed and shook my head. 'And this stump of candle and this little earthenware bowl. Oh, and this twisted stick.'

Dan turned the stick over in his hands. 'Rowan,' he confirmed, 'the tree of protection. You don't find these often. It's had honeysuckle growing around the branch which has given it the twisted effect.' His fingers gently caressed the silver wood before laying it down and picking up the objects one by one, inspecting them carefully. 'These were Rose's tools,' he commented after a while. 'The chalice, the bowl, the candle, the stick - wand if you want to be precise - they're all to do with working magic.'

'Really?'

'Course they are,' replied Dan. 'I've told you before, hers would have been a simple magic, no flashes and bangs or streaks of lightning. Just a candle for fire, a handful of earth, some herbs for the air and water in the bowl, or the chalice used on special

337

occasions, and there's even a wand here to direct the energy.'

I gazed at the items afresh, finally understanding their significance after so many years.

'And there's this.' I fished out the brown, flint, spearhead and dropped it into his hand. At the same moment a shadow passed fleetingly across the face of the descending sun and Dan blinked. 'Now that really is old,' he said.

'I had someone look at it once, and they thought it was probably Bronze Age. Three thousand years ago or more.' I paused. 'Makes my head spin just to think of it sometimes. That someone so long ago crafted it, used it, lost it maybe, so it was found again and ended up here.' I shivered in the sunlight. 'You okay?' I noticed Dan was turning the spearhead over and over in his hands, as if he was unable to believe what he was seeing or was trying to retrieve a memory he could not quite grasp.

He shrugged. 'Like you say, makes your head spin.'

I nodded as Dan carefully placed everything back into the box. 'And each one has a tale to tell,' he murmured as he dropped the spearhead in and closed the lid. 'I wonder if anyone will ever know what their stories are.'

We sat a while longer, finishing the flask of tea as the sun sank towards the horizon. 'D'you want to wait to see the sun go down?' I asked.

There was no reply.

'Dan?' I repeated. 'Do you want to see the sunset or shall we go back?'

I turned, expecting to find him stretched out and dozing but his eyes were wide open and he was staring at the vanishing sun as if he was unable to tear himself away.

'I hate it,' he whispered. 'The twilight, the darkness. Especially at this time of year when the nights get longer and it seems for ever until the days begin to lengthen again.' He looked at me and I saw real fear in his eyes.

'But there's nothing to harm you.' I took his hand in mine and held it firmly, realising he was trembling. 'The darkness can't hurt and there's nothing to be afraid of.'

'I know.' He nodded and gulped, holding my hand even more tightly. 'But it's always been with me, ever since I was a child, and the fear, it starts deep down here, in my stomach, and fills my entire body.' He swallowed. 'There's something to do with the twilight, the deepening twilight moving into darkness and a fear of being left, alone, abandoned.'

I put my arms around him and pulled his head onto my shoulder. 'You'll never be alone,' I whispered, tears chocking my voice. 'I'll always be here for you, I promise.'

The evening was darkening, the twilight turning to blackness. We sat in silence for some time, my arms encompassing Dan, his head turned into my shoulder as if he was unable to face the dark.

I swallowed, unsure of what to do next. Slowly, as the darkness closed around us, the stars began to appear one by one in the night sky. I was aware we were getting cold and pulled the blanket we had been sitting on around us both. 'When I was a little girl,' I began, 'I used to make up stories in the stars. I used to join the dots of the pinpricks of light in the sky and create pictures in my mind and from those pictures make up tales of long ago.'

There was silence but I knew he was listening.

'And I learnt from the stars and my stories that there's nothing to be afraid of, not really. Everything moves in its own cycle, the sun, the moon, the earth, the seasons, the days, hours, minutes, seconds. There needs to be a balance in all things, darkness and light, happiness and sadness, for without one, the other cannot exist. The higher we climb, the further we fall. The deeper we love, the greater the pain of loss. And the darkness and winter months are merely the other side of the coin to the sunlight and the summer.' I paused, wondering what to say next.

'I know,' came Dan's muffled reply. 'I know, but it doesn't stop me feeling the way I do.'

I cast around in my mind, trying to think of a way to replace the negative thoughts which had taken hold of his mind with positive ones. 'You're never alone,' I whispered eventually. 'You of all people should know that. Even if you can't see them, there are spirits watching over us and, as you so often say, their message is subtle, you only have to look for it.'

'Then,' whispered Dan, 'why can't I see it? Why is it all I can see is darkness?'

I drew a breath, unsure of how to reply, for if Dan felt this way despite the strength of his faith how could I possibly show him otherwise?

Then I saw it.

'Dan.' I pushed him gently away from me. 'Dan,' I repeated. 'Look. Look now.'

He raised his head and there were tear stains upon his face. 'Darkness,' he murmured. 'That's all I can see.'

'No.' I shook my head, taking his hands in mine.

'Take your own advice, you're looking in the wrong direction. Look down into the valley, towards the earth.'

While we had been sitting, Jowan, for I could see him clearly silhouetted in the doorway, had visited the little chapel and lit candles all around and now it blazed with light, a beacon of love and hope in the darkness of the night.

'You see.' I put my arms around Dan once more and kissed him. 'It's all still here, even though you can't see it. Nothing is ever truly lost, only hidden. You were just looking in the wrong place. The spirits, friends, love and light are all around us. You need never feel alone again.'

Sixty One

Samhain

The first of what I came to call my 'days' dawned fair, even though it was early November and could have been cold, damp and miserable. But it was as if the Gods smiled upon us and sent warmth and sunshine to the early winter light, giving the valley a feeling of new beginnings, and once again I felt the dots joining and the pattern of my life emerging.

I arrived early. Although no one else would be appearing until mid morning, not even Dan, Jowan and Cornelius who had all promised to help, I wanted everything to be perfect and needed to do it alone. As I walked along the path from the church to the chapel the frost was fading from the ground, remaining only where the grass lay in shadow and any mist still hovering over the river and in the folds of the valley dissipated fast. I clicked open the gate and my day began.

The previous afternoon I had decorated the chapel with flowers and foliage, fitting for the time of year, bracken turning from green to brown, branches covered in lichen, berries of rowan, and candles all around. Samhain, All Saints Day, and even St Clether's Feast Day seemed to be about remembering the past, and the chapel had even more than its usual air of peace and tranquility about it. As I was to do many times in the future, I checked all was well and lit the candles, their warm glow chasing away the last of the chill in the air, giving the building a feeling of reverence.

Outside the holy water ran swiftly, carrying its melodic song into the chapel and through to the lower well, and here too, I lit candles in any sheltered crevices I could find.

I set up everything for the day. After all, I was a Maiden of the Well, and it felt fitting to offer refreshments to those who visited. With a gas burner and a silver cauldron I brewed hot, spicy, punch and placed out a tray of home baked biscuits. Finally, I was ready and waiting.

It was still early when I eventually sank down upon the wooden bench and surveyed the landscape around me, a landscape I had seen a thousand times yet never tired of watching, for it was never exactly the same. I felt comfortable sitting alone in the cool air of an early winter morning, the ravens calling overhead as though welcoming me back and wishing me good fortune for the day as I warmed my hands on my first cup of hot punch.

I closed my eyes and waited. There was no sign

of anyone and I tried to imagine how it would be when people eventually began to arrive, to traverse the pathway from the church, to visit the valley, to be welcomed, to find their own peace. I hoped they found their journey worthwhile. I hoped they would enjoy and find pleasure in everything I had prepared for them. I hoped...

And then the doubts began to set in. What on earth was I doing, I wondered, sitting here in the middle of nowhere on a November day, surrounded by food and drink and actually expecting people to turn up? And if they did, what would they find? A perfectly ordinary woman who thought she was different, who imagined she was doing something special, but was very likely deluded and would end up looking a fool. After all, the inner voice which was taking an increasing hold on me whispered, who was I to do this? Who was I to presume anyone would be interested and how could I possibly organise such an event and be the right person to do so? There must, I finally concluded, be a hundred other more worthy people who should be sitting here now. Not me, Rowena, of parentage unknown, who just happened, quite by chance, to be given a chapel and believe she was the Guardian of the Well.

I closed my eyes, felt the prick of tears which I knew were about to fall and was aware that, once started, nothing would stop them. For in the great scheme of things I was of no importance at all. I wondered if it was too late to run back to my cottage, leaving everything as it was for anyone to find, should they arrive, and if they enjoyed their visit all well and good, but it would be nothing to do with me. I wondered how I would explain my actions to Cornelius,

Jowan and Dan, who had been so supportive, and in that moment I felt all my plans were no more than sunlight and shadows dancing on water, which could dissipate at any moment.

The click of the gate roused me and I opened my eyes but no one was there, only a flurry of white wings in the distance and the rustle of a small animal in the undergrowth.

'Why me?' I asked silently. 'How did I possibly think I could be the one to do this?'

And a whisper crossed my mind. *Because you are the only person who can. You are the chosen one.*

I looked up again. Still no one around, yet I had the sensation I was not alone, as if someone had passed behind the chapel in the direction of the holy well and, so strong was the feeling, I rose to follow.

Wear the crown, Rowena. Wear the crown.

I paused. There it was again, no more than a whisper at the back of my consciousness, so soft and subtle I could barely hear it. But I knew I had.

Wear the crown. What did it mean? What crown? And all at once I saw myself, as if from a great distance, standing in the place I had loved so many times before, over many lifetimes, and I knew this was my crown and I had returned to receive it. Everything which had happened all through the years, since the beginning of time, rushed towards me as if on wings and I realised I had been the Maiden, the Mother and now it was time for me to wear the Crown, the crown of wisdom, the crown of a job well done.

My feet moving of their own accord, I made my way to the holy well fully expecting to find my first visitor there, the words offering refreshment already forming on my lips, for in that moment I found my destiny and knew without a doubt, I was the right person, in the right place, at the right time.

I stopped, my words dying even before they were formed, for no one stood at the holy well, indeed, there was no one around at all. Only, on the granite arm of the well, glinting in the morning sunshine, lay a wreath of rowan, hawthorn, meadowsweet, wild roses and honeysuckle, the dew fresh upon the leaves, their perfumes mingling on the morning air.

There lay my crown.

Sixty Two

Afterwards, everything seemed to flow like the river rushing towards the sea, clearing all obstacles in its path.

The cycle of the festivals began on St Clether's Feast Day, 4th November, and continued on through Midwinter Solstice, Imbolc, Spring Equinox, Beltane, Midsummer Solstice, Lammas, Autumn Equinox and back to Samhain and St Clether's Feast Day once again.

Each day I arrived early to take time to sit quietly before anyone arrived and always it was special, although never quite as poignant as the first.

After Samhain came Midwinter Solstice, the chapel adorned with holly, ivy and fir, the candles points of light at the darkest time of the year. Imbolc saw the first snowdrops and a feeling of spring, freshness and new growth. At Spring Equinox the chapel was a blaze of yellow daffodils and Beltane saw the spring flowers of red campion, cow parsley, bluebells and the scent of the hawthorn blossom throughout the valley. Midsummer brought tall, swaying foxgloves, golden buttercups, meadowsweet and a swathe of greenery, followed by the first harvest at Lammas and high summer with purple thistles and swaying grasses. The Autumn Equinox brought berries, fruits and seeds, and then we were back to Samhain, the close of the Celtic year with autumn leaves, lichens and twisting branches - and the cycle began once more.

And people came. They came to visit the chapel, to light candles and they came to witness the turning of the seasons, for although there were only six weeks or so between each festival, the valley changed dramatically as the year progressed, from the resting of the winter to the new growth of spring, the harvest of high summer to the fruitfulness of autumn. At each festival, I wrote a short leaflet explaining its significance and how it might have been celebrated in times past and these eventually came together as a booklet, *The Wheel of the Celtic Year: A journey through the turning of the seasons and their festivals.*

A wide variety of people visited, from those simply enjoying the peace and beauty of the valley, to others seeking their own spiritualty or religious beliefs. All were welcome, for none are wrong and everyone of equal importance. And people helped. They sponsored slates, raised money, made donations, gave concerts, painted fences, scrubbed floors, cut grass, and as time progressed I knew the chapel was loved and appreciated by others, almost as much as I loved it myself.

In time there was enough money for the roof repairs and I finally knew all was safe for another hundred years.

Dan and I were handfasted at Beltane, when the scent of the hawthorn drifted through the valley, the magical water collected on the day we met upon the altar. I wore my crown of rowan, hawthorn, meadowsweet, wild roses and honeysuckle, and I will never forget the moment when a sudden breeze caused the white mayflower blossom to swirl around us like confetti, as we stood outside the chapel surrounded by our friends.

They were all there, of course. Cornelius and Jowan, *The Maidens* - Tamsyn, Morwenna and Demelza, and The Green Knights - Art, Will, Sean and Stu, accompanied by Lance, Perce and Tristy; and other travellers we had encountered along the way who felt as deeply about the chapel and found as much beauty in nature as we did.

'I suppose you'll be having a Pagan or Druid to officiate?' Cornelius had commented when we told him of our plans, but he had been surprised, and I think quietly pleased, when we said we would have none but him, for he had always maintained all religions were simply different paths up the same mountain, and he was our dearest friend.

Cornelius eventually decided not to sell the farmhouse after all but to rent it to Dan and myself so Dan could work the land and there would be plenty of room for our growing family – the new dynasty of Maidens of the Wells, as he jokingly called them.

And in due course our daughters arrived – one born at Midwinter with eyes as grey as the snow ridden sky and hair as black as the raven's wing; the other at Midsummer, whose eyes shone with the brilliance of the bluest sky, hair as fair as the grasses which rippled gently in the fields. I knew then our happiness was complete. This time around we really had done it properly and the next generations of Maidens had arrived; but theirs is another tale to tell, for the paths of light and darkness seldom run smoothly but are ever intertwined and filled with unexpected twists and turns.

There was one last thing to do before I could rest and truly feel I had accomplished all which was required of me. Increasingly, the stories of the former Guardians of the well had been in my mind, ever since I read Rose's writings and Dan and I looked at the contents of my box, wondering what tales might be held there. Although I never saw the monk myself nor any of the others, except perhaps without realising it, their stories called to me and the time came when I knew they needed to be brought into the world, for there is no one Guardian of the well but a number, all who have played their parts for three thousand years and more and will continue to do so into the future.

It is not merely the holy wells which should be revered and kept safe, but all the wild and sacred places which hold the timeless magic so special in the world today; and so in remembrance of the times I had looked into the still, clear waters of the holy well and found solace there, I decided to write, *Reflections of the Past: A Story of the Guardians of the Well,* in honour of all those who had passed before me.

Sixty Three

But all things change in time, just as the cycle of the year brings birth, fruition, resting and renewal, so it is with people and, as the years crept by, I knew my time was coming to a close.

I saw it first as a shimmering white void upon the horizon. Whereas before I had always been able to see the pathway of my life ahead, sometimes clear and straight, at others misty with many twists and turns, there came a time when I could see nothing and knew not what the future might hold.

I have waited a long time for them to join me - or perhaps it has been merely the blink of an eye - but the time has passed pleasantly enough. Our beautiful daughters are grown with children of their own and I have watched them visit the well, continuing the tradition, perhaps in different ways, but all things have their season and their passing.

And people visit, from all walks of life and all religions, each finding spiritual refreshment and their own particular path to the top of the same mountain.

More spirits rest here than I could ever have imagined, gentle spirits from time immemorial, guarding the holy well and the chapel in their own special way, creating its atmosphere of peace and tranquility.

Sometimes I stand watching the stars in the night sky and making up stories, whilst at others I see the sun and shadows play upon the hillside opposite and wonder what tales are hidden there, waiting to be told.

Cornelius was the first to join me and we were reunited again, although I had watched over him for many years. Jowan will be a while yet for he has much left to do in life, but in time his spirit will return here once more.

And Dan? I have stayed with Dan every moment he has spent in the valley and the chapel. I have been beside him as he fished the river, walked the paths, lain in the sun on the top of the highest rock and rested on the wooden bench – and known he has thought of no one but me.

But today is a day of celebration for he is coming home and we will be reunited once again, for I now know we have spent many lifetimes together in one guise or another and this is not the end, merely a continuation until the next time. Deerman, Dominic, Duncan, Davy and Dan are all but different facets of the same spirit, for although we have many lives, one spirit traverses them all, just as Cornelius, Jowan and myself have lived many times before.

I see him now, making his way towards me from the riverbank, the sunlight flashing on the water behind him and all at once he is young and old, the young man I fell in love with thousands of years ago and the wise, Green Man, the spirit of the earth.

By coincidence - or perhaps not, for does coincidence really exist – it is Midsummer's Eve and Jowan is sitting on the bench, as he does without fail at this time every year. He cannot see Dan making his way towards us from the river although he will hear of his passing upon his return, nor is he aware of Cornelius and myself sitting on either side of him waiting patiently, yet a part of him knows and a feeling of peace encompasses us all.

For in the end we all are one. The nurturing earth beneath our feet and the sun above us, sending warmth and light in order that the crops may grow. The moon, lighting the darkness of the night, the breeze which whispers its way through the valley and the sound of the ever rushing water, singing its soft melodies and telling its own story to all who care to listen. The earth mother and the green father, who give us life, and hold the answers to all the questions we might ever wish to ask.

During the daytime the ravens call and tumble in the skies and at night the moon rises, casting her magical light all around and, if you wait for long enough, you will hear the rustle of the undergrowth as a stoat quietly passes and you will see the great white owl, swooping down the valley on its never ending flight.

'Take my hand.' I reach out, his hand is in mine and we are reunited once again. The dots have been joined, the picture complete, for the moment at least. We stand together, our spirits entwined as one, watching the sun set over the brow of the hill as we have done so many times in the past, and yet there is never an end, merely a resting, until our spirits return and a new journey begins once more.

*   *   *

Bibliography

Clarke, Matthew. *Fenten Glether.* 2007.

Cunningham, Scott. *Cunningham's Encyclopedia of Magical Herbs.* Llewellyn Publications, USA. 2002.

Freeman, Mara. *Kindling the Celtic Spirit: Ancient traditions to illumine your life throughout the seasons.* Harper Collins, San Francisco. 2001.

Inman, Vanda. *The Awakening.* Vanda Inman's Write Space, Cornwall. 2007.

Inman, Vanda. *The Dawning.* Vanda Inman's Write Space, Cornwall. 2006.

Inman, Vanda. *Legacy of a Cornish Saint.* Inman, Cornwall. 2005.

Inman, Vanda. *The Scent of Meadowsweet.* Scryfa, Cornwall. Volume 11. Autumn, 2008.

Inman, Vanda. *The Wheel of the Celtic Year: A journey through the turning of the seasons and their festivals.* Vanda Inman's Write Space, Cornwall. 2008.

Quiller Couch, M and L. *Ancient and Holy Wells of Cornwall* (2nd ed). Tamara Publications, Cornwall. 1994

The Well Wishers

Supporters of St Clether Holy Well Chapel

Following the recent restoration work at St Clether Holy Well Chapel, we have set up a small group to help with the continued upkeep.

There are many areas in which people can be involved, including helping to maintain the building, enclosure and surrounding area, assisting on celebratory days or contributing an annual donation.

The Well Wishers receive a twice yearly newsletter, 'The Well Spring', providing details of events and general progress concerning the chapel and holy well.

If you are interested in becoming involved, please feel free to contact us.

Vanda Inman, Rivendell, St Clether, Launceston, Cornwall.
PL15 8QH   Tel: 01566 86533
www.peaceland.org.uk - vanda@peaceland.org.uk

No longer a wisht well.

St Clether Holy Well Chapel is situated in North Cornwall, near Launceston, approximately a third of a mile along the valley from the parish church, (signposted on the A395). It is advisable to wear sensible footwear, especially in winter, as the path can be difficult in places. NGR 202846.